The Hidden Beach

Karen Swan is the *Sunday Times* top three bestselling author of seventeen books and her novels sell all over the world. She writes two books each year – one for the summer period and one for the Christmas season. Previous winter titles include *Christmas at Tiffany's*, *The Christmas Lights*, *The Christmas Party* and for summer, *The Rome Affair*, *The Greek Escape* and *The Spanish Promise*.

Her books are known for their evocative locations and Karen sees travel as vital research for each story. She loves to set deep, complicated love stories within twisty plots, sometimes telling two stories in the same book.

Previously a fashion editor, she lives in Sussex with her husband, three children and two dogs.

Visit Karen's author page on Facebook, follow her on Twitter @KarenSwan1, on Instagram @swannywrites, and her website www.karenswan.com.

Also by Karen Swan

The Hidden Beach

KAREN SWAN

MACMILLAN

First published 2020 by Macmillan
an imprint of Pan Macmillan
The Smithson, 6 Briset Street, London EC1M 5NR
Associated companies throughout the world
www.panmacmillan.com

ISBN 978-1-5290-0621-6

3 5 7 9 8 6 4 2

A CIP catalogue record for this book is available from the British Library.

Typeset in Palatino by Palimpsest Book Production Limited, Falkirk, Stirlingshire
Printed and bound by CPI Group (UK) Ltd, Croydon, CR0 4YY

Visit **www.panmacmillan.com** to read more about all our books
and to buy them. You will also find features, author interviews and
news of any author events, and you can sign up for e-newsletters
so that you're always first to hear about our new releases.

In loving memory of
Sophie Lowry

'I had a dream I was awake and I woke up to find myself asleep'

Stan Laurel

Prologue

Stockholm, March 2013

In the final moments of his life, it was her face that filled his mind. Images spun round and round, of the light catching her pale hair, her head thrown back so that her long neck was exposed, eyes slitted with heady pleasure. Everything about her was radiance and beatific grace, as though she was not solid at all but a heavenly conceit, a constellation of stardust fallen from the skies into one deft, perfect form . . .

In seeing all this, there was much that he missed – the early autumn puddle glinting darkly, deeply; the low, discernible electric burr of the tram behind; the singular scream that pitched into the air and tore through the city's sky. He knew none of it.

For him there was only light.

And then darkness.

Part One

Chapter One

Stockholm, December 2019

Bell wheeled through the lights, standing on the pedals, her trousers tucked into her socks and her breath still coming hard from the last hill. She was one of the few cyclists on the road actually pedalling; all around her were commuters on their electric bikes and scooters, looking a lot more composed – and a lot less late. At least the Baltic blast that had chilled her as she'd stepped out of her apartment ten minutes ago was now merely notional, her cheeks stained with a laboured flush.

She swerved right into a narrow street and, leaning harder on the handlebars, began her ascent up the short but steep hill that she would be walking straight back down again in a few minutes' time. Glossy black cars flanked either side of the road, some with drivers already in the front seats – for this was embassy-land, the handsome townhouses painted in deeply pigmented shades of loden, umber and terracotta red.

Reaching the top with a gasp, she finally allowed herself to sink back onto her seat again, knowing she could glide the rest of the way from here. The background drone of rush-hour traffic became muted, the birdsong and buzz of her spinning wheels amplifying as the streets fanned out, becoming wider and brighter. Parked Volvos, Audis and Jaguars stood outside plain but generous townhouses, as indicative of the family neighbourhood as the playground set atop the small, anomalous hill in the middle of the square: a rocky outcrop that the bulldozers had been unable to flatten when the city was being developed, so they had been forced to build around it instead. Bell loved the curious anomaly – the city's smooth, ordered surfaces disrupted by a jagged poke of something older and wilder. Feral. It was probably the reason why families had settled in this district in the first place. There wasn't a child in Stockholm who didn't love to run and climb over it; teenagers snuck their first cigarettes and kisses on it . . .

She rounded the Rock and saw the house that was, these days, her second home. Set on the corner, it was unmissable on the block – a four-storeyed, stocky building with canti-levered Crittall bay windows running down a central column, the dark, time-blackened bricks offset by the bright verdigris of the copper mansard roof and downpipes. A high garden wall obscured the surprisingly leafy and pretty courtyard within; Oddjob, the family's tabby cat, was sitting on top and surveying his kingdom. As she drew closer, she saw the gate set within the garden wall begin to open. She wasn't the only one behind time today, then? An electric scooter was swung through, followed by a bespectacled man in a mid-thigh navy pea coat, a Missoni striped scarf at his neck and a brown satchel worn across his body, his lightly salted dark hair largely obscured by a ribbed beanie.

'Hi, Max,' she panted, her brakes squeaking slightly as she lifted over her left leg and came to a stop standing on the pedal.

'Morning, Bell,' he said, holding the gate open for her, and she dipped through with brisk, practised efficiency, as though this were a dance.

'How's it going in there today?' she asked, propping the bike up against the garden wall and pulling off her pom-pom hat; her long dark hair immediately stood with static.

He shook his head with a roll of his eyes. 'It's a madhouse. I'm escaping with my sanity while I still can.'

She laughed. 'That explains why I like it here, then. I lost mine years ago,' she grinned, running up the back steps and opening the fully glazed back door. The ground floor of the house stood a couple of metres off the ground, to allow light into the sub-basement below.

'Morning, everyone,' she said cheerily, walking into the kitchen and twisting up her hair into a topknot with a band she kept on her wrist. Her eyes automatically scanned the dirty breakfast dishes in the sink, the orange juice getting warm on the island; without thought, she returned it to the fridge.

'Oh Bell, thank heavens you're here. I've got to dash. A client's just booked an emergency appointment and they're waiting for me.' If Hanna's voice suggested urgency, her movements didn't as she shrugged on a berry-coloured coat that looked sensational against her pale blonde hair and double-checked her appearance in the mirror. As ever, her discreet make-up was expertly applied, not a hair out of place. In the three years she'd been working for the Mogert family, Bell had never seen her look anything less than flawless. Her kitchen, on the other hand . . .

Feeling a tug at her ankles, Bell looked down to find Elise, the older of the twins by nine minutes, tugging her tucked-in trousers out of her socks with a disapproving pout. Even at the tender age of three and three quarters, she had her mother's innate sense of style.

'Thanks, Elise,' she smiled. 'That's saved me a job. Now, have you brushed your teeth and washed your face?'

Elise nodded.

Bell bent down and gently wiped a lick of jam off the girl's pudgy cheek with a finger. She showed it to her with one of her famous bemused looks. *'Have* you?'

Elise gasped and ran from the room, scarcely able to believe she'd been rumbled.

'She's a rascal,' Hanna chuckled as she grabbed her slim leather file case off the kitchen stool. 'So, you remember Max won't be back for dinner tonight?'

'Yes. I'm making meatballs, so I'll freeze whatever's left over,' Bell said, looking in the fridge to make sure she had all the ingredients. It looked like they were low on lingonberry jam.

'Great. And I was supposed to get to the parents' meeting with Linus's teacher this evening, but this emergency might throw the whole schedule out the window. Can we play it by ear and, worst case, you can get over there for me?'

'Oh –' She was supposed to be seeing Ivan again tonight. It was going to be their third date and, she expected, *the* night. Bell looked across at the nine-year-old watching them both from the kitchen table. He had the face of an angel – softly curled muddy-blonde hair and wide grey-green eyes, a smudge of freckles across his nose. He had a gentle manner, manifested in a love for animals and the outdoors, but a mischievous sense of humour often winked through his eyes too, and the first hints of pubescence were beginning to show themselves: wanting a skateboard, cooler trainers, a Snapchat account . . .

Bell winked at him. 'Sure, no problem.'

She watched as Hanna skittered over to him and gave him a noisy kiss on his cheek, making him scrunch his face in a look of delighted disdain. 'I love you, my Liney . . . And thanks, Bell, *you* are a lifesaver!' she said with an appreciative point of her finger, before throwing Linus another kiss from across the room and exiting through the back door in an elegant streak.

It clicked shut behind her, but not before Blofeld, the family's other cat, slipped in and trotted across the kitchen floor. Bell looked across at Linus again, seeing how he watched until Hanna disappeared from sight down the steps. A room always felt different when she left it, as though the oxygen–nitrogen balance of the air itself changed; she was somehow all things – elegant yet chaotic, softly spoken yet commanding.

'Right, champ, you just about ready to shoot? One of us overslept her alarm this morning, and you've got your maths quiz today. We don't want to be late,' she said, immediately setting about gathering the dirty plates off the kitchen table and putting them in the sink – out of sight until she could deal with them later.

'I don't want to go,' he said, watching as Bell wiped a blob of honey off the worktop with a tear of kitchen paper.

'Sure you do.' It was the same every Wednesday morning, maths not being his strong point. 'What's eight times four?'

'Thirty-two.' The hesitation had been only fractional. They had spent every morning and afternoon walk to and from school this week learning this times table.

'Nine times eight.' She glanced up at him as she scooped up the carton of oat milk and replaced it in the fridge, along with the jam, cheese and pickles.

'. . . Seventy-two.'

She gave an impressed nod. He hated the numbers higher up the ladder. 'Eleven eights.'

'Too easy,' he scolded. 'That's a cheat one.'

She shrugged. 'If you think that, then you're totally ready. You're going to slay it today and that gold star *will* be yours.'

'Nils will beat me. He always does.'

'Not this time. You've got this. He got the fours and the sevens and the threes, but you got the fives, sixes and nines. And now the eights will belong to you too.'

He stared at her. Could it be true? Could he really beat his old foe? She gave a nod in silent affirmation and he slid off the chair. 'Good boy – shoes on. And tell your sisters they're wearing their hats. No arguments. It's bitter out there this morning.'

He darted out of the kitchen, hollering up the stairs at the twins as Bell rinsed the coffee machine's foamer before the milk dried to a stubborn crust. Twenty seconds later, there came the stampede of tiny feet down the stairs.

'Let me see,' Bell said as they skidded to a stop in front of her, mouths pulled back in rictus grins to show their gleaming milk teeth. 'Very good,' she smiled, wiping a bit of toothpaste from the corner of Tilde's mouth and taking the hairbrush from her hand. 'Now who's having plaits today?'

'Me!' Elise's hand shot up first.

Hanna and Max didn't mind the girls wearing the same clothes – as was often their wont – but they liked their hair to be worn in separate styles to impose some sense of difference between them. The point of the exercise was to promote the girls' individuality but it was a helpful marker of distinction for the outside world too: they really were truly identical. When she had first started, it had taken Bell several weeks to confidently know which twin was which, but now she saw their differences easily. Both had what Max called his 'buggy' blue eyes and long limbs, but whilst Elise had their mother's self-composed Mona Lisa smile and confidence, there was a tiny crook to the left in Tilde's grin, and her left foot was fractionally pigeon-toed – the faintest strain of a palsy? It was common in twins.

With practised deftness, Bell quickly brushed Elise's white-blonde hair free of her bedtime tangles, ignoring her dramatic squeals of protest, and plaited it into pigtails. Tilde had a half-ponytail with a blue gingham beribboned band. 'Okay, very smart. Now boots on. Hats on. Gloves on. Quick-quick-quick.'

Linus walked back in, fully dressed and with his backpack already shrugged on his shoulders. His lips were moving but no sound escaped them as he ran through the eights again.

'Five eights?' Bell said, knotting the girls' scarves.

'Forty-eight.'

She hitched an eyebrow fractionally as she pulled their hats down over their ears.

'Forty! Five eights are forty,' he corrected himself quickly, the panic evident in his voice.

'Good boy. Don't worry. It was just a slip. Remember to breathe.'

He shot her an annoyed look. Nine-year-old boys didn't appreciate mindful reminders such as remembering to breathe.

'Okay. Have we got everything?' She assessed them swiftly. Everyone was clean and bundled up. 'Right, quick march. We'll have to walk fast if we're not going to be late.'

'Did you oversleep again Bell?' Elise asked.

Bell shot her a bemused grin. 'Cheeky . . . And yes, I did.'

'I can take my board and go on ahead,' Linus said immediately, as though helpfully.

Now it was Bell's turn to shoot him a look. He knew perfectly well his mother's views on that, with all the hills in their neighbourhood.

'Fine,' he muttered, walking to the back door and holding it open as the twins followed after him – a reluctant young gentleman, but a gentleman nonetheless.

'Twelve eights,' Bell said, locking the door as the girls ran down the steps to see whether the birds had eaten any of the seeds they had left out on the bistro table overnight. The frosts were still hard at the moment, and all four of them had been broken-hearted to find a dead sparrow on the ground the other morning.

Inside the house, the phone started ringing just as Bell pulled the key from the lock. She sighed and hesitated, staring back in at the superficially tidy kitchen – the dirty dishes hidden from view here, the crumbs too small to see on the counters. But the signs of a sprawling, unwieldy life lay scattered everywhere: a basket of laundry had been brought up from the utility room, ready for ironing; a raincoat from last night's showers was slung across the back of a hemp linen armchair, rather than hanging from its designated hook, no doubt leaving a water mark. The weekend's newspapers had been carried through from the living room, almost but not quite making it to the recycling bin. The water in the glass vase of lilies had been used up, she saw, and needed immediate refreshing . . .

She dithered as she listened to the phone ring on the other side of the glass. They would be late if she answered it, but there was something always so urgent, so insistent about a ringing phone. The ringtone for her mobile was set to 'Lark', far less . . . pressing. What if it was Hanna or Max? Had they forgotten something? Hanna had been in her version of a rush, with that emergency . . .

'. . . Ninety-four.'

Huh? She glanced back towards the outdoor table. The girls were kneeling on the cafe chairs, freeing the sunflower seeds from their stuck-down positions with little fingertips. She made a mental note to remind them to wash their hands if they handled the chicks that had recently hatched at their nursery; now that the babies were a couple of weeks old, the children were allowed to pet them.

'Twelve eights are ninety-four . . .' Linus frowned. 'No – wait . . .'

'I'm just going to answer that quickly,' she said with an impatient sigh, pushing the key back into the lock. It might make them a minute later, but it would be sod's law Hanna did need something, and then she'd have to do an extra trip back here later. 'It might be Mamma.'

Unlocking the house, she ran back in again, eyes fixed on the handset and the glowing blue digital screen. It would go to voicemail any –

'Hello?' she panted, reaching it just in time.

'Hanna? Hanna Mogert?'

Her shoulders sagged. 'No, I'm sorry, she's not here. Who is calling, please?' she asked in brisk Swedish.

'This is Dr Sorensen from the Larna Klinik.' The woman's voice was officious and clear. As a psychotherapist, Hanna worked with a lot of different institutions and facilities, although this one was new to Bell. 'I tried her cell just now but it wouldn't connect.'

'Yes, she's rushing to work. She probably didn't hear it in her bag. Can I take a message for her?' She tried not to sound as impatient as she felt. Glancing back, she saw Linus on the top step, a look of panic dawning on his beautiful face, lips moving rapidly as he tore through his repetitions again. 'Ninety-six,' she mouthed to him.

'It would be preferable to speak to her directly. It is urgent.'

13

Bell suppressed a sigh. 'Well, you're welcome to keep trying her. But she's dealing with an emergency herself, so I'm not sure how contactable she will be this morning.'

There was a pause down the line as options were considered, weighed, discarded, accepted. 'And to whom am I speaking?'

'I'm her nanny.'

'Of long standing?'

Bell frowned. Was she being interviewed? 'Three years.'

'I see.' That appeared to pass muster. 'Well, then, if you could pass a message on to her, please.'

'Sure. It was Dr Sorensen, you said . . .' she muttered, grabbing a biro that had been left beside a half-done crossword and writing it on the top of the newspaper. 'From the . . . ?'

'Larna Klinik. She has my number.'

'Okay.'

'It is really very urgent. If you can please pass on to her –'

Linus stepped back over the threshold, eyes wide, tears threatening. 'Bell, I can't remember them. They've gone.'

'– so the sooner she can get here the better.'

What? Bell blinked at Linus blindly as the two simultaneous pronouncements clashed and clattered in her brain, each one vying for her attention. She turned away from him, certain she had misheard the voice on the phone.

'I'm sorry, that makes no sense. I think you must have the wrong number . . .' But even as she said it, she frowned; the doctor had clearly asked for Hanna Mogert. 'Hello? . . . Dr Sorensen? . . . Are you there?'

Chapter Two

The day ticked past with leaden boots. Somehow she had managed to get the kids to school and kindergarten only a few minutes past the bell; somehow she had managed to tidy the kitchen, buy lingonberry jam, make dinner and get the ironing done before collecting the girls again and giving them lunch. Somehow she had managed to sing songs and read stories to them, and even more surprisingly, somehow she had managed to get them to tidy their bedroom. But what she hadn't managed was to get hold of Hanna.

Ninny, her secretary, had confided that Hanna was dealing with a patient in the midst of a psychotic break – but that if it was about the kids, she could get hold of her for Bell. Reluctantly, Bell had declined. It wasn't about the kids, and she didn't think her message – bewildering though it was – could compete with the needs of someone in such acute mental distress. Not to mention, it might all turn out to be a mistake anyway. Perhaps Dr Sorensen had in fact been trying to get hold of *another* Hanna Mogert, a Hanna to whom this scenario would make perfect sense.

Max had called in a short while ago to talk to the kids before going on to his client's dinner; but although the message had sat poised at her throat, ready to be shared and diluted and expelled, explained and clarified and laughed upon, Bell had stayed silent. It might just be that he was the very last person she should tell.

Holding a coffee cup between cold hands, she glanced anxiously at the kitchen clock for the thousandth time. But it didn't matter how often she checked it, she couldn't seem to make those little hands move around more quickly. Five twenty-five. Linus was in the playroom downstairs, dejectedly watching TV, having lost the eights not to Nils but to quiet little Brigitte Carlsson.

His teacher talk was in just over half an hour, and with no word from Hanna at all, Bell was resigned to the fate of her evening plans. She had already texted Ivan asking for a rain check, but taking the girls out after dinner to sit quietly whilst she listened to Linus's school report was not going to be fun. She would need to find something to occupy them – Elise was a terrible fidget, and Tilde was always prone to getting overtired after supper.

Her hand trailed over the sludgy grey-green handrail as she skipped downstairs, past the crowded gallery of black-and-white family photographs which had been carefully framed, but always seemed to have one or two askew. She stopped and straightened a small one of Hanna and Linus taken when he was a toddler: they were sitting on a sandy beach, their matching blonde hair streaming in the wind as their cheeks pressed together, eyes slitted against the bright sun. It was a snapshot of joy, and all of the other pictures told the same story – that this was a happy family.

Was it?

She frowned, continuing down into the basement. The washing machine in the utility to the left was drumming away quietly, tossing and turning and soaping and rinsing the children's clothes from their muddy play in the park yesterday.

The door left ajar into the small WC gave a glimpse of the patterned Moroccan clay tiles Hanna had fallen in love with on a trip to Marrakesh with Max.

She peered around the playroom door. It had high-level windows that allowed natural daylight to, if not flood the room, certainly trickle into it; all-white walls and a pale larch floor helped too. To her relief, it was still tidy. More days of her life than she wanted to count had been devoted to taming this one space, but for the moment at least, the paint brushes and pencils were still in their pots on the lime-green Ikea craft table; jigsaws and books were stacked in colourful neatness along the wall-to-wall bookcase; there were no tiny Sylvanian Family characters hiding in the bright swirls of the rug, waiting for a bare foot to tread on them.

Linus was lying on the red beanbag, a packet of sour peach sweets perched on his tummy and his curls splayed out. Only a heap of Lego bricks lay scattered to his far side, the progress on a half-made F1 car no doubt stalled by the absence of a single, vital piece.

He was watching *Doctor Who* in English; all the children were fully bilingual with barely a trace of an accent, and Bell's own Englishness had been one of the reasons they'd been so keen to employ her, even though she'd never nannied before. Hanna and Max had asked her to always converse with the children in English, even though she was fluent in Swedish herself; her grandmother had hailed from Gothenburg on the west coast and until the day she'd died, when Bell was twelve, had always insisted on addressing her in her native language.

'Hey.'

He twisted to look back at her, his eyes seeming wider than ever in his upside-down position.

'You ready? We should head off in a few minutes.'

'Oh . . . I guess.' He turned away again, and she saw the disappointment in the stiffness of his little body. He was a perfectionist and a worrier, always seeming to expect so much of himself.

She walked over to him and tried to perch as lightly as she could on the side of the beanbag, but it still rose up beneath him like a souffle. 'It's going to be okay, you know,' she said, gently winding her index finger into one of his curls. 'Forget about today; you're one of the smartest boys in your class and Miss Olsson *loves* you. Going to your teacher's evening is like . . . playing with puppies. A total feel-good session.' Linus shot her a sceptical sideways look. 'Your naughty little sister, on the other hand . . .'

That got his attention. 'What did she do now?' he asked, alert, not even having to ask which one.

'Promise you won't tell?' With a five-year age gap between him and the girls, and the twins sharing such a tight bond, Bell often sensed he felt like a third wheel: too big and strong for some of their games, bored by others, and a boy to boot. She occasionally shared these little snippets to make a virtue of his age and bond them as the 'grown-ups'.

'I promise,' he said eagerly.

She lowered her voice for conspiratorial effect. 'Well, you know the chicks have hatched?'

He nodded. How could he forget? It was all anyone in his family had discussed at breakfast or tea for the past few weeks.

'When I picked the girls up at lunchtime, I was taken to one side and informed that Elise had sneaked off with one in her pocket –'

His mouth opened in surprise, hovering between horror and hilarity until he knew the full extent of the chick's fate.

'– painted it green –'

18

It opened wider still.

'– and sprinkled its feathers with glitter.'

There was a moment of abeyance as he concluded the chick was – in the life or death sense – technically unharmed, and his eyes suddenly sparkled with delight. 'She did not!' he laughed.

'Oh yes. Apparently she thought it might prefer to be a mermaid chick.'

He laughed harder and Bell smiled, loving his delight. 'So, *that* will be an interesting parents' meeting. Yours, on the other hand?' She shrugged. 'Really not so much.'

'She's crazy!'

'She's certainly not dull.' She tickled his tummy, making him laugh and wriggle again. 'Come on, champ. Let's go hear how great you are.' With a puff of effort, she got up from the beanbag. 'I'll round up the girls while you put that Lego away.'

She jogged back upstairs, straightening another picture as she passed – this time, one of Linus and the twins in the bath, their chubby, pinked faces peering over the enamel rim.

'Elise, Tilde!' she called, stepping into the hall and staring up through the narrow gap of the winding staircase. The girls' rooms were on the third floor, and she'd rather not have to run all the way up there to get them. 'Come on, it's time to—' Her eyes widened in surprise. 'Hanna! You're back.'

Hanna peered down from the first-floor landing, her hair hanging like a sheet of spun flax. 'Only just.'

'I – I didn't hear you come in.'

'I think you were in the basement. I hoped there might be time for a five-minute rest, but –' She shrugged. 'Anyway, I'll take it from here. You get off. Your day has been long enough already.'

So had hers, apparently. Bell stared up at her, seeing the exhaustion on her boss's face, and she wondered what it was like dealing with someone in the midst of a psychotic break. It suggested delusion, violence, wildness, blades, blood . . . This teacher meeting was poorly timed.

'Thanks again, Bell. See you tomorrow.' Hanna turned and disappeared back into her bedroom.

'Hanna, wait,' Bell said, bounding up the stairs two at a time and rushing to the door. She peered into the room. It was large, with what Bell always considered to be a very masculine energy. It had aubergine walls, finished with some kind of lacquer effect, and the exposed floorboards that ran throughout the house were covered with a vast charcoal-grey sheepskin rug. Hanna was standing by the end of the bed – a fine black four-poster with heavy ivory linen hangings – pulling off her shoe with the other foot and untucking her blouse from her trousers. The right way up, she looked even more drained than she had from downstairs.

'I've been trying to reach you all day.'

'Oh, I'm sorry.' Exhaustion suffused her voice, making it thick and slow. 'I had to switch my cell off.' She looked up suddenly, concern on her face. 'Something—?'

'No, no, the kids are fine,' Bell said quickly, coming into the room. It was probably best that the children didn't over-hear this. 'But I took an urgent phone call this morning, only minutes after you left.'

Hanna relaxed again. 'Oh?' She unbuttoned her trousers and stepped out of them, walking across the room as she arranged them on a hanger and replaced them in the wardrobe. She put on her jeans instead.

Bell didn't blink an eye; she had grown accustomed to the Swedes' lack of inhibitions. Hanna and Max routinely moved around – certainly upstairs – in their underwear, and they all swam nude in the sea at the summer house (although Bell usually excused herself on the pretext of urgently needing to buy milk. Or bread. Or hazelnuts).

'Yes, a – uh – Dr Sorensen called for you,' Bell said quietly, seeing how Hanna fell still at the mention of the name.

'Oh?' But her voice was hesitant now. 'What did she want?'

She? She knew Dr Sorensen was a woman? So Hanna did know her, then. It wasn't a coincidence or a mistake. This might be . . . this might be *true*?

Bell opened her mouth to speak, but nothing came out. How could she repeat the message, say those words, when they made no sense?

Hanna turned back to face her, but the depleted energy she had radiated only a few seconds ago had suddenly switched to a quivering intensity. Her mouth was stretched thin, the sinews in her neck pronounced, but her eyes were fiercely focused. 'Bell? What did Dr Sorensen want?'

'She wanted you to know . . .' But still the words failed her. She couldn't give them a shape. It was preposterous. Nonsensical.

Suddenly Hanna was before her. She was tall, at least four inches taller than Bell, and her hands were on Bell's arms, as though *she* was the one in need of consolation. 'Tell me. What did she want me to know?'

Bell looked up at her, sensing change, some sort of seismic shift. 'Your husband has woken up.'

Chapter Three

Kris looked up from his favoured spot at the stove, his lobster-print apron looking anachronistic against the faded and torn Metallica t-shirt. The smell of chorizo, prawns and peppers filled the small flat. 'Hey! You're late!'

Bell, positioning the bike on its rack behind the front door, kicked off her trainers, pulled her beanie from her head and let her hand fall against her thigh. 'Yeah,' she sighed, lethargically shrugging off her coat and limping in. 'Oh – hi.'

Tove waved from her sprawled position on the sofa, blowing smoke from her roll-up towards the ceiling. 'Hi, babe. I'm not here. You haven't seen me.'

That was easier said than done. At five foot eleven, with legs up to Bell's armpits, Tove wasn't particularly easy to hide. But Bell nodded, knowing the drill; her lanky, irreverent friend, who worked in the Star Bar two floors below the flat, often escaped up here on her breaks. Invariably, they slid well past the official twenty minutes.

Kris frowned at Bell as she dragged herself into the room. 'You look like shit,' he said fondly. 'Tough day?' He finished slicing a Romano pepper and scraped it off the board into the pan. It instantly sizzled and hissed, and he shook the pan several times, biceps flexing under the harsh under-cupboard lights.

'. . . You could say that,' she said after a moment, collapsing onto the battered black leather sofa opposite Tove and stretching out, letting her feet dangle over the arm. She closed her eyes as if that would still her mind, but the thoughts continued rushing like a river in flood.

'Here.'

She looked up to see Kris standing over her and holding out a chilled bottle of beer. She gave a happy sigh of contentment. 'I love you,' she smiled. His dirty blonde hair was pulled up into his signature man-bun and he looked unseasonably tanned, thanks to a recent gig for some surf brand in Sydney. His modelling jobs easily paid the rent, but cooking was his real passion, and he was saving to get enough to open his own place – a small bar specializing in craft beers and Hawaiian food.

She pushed herself up to a sitting position and crossed her legs, feeling none of Elise's urge to untuck her black trousers from her purple socks.

'I thought you were seeing Ivan tonight?'

'Yeah, so did he. But Hanna had an emergency at work, so I had to stay late.'

'Again?' Tove lamented. She took a serious interest in the state of Bell's love life, which she proclaimed as being 'dire'. 'That's how many times you've blown him out now?'

'I don't know.'

'More times than you've seen him, for sure.'

'Well, it couldn't be avoided this time.'

'And why couldn't Max deal with it?'

'Because he's pitching for a big deal with a client, and he's got some fancy dinner set up for tonight.'

'So yet again, you have to pick up the pieces?' Tove sighed, tutting. 'Honestly, I don't know how you think you can ever get your life back on track when you're constantly putting yourself second.'

Bell met Kris's eyes as she took a swig of her beer. They both knew Tove meant well; it was just that she had the subtlety of a sledgehammer.

'So, what made your day so tough, then?' Kris asked, rescuing her as he moved about their kitchenette. The apartment was largely open-plan, with an old eighties pine kitchen spread against the back wall and delineated from the sofas and table area by a marble-effect linoleum counter.

'Well, if I tell you, do you promise to keep it to yourself?'

It was a rhetorical question to *one* of her friends, and Kris gave one of his easy shrugs in reply. He wasn't big on rumour and innuendo; he'd been on the wrong end of it too many times. Tove dramatically drew a cross above her heart, and then kissed her fingers.

Bell rested her elbows on her knees, as though an approximation of the lotus position was going to give her any more peace. Her topknot flopped limply to one side of her head, but she ignored it. 'So, I took a phone call today –'

Instantly Tove began clapping and kicking out her long legs. 'Yes! Yes! I knew you could do it! Didn't I say?'

Kris shook his head with a weary, wry grin as he shook the pan again.

Bell gave her the bird, and a sarcastic smile. 'It was some doctor asking for Hanna. She said it was urgent, and gave me a message – but it made no sense, right? Like, none at all.'

Tove nodded impatiently, whirling her hands in a 'get on with it' motion, puffing more smoke towards the ceiling pendant.

'Only, I couldn't get hold of Hanna all day – like I said, she had a client emergency of her own going on. I wasn't that worried about it, because I really figured they must have had the wrong number, or the wrong Hanna, at least, because her message made *no sense.*' She took a swig of her beer. 'But then, when Hanna got back this evening . . .'

Kris, tossing the peppers to let them char on the other side, watched her, waiting. Unlike Tove – ever impatient and restless – he understood that she had to run it through in her mind again exactly as it had happened, in case there *had* been a mistake . . . She looked straight up at him. 'It turns out that before she was with Max, Hanna was married to some other guy.'

Kris frowned. 'Did we know that?'

'Nope. He's never been mentioned. There's no photos of the dude anywhere.'

'Oooh, a secret husband – how fabulous!' Tove said, lifting one endless leg into the air. Bell always joked that her legs were like strings with knots in them, but they both knew she was just jealous. If Tove was lean and lanky – with a tendency towards elegance in her more mature moments – Bell was rounded and, in Tove's words, 'juicy'. Five foot four but with a figure like a cello, she had curves where Tove had straight lines.

'Well, he was secret for a reason. Apparently the poor guy's spent the past seven years in a coma.'

Kris stopped what he was doing. Tove's leg swung down, and her arm dangled off the side of the sofa. *'What?'* they asked in unison.

Bell nodded, feeling gratified by their shock. It roughly matched her own. 'Yeah. And today he woke up.'

'Holy shit!' Kris returned the pan to the heat as though unable to keep holding it. He stared at her as though she had the answers. 'How?'

'What do you mean, how?' Tove asked him, sitting up herself now, her short skirt riding all the way up her thighs to flash her knickers – no one in the room caring, least of all

25

her. Bell was just grateful she was wearing some. 'Her husband was asleep and now he's awake! He opened his eyes and woke up!'

'Well, if it was that simple, you'd have thought he'd have done it before now, surely?' Kris exclaimed.

'Hmm.' Tove conceded the point.

'I'm not really sure how they did it,' Bell replied. 'It was a lot of different things combined, I think. Hanna said something about stimulating the vagus nerve . . . ? It's some pioneering treatment. I don't think they thought it would actually work.'

'Fuck,' Tove whispered under her breath. 'The vagus nerve.' It was clear none of them had ever heard of this before.

'How did Hanna take the news?'

'She was very shocked. She collapsed, actually.' Bell bit her lip, remembering how Hanna had paled and then fallen, her legs giving way, both of them sitting on the floor until Max arrived home.

'Shit,' Tove murmured, as though this was proof of the seriousness of the situation. She had met Hanna only once, but had rhapsodized afterwards about her skin and flashing aquamarine ring and good shoes. 'She's such a grown-up!' Tove had cooed, and Bell hadn't liked to point out that there was only three years between Tove and Hanna – and six years between her and her boss.

'What happened to the guy? How did he end up in a coma in the first place?'

'Traffic accident, I think. To be honest, she didn't say much that was coherent, and I didn't feel I could ask too much. She was so shocked; I've never seen her like that. Hanna never loses control.' Bell took a swig of her beer.

'So has she gone to see him?'

'She can't. Not tonight, it's too late now. He's in some clinic in Uppsala and they've got strict visiting hours. She and Max are going up in the morning.'

Kris put down the knife again. 'Christ, that'll be a head-fuck for him, won't it? His wife's first husband suddenly back on the scene again?'

'Well, technically, he's her husband, end of. Hanna and Max aren't married.'

He hesitated. 'I take it *he* knew about him?'

'Yeah, seemed to. He was at this client dinner but I couldn't leave Hanna in that state, so as soon as I rang and told him what had happened, he came straight back.'

'And the kids?' Tove asked.

'They don't know. Yet.'

Kris shook his head with a weary sigh. 'Hell, Bell.' It was his signature catchphrase to her but there was no laughter in his eyes today. 'That's one mighty mess.'

'I know.' She sank back into the sofa again, as though depleted by the message she had conveyed, and stared at the wall. But she was gazing far beyond the neon 'love' sign that sufficed as lighting in that corner of the room; she was trying to imagine how it must have felt to have been Hanna when the doctors had given her the prognosis . . . her husband alive, but to all intents and purposes dead. Hanna had said the doctors had told her that there was very little hope he would ever emerge from the coma.

She went to take another swig of her beer and realized she had finished it.

'I'll get you another one,' Tove sighed, getting up and walking over to the fridge. 'I've got to shoot anyway.' She glanced at the clock and gave a small spasm of surprise. 'Oh fuck. Not again.'

Bell glanced over. She knew Tove's schedules well enough

to know she should have come off her break twenty three minutes ago. She gave a small tut and a grin as Tove jogged over and handed her the fresh beer. 'Thanks, hon.'

'Laters alligators,' Tove called over her shoulder in English – one of the more sedate phrases she had insisted Bell teach her – as she headed towards the front door. The door slammed shut a moment later, making the furniture vibrate; Tove was incapable of doing anything quietly.

Kris gave a sympathetic tut and frown as he picked up several nests of noodles and threw them into a pan of boiling water. Bell sat quietly on the sofa for a few minutes, enjoying her beer and the little moment of peace. She peered over the back of the sofa, towards the kitchen. 'Hey, Kris, how long do you think it is to Uppsala from here – an hour-ish?'

He nodded in agreement.

'Right,' she sighed. That would be an extra early start for her, then. Hanna had asked her to get in early tomorrow so that she and Max could head straight off to the clinic, before the commuter traffic built up.

She'd made light of it to her friends, but she felt rattled by the day's events. It frightened her when life slipped off its rails like that, the straight tramlines of expectation suddenly hijacked by a too-sharp curve that sent everything flying. Lives could turn on a sixpence, she knew that only too well – the entire reason she was here and living in Sweden was down to one such curve ball – but it was just as unsettling to watch it happening from a close remove. She was near enough to care, but just outside of the involved circle.

'Come. Eat,' Kris said, draining the pan so that great plumes of steam billowed in his face. He tonged the food into colourful and artful heaps in the bowls, and slid one towards her on the island.

'Oh, I'm not sure I ca—' It was almost ten. Eating late was hardly conducive to whittling out that bikini body she was determined to find.

'You can and you will,' he said firmly. 'You cannot spend all day looking after other people and neglecting yourself.'

'I really didn't neglect myself when I was serving the kids their dinner earlier,' she said, getting up anyway as her stomach growled appreciatively. She took her bowl with a grateful smile and they sat down together at the small circular table that was only big enough for two, or a pot plant. Every third Friday, for Kris's renowned and sought-after supper clubs, it was moved to the bathroom and set in the bath out of the way, as six trestle tables and benches were carried in, the rest of the furniture hidden in the bedrooms or pushed to the walls.

'I thought Marc was coming over?' she said, her mouth full, as they tucked in in appreciative silence, elbows out, heads dipped low, beers fizzing in their bottles.

'He is.' Kris's gaze flickered over to the reclaimed train clock on the opposite wall. 'After his shift, in twenty minutes hopefully.'

'Ah.' Marc was a junior doctor at St Görans Hospital. He was almost the same height and build as Kris, but where Kris was blonde and stubbled and rocking a chiselled indy traveller vibe, Marc was clean-shaven and preppy. Tove had said it was like choosing between Redford and Newman the first time she'd seen them together, and Bell had had to break it to her that she sadly wouldn't ever get to choose either one of them. 'Did his consultant apologize for screaming at him?'

'Of course not.'

'Outrageous,' she tutted. Marc had been late to a meeting on account of sitting with a terminal patient, literally holding their hand as they died. She forked another heaped bite and gave an immediate groan of appreciation. 'Ohmigod, *so* good.'

His eyes gleamed appreciatively. 'So how about you? Was Tove right just now? Are you deliberately sabotaging your own dates?'

'Kris, *no one* could have foreseen what was coming our way today. Not even Hanna. Long-forgotten husbands waking up from comas is not all in a day's work for me.'

'No, I guess not,' he conceded, looking up at her from beneath his ridiculously long eyelashes as he twirled his noodles. 'All the same, you really need to start insisting on extra pay if you're gonna be doing extra hours. You help her out a lot. *A lot* a lot.'

'I know.'

'You know – but you won't,' he said, watching her, knowing her too well. 'You're too soft.'

'It's not a matter of being soft. I just . . . don't mind if things over-run. It feels sort of wrong monetizing looking after children.'

Kris burst out laughing. 'But that is the very definition of your job!'

She couldn't help but crack a smile. She had walked into that one. 'You know what I mean. Those kids are so cute.'

'Elise is not cute! She is a diva-in-training. Mariah Carey in miniature and fucking terrifying.'

'Okay, fine, but Linus then – you haven't seen his puppy-dog eyes. He didn't win the times table test today and he was heartbroken. Big, fat tears rolling down his cheeks . . .' She trailed a finger down her own cheek, her mouth downturned sadly to make her point.

Kris sighed and shook his head, looking entirely unconvinced, before suddenly stabbing the air decisively with his fork. 'Give him a booty call.'

She frowned in disbelief. *'Linus?'*

He banged the ends of his cutlery on the table. 'Ivan!'

'Ha, yeah right.' Quickly she stuffed another overloaded forkful into her mouth, trying to distract herself from his words with a taste-bud explosion.

He dipped his head and looked closely at her. 'Listen, I know you love that family, but you *need* to start imposing some boundaries. Puppy-dog eyes or not, Tove's right – you've got a life to live too. You need to start saying no. Except when it's to a guy – then you need to start saying yes.' He reached over and put a hand on hers. 'You know what I'm saying.'

She nodded. She knew exactly what he was saying.

He winked at her kindly, heart-stoppingly. 'Remember – it's just a job, and you're just the nanny, Bell.'

It was exactly 5.28 a.m. as she closed the door behind her with a shiver, holding the bike steady with one hand as she tucked her trousers into her socks with the other. She glanced up and down the arm's-width narrow street but no one else was around: a few bottle crates were stacked in a tower, ready for pickup, and the hand-painted A-frame advertising the craft beers in the Star Bar was propped against the wall. Quickly, she stepped on the pedal and swung her leg over the bike, gliding silently past the tiny, narrow antique shop selling ceramics and glassware, past the ancient wooden door of the rare comic emporium sited thirty feet below the street in an old wine cellar.

The cobbles glistened from the overnight rain. Her tyres sluiced through shallow puddles as she darted from alley to alley, cutting across the pedestrian thoroughfares that would soon be heaving with tourists looking for wooden Dala horses and bakeries to have *fika* in. In these long, thin alleys she was protected from the wind that came straight off the Baltic, but she knew that as soon as she took the left onto Stora Nygatan and over the bridge it would push at her back all the way to Ostermalm, until she closed the Mogerts' garden gate behind her.

Traffic was light, with few commuters out yet. Small clusters of electric scooters stood poised by the bridge, outside the main station, at street corners and by bike racks. There weren't even any drivers in the embassy cars as Bell powered up the colourful street, and she had a sense of suspension, as though the city was holding its breath – just about to exhale, just about to start up again. What would today hold?

She had slept well, awaking in the starfish position on her double bed, although she'd still wished she could stay there for another four hours. But one glance at her employers' faces as she walked in, and it was clear they had had a very different night. Both of them were pale and tense, sitting stiffly and in silence at the whitewashed kitchen table as she shut the back door quietly behind her.

'Hey,' she said in a low voice, partly so as not to wake the children, but also in deference to the sombre mood in the house. She pulled off her beanie and automatically twisted her hair into the topknot, seeing that they had managed only coffee; the island was spotlessly clean and tidy.

Hanna was dressed but Max was still in his pyjamas, and his eyes followed his partner as she got up to rinse her cup.

'Bell, thank you for coming so early. I really appreciate it.' Hanna's poise was in stark contrast to the sucker-punched disbelief of last night, but Bell could see the effort it was taking her just to present this veneer. Her mouth was pulled down at the corners, the sinews strained in her neck.

'It's the very least I could do. How are you both?'

She made a point of including Max in the question, seeing that Hanna was using manners as a mask, and he answered her with a weary nod that told her more in its fragile silence than words would.

'Did you manage to sleep at all?'

A silence followed; they seemed to be deferring to each other to answer.

'Not really,' Max said finally. His voice, usually spry and infused with an untold joke, was flat and heavy.

'No.' She bit her lip, watching as Hanna cleaned the coffee cup vigorously before immediately drying it and returning it to the cupboard. Bell wasn't sure any implement in this kitchen had ever been returned to its home without first spending at least four days on the draining board. She watched as Hanna stood, unseeing, at the cabinet for a moment, her shoulders pitched a good two inches above their usual setting, before turning around with possibly the most implausible smile Bell had ever seen – but one of the bravest.

'Right. Well, we should head off then. Traffic will get sticky if we hit rush hour.'

'Sure,' Bell agreed, offering her most reassuring smile in return, although she felt a guilty wave of relief at the prospect of stepping clear of their suffocating gloom. 'And I'll take care of everything here. Don't worry about a single thing –'

Hanna straightened her back. 'Actually, Max and I have discussed it, and we think it would be best if *you* came with me.'

Bell blinked at her, confused. '. . . Me?'

'To Uppsala, yes.'

33

She looked across at Max, who was staring into his coffee cup.

Hanna stood stiffly. 'It could be too . . . confusing.' Her voice was as brittle as toffee.

'Oh, yes,' Bell murmured. 'I can see how that . . . But what about –?'

'Max is going to work from home today. He'll take the girls to nursery.'

'. . . And Linus?'

'He's coming with us.' Hanna flinched, as though hating the indecision in her voice. 'But we don't know yet if . . . well, whether he should actually come in. That's why I need you there.' Her eyes flickered towards Max and away again without resting on him, and Bell understood they were at odds on this.

Bell went still as suddenly the maths presented itself. Linus was nine. The ex had been in a coma for seven years. 'He's . . . Linus's father?' She looked between them both. Max nodded.

Bell was stunned. In the three years she'd been working here, it had never been mentioned. She supposed she could have worked it out last night if she'd stopped to consider it, but she hadn't thought to make mathematical calculations. 'Does he know?'

Hanna whirled back to face her sharply. 'No. And I'd like it to stay that way until we get up there and I . . . I know what we're dealing with.'

Bell nodded, looking from Hanna back to Max again. He looked suitably bitten back too.

'He's awake, but we don't yet know how cognizant he will be of what's happened to him. It could upset him to see Linus so changed – he was little more than a baby when the accident happened.' Her voice was brittle and hard, shining with jagged edges that could, at any moment, draw blood. She was a mother in defence. 'On the other hand, he could be absolutely the man he was and the first person he'll want to see is his

34

son.' She gave a helpless, exaggerated shrug and stretched her mouth into a grimace, tears in her eyes. 'I have absolutely no idea what we're walking into.'

'Which is why you would be better to play it on the safe side and keep Linus here until you know the score,' Max said to her back.

'He's been in a coma for seven years, Max!' Hanna snapped, whirling round, and Bell could tell by her tone they had been arguing about this for hours. 'What if Linus is all he wants? What if he's distressed by his not being there? It could make things worse for him.'

'I sincerely doubt he's going to be that lucid.'

'Oh, because you're the expert?'

Max sighed, looking away with a shake of his head.

Hanna looked back at her. 'I need to have options, Bell. I need to go in first and assess how he is. If he's calm and lucid, Linus can come in. If he's confused or distressed or . . . not right, he doesn't.'

Bell nodded. 'Okay.'

'And if he *is* alert and okay, what are you going to say to Linus?' Max asked, his voice sounding choked. 'Are you honestly going to break it to him, in the doorway of that hospital room, that the man he's about to meet is his real father?' He stared at his wife with shining eyes. 'How do you think he's going to react to that? I mean, the shock – Jesus, the poor child! He needs time to process the facts before he's presented with the reality! We always said we would tell him together, when he was old enough – the two of us, together –'

'But we don't have that luxury now! He's woken up, and there's no time left. He's been nearer to being dead than alive, and we have to put his needs before ours – and before even Linus's. It's the very least he deserves.'

35

Max exhaled forcefully, his body rigid with anger and tension as Hanna suddenly dropped her head into her hands.

'God, this is an impossible situation,' Bell said quietly, walking over to her quickly and squeezing her shoulder comfortingly. It was a strange reversal of roles. Though her boss was only six years her senior, their very different lifestyles and choices often left Bell feeling almost adolescent in her company.

Hanna lifted her head again. 'I just need options, Max, until I know what's the best thing to do.'

'Well, you're his mother,' Max retorted snippily. 'So I don't get a final say in it. I'm not even his adoptive father. When it comes down to it, I have no legal rights.'

'This isn't about legalities.'

'Not yet it isn't,' Max said bleakly.

Hanna's mouth parted. Bell's, too. What exactly *was* ahead of them?

'Uh, look, I'll keep Linus occupied until you've seen him and you know what's best to do,' Bell murmured. Hanna nodded, but Bell could feel the tension in her arms, and her skin was icy. 'Just so I'm up to speed – what exactly has he been told about today? I'm assuming he'll be suspicious as to the early start and not going in to school?'

'I've told him we're going on a road trip and having some special time together, just the three of us.'

'. . . Okay.' It wasn't the most convincing cover story Bell had ever heard. She glanced at Max again. His arm was outstretched on the table, his body slumped against the chair. He looked . . . lost. Defeated, almost.

The sound of footsteps on the stairs made them all stiffen, Hanna withdrawing quickly and running her hands over her face and through her hair, as though prepping herself for another day at the office.

'Liney, are you ready?' she asked, turning her back to him but making an effort to sound distracted and busy as he trudged into the kitchen. His backpack was bulging, and his shoes were already on.

'Yes.' His face was still kissed with sleep, his eyes heavy. Bell knew he'd fall straight back asleep in the car.

'Now, seeing as this is a special occasion today, do you want to bring the iPad?'

The boy frowned, roused from his early-morning stupor by the question. 'Huh? You never let me take the iPad from the house.'

'But today . . .' Hanna's voice fractured and she quickly forced another grim smile. 'Today is our special day. A one-off. Go get it.'

'I can bring it?'

'That's what I said, didn't I? But hurry. We're just about to leave.'

Linus gave a small squeal of delight.

'Agh!' Hanna said, hushing him before he got too excited. 'And go up the stairs quietly, please. Your sisters are sleeping.'

'Yesss!' Linus stage-whispered, punching the air, his gaze sliding over to Bell. 'Did you hear, Bell? We're going on an adventure, just the three of us.'

'I did!' Bell gasped happily, falling into her role and pressing a hand over her heart. 'How lucky are we?'

'It's going to be the best day ever!' he said, dropping his rucksack to the floor and running from the room and back up the stairs like a stampeding wildebeest.

Bell looked back at Hanna to find her and Max staring across the room at one another in agonized silence.

No, today definitely wasn't going to be that.

Chapter Four

They stole away from the city, leaving Stockholm's waterways and copper roofs at their backs as they headed north on the E4, passing beneath vast green signs and a rosy sky until endless forests of pines lined the route. Linus remained resolutely awake, the novelty of his tablet on his lap keeping him engaged. Conversation between Bell and Hanna was muted.

Bell had so many questions she wanted to ask, but it was impossible with Linus sitting in the back seat. Every so often she glanced across at her boss, seeing how Hanna's knuckles blanched white on the steering wheel, her gaze set dead ahead with laser-beam focus, even though traffic was light. What must it be like to be driving towards a husband she hadn't had a conversation with in seven years – a father whose son had almost grown up without him? What would their first words be? *Hello? How are you? What's the weather like out there? You grew your hair? You cut your hair?* She frowned. Would the physical changes in Hanna alert him to the time he had lost? Did he know that almost a decade of his life had slipped past?

So many questions, and not one answer. It wasn't her business and yet, she had been pulled into this story too.

They arrived in Uppsala before eight, Hanna pulling into a car park with an easy familiarity that suggested she knew it well. Bell looked around with mild curiosity as she stepped out of the car. Kris had told her it was Sweden's fourth city, but there was nonetheless a quaint, small-town feel to the place, the skyline pierced by the dramatic gothic towers of a cathedral to the west. There were immediate similarities to Stockholm: the coloured buildings in red and yellow, every wall punctuated by multitudes of windows to maximize the northern light, barrelled mansard roofs. But unlike the capital's wide, pale roads, here the streets were cobbled and shaded with a froth of trees; and the city was bisected not by the sea but a rushing river with cafes strung along its banks.

Linus, sensing food, allowed Bell to take his hand, and the two of them followed after Hanna's brisk steps as she led them directly to a small cafe with a glass room at the back that overlooked the water. They ordered breakfast quickly, Linus eager to pull out his iPad again as soon as they were seated. Ordinarily Bell would have insisted he put it away at the table, but only because Hanna would have insisted on it first – and she wasn't doing that today. Special rules applied here; seemingly everyone was being cut some slack.

Hanna gazed through the window, watching a couple of ducks swimming beside the riverbank. Two young women jogged past with earbuds in, ponytails swinging.

'It seems like you know this place well,' Bell posited, not wanting to intrude on Hanna's thoughts, but not wanting either to alert Linus to the strangeness of how their day was proceeding. Several times already she had caught him glancing up at his mother with a quizzical look, and he couldn't have failed to notice their silence on the journey.

It took Hanna a moment to process her words. 'Yes, I studied here. The university is just over there.' She nodded her chin vaguely over Bell's shoulder, her voice so low that Bell had to strain to hear her. 'It's where we met.'

'You and Ma—?'

The almost imperceptible shake of Hanna's head stopped her.

'Oh,' Bell murmured, wanting to kick herself. Hanna and Max were the automatic couple, in her mind.

Hanna's stare was distant, seeing back into the past, reaching out for a life that had since slipped from their grasp, like a rope in the water snaking away and leaving ripples long after it disappeared.

'How did you meet?'

'At a party.' Hanna shrugged her eyebrows wryly. 'I was going out with a friend of his at the time.'

'Oh.'

'Yes, it was a tricky start.' Her gaze darted like a dragonfly, nervous and flighty, never settling; Bell thought she was like a hologram of herself, there but not there. 'But you know how university life is. My friends and I fell in love several times a week. I think we were in love with the idea of being in love.'

'What made him different? How did he stand out for you?'

Hanna gave a tiny smile that seemed to convey only sadness. 'Oh, it was impossible for him *not* to stand out. Blending in was never an option; every room he entered, he became the centre of it. Everyone knew who he was.'

Bell saw Hanna's gaze track over to Linus – his head was bent, immersed in some shapes-logic game Max had picked out for him.

The waitress came over with their drinks. Hanna was looking back out of the window, lost to the past again, and Bell glanced down as her phone buzzed with a new text.

'Tonight? I want to see your pretty face.' Ivan. Giving her yet another chance.

She quickly switched off the screen and turned the phone over, not wanting the distraction. But Hanna didn't want conversation either – or at least, she wasn't up to it – and they sat in distracted silence, the minutes dragging, until the food came. Bell ate as if in competition with Linus, both of them feeling ravenous after the early start and car journey, but Hanna nursed her coffee like she was just using it to warm her hands, her unseeing gaze fixed on the river rushing past outside.

'So where shall we meet you?' Bell asked her, as they all walked back to the car afterwards. The hands on the church clock were nudging nine.

'I don't know yet. Keep your phone in your pocket. I'll call you as soon as I know what's what.' Hanna's eyes slid warily over to Linus again. He was leaning against the car, his cheek pressed against the window tiredly. He looked bored. He'd been promised an adventure, after all. 'You may need to take a cab to the clinic,' she said in a low voice. 'Or else I'll meet you back here again. Either way, we'll speak.'

'Sure,' Bell nodded.

Linus automatically opened the back door as she bleeped the locks.

'No, Linus,' Hanna said, stopping him from getting in. 'Not yet. I want you to go with Bell for a bit and be a good boy for her, okay?'

His face fell. 'But where are you going?'

'I've just got a couple of things to do first, but I'm going to meet up with you in a little while.'

'But I want to stay with you.'

'Well, you can't,' Hanna said curtly, her body stiff as he reached for her arm. 'Not yet.' She looked like she was about to burst into tears.

41

Bell crouched down on her heels beside him. 'Linus, you know that saying "Spoiler Alert"?' He looked back at her sullenly and she wrinkled her brow, tapping a finger thoughtfully against her lips. 'Well, isn't it someone's birthday coming up soon . . . ?' His eyes widened. He'd been counting down to ten for the past nine weeks. Double figures, at last. 'And wouldn't it be a shame if a special surprise got ruined . . . ?'

A delighted smile spread across his lips as he got her point and she smiled back, inwardly cursing that this meant she was going to have to set up some sort of surprise on Hanna's behalf for his birthday.

Hanna shot her a grateful look as she squeezed Linus briefly. 'I won't be long, okay? You be good for Bell, and I'll see you in a bit. Quick as I can.'

They watched as she got into the car and drove away, her face pale behind the glass.

'Mamma looks sad,' Linus said, watching the car pull into the rush-hour traffic.

'No, she's not sad,' Bell said, thinking the same. 'She's just tired, that's all.'

'Because we all just woke up?'

Bell looked down at him as he slipped his hand into hers. 'Exactly. Because we all just woke up.'

He was staring straight ahead, but the view kept disappearing every few moments, his eyes opening but always closing again too, as though the darkness that had claimed him was something sticky, unable to quite let go of him. He felt a dread he couldn't explain, a fear that crept through him on hands and knees, circulating to every crevice and nook inside him. He knew what they had told him: this body that now moved at will and responded on cue had been a prison – his prison –

for years. It had been a testing site, a laboratory, as they cut and excised, prodded, poked, manipulated, bathed, turned, experimented, tweaked . . .

He was lucky, they said, but it didn't feel like that. Black shadows lingered not just around the periphery of his vision, but inside him too – a hole that threatened to grow and swallow him whole. Something was missing. He was alive, he was awake, and yet . . .

No one was speaking. After all the fuss and the shouts and the lights and the beeps and the faces, now everything was quiet and still. He didn't like it. Silence held threat for him – it was the land of the sleeping, the unconscious, the dead.

He wasn't dead – was he?

But then something came to his ear – a sweep, like the hiss of a wave – and to his eyes, a light. It was a light that grew brighter as it drew nearer, something pale and golden filling his blurry field of view. Two eyes, pale as Arctic ice, linked with his, reconnecting him to the world and blotting out the shadows. Filling him up.

No, he wasn't dead. This was life. *She* was life. She was his life.

His wife.

They were in the Stadstradgarden, watching the skateboarders and chasing pigeons, when the call came an hour and ten minutes later. Hanna's voice was like porcelain: thin, fragile, but with light shining through. 'Come now.'

She texted the address and Bell booked an Uber, running with Linus through the park together in a race, back to the street, to catch him in time. Bell pipped him to the post, just. 'Where are we going?' Linus panted, worn out but excited as they slid onto the back seat.

Bell hesitated, a twist of anxiety in her gut. It wasn't her place to tell this child the full truth that was awaiting him. 'We're meeting up with Mamma now. There's something she wants to show you.'

'You're fast,' he sighed, dropping his head back on the seat as the driver took them across town. 'Considering.'

'Considering what?' Bell asked in mock outrage. 'That I'm a *girl*?'

'That you're a grown-up. Most grown-ups can't race.'

'I'll let you into a secret,' she said, dropping her head back against the seat too. 'I'm not really a grown-up.'

He frowned. 'But you're old.'

'I'm twenty-six!' she laughed, tickling him by squeezing his thigh.

'That's old.'

'Yeah, fair enough. I've still got stride length on you, though. See?' She extended her leg and pressed it against his. 'A good six inches, I reckon. You'll be overtaking me soon, and then it'll be game over.'

'Do you think I'll be taller than you?'

'I know it. You'll take after your parents and they're both t–tall, aren't they?' She stumbled, realizing she had no idea how tall his biological father was. And *he* had no idea Max wasn't that man.

It was still such an unbelievable shock, even to her. She put her hand on his head and ruffled his hair. The poor child. He had no idea what they were driving towards.

They sank into an easy silence as they wove through the city, past a pink castle and garden squares. Bell checked her phone for new messages again – one from Kris reminding her he was working tonight and to finish the chilli in the fridge for dinner; one from Tove asking if she wanted to meet

44

up for a run – and she went back to Ivan as well, reluctantly having to decline meeting up tonight too. Even if she was back in time, she was going to be wiped out by the early start this morning. She finished the text with sad face emojis, hoping he'd understand but already half expecting him to give up on her. He had three nightclubs in Södermalm, but when she'd told him she was a nanny, he probably hadn't banked on it being *her* job that would make it so hard for them to meet.

She was just pressing send when the taxi pulled to a stop and she looked up to see they had stopped outside a modern, glass-fronted building, with 'Larna Klinik' engraved in a vast granite column.

'What are we doing here?' Linus asked as they walked through the automatic sliding doors into a minimalist atrium, softened only by feathery potted trees.

Bell scanned the stark space, her gaze skimming over the dark-suited receptionist tapping a keyboard behind a walnut desk. She was looking for Hanna's distinctive berry coat amidst the smartly dressed professionals standing, talking, in small groups and hushed voices, or reading on the leather chairs. It looked more like the lobby of a corporate hotel than a hospital.

'Bell. Linus.'

They both turned at the sound of Hanna's voice, and saw her waving to them excitedly from the mezzanine. She pointed to the staircase off to the far side, and Bell jogged after Linus as he took off to join her. Hanna had taken off her coat to reveal a camel turtleneck jumper and trousers which, from a distance and against her light hair and pale skin, gave her an impression of being indistinct and amorphous. But there had been energy in her movement, and as Bell got to the top of the stairs she saw an intensity in Hanna's blue eyes as she hugged her son.

Bell felt her own anxiety lift a little. 'All okay?' she asked lightly.

'Better than okay. Incredible,' Hanna said breathily, taking Linus by the hand and patting Bell's arm warmly. 'More than we could ever have hoped. It's a miracle.'

'Wow,' Bell beamed. 'That's so great.' After the scene she'd been greeted with last night and again in the kitchen this morning, she'd been braced for the worst, worrying what the hell Linus was going to see here today.

They walked briskly down a wide, all-white corridor that was lined on one side with vast glass windows looking onto the main thoroughfare in and out of the town. Although it was busy with sluggish traffic, no noise permeated here, a muffled hush maintained by murmuring voices, soundproofed walls and soft-close doors.

'Mamma, why are we in a hospital?' Linus asked her curiously, ogling a tray of filled specimen pots being wheeled past on a trolley.

Hanna stopped outside a door and crouched down so that they were eye to eye. She fiddled with the collar of his jacket and smoothed his hair behind one ear, gazing at him lovingly but seeming to see beyond him somehow too, as though searching for another face within his. 'Because they serve the best – the very best – ice cream in town. Right here.'

Linus blinked back at her. His expression was complacently blank, but Bell knew he was perplexed as to why anyone – even a nine-year-old boy – would want ice cream at ten o'clock on a cold December morning. 'Oh. Okay.'

'Do you want an ice cream?'

He nodded unenthusiastically. 'Sure.'

46

The door to their right opened and a nurse came out, smiling over at them perfunctorily as she began walking down the corridor, carrying various utensils on a tray. The door immediately began to swing closed on its hinges, but not before Bell glimpsed a narrow montage of the scene within: several doctors were standing around a bed. There was the usual array of high-tech machinery banking the room, and – rather less usual – a large contemporary abstract print on the wall.

'But, before we do that –'

Bell turned back to them, hearing the tension flex in Hanna's voice again. How was she going to do this? How was she going to reintroduce her son to his long-absent father?

Hanna took a big breath. 'There's someone I thought you'd like to meet.'

Linus blinked back at her, perfectly still. 'Who?'

Hanna froze momentarily. '. . . An old friend.'

'Of yours?'

'Of both of ours. But you were very little the last time you met, so you may not remember.' Hanna tipped her head fractionally to one side, as though it was a question, a nudge *to* remember a long-forgotten face.

Linus glanced over towards the wide door, as though sensing the mystery friend was behind it. 'Did I like her?'

'Actually, she's a he. And yes, you did, very much. You were the –' Her voice faltered suddenly. 'You were the best of friends.'

'What's his name?' Linus asked.

Hanna blinked, her smile stuck on her face but the fear gathering in her eyes again. Bell could see her courage slipping away like a tide; her body seemed to stiffen in the pose, becoming implacable and defensive. '. . . Well, why don't we go in and you can introduce yourself?'

What?

Bell frowned. Hanna wasn't going to leave it to Linus to work out the connection on his own, surely? But though her mouth opened in protest – like Max's – he wasn't her son, and she had to stay quiet as Hanna rose up, holding his hand. They turned to go in.

The door opened with a swoosh, the faint suckering of the draughtproofing brushes punctuating the quiet, and the group of doctors surrounding the bed turned as one. Their gazes swept over Hanna and settled downwards, on Linus.

'Ah, Hanna, you're back,' one of them said from the far side of the bed, and Bell recognized the woman's voice from the phone call yesterday. Dr Sorensen. Her voice had a pointed quality to it, as though her words carried hidden meaning.

The door closed, clamping down on any leaky audio from the outside world, hermetically sealing them in a pristine environment. Bell hung back against the wall, casting a curious gaze around the room and immediately feeling her own past reattach to her with sticky fingers. She was, sadly, no stranger to hospital rooms, but this was unlike any she had ever seen. She could still see at night, when she closed her eyes, the metal bed frames, the linoleum floor, the smell of antiseptic, the blue-tinged strip lights. But in here, there were framed photographs on a cabinet by the bed, expensive bed linen with a camel-coloured Hermes 'H' cashmere blanket, a potted weeping fig tree in one corner, a comfortable red linen armchair, and artwork on the walls that looked like it required insurance certificates. Was this the reality of long-term care? Personalize the environment in case he wakes up, disoriented, confused? She would have been overjoyed if this was her bedroom, full stop, much less in a hospital.

Hanna and Linus were standing by the bed, the doctors

flanking them like bodyguards so that all she could see was the line of a leg beneath a sheet, a glimpse of an almost-shaved head, dark stubble grazing the shockingly white scalp. She saw the head move as the doctor in charge touched his arm – responsive, alert, functions which had seemingly been impossible even the day before yesterday.

'I've brought a special visitor for you,' she heard Hanna say, also in an altered voice. 'Do you remember I said I would bring someone very special?'

On cue, Linus took a micro-step forward. His head was dipped and even from behind, Bell could see he was feeling shy and reluctant.

A silence billowed through the room, punctuated only by the rhythmic beat of machines monitoring his blood pressure, oxygen saturation levels . . . One of them started flashing, and the nearest doctor turned and began pressing buttons.

In the gap that opened up, Bell saw his profile. He was staring back at his son with a blank look, his skin pallid, the bony nub of his shoulders smooth beneath his hospital gown. She felt herself recoil. He was awake and he was alive, but he was not living. Not yet. His was a body that hadn't seen daylight in seven years, skin that hadn't felt sunshine or a cold breeze in almost a decade. For all those years, he had hovered in the realm of the unconscious, with only a hair's breadth between the sleeping and the dead.

By contrast, Linus was overstuffed with life force – radiant and rosy, glossy and glowing from his run in the park. His curls shone like golden leaves, and there was something about the outward curve of his plump cheeks that seemed a rebuke to the sunken dip of his father's. There was no mirror in the room, but his father's hand must have travelled upon his face; he surely knew the hard shapes he made in that bed.

49

'Hello, I'm Linus. I'm nearly ten.' His arm rose like a lever, Hanna standing crooked and immobile beside him, like a twig caught in a frozen lake. The moment stretched out – elastic, expansive – as the small arm stayed pointing towards him until slowly, he lowered it again.

Linus looked up at his mother, a dawning look of panic on his face. 'Did I do something wrong?' he whispered. Bell felt a pinch of concern.

'It's okay, it's fine,' Hanna whispered, placing a hand on his head.

Another doctor, an Asian woman standing closest to them, crouched down and smiled at him encouragingly. 'Don't take it to heart, Linus, your father is still very weak –'

Silence cracked like a clap of thunder, a brilliant white light exploding in the room as the mistake was realized, and for several moments, the room was held in a suspended state. No one breathed, stirred, spoke. But then a sound started up – a sound made from fright, the moment before a scream – and the energy in the room shifted like a hibernating bear turning over in its cave, a great immobile mass suddenly moved and unsettled from position.

The sound yawned into the room, a moan that rapidly became a siren wail – and through the gaps, as the doctors suddenly converged, Bell saw the emaciated, atrophied body on the bed beginning to thrash with surprising force.

Linus gave a scream of fright and began to cry, but Hanna was rooted still, unable to tear her gaze from the unravelling scene on the bed.

'Get them out!' Dr Sorensen barked as the doctors all grabbed a limb and tried to restrain their patient. There were six of them, and still it was a challenge.

Hanna, somehow, bundled Linus to her and they staggered

back two paces from the bed, watching on in horror as bed straps were buckled onto his wrists and ankles, pinning him in place. But it wasn't enough. His body still writhed, his head banging against the pillow, screams and obscenities crashing around the room with frightening violence. The chaos bloomed into deeper colours, spreading wide its petals so that everything lay exposed and vulnerable, screams echoing in the stark space and raining down on them all, wails and moans and shouts blending into an indistinct maw.

Bell ran over to the mother and son, both of them frozen, Hanna's body rigid in her grip.

'We need to leave,' she said, shaking Hanna firmly, wrenching her attention off the horror in the bed. 'We need to get Linus out of here. *Now.*' And she forcibly pushed them both towards the door, their footsteps stumbling and leaden.

She flung open the door and the screams and curses and profanities and moans escaped into the corridor with them, like a rush of ghouls. A nurse walking by startled at the tumult, silence dropping as suddenly as a velvet curtain again as soon as the door swished shut.

'Can I help?' she asked, seeing their ashen faces.

'We're fine. But thank you,' Bell managed, seeing how Hanna was trembling, as white as the walls. The nurse walked on.

'Come and sit down, you look faint,' Bell said, tugging Hanna forward by the arm to a leather tub chair. She collapsed into it, staring into nowhere, caught in her own head.

Bell crouched down to clasp her arms around Linus. 'Hey, are you okay?' she whispered, pulling back to look into his eyes, to smooth his hair back from that beautiful face, to reassure him that it was all okay again. His sobs had subsided, but his eyelashes were glossy with hot tears. He nodded, but the movement was shaky, the movement of a child wanting to make his mother happy again; his eyes kept tracking back to her, fearful.

'Are you sure?'

He nodded again, but he would only look at his mother.

'Hanna?' she asked, turning to her too and touching her arm lightly.

Hanna blinked, her eyes darting everywhere. 'I'm . . . I'm fine.'

Bell felt the silence expand as they each recovered. Away from the distraction of the confusion and chaos in that room, in the calm of this corridor, it was filled with something heavy – something that had been said and couldn't be unsaid. She felt a rush of anger that Hanna had allowed this to happen. To have handled it that badly . . . Max had been right. Linus should never have come here; and if Hanna was adamant he must, she should have told him the truth before they'd gone in. She should have explained exactly who that man was, and what had happened to him – and what might happen when he was reunited with the poppy-tall son he had last seen as a toddler. Instead, she'd left it to chance, and it had blown up in the most terrible of ways.

'She called him my father.' It was a statement, a question, an accusation.

Oh God. Bell felt her stomach twist as she saw the uncomprehending expression on Linus's tear-streaked face. He had been told the truth, and now Hanna had to explain it to him. Everything was back to front; it should never have happened this way . . .

Hanna looked back at him, finally, and with outstretched arms, drew him towards her. Her hands were trembling still, her smile sketchy and weak. Bell swallowed. How could she say these words, here, in a hospital corridor? Max, fifty miles away, unable to tell the boy he had raised as his own that he was still his father, would always be that.

'. . . That doctor was just confused, sweetheart.'

Linus blinked, not so easily fooled. He was nearly ten, almost in double figures, a few years from being a teenager. 'But she said—'

'I know, but she was wrong. He's just an old friend of mine. He's your *godfather*.'

Bell stared at her in horror. What the hell was she doing? She could understand why Hanna hadn't told Linus about his real father before he had woken up: Linus would have been just a toddler when the accident had happened, and if the prognosis had been so poor . . . And Max had been an excellent father to him. There had never been any sense of difference that even she had discerned between his affection for Linus and for his sisters. But all of that was irrelevant now that the man in there was awake and was, in one way or another, going to be back in their lives. Linus had to know the truth. It couldn't be kept from him. And yet –

'*You* know who your daddy is.'

Linus looked confused. Of course he knew his own father. Max. The man at breakfast and dinner, kicking a ball in the park on Saturdays and there at every school concert and play. The man who made the World's Best BLT and tickled him till he wet himself, who had never yet beaten him at Fortnite and yet still played without complaint, who took him to the Hammarby IF handball games in Eriksdalshallen and went skiing off-piste with him whilst the girls did the bunny runs, who watched all the Bond films in one week with him when he'd broken his leg. He had never even questioned it.

53

He looked back towards the room, its door firmly shut, no sound escaping from it now. 'So he's my godfather?'

Hanna hesitated, then gave another shrug, the action careless and cold. 'Yes.' She took his hand in hers and kissed it, her decision made, her resolve growing again. 'Like I said, just someone I used to know.'

Linus softened, accepting the lie, the tension slackening in his face. 'So then, can we get ice cream now?'

Another pause, and Bell saw invisible doors to the truth slamming between them and clicking to a lock.

'Sure,' Hanna smiled, getting up and – still holding his hand – beginning to swing his arm as they turned and walked down the corridor, as though they were in the park.

Bell stood rooted to the spot as she watched them go ahead, walking without a backward glance from the room where a man lay distressed, withered – and now abandoned. He had spent seven years here on the brink of death, trapped in a half-life, but his injuries had robbed him of far more than his consciousness. He couldn't know it yet, but, Bell thought as she followed slowly after his wife and son in silent dismay, he was soon going to realize that waking up had been the easy part.

Part Two

Part Two

Chapter Five

Six months later – June 2020

'The dolls' house? *Really*?' Bell asked, looking down at the pink plastic monstrosity. It had a purple handle shaped like a hairbrush. An oversized doll had been squashed into one of the rooms, leaving its backside dangling alarmingly through the window.

'Mamma said we could!' Tilde protested, looking up at her imploringly.

'Well, I guess if Mamma says it's okay . . .' Bell sighed, blowing out through her cheeks as she looked around at the ever-increasing pile of toys surrounding the never-diminishing pile of bags on the floor.

Max came running back through, ready to cart the next load into the car. 'Right, we're nearly – Oh!'

Bell gave him an 'exactly' look.

'That wasn't there a minute ago, was it?'

'Mamma said we could!' Tilde repeated, just as Hanna herself came down the stairs with a gently enquiring glance.

'Well, if Mamma says it's okay, I guess it's okay,' Max shrugged, picking up the dolls' house in one hand and Linus's new skateboard and ramp in the other, soft bags shoved under his arms.

Hanna shot them all a distracted smile as she walked through into the kitchen. It was the usual chaotic mess in spite of Bell's best efforts to keep it tidy; the weaponry involved in making Linus's emergency sandwich was still on the counter, Max's files were spread across the table, and the twins' costumes for the upcoming *Midsommar* festival had once again been pulled from the dressing-up box and strewn across the floor during a game of 'weddings'.

Bell grabbed the stray garments as she jogged in, folded them expertly into neat piles, and set to wiping off the crumbs and putting the dirty cutlery into the dishwasher, ready for Max to put it on tonight. He was on a deadline for his new client, and would be only coming to join them at the end of the week.

'Did you find the beach towels?' Hanna asked her, checking for something in her purse.

'Yes. They were in the blue Ikea bag at the top of the wardrobe in the spare room.'

Hanna stopped, as if to consider this. 'Oh yes. I didn't think to look there. Huh.'

'And Linus has packed his project,' Bell said, half over her shoulder as she rinsed the glasses that had been left in the sink.

She stopped again. 'Remind me . . . ?'

'Glacial retreat in the Arctic Circle.'

'Oh yes.' Hanna zipped up her purse and replaced it in her bag, pulling out the tickets and casually skimmed over the details; but Bell already knew the reason Max was red-cheeked and wild-eyed was because they had to leave in precisely six minutes if they were going to make it to the ferry.

She turned off the tap and shook her hands dry, realizing too late that she had forgotten to plant out the potted rose Hanna had received as a gift from a patient.

'Are you ready? Where is everybody?' Max's voice came through the house, his shadow long and angular in the bright sunlit pool on the hall floor. 'It's going to leave without you if you don't get a move on!'

The sound of stampeding feet on the stairs heralded the twins' call to action, and the slow thud coming up from the playroom reintroduced Linus into the scene, a smear of jam at the corner of his mouth.

'Have you got everything?' Hanna asked him, seeing the iPad in his hands again. That and his skateboard were increasingly all he wanted. 'Did you bring a book?'

'No, should I?'

'*Should* you?' Hanna tutted. 'Honestly, Linus, we discussed this.'

'I'll go find something now, then.'

'Hurry up!' Max's voice carried through again, growing in impatience. 'Move faster! You all need to get into the car. Now, now, now.'

Hanna sighed, sounding as exasperated by Max as she was by her son. She swung her handbag over her shoulder. 'You'll have to read something already out there then, although I doubt there'll be much of interest to a ten-year-old boy. *Moby-Dick*?' She put her hand on his shoulder, directing him into the square hall and towards the front door. 'Perhaps that'll teach you to do as you're told next time.'

Bell grabbed her own bag – a Sandqvist rolled backpack – and did another visual sweep of the room. It was as well Max was coming on afterwards, as they had no doubt forgotten half of what they needed and brought double of what they didn't.

She grabbed the electric scooter she'd left rather naughtily propped up in the hall – they weren't supposed to be taken into private premises, but she hadn't been able to risk someone else taking it. There were far fewer left lying around in the Ostermalm district, and there wasn't room for the entire family *and* their luggage *and* her in the car. She pulled the front door shut behind her. Poor Max was attempting to close the boot, only for it to bounce off the bulging contents within. It took three attempts and all his body weight before it finally clicked shut.

'I'll see you down there,' she said cheerily, stepping onto the board and scooting past them all, but no one noticed. Linus was back on his screen again, head bent at that pronounced angle that was no doubt going to make chiropractors rich in the coming generation, and the girls were too busy fighting over a Pippi Longstocking doll to see her go. Hanna was staring into space, her mouth slightly parted as though she was watching television on the windscreen.

Bell turned around the corner, happy to have a few precious minutes to herself – she sensed there wasn't going to be any let-up for the next four days – and let the breeze whistle around her neck as she zipped easily through the streets. Many families had left already; the surplus of empty parking spaces was the signature of summer in the capital. The horse chestnut, alder and beech trees were bushy-headed and thronging with life, squirrels leaping from branch to branch; choirs of birds sang riotously, hidden by the leaves. Window boxes rippled with bold colours, tulips and lavender, and everyone walked with the slight bounce that came with warm, sunny days in the holidays. There were people everywhere – tourists sitting in cafes, students perched on low walls – but traffic was still light as she emerged from the residential streets and joined the main flow downtown.

Getting to the city's beating heart took only four minutes

by scooter but as she wove along the widening streets, it was like a chameleon changing colour – the same, but different. High street stores and commercial offices lining the avenues, museums and libraries replacing townhouses, playgrounds swapped for imperial bronze statues, gardens for parks; and around every corner, the sea, a glistening sliver of ice blue, like the ribbon round a wedding cake.

The Nybroviken port was a horseshoe-shaped basin, flanked on all sides by the city's grandest luxury hotels. Seagulls wheeled overhead, cawing loudly, some roosting contentedly, others waddling heavily along the promenade like grey-suited businessmen with big bellies and their hands behind their backs. Fleets of white ferries nodded and bumped against the harbour walls, their gangplanks laid down like medieval drawbridges as passengers stepped aboard with bags, or sometimes just a newspaper. The earliest birds were already sitting on the open decks out back, sunning themselves and waiting patiently to be whisked to the archipelago.

Not the Mogerts, though. They had beaten her down, but Bell cracked a wry smile at the sight of her adopted family, the chaos amidst the calm: Max illegally parked, hazard lights flashing as he frantically disgorged almost the entire contents of their home onto a small flatbed trailer one of the crew had brought over to them. Hanna was talking to the captain, who was nodding at something she was saying and looking over her shoulder at Max's efforts. Linus was leaning against the lamp post, still absorbed in the game on the iPad, the girls having seemingly made up and Tilde examining something on Elise's palm.

Bell rode up to Max, who had by now worked up a sweat. She left the scooter beside a bench for the next punter and helped him place the last of their luggage onto the trailer: a fishing net and a guitar.

'You play?' she asked in surprise, as together they followed the crewman across the cobbles. She'd never heard anyone in the house playing an instrument before; they were a creative family, but not particularly a musical one.

He rolled his eyes. 'Not me, no.'

'Oh good, you made it,' Hanna said, turning to them both, and Bell wasn't sure to which of them her comment was directed.

'Yes,' Max sighed, removing his glasses and rubbing the sweat off his face. He was dressed in shorts and a linen shirt, driving shoes with no socks; he looked ready for a morning on a boat, rather than sitting alone in a large, empty house, working at the kitchen table. Not for the first time lately, Bell felt sorry for him.

She saw how his gaze snagged and caught on Hanna, as though to look at her was somehow illicit.

'Come on, kids, say bye to Daddy,' Bell said quickly, deciding they needed privacy and hustling the children towards him for alternately bashful (Linus) and exuberant (the twins) hugs.

'See you in a few days, Max,' she said with a brisk nod as the kids crossed the gangplank ahead of her. She would be getting on the same ferry he'd be disembarking from on Friday afternoon. She hurried the children into the boat, sighing as they automatically ran up to the food counter and pleaded for muffins. Getting them apples instead, she also ordered coffees for herself and Hanna, glancing back as she reached into her pocket for change. Hanna and Max were standing on the gangplank, his hands on her waist, eyes locked. Even from a distance, it was evident the world had fallen away for them. Lovers in love.

'Can we go on the top deck?' Tilde asked her excitedly, pulling her back. 'I want to make my face hot.'

Bell groaned. Such was the substance of *her* days. 'Well, not too hot, I hope,' she said, allowing herself to be led towards the stairs. 'We wouldn't want it melting off now, would we?'

The ferry pulled away with a peremptory dismissal of the maritime city, leaving it behind in its island chunks, the bright copper roofs and colourful, canopied windows of Gamla Stan quickly giving way to contemporary-looking tower blocks and duplexes, and then to ever larger and grander suburban houses. Bell felt the equation shift quickly, the solid mass of urban sprawl diminishing against the mercurial body of the vast sea, land breaking down into crumbs until it was water, water as far as the eye could see. It was an idyllic, sparkling blue under these clear skies today, but she had seen the archipelago turn on numerous occasions – brown and churning – and she knew this was a fragile peace.

They found a table at the very back of the top deck, just out of reach of the protective covered area, leaving them to the mercy of the elements, the wind wildly whipping everyone's hair. It was a beautiful day, so they weren't cold, but Bell knew that by the time they disembarked in two hours they would look like crows had nested on them – and that they'd be burned. She dug out the suncream and began slathering it onto Elise's face.

Hanna was sitting inside, downstairs, doing some work on her laptop, and Bell had to keep the girls from running down to her every ten minutes. They passed much of the journey playing I Spy and Would You Rather, Elise setting everyone into deep contemplation with her conundrum of 'would you rather eat a whole raw onion or drink mustard'?

Bell's gaze kept returning to the archipelago; it was impossible not to. There were so many tiny, almost fragment-like, islets and islands and skerries – Kris had once mentioned a figure of 30,000 – that on a map, they looked like smashed glass on a stone floor. Some were nothing but smooth rock plateaus, breaching the glassy surface like beluga whales; others were fully forested and bushy, like distant, dark clumps of moss floating upon the water.

This would be her third summer on the archipelago; it was where she had truly fallen in love with the country, why she'd decided to stay. Stockholm was great – smaller than London, friendlier than Paris, calmer than Rome, even cooler than Berlin – but experiencing the Swedes' summer lifestyles at their island cabins and houses had been a game-changer for Bell. Her own childhood had been spent summering on the North Norfolk coast, sailing and crabbing and playing tennis, but the version here was even more stripped back, raw. Pure. Some of the islets were so incredibly tiny that there was barely enough room for a single-room cabin to perch on the rocks; clearly, electricity and heating and running water weren't options. There was really nothing for the occupants to do but sit on the shore and read, fish, swim and watch the boats go by.

And there were a *lot* of boats to watch. Saturday mornings in particular looked like regattas, with low-lying yawls and ketches and sloops in full sail, small speedboats zipping over the water's surface, some towing inflatables or water-skiers, jet-bikers carving into tight turns and trying to catch air over the ferries' wakes.

Bell always loved the two months she spent with the Mogerts here. Their island – known in the family as Summer Isle – was still small compared to some; it took just fifteen minutes to walk around, whereas the larger ones would take perhaps an hour and the very smallest, just a couple of minutes. But they had a few neighbours, including Gustav Persson, an elderly man who spent ten months of the year in an almost defiantly rudimentary cabin on the northern tip; it got the worst of the weather and had been patched numerous times with squares of corrugated tin, so that the effect on approach was of a patchwork house. There was another house, too, further up from the main jetty on the eastern side, owned by a middle-aged couple, the Janssons, from Halmstad. It was painted in the traditional brownish-red, with white square windows and a Swedish flag flapping from a pole out front. None of the gardens had delineated boundaries, and it had taken Bell a while to adapt to the idea that the island was theirs collectively; people were largely sensible about respecting each other's privacy without the need for fences, walls or gates.

Her own accommodation was a tiny cabin set twenty metres or so back from the family's main house. They were both painted black, as though to demonstrate the connection to passers-by or trespassers. But where the main house sat dead centre, back from a curved private beach, her tiny cabin was tucked into a thicket of trees at the far end, with a path leading through the moss to a narrow inlet in the rocks. From there, she could step straight down into the water, and it had become something of a private ritual for her to skinny-dip under the midnight sun before bed each night.

The space was almost unimaginably small when she was away from it – just big enough for a bed, table and chair, and tiny kitchenette hidden in a cupboard. The toilet was housed in an add-on room around the back, old-school style, and the shower was outdoors, clad with rickety timber panels and prone to spitting water. It wasn't the easiest way to live, but the vast majority of her time was spent in comfort at the family house anyway, and she was grateful for the brief respite of peace and solitude at the beginning and end of each day.

The truth was, she could hardly wait to get back there and she felt a small thrill as she began to recognize elements of the nautical landscape. Last year, she had spent a lot of time with Linus particularly, pootling around the neighbouring islands while the girls – only two years old at the time – played on the beach and napped with their parents. She and Linus had kayaked together along the coves almost every day, looking out for orcas and herons and choosing which houses or boats they liked best, so the landmarks from those adventures stood out to her now: the bright-yellow lichen-covered rock at the tip of the island with the freshwater pool in the middle; the ragged flag by the tumbledown, storm-ruined jetty on the island three away from them; the deep cove where they'd found a dead gull in the water. And then, up ahead, the tip of the steepled Sandhamn tower peeking through the trees and announcing itself to passing sailors and travellers. It was set on a tall scaffold, rather like a gigantic dovecote. Max had told her last year that it had originally served as the piloting bridge, or lookout, back when piloting – navigating ships through the straits to Stockholm as commercial trading developed – had been the islanders' primary income.

The land bellied out and swooped back in again in dynamic curves, the cabins beginning to cluster close together on the rocks like barnacles, and she saw the ferry channel up ahead narrow into a wincingly tight strait as Sandhamn's shores all but kissed those of its neighbour Lökholmen. Inching through, they rounded a headland and suddenly a small harbour opened out and stretched away from them; fronting the town, it was a mini metropolis in the Baltic vastness.

They had arrived.

'Okay, everyone, have you all got your things?' Bell asked, checking that backpacks were zipped shut and nothing had been left on their seats. 'Let's join Mamma downstairs. Now remember, you're all going to need to be patient while we get the stuff off the boat. Linus, you're in charge of looking after your sisters, okay?'

He nodded nonchalantly.

'I don't need him to look after me,' Elise protested. 'I'm big enough to look after myself.'

Linus and Bell made eye contact, but said nothing. She gave him a wink instead.

They all walked carefully down the stairs and back into the cabin, where Hanna was sitting with her laptop shut, her hands resting one upon the other as she stared out of the window. Who could blame her? Even from inside, it was a magnificent sight. The approach past the neighbouring islands, Telegrafholmen, Lökholmen and Krokso, was so tight, it was a constant marvel to Bell that the big boats could get through it. She could easily throw a stone from one isle to the next, and even just coming in on the little putt-putt for morning bread and papers, it felt confined, like a canal.

The rocks on either side of the strait swelled like mini mounts, twenty, thirty feet high, their lower edges draped with seaweed, a tide line marking the stone. The tiny port fanned out gently to the sides; everything seemed gentle here – weather-worn, accepting, welcoming. To the right was the police and fire station, an orange helicopter sitting idle as a couple of uniformed officers talked about something that probably wasn't crime-related. The island had a grand total of ninety full-time residents, and although that number swelled to 3,000 in the summer months – with a further 100,000 visitors and day-trippers annually – the worst thing that usually happened on the island was someone illegally mooring on a berth, or dropping litter.

There was a pub, the well-stocked grocery store Westerbergs, a bakery, gift shop, art gallery, clothing boutique – and, to the left of the harbour, the grand Yacht Hotel, which had once been the headquarters of the Royal Swedish Yacht Club. It was by far the swankiest place on the island, with a smart restaurant for dinner dates and a beach club vibe at its outdoor pool and grill. Bell knew it well, for all the big summer festivals and parties usually ended up being celebrated there.

She looked over now as they disembarked, hearing the distant shouts and splashes coming from the pool just out of sight. She wished she could take the kids over there for an ice cream, just to get her eye in on the scene again; but Hanna was already talking intently to a man she had known for years, Jakob Cedergren, the harbourmaster. A bearded man with a pronounced limp and ready smile, he was one of The Ninety, and he clearly loved his job, his family and his life. As far as he was concerned, his world might not be big but it was pretty close to perfect. Bell had left last summer on cheery 'hai hai' terms with him, but would he remember her now? She would never be on the inside track like Hanna and Max, who had been coming here all their adult lives.

'Linus, if you stand with the girls there,' she said, taking them to the nearby hut where fizzy drinks, ice creams and newspapers were for sale, 'I'm going to start unloading our stuff.'

'You're not in charge of me,' she heard Elise say bossily to Linus as she hurried back up the gangplank. She found one of the crew standing in front of their not so much luggage as *home*, scratching his head in bafflement. Everything had been stacked into a precarious tower beside a door that led down to the bilge pumps.

'Don't worry, it's ours. I'm here,' Bell called, jogging up behind him and reaching down for the first load. 'I'll get it cleared out.'

'How are *you* going to manage all that?' he asked, frowning at the sight of her and all the luggage. At five feet four inches, she wasn't small, but neither was she a seven-foot power-lifter. 'You know we leave again in an hour?'

'Not a problem. Our boat's just . . . there,' she huffed, hoisting a bulging soft leather holdall under each arm, along with three tennis racquets, the dolls' house and the guitar. She jerked her chin towards the nearest porthole and beyond it, the Mogerts' humble boat, *Nymphea*. In spite of the name, she was no beauty: she had a tired white hull, a dated red-painted water- and bowline, with a semi-enclosed cabin and just enough room for sitting out in front, more on the bench seats at the back. Max's father had bought her when he was a teenager, Max 'inheriting' her when the twins were born (and, as Max muttered, the maintenance bills became unsustainable). Max called her a plodder: she was unimaginative but dependable for ferrying the family and small groups from their island to others in the vicinity and, of course, back to here. Sandhamn was their portal back to the real world again, where they came for bread, papers, human contact and medical help.

The crewman gave her a sceptical look. 'Let me help.'

'Oh, really?' she asked, smiling gratefully.

He shrugged. 'I can hardly leave you to do it alone. There must be slavery laws against that sort of thing.'

She grinned. He was young, good-looking . . . Hanna was still engrossed in conversation; it apparently hadn't crossed her mind to help Bell unload their belongings. 'Well, thanks,' she said, giving a wriggle and small jump to hoist the bags higher under her arms again. 'I'm Bell, by the way.'

'Per.'

Together they carried the first of the piles to the boat, Bell glancing over every few strides to check on the children; they were sitting slumped on a low wall, looking very bored.

Nymphea was thankfully moored close by, in her usual berth at the near end of the jetty. The chandlery yard had serviced her and put her back in the water in time for the summer. Bell dropped her pile carefully on the ground, but Per was a few steps ahead of her and had hopped onto the deck before she could even pull in the bowline. He held out his hands for the first consignment.

'Anywhere's fine,' she said as he looked around the modest deck for a place to put their stuff. Hanna had the key, so the cabin was still locked. Bell tried not to think about having to unload it all at the other end as well.

It was another two runs before they had everything transferred.

'Finally! Lugging all that across really would have killed me if I'd had to do it on my own,' she said with a roll of her eyes. 'Thanks.'

'No problem.' He smiled.

She felt his interest creep towards her like a tide coming in, and she knew what he was going to ask as they began walking back towards the hard standing again; but she was distracted, her gaze constantly strobing for the kids. It always worried her, the girls being so near to the water, even though Linus and Hanna were close by. They weren't yet strong swimmers, and there'd been a fright when Elise had fallen in the pool at a friend's house the year before and Max had had to jump in to save her, fully clothed.

Per turned to her as they approached. '. . . So listen, are you hungry? We could get some lunch if you've got time?'

'Oh sorry, I'm working.' She jerked her head towards the children; at least they were sitting in the shade. 'I'm on duty.' She gave an apologetic grimace.

'Oh.' He looked disappointed. It was like she'd kicked a puppy.

'But another time, perhaps?' She liked his manners and he was roughly her age – okay, maybe a *bit* younger, but why not?

'You'll be here long?'

'All summer,' she shrugged. 'My employers have a place on the lagoon past Krokso.'

'Okay, so then I'm bound to see you around. We come over every day,' he said excitedly.

'Yeah,' she shrugged, not minding either way. 'And I'm back in the city at weekends, so . . . y'know. Whatever.' She got her phone out and gave him her Snapchat details.

'Great. We'll set something up.'

'Sure.' She glanced over again, knowing she should get back to the kids, seeing how Hanna and Jakob were still locked in conversation. 'Honestly. What *are* they talking about?'

Per sighed, looking used to it. 'Catching up on all the gossip. This is Jakob's favourite time of year. He calls it 'reconnecting' with everyone but really, he's just an old woman blathering at the garden gate. He does this to someone on every drop we make.'

'*Is* there really that much gossip to be had here?' she asked sceptically.

'More than you'd believe. A beluga was spotted a mile from here last week; the local reclusive billionaire's back on the scene; there's already a scandal around the Gotland Cup –'

He stopped talking suddenly and flashed her a grin. 'But I won't tell you too much. That way you'll be incentivized to have that lunch with me. Or drink.'

She looked back at him. 'It sounds like there's a lot I need to hear.'

'Oh yeah,' he said, his gaze locking with hers flirtatiously. 'The summer season has officially kicked off.'

Chapter Six

The water lay stretched and tight like a bolt of sapphire silk, not so much as a wrinkle on its surface as *Nymphea* chugged efficiently out of the marina and into the narrow sound. They passed within metres of the opposite islands of Lökholmen and Krokso, which stood as buffers between Sandhamn and the open sea, heading back towards the strait.

Summer Isle, officially called Strommskar, lay a short distance behind them as part of a separate constellation of small, semi-linked holms, some so close to one another it was as though they were holding hands underwater. Max had described it for her as roughly forming the shape of a number six, with several breaches in the perimeter of the belly where occasionally curious sailors would glide silently through on their way back to the strait.

The children (Linus, really) had named the islands individually – Dead Man's Bones on account of the hop-skip-and-jump collection of rocks that looked like a floating skeleton; Rockpools because of the inland ponds where they fished for minnows; Little Summer, which was right next to them; 007 because it had a big house that couldn't be seen from the water, and the entire island was privately owned by a secretive rich family; Swan's Nest after they were chased away by an aggressive cob . . .

Summer Isle was perhaps a square kilometre in total and was one of the more forested isles, with bare rock only on the perimeter; moss and pine needles carpeted the ground, and the light fell through the shimmying canopies in golden splinters. Last summer, Bell had spent hours exploring the island's nooks and crannies with the children, fishing nets tightly gripped in their small fists as they pretended the smooth, pinkish rocks were sleeping hippos, the four of them spinning in circles, arms outstretched and their faces turned upwards like daisies, in the sunny pools of the scattered glades.

The children sat beside her now on the bench seats, wearing their lifejackets and enjoying the breeze on their faces as Hanna expertly guided the boat in closer. She knew instinctively where to avoid and turn, and had no need of the warning sticks alerting her to submerged rocks just below the surface. Max had been coming here since he was a boy and he had taught Hanna well.

The jetty was already visible, the Janssons' sun-bleached flag flapping limply further up the shoreline. Bell joined the children as they instinctively twisted in their seats and looked down into the water as they drew ever closer, spotting the small stones on the sandy bottom, the delicate lacy fronds of spiracea and strife lilting with the tide; a crab scuttling nimbly across the seafloor, falling still as the shadow of the boat passed over.

Hanna docked with precision and she and Bell helped the children safely off the boat, Bell passing up the luggage bags for the two of them to carry between them. The rest of the children's toys and sports kit would have to come up on separate trips.

They followed the grassy path through the trees, the girls stepping onto old stumps, picking up jumbo fir cones and stopping to nibble on wild blueberries. It had taken Bell several weeks on her first visit to successfully navigate her way through the forest to the Mogerts' house without circumventing the entire island, doubling back on herself or inadvertently dropping in on the neighbours. But her eye had found the clues eventually – look for the broken branch, go past that fallen tree, turn left at the salty marsh where the frogs chirrup at night.

It was never dark anywhere here in the summer months, but light only fell in narrow blades at the very centre of the island, cutting past the trees in whisper-thin arrows as they wound through the slim-legged trunks one after the other. Linus was managing to carry a couple of bags too, the guitar slung across his body, but Bell seemed to have the heaviest load and her muscles were burning as she held and braced them at awkward angles. The cut-through across to the other side was probably only an eight-minute walk from the jetty to the cabin, but every minute felt quadruple that. She felt a wave of relief when the sea gradually emerged as a backdrop to the trees, growing ever bluer and brighter, until eventually they stepped out of the shady woods and the blue sea met the bright sky again.

'Thank God,' she groaned, letting the bags drop to the ground with a soft thud as the girls immediately shrieked at the sight of their familiar playground and ran down to the gentle scoop of sand. Tilde found a driftwood stick, and proudly wrote her name. Linus sank onto the bottom step of the deck and watched them, left out and looking overdressed now in his jeans and grey sweatshirt.

Bell looked back at her home for the next six weeks, bar weekends when she could escape back to the city for some much needed time out with her friends. Built on the site of the original cabin that had belonged to Max's grandparents and parents – and which had eventually succumbed to a storm – the Mogerts' place was a largish, modernist cabin with black pine cladding and walls of huge sliding plate-glass windows. It was surrounded on all sides by a large deck set on a bed of smooth rocks. Their shallow cove was on the lee shore on the south-westerly side of the island, away from the main nautical thoroughfare. Good for privacy, less so for prevailing winds.

Hanna walked up the steps and over the deck, reaching into a battered, fraying fishing creel propped up against the back wall that looked distinctly at odds with the pristine minimalism of the rest of the house. It was an inherited piece too; much of the 'kit' here was – repaired fishing nets, sun-bleached buckets, hand-whittled rods – but inside the newly built house, everything was pale blonde and white, the furniture bent wood and minimal. It was so sparse that in winter the effect would have been cold and severe, but the family never came out before June, and for summer it was perfect.

Hanna slid open the door, having 'aired' the place on a weekend in May with Max, checking for any over-winter repairs that needed seeing to and stocking up the larder with non-perishables. 'Home sweet home,' she sighed, stepping in with a curious gaze before beginning to slide back the rest of the walls.

Bell picked up the bags for one last time and lumbered them into the house. With all the doors opened on three sides, the breeze blew happily through the cabin, carrying in the sharp briny tang of the sea, dragonflies darting in curiously, the hiss of the tide sinking into the sand, the girls' chattering voices . . . Outside became inside here; it was all one.

Linus went straight to his room, Hanna's eyes following him as she let the taps run for a moment. She looked tired.

Bell took the girls' bags to their bedroom and immediately began unpacking their clothes. They were so tiny that even to the power of two, they took up no space at all. She opened the window in there and shook the duvets, plumping and turning over the pillows, checking for spiders or anything else that might cause a fit of hysteria.

'Need any help unpacking?' she asked, popping her head in through Linus's door.

He was lying on the bed, staring up at the ceiling. His bed was made up with a red-and-blue-starred bed set, a dark-blue blanket draped artfully across the bottom. There was a fake-fur beanbag by the sliding window that looked back into the trees, the neon print of a dinosaur on the wall – several years too young for him now – and a striped hooded towel poncho hung from a hook on the back of the door.

'Linus?'

He startled. 'Huh?'

She frowned. 'Are you okay?'

'Sure.'

'Tired?' The ferry journey – at two hours long – was surprisingly wearing in the wind and sun.

He gave a shrug that was supposed to be nonchalant but wasn't. 'Maybe.'

She watched him for another moment, seeing how he stared at the ceiling with a studied intensity. She walked over, sinking down with a 'whoosh' into the jumbo beanbag. 'What is it?'

'I'm just bored, I guess.'

'We only just got here!' she laughed.

He was growing fast now – those jeans that had fit him at

Christmas were already too short at the ankle – and his mood often seemed more sullen and reluctant.

Bell dropped her head back on the bag and turned it slightly, looking out into the forest. Some of the larger islands had rabbits and foxes, even deer; the best they had had was a grouse scuttling through the undergrowth. They lay in easy silence, both staring at nothing, listening to everything: Hanna opening and closing cupboards in the kitchen, the sound of bottles and jars being set down on the counter, the suckering of the fridge door. Bell knew she ought to get up and help. This, lying on a beanbag, couldn't technically be classified as 'working'.

'So what do you want to do most, now that we're here?' she asked, looking back at Linus, seeing how he stared and stared at the ceiling. 'We could go on an afternoon paddle, round to Blind Man's Bay?'

'Maybe.'

'We could put out the nets and see what we can catch for supper?'

'I want pasta.'

'Okay. Well, how about we just go on an exploring walk and see if anything's changed?'

'Like what? Nothing changes here.'

'Linus, what a thing to say,' she gasped in mock horror. 'Everything changes here. Summer Isle is the very crucible of change.'

'The very what?'

She smiled, knowing the unfamiliar English word would pique his interest. 'You never know, the Big Ash might have fallen in a storm. Or old Persson's shack might have been blown away, and he's now living under a palm leaf that blew in from the East Indies.'

Linus cracked a tiny smile at that. 'Or he might have died seven months ago and his body's lying undiscovered on the floor.'

Bell gave a grimace. 'Eww, I hope not!' She winked. 'But we should probably check. Stealth mission?'

'What's our cover story?'

She thought for a moment. 'Collecting kindling.'

He gave a smile, but then it faded. 'No. I don't want to.'

'Oh Linus! Why not?'

He shot her a look. 'Because I'm ten now, and that's babyish.'

She gave a frustrated sigh, giving up. 'Right, fine – well, if you're too old to play, you can help me do some chores. Come on; I need to get the rest of the stuff from the boat. Then we'll kayak back to Sandhamn. We forgot milk. You can take your skateboard and have a run on the roads out there.'

'But it'll take twenty minutes each way to get over there.'

'Yeah. What's your point?'

'That'll take *ages*.'

'Precisely,' she said briskly, patting his knee and getting up. 'What else are we gonna do? We're on island time now, champ.'

Her cabin was exactly as she had left it: narrow pine bed dressed with fluffy duvet and a jumbo-stitched knitted blanket; a trendy charcoal-grey knotted wool rug over the floorboards; a replica Egg chair in the near corner; on the wall a black-and-white print of pine trees silhouetted by a frozen lake; books in English and Swedish – mainly thrillers – laid along the window edges, sagging slightly from the condensation build-up; the kitchen units – sink, fridge – hidden from sight, set inside what looked like a wall of cupboards.along the far gable end.

Bell set down her bag and went straight to the fridge. With a moan of relief, she saw that the bottle of vodka she had left last summer was still in the shallow freezer compartment. A can of Coke was in the fridge door, and within seconds, she had poured herself a chilled reward for the day's labours.

She walked back out onto the deck and sank into the low timber Adirondack chair, tucking her feet in close to her bottom and letting her chin rest on her knees as she gazed out to sea. They were just at the end point of the island, where the rocks swooped back on themselves in an irregular ellipse, and she had a partial view east, back towards the lagoon and the island opposite, which was maybe two hundred metres away. It was the one Linus had called 007, in the hope that a rich villain lived there. Everyone knew the owners were rich. But villains, too? Linus hoped so. It was the largest island in their little constellation, and deeply wooded. Unlike many of the other skerries and isles here, it was privately owned, and even though Swedish law took a relaxed view of ownership and trespass law – stating that anyone could camp anywhere for a period of up to twenty-four hours – no one ever *did* seem to dock or land there. The jetty was always noticeably bare, pointing into the water like a threatening finger, a warning to stay back.

Looking further left – or westwards – Bell could see the Baltic swing out on an expansive curve, the horizon pushed back and distant, the next islands of the archipelago merely fuzzy blots, before the view turned tightly back to the Mogerts' crescent beach and contemporary cabin. They were only twenty or so metres behind her, but the swathe of trees at the end of the beach provided a natural privacy barrier for both parties. The rock bed on her little patch was largely level, although it undulated into shallow dips and rises, catching the rain in little rock pools before dropping in smooth slopes, two metres down to the water's edge.

She knew she ought to unpack and organize herself the way she'd organized the family – after getting the milk with Linus, whilst Hanna wrote up some patient reports, she had spent the afternoon unpacking everyone's bags, setting up toys and cooking a chilli (her freezer and store cupboard fall-back), keeping a close eye on the girls' frolics on the sand, although they were so excitable, they could be heard at all times. But she didn't move; this was the first moment of the day she'd had to herself. It was well after nine, the children having been finally coerced and settled into bed, but the night sky still glowed brightly, with only a deepening blush of colour to indicate the day's end. She hoped she'd remembered to pack her sleep mask.

She took another sip of her drink, feeling the vodka begin to take effect, relaxing her. Over her right shoulder, the forest stood shadowy and silent, not so much as a mouse picking its way across the grass. Her eyes grazed idly over the tufts of yellow sedum peeking through the crevices of the rocks, and she watched as a tern swooped from the sky and tore a neat slit through the water's glassy surface. It was pale and still now the breeze had dropped. The fierce heat of the day had lifted, but it was still humid, and her skin felt tacky with dried sweat, her hair tangled around her face from where she had repeatedly pushed it back.

'You would have loved this, Jack,' she whispered to the sky, her index finger tapping against the chilled glass. '. . . You should have stayed.'

A sob gathered in her throat, tears pricking her eyes and she squeezed them shut, her mouth drawn in a flat, angry line. No . . . She felt a contradictory kick of exhaustion and agitation and she stretched her legs out, trying to adapt to the feeling of nothingness – nothing to do, nowhere to be. It always took a while to adjust to the change of pace on the islands; Linus wasn't alone in his restlessness. The usual distractions didn't apply – there was no TV in her tiny hut, of course, only electricity generators and gas. A small solar panel on the roof was enough to power the fridge, but a kettle was a luxury too far for her tiny annexe, and a cup of tea meant a trek back to the main house. If she wanted to charge her phone, she had to use a solar-powered battery (which had naturally been packed away in her bag all day), and right now she was too tired to read. She supposed she could have an outdoor shower . . .

She glanced over towards the rudimentary vestibule Max had cobbled together long before she had come to work for the family – old copper pipes snaking up to a shower head that sprayed in all directions but down, the weathered timber privacy boards beginning to split and warp.

Or . . .

She looked back at the sea again. It would be the same temperature anyway, and being brackish, the water here always left her feeling clean afterwards. Could there be a more perfect wind-down from her day: a cooling, cleansing swim in silky water before she fell headlong into bed?

She got up and stripped off where she stood, her clothes falling in a heap at her feet. She took another, large gulp of her vodka and tiptoed, naked as a baby, over the rocks towards the small cleft dug into the outermost knuckle of the isle. It stepped down in narrow, banded ledges to the water, looking clear and inviting, but she still gave a little gasp as it closed coldly over her feet. She sucked in her breath, tensing her muscles as she tried to adjust to the shock. The short channel here was narrow but the water was deep and she swung her arms above her head and dived in, feeling the icy grip and then release of the water's embrace. She glided for several moments, surfacing with her face upturned so that her hair streamed back, before launching into a ferocious front crawl for several minutes to warm herself up.

She felt the city slough off her, the familiar rumble of traffic on Stockholm's Centralbron, always in the background, replaced by an echoing silence. She felt her soul begin to shift, Summer Isle's tranquillity sliding like a glove over exposed nerve endings.

She felt like she was home.

Chapter Seven

They settled quickly into the new routine, the first few days a blur of sandwich-making, sandcastle-building, rock-pool-exploring activity. They went out on the little boat with picnics wrapped and knotted up in a blue-and-white checked table-cloth, the children awkward in their bulky yellow buoyancy vests, their faces already turning berry-brown, their hair salty and increasingly tangled. They explored the nearby bays and coves of the neighbouring islands on the lagoon side, where the water was warmest and most protected. But although their world here was remote and small, it was not without incident – already there had been one allergy-inducing spider bite (Elise), a bleeding toe from standing on a piece of glass (also Elise) and a bright strip of sunburned back (Tilde) which had been missed in the regular suncream-slathering sessions.

With every dawn, the sun seemed to beat with growing intensity, each day hotter than the last so that bobbing, gliding and diving in the water was the only relief to be had. And when their skin was wrinkled, they took refuge in the speckled shade of the pines, idly pulling apart needles as Bell read to the girls after lunch and lulled them into drowsy naps on the blanket, giving her, Hanna and Linus – who seemed to be grouped with the adults this year – a few precious hours of peace.

They couldn't sleep hard enough, it seemed, their little

bodies woken too early and nudged too late by the almost endless sunlight, and she kept forgetting to ask Hanna to ask Max to bring the blackout linings from home when he came out this weekend.

The long days left her worn out too, and after the initial challenge of sudden digital detox, she was just about adjusting to not having wifi. She had to catch the news on her old radio and actual newspapers, and depend on WhatsApps– mobile coverage permitting, depending on the weather systems – from Kris and Tove to keep her in the loop with the Stockholm scene. Not to mention fixing up a social life.

Tonight was her date with Per, the crewman from the ferry. He had invited her for a drink at the pub, having docked that afternoon and swapped a shift so that he could stay over on Sandhamn tonight. Bell stared at her reflection in the mirror, somewhat surprised by what she saw; there'd scarcely been a moment to stop all week, much less consider what she looked like. Most mornings she took it as a win if she had time to drag a brush through her hair and find a dry bikini. But she had caught the sun, too, even in just four days – her hazel eyes looked vivid against her tanned skin, and there were a few freckles smattered across the bridge of her nose.

She brushed her hair to a shine, pulling it up into a high ponytail and finishing it with a thin black velvet ribbon. That and a pair of earrings were her only nod to accessorizing, as she buttoned up her denim shorts and tugged on the red-and-white striped tank. She gave herself one last appraising look in the mirror – sporty, fresh, natural, not too try-hard. It wasn't like she particularly fancied Per, but she could probably be persuaded into it for a while. More than anything it would just be nice to talk to another adult about something other than sandwich fillings and suncream.

Sliding on her Birkenstocks, she cast about for her phone. It was ten to eight and it would take roughly ten minutes to putter over to Sandhamn and dock in the marina, then a few minutes' walk across the harbour to the pub on the far side.

Where was it?

She checked on the bed again, inside the kitchen cupboard, ran out to check in the loo, the Adirondack chair, the window-sill, the rock where she sometimes just about caught a phone signal, the bed again – before remembering she'd left it on the worktop in the main cabin kitchen.

She had to go past the main house anyway to get the boat; Hanna had told her she had free use of it. Panic over, she shut the cabin door behind her and began walking through the trees back towards the little beach. The path was narrow, with moss springing up on both sides, patches of rock peeking through like bare skin beneath the worn grass and scattered pine needles.

Hanna wasn't on the deck as she stepped into the clearing, although a half-empty wine bottle and glass stood on the small table.

'Hanna, it's just me,' she stage-whispered as she opened the door and walked into the open-plan space. There was no one on the sofas either, and the TV was off, but she could see her phone on the worktop, beside the fruit bowl. 'I forgot my phone.'

She picked it up and waited a moment, expecting the sound of her boss's barefooted steps on the wooden floor. With everything on one level in the cabin, noise travelled easily.

'Hanna?'

Still nothing. Was she in the bathroom?

With a shrug, she turned and left, closing the door softly behind her. She walked down to the beach, checking her phone for missed messages and calls. Just one from her hairdresser, putting back an appointment she had forgotten even booking. At the water's edge, she slid off her shoes and held them in one hand, beginning to wade into the water, before stopping suddenly.

What?

She frowned, blinking once, twice, at the distant horizon. There was no boat blotting its perfect curve. She kept staring at it, trying to comprehend the situation. The boat wasn't there. It clearly wasn't there. But no one apart from her and Hanna had a set of keys.

With a gasp, she turned back to the cabin. The never-quite-setting sun reflected dazzlingly on the sliding glass doors, like the pink-tinted lenses of Ray-Ban aviators, mirroring the world back to itself.

Running, feeling the sand clump between her wet toes, she dashed up the beach and up the steps onto the deck. She was supposed to dunk her feet in the yellow water bucket by the door before she went in – it was a cardinal rule in the Mogerts' summer house – but she ran straight through, oblivious to the sandy footprints marking a path behind her. She looked into the bathroom as she went past. Empty.

Hanna and Max's bedroom.

Empty.

Heart clattering, she peered in to the children's bedrooms too – but they were all sleeping soundly, skinny limbs thrown atop the covers in the heat.

Bell stood breathless in the hall, trying to make sense of what was going on, trying to find another explanation for what the facts were showing her. But there was only one truth. The boat was gone. Hanna was gone. And her children had been left alone in this cabin on an island.

Had there been an emergency? There must have been. And yet, if so, why hadn't she told Bell and asked her to come back down here? To just . . . *leave* them here? Alone and vulnerable whilst they slept?

Bell felt an uneasy sensation swirling in the pit of her stomach, a small monster settling into a restless sleep. She walked back out onto the deck, scanning the dusky millpond water for signs of a small boat puttering back into view; but there was only that big, blushing, empty sky and the vast, unbroken stretch of sea.

She couldn't leave, clearly. She couldn't get there, for one thing, but to leave the children alone . . . With a sigh of disbelief, she sank into the chair and texted the bad news to Per, staring at the half-drunk wine bottle and the glass with a smear of lipstick on the rim. She could already imagine her friends' responses when they heard she'd cancelled on another date.

She waited in the growing dusk, with just one question going over and over in her mind.

What the hell was going on?

It was gone two when she heard the sound of the motor, raising her head from the sofa and looking out through the giant window. There was still light out there, but darkness hovered like a gauze veil, a suggestion rather than fact, and Hanna was an inky silhouette as she jumped into the thigh-deep silvery water and began to wade to shore. There was something exaggerated in her movements, her arms held that bit too extravagantly above her head, her legs kicking with an excitable flourish through the water.

Bell sat up, pushing her hair back as she tried to bite back her anger. There would be a good reason for this. Hanna wouldn't have left her children – her babies – unattended here without a damned good reason.

The door slid open, almost silent on its tracks.

'Bell!'

Bell saw how Hanna's legs buckled at the knee in sudden fright at the sight of her sitting on the sofa, a blanket over her legs. But there was no relief in her voice. No 'thank God you came'.

'What are you doing here?'

Bell took a moment to respond. How could she reply without betraying the accusation in her voice? 'I left my phone on the counter,' she said steadily, quietly, not wanting to waken the children. Hanna's voice, by contrast, was slightly too loud. Too . . . appeasing. She was drunk. 'I came back to get it before I went out, and saw that . . . no one was here.'

She gave Hanna a moment to reply, but her boss merely nodded, open-mouthed, looking around the cabin as though somewhat surprised to find herself there. 'Uh-huh.'

'So I thought I should stay here. With the children.' She waited again, giving Hanna another chance to explain, to make this all okay. '. . . I assumed something must have happened.'

Hanna looked back at her in apparent confusion, her eyes catching on Bell's stained lipgloss, her hoop earrings (a complete no-no during the day, with the girls around). Suddenly, she slapped her forehead with a hand. 'Oh my God, you were supposed to use the boat tonight!' she cried.

Bell glanced in alarm towards the children's bedrooms. Instinctively, she pressed a finger to her lips. 'Sssh. The children are asleep.'

Hanna copied her, the movement clownish. 'Ooops. Sorry.' As though it was Bell's kids she was disturbing, not her own.

'I'm so sorry. I can't believe I forgot that. It completely slipped my mind.'

'It doesn't matter about the boat, Hanna,' she said. Exactly how much had she had to drink? 'But I was worried about the kids.'

Hanna tipped her head to the side, and the movement seemed to be enough to unbalance her, as she lurched several paces to the side, having to grab at the wall. 'Aww, you are so sweet. Always worrying about us. Looking after us so well.' She sighed dramatically and hiccuped. 'I don't know what we'd do without you. I really don't. I'm always saying it to Max. You are our angel. Heaven sent.'

'Hanna—'

'You must let me make it up to you.'

'Hanna, I don't care about the boat. I was worried that the children had been le—'

'I *insist*. Tomorrow you are to have the day off. The whole day!'

Bell glanced down the corridor again, certain Linus would wake up. His mother was paralytically drunk, holding on to the wall and waving her arms about.

'Sleep late. Go to Sandhamn. Go back to Stockholm, if you like. Have a three-day weekend, on me.'

Bell stared at her. 'Hanna, it's *Midsommar* this weekend. I was going to help you with the girls' floral crowns tomorrow and get things ready before I went.'

'*I* can do that!' Hanna exclaimed, batting a hand dramatically.

'Ssh!' Bell pressed a finger to her lips again, beseeching her for a little consideration for the children.

Hanna followed suit again. 'Oh yes, I keep forgetting,' she giggled, whispering again. 'Well, now, you get off to bed and don't worry about a thing here. We're *fine*. Off you go now, and we'll see you on Monday. You work too hard. Go have some *fun*. Go,' she shooed, flapping her hands.

Reluctantly, and only because she didn't want the children to be disturbed, Bell turned and walked slowly towards the door. She glanced back to see Hanna lurching down the corridor, arms outstretched as she bounced off the walls, leaving grubby handprints on the pristine white paint. She stumbled into the bedroom, closing the door with a slam. Bell winced and waited for a small tousle-haired head to appear at one of the other doors; but after a few minutes, when no one stirred, she let herself relax. They must be in the dead of sleep.

Lucky for them.

Lucky for Hanna.

Chapter Eight

Sunlight freckled the air as it percolated through the upper canopies of the pine and silver birch trees, squirrels running through the bright spots, tails aloft, birds trilling from the high branches. Bell pulled her knees up under her chin and cradled the coffee mug in her hand, looking out over the neighbourhood. It was quiet, most people still asleep in the red-roofed, low-slung cabins. They were clustered close together on the shallow hill, accessed by bleached-silver gang-planks that wound through the trees, their small private yards filled with the accoutrements of summer island life – barbecues and tables and chairs, kayaks, SUP boards, water-skis, buckets and spades, inflatables, bikes propped against walls . . .

It wasn't a glamorous scene. In fact, through a critical eye, it was a mess. This wasn't the Hamptons. Nothing was groomed or manicured or clipped here – the very smartest properties were identified by a whimsical patterning of the whittled birch used for fencing – but that was the point. To know its scruffiness was to love it. The place had a rustic, low-key vibe that was the antithesis of slick city living, and the people coming out here, right on the farthest edge of the country's landmass, weren't just getting back to nature, they were getting back to themselves.

The first time she had come here had been like stepping

back in time fifty years. No one locked their doors, children played without adults hovering over them, everyone cycled everywhere, fished for their dinner and cooked it . . . She loved that the ground was permanently carpeted with pine cones and needles, that the tree roots protruded like veins, the grass sprinkled with sand and vice versa on the beach. Everything felt like it was on the brink of going feral. Rewilded.

Even Kris and Marc – urban creatures who cared about 'the right black' and genuinely fretted over dado profilings – couldn't resist its pull. When they had bought this place, with its bright-yellow clapboard and blue windows, they had sworn to paint it a matt blackish-green and open up the back with an all-glass wall. But two years later, the primary colours were still there, and even the previous owners' geranium pots were still balancing on the deck's handrail – because when they came out here, all they wanted was to stop and relax.

Bell had found the key in its usual place: in the faded red Croc beside the ash bucket, which the previous owners had also left. She knew her friends were coming out tonight. It was *Midsommar* tomorrow, which meant no one was going to be sleeping this weekend; the longest day of the year – or shortest night, depending on your proclivities – always heralded party time. But they wouldn't be out till tonight at the earliest, possibly even tomorrow morning depending on Marc's hospital shifts, giving her at least a day on her own, and she was grateful for that. She had come over early on the kayak, unable to sleep in spite of her exhaustion, the evening's events nagging in her mind all night.

She still couldn't believe what had gone down – Hanna leaving her children alone in their beds, unattended. It was so reckless, so completely unlike her. Had she thought it was okay because Linus was ten and therefore 'old enough'? Or had she thought it was okay because Bell was just through the trees – even though Hanna knew she had plans?

It made no sense. She was a good mother. Yes, she'd been strained lately – she'd lost weight, her face was often pinched and several times, Bell had overheard her and Max exchanging sharp words behind closed doors. She thought she could probably guess as to the source of their stresses; though the ex-husband hadn't materialized, as poor Max had feared, into their lives, he must still be a background figure. The guy was Linus's biological father, after all, and there would likely be paternal rights issues to co-ordinate. But not yet, clearly. Hanna hadn't mentioned him once since their return from Uppsala, and she (and Linus) had all but put the day out of their minds. But to do something so wilfully dangerous as to leave the children alone on an island . . . whatever issues Hanna and Max might be facing right now, it was no excuse. What if Tilde had woken up needing the loo, or Elise had wanted water, or Linus had had a nightmare? There were so many ways this could have been a disaster.

She checked her phone. Eight ten. She wondered whether Hanna was awake, or still sleeping it off. Part of her wanted to go back there and confront her, for the children's sake. But how? She couldn't just accuse Hanna of neglect or abandonment or endangerment – even though she was guilty of all those things – without serious risk of losing her job. On the other hand, what if Hanna did it again tonight? Just the thought of it made Bell feel sick; and how, in all good conscience, could she expose those children to that risk? But then *again*, if she reported Hanna to the authorities, it could spark a chain reaction equally as devastating to the kids. She was caught in a bind; to act and not to act seemed equally dangerous.

An idea came to her, and she fired off a text: *'Hi Max, are you coming out today?'*

His reply was almost immediate, and she knew his working day would have started an hour ago at least. *'Yes. Catching the 18h00. Need anything? M'*

She tried to think of a reason why she would normally have asked the question. *'Can you bring the blackout blinds? Rolled up in the airing cupboard, top shelf.'*

'OK, will bring.'

Bell gave a sigh of relief. Max would be there tonight; there'd be no repeat of last night's horror show. That was something, at least. But it was no solution, just a stay of execution. Bell had a strong feeling that whatever was going on with Hanna, it wasn't done yet.

She walked along the back lanes, through the tangle of bird-song, snipping clutches of wildflowers she saw along the way – forget-me-nots, ox-eye daisies, buttercups, wild rosemary, white willow, bird-cherry blossoms . . .

'Good morning,' she smiled as she passed a pair of older gentlemen playing boules on the sandy path. A black-and-white terrier was lying on the grass verge, watching them from between his paws.

The island had woken up now, residents buzzing around their summer homes – watering plants, fixing punctures, hanging up laundry. She could hear the rhythmic *thwack* of tennis balls coming from the club just through the trees, joggers running in pairs along the dirt road that circumnavigated the island. She herself had had a busy morning airing and doing a light clean of the cabin. Rest was still impossible, and Marc's stash of industrial-strength coffee – to help him with the night shifts – had done what sleep couldn't and kept her going. She had texted Kris, Marc and Tove, telling them she'd arrived a day early and was on the case with bagging the strawberries (Westerbergs had run out last year) and beer. Marc had come back asking her to buy some gardening twine. Tove had asked whether she'd brought her 'sex underwear', and if not, should she collect it? Kris had asked if she'd been fired. Her replies had been *'Sure'*, *'Of course'* (total lie) and *'Might be'*.

She turned towards town, ambling down the hill, the sea pale and glinting beyond the red rooftops, the sun warming her face and bare legs as she walked in her yellow-checked Vans and poppy-printed romper, her hair caught up in her usual bird's-nest topknot. Some locals were pushing their bags up to their house in a wheelbarrow, and she guessed the ferry had just come in.

Sure enough, she turned the corner onto the main street and saw a mass of Stockholmers and tourists disgorging into the square, suitcases being wheeled along the boardwalks to the grand Yacht Hotel or towards boats, bare legs flashing, flip-flops slapping. The place was heaving, a flotilla of sleek, high-masted yachts moored in the deeper waters offshore, the marina already crammed with day-trip speedboats and smaller sailing vessels whose rigging laced the sky like spiders' webs. A small, rather tatty-looking cabin boat was chugging through the sound towards what appeared to be the only empty berth, its underpowered engine causing barely a ripple of wake behind it.

She headed to the bakery and stocked up on pastries for breakfast for everyone tomorrow, and crispbreads; then on to Westerbergs, the general store that was the focus of island life – food was bought there, services advertised, news exchanged and shared. The place had everything, from batteries to plants; bags of compost were piled up by the steps, potted geraniums and bright watering cans beside them. She caught sight of one of the delivery trikes standing inert in the shade – a rare sight; Kris called them the unicorns. It was sky blue, with rust patches, and had been fitted with a large wooden tray to the front that could take everything from shopping to suitcases. This particular one had also been fitted with an electric motor. There was a problem, though – they couldn't be pre-booked. It was first come, first served. She'd need to be quick!

She jogged in. The bright, functional arrangement of the stacked shelves was always somehow a surprise, with trays of glossy fruit and vegetables set out like colour-coded Lego bricks. The shop was busy, but no customers were at the till, although the shelves were looking alarmingly scant, as though everyone had already stocked up for their *Midsommar* parties. Obviously she could ask the others to bring what else they needed from the city, but she would do her best here first. She scooped up two baskets and, with the speed of a seasoned local, quickly filled it with some milk and cereal, pasta, herrings, potatoes, cream, sugar, two punnets of strawberries, some twine and several loops of picture wire. She needed beer, too, but it was impossible to carry with a basket in each hand.

'I've just got to get some beers too,' she said to the till operator, setting it all down carefully. Someone else was doing the same at the other till, but he had almost nothing in his basket; a small cardboard box would take his shopping. She ran back to the alcohol aisle. There had been three six-packs left of Evil Twin, Kris's favourite. She had come in for two, but the sight of 'only' three put her into panic mode, so she took them all.

The girl at the till was already scanning the barcodes and

packing everything into a box for her. 'And can I hire the bike outside, please?' Bell said breathlessly, as she set the bottles down and pulled out her bank card.

'I'm sorry, but the gentleman over there has just rented it,' the girl said, nodding her head towards the other till. Bell looked over just as the man standing by the register glanced up, as though he had overheard.

Dark hair, faded baseball cap, expensive-looking anthracite-grey metal sunglasses. He looked to be mid-thirties or there-abouts. His face and forearms were incredibly tanned but his upper arms, peeking from the sleeves of his t-shirt, were paler. He gave an unsmiling nod and she looked away – he was one of the proverbial yachtie types that swarmed here in the summer months. No doubt his wife and kids were sitting by the Sea Club pool, or buying Ralph Lauren knits in the expensive boutique that fronted the harbour like a civic proclamation of the island's good style and stealth wealth.

She looked again at his shopping haul – some bottles of wine, a wriggling bag of pinched lobsters, a carton of juice and the weekend papers. She frowned. Whilst the bag of lobsters might not be much fun to carry, did he really need the trike?

'That'll be four hundred and thirty-two kroner,' the shop girl said.

'Huh?' Bell glanced back again.

'Four thirty-two, please.'

'Oh.' She looked down at her shop – the girl had packed everything into a box for her, but with her cuttings basket and the cases of beer too . . . She handed over her card. How the hell was she supposed to carry this all the way home? The extra beer had been a mistake. 'I'll . . . I'll have to come back for the beer later,' she muttered as the man walked past, carrying his shopping perfectly easily. She stared daggers at his back, feeling her good mood dissipate.

'I'm sorry, but we can't keep anything by the tills today. We have a very large order coming in for the weekend. It's our biggest delivery of the year.' The girl jerked a thumb over her shoulder, towards the window. Sure enough, pallets of boxes were being unloaded from the ferry, destined for here.

'Oh, what?' Bell cried, noticing the long queue forming behind her. Great! 'For God's sake . . .' she tutted. 'Well, can you at least help load me up, then?' She wondered if there was someone's wheelbarrow she could use. Surely an enter-prising teenager would be happy to earn some easy cash? The girl, shooting her an annoyed look, put the box into her outstretched arms, then two of the six-pack cartons on top, with the third six-pack just under her chin and the basket of flowers resting in front of that. It was very precariously balanced.

'Are you going to be okay?' the girl asked, looking concerned as Bell started to stagger away. She could barely see anything, certainly not her feet.

'Well, I'm going to have to be, aren't I?' she muttered. 'If someone would be so kind as to open the door . . . ?'

Someone – she couldn't see who – did, and she walked carefully down the ramp, people side-stepping out of her way as they saw her overloaded progress. 'Talk about beast of burden,' she muttered under her breath as she passed the man easily dropping his small box and folded newspaper onto the trike's vast wooden tray.

She walked eight paces, stopped and turned back. 'Excuse me.'

He took a moment to respond, turning around with a quiz-zical look. 'Yes?'

'That trike.'

He looked down at it, as though needing to confirm first. '. . . Yes?'

'Do you *really* need it?' He frowned, perhaps because he had picked up on the indignation in her voice. 'Because I would happily pay twice what you've just paid to hire it.'

'Oh. I'm sorry, but I do need it.'

'As much as me?' she panted, her arms already beginning to ache.

'Yes, I—'

'Three times, then.'

'Miss, it's not a question of money.'

'No, you're quite right, it's a question of need and forgive me if I'm sounding rude, but right now, honestly? My need *is* greater than yours.' She changed her stance and improved her grip. 'So tell me, how much will it take for you to let me put this lot down?'

He stared at her for a moment. She wasn't a tall woman anyway, but she was truly dwarfed by the pile of shopping in her arms. 'Let me.' And he reached for the beers and set them down on the wooden tray; immediately, the load on her reduced by half. She gave a groan of relief.

'Thank you,' she said as he took the box and basket from her too, and she stretched her arms out. They were already stiff. But any hopes that he might be a knight in shining armour were short-lived.

'Why did you buy so much if you knew you couldn't carry it?' he asked.

'Well . . . because I saw the trike out here.'

'Didn't you know it was first come, first served?' he asked. 'Didn't you see me ahead of you at the till?'

'I did, but it didn't look like you were going to need the

trike,' she said, a hint of sarcasm in the words as she scanned the scant, utterly middle-class provisions.

'I've bought some gas,' he said, kicking his foot lightly towards three large canisters set beside the bags of compost outside.

'Oh.' Dammit. She looked back at him, embarrassed. 'I see.' An awkward silence bloomed. 'Well then, I'm sorry about that. Clearly you do need the trike. I'll just . . .' She sighed and bent down to pick up the box again, immediately feeling the strain in her arms. 'If you wouldn't mind reloading me up again?'

She waited as he stared at her with an air of bafflement. She could scarcely see his face behind his glasses and cap. 'Where do you need to get to?' he asked finally.

Oh thank God! 'Just past the Yacht Hotel, that first right up the hill.'

His mouth pursed a little. 'That's gangplank access.'

'Yes – but I usually go up and across the back when I've got the wheelbarrow.'

'Why didn't you bring the wheelbarrow today, then?'

She gave a gasp of despair. 'Ugh, because it's got a puncture. Oh my God, forget it, I'll walk back. Don't put yourself to any trouble! Just load me up.'

'It's fine, I'll drop you.'

'No, really, I've clearly inconvenienced you quite enough already!' The sarcasm was plainly apparent now.

'Are you always this rude to complete strangers?'

'Just give me my beer!'

He leaned forward and took the box from her arms. 'Get on,' he said, exhaling like the frustrated father of a teenager. 'You'll have to show me where.'

She stood in equally frustrated silence. On the one hand,

she didn't *want* to accept his help now. On the other, she had asked for it – and needed it. While she prevaricated, he reached down and loaded the gas canisters, securing them to the back of the tray with webbing straps. He threw a leg over the bike and cast her an enquiring look.

Without a word, she indignantly climbed onto the tray and sat down cross-legged between the packs of beers, her flower basket, the gas canisters and his lobsters. Their pincers had been taped together, but they were still moving, the bag rustling and creeping towards her. She gave a small squeal and tried to inch out of the way.

'It's best to track back that way,' she said, jerking her thumb over her shoulder. He started up the trike, turning a full circle away from the marina. He took the first left inland, and immediately the path became narrow and sandy as they wound their way up the gentle hill between picket-fenced gardens and the small reddish-brown historic cabins. With nothing to hold on to, she had to splay her arms out and down on the tray, trying to balance as they went over the rough ground. The bike struggled a little with the load as they went up the hill, but soon enough they were at the top and it was an easy, level cruise the rest of the way back through the trees.

The runners were out in force now, and they attracted some amused looks from passing joggers, with Bell cross-legged on the tray and trying to avoid the wriggling lobster bag.

'This one here,' she said finally, pointing to the narrow lane at the end that had the gangplank running down the length of it.

He came to a stop and she jumped off.

'How far down are you?' he asked, squinting at the cascade of cabin roofs all the way down to the marina again.

'It's fine. I can get the rest of the way. It's not far now.' She picked up the box again and waited with her arms outstretched.

Without offering to help any further, he loaded her up with the beers and the flower basket again. 'Thank you,' she said resentfully. 'You've been very kind.' He hadn't been kind at all. He had been reluctantly polite. 'Can I pay you for your help?'

He looked baffled again. '. . . No.'

'Okay then. Well, thanks,' she said briskly and turned away, walking carefully and wondering how she was going to manage on the gangways when she couldn't see her feet. But she didn't need to worry about falling and making a fool of herself in front of him. Her foot wasn't even on the first tread when she heard the bike start up again, and he drove off.

Sandhamn, 27 July 2009

He ran the produce past the scanner, the *beep-beep-beep*s like a meditation as the customers shuffled forwards in the queue, one after another. It was the end of July and he hadn't moved from here all day, his body stiff from standing, his mind numbed to the monotony of repeating the same words on a loop. 'Do you have a loyalty card?'; 'Do you need a box?'; 'Would you like a token?'; 'Thank you, please come again.'

'It's good discipline,' his father had said.

'Thank you, please come again . . . Hello.'

Schnapps. Fizzy cola bottles. Cigarettes. Durex –

He looked up automatically, and she smiled back at him. 'Hi.'

'Hi.' He looked down again, away, unable to maintain a gaze with those blue eyes. He felt like he'd been zapped with an electric current. The air suddenly felt thick, like a duvet; he could scarcely breathe through it. 'Do you have a loyalty card?' His voice was strange too.

'No.'

He kept his eyes on the produce, the scanner beeping like a heart monitor. Regular. Rhythmic. 'Will you be coming here frequently this summer?'

'. . . I hope so.'

'Then a loyalty card would be beneficial for you.'

'Okay.' He heard the smile in the word, though he didn't dare look back at her again.

'I'll need to ask you to fill this in.' He reached under the counter and pulled out one of the forms. He got a commission for every new loyalty account he bagged, but it wasn't percentages on his mind right now. 'You need to put your name and address there, and your telephone number there.'

Her eyes met his. 'Right here? Where it says name, address and number?'

He looked down again. She was teasing him. 'Ah, you're cute,' she said quietly, like it was a secret, writing her details in clear handwriting, the pink tip of her tongue peeking out through her teeth as she wrote.

She handed it back. 'There. Can you read it okay? It's important you can see my details clearly.'

'Thanks, they're clear.' He scarcely had to look at it to commit it to memory. 'That's two hundred and forty-nine kroner, seventy. Do you need a box?'

Her smile grew as she handed over the money. 'Just a little one, please.'

He found one that the gum had been packed in.

'Thank you.'

He could feel her staring at him. 'Do you want a token?' he asked, handing back her change and managing to avoid eye contact.

There was a slight hesitation, then she leaned in towards

him, her hands pressed flat on the conveyor belt. 'I think I want you to call me,' she whispered.

'Why?'

She laughed and as his eyes flickered up to hers, just for a moment, he felt the electric shock again. 'You know why.'

He watched her pick up her shopping and walk towards the door. 'Thank you, please come again . . .' he croaked, checking the form in his hands. 'Hanna.'

Chapter Nine

'There! How's that?' Bell asked, placing the floral crown lightly upon her head.

'My queen!' Kris crooned, clapping delightedly as she got up and gave a twirl. 'Sensational. You should wear your hair down more often.'

She shrugged. 'Not practical with three kids to keep an eye on. It'd be permanently dipping in paint or ketchup.'

'Eww.'

'Ta-da!' Tove cried, finishing off her crown, which she had made more 'fabulous' by fashioning and embellishing picture wire strips that met and dipped in a central point, like a jubilee crown and intertwining them with ivy.

'Nice!' Kris grinned.

'Nice? She gets called a queen and I get *nice*?' She planted her hands on her narrow hips in mock indignation.

They were all sitting on the deck, post-lunch – Kris's superlative herrings and potatoes, followed by strawberry cream cake, completely demolished. They had polished off two of the three cases of beer, and all around them the island was humming to the sounds of *Midsommar* celebrations. Cheers and singing could be heard from distant houses, children running down the gangplanks in national dress costumes, flags flying from poles. *Midsommar* wasn't officially the

Swedes' national day, but to many, it was as important – if not more so – than Christmas itself. After the long, dark Scandinavian winters, the unsetting midsummer sun was a national celebration of light and levity, their reward for enduring the hard seasons.

'Shall we go, then?' Marc asked, coming through and drying his hands on a tea towel. 'We don't want to miss it.'

'But I don't think I can move,' Kris protested, patting his hands around his six-pack.

'You can dance it off with me,' Marc said, kissing him with a wink.

'Well, before we go . . .' Tove reached behind her and grabbed the bottle of schnapps from the ice bucket. She poured it into shot glasses. 'Happy *Midsommar*!'

They cheered and drank, knocking it back with vim.

Like everyone else, they left the house unlocked as they ran merrily down the gangplanks, beer bottles in hand, joining the throngs all streaming towards the same grassy patch where the maypole was erected. It was set in a large grassy parcel of land surrounded by houses, on the opposite side of town, and hundreds were gathered there. The sheer number of people was always amazing to Bell. It was a tiny island, with a year-round population of less than a hundred – where did everybody go to after this?

They stood for a moment taking in the scene, looking for friends' faces and deciding where to stand. A fiddlers' group was playing, smorgasbords were set out on tables around the edges, young and old were talking and laughing. The maypole – decorated with greenery and flowers – had already been hoisted into position, and everyone was preparing for the next dance. Bell scanned the crowd, looking for Hanna and Max. The kids *loved* the maypole dancing – although Linus was becoming more reluctant with age – but even he couldn't resist the 'Små Grodorna' song, where everyone pretended to be frogs. *Frogs.* As a non-Swede, it was the one custom that baffled her and she always made her excuses to duck out, looking on with bemusement as Kris, Marc and Tove went crazy for it.

Her frown puckered as she scanned and looked and searched. Where were they? There were dozens of children here, but Tilde and Elise were still so small, she would expect to see them on their parents' shoulders in a crowd of this size. They should be easy to spot.

'Oh God, they're off!' Tove laughed, beginning to film on her phone as Marc dragged Kris into the dancers' circle and they began galloping one way, then the other. 'I'm going to blackmail them with this later. I reckon I can probably get Marc to give me that denim jacket of his in return for not showing this to his boss.'

'Ha.'

Tove glanced down at her, hearing her distracted tone. 'Who are you looking for?'

'The Mogerts. I thought they'd be here.'

'Oh, they will be. They're always here. That little girl, the feisty one –'

'Elise.'

'Yeah, Elise. She stung me for double-scoop ice creams last time.'

Bell chuckled. 'Don't mess with Elise. She's fierce.'

Tove threw her head back and laughed at a memory. 'Do you remember last year when we saw them on the boat just as I did my streak down the jetty?' She gave a cackle of laughter.

'Oh, I remember all right,' Bell groaned, but grinning too.

Poor Max had almost fallen overboard, and he still looked terrified anytime he and Tove met. Her smile faded again. 'Hmm, it's odd, I just can't see them. Maybe we missed them.' But a kernel of worry was worming into the pit of her stomach. It was highly unusual that they weren't here. 'I'm just going to look over there. I'll be right back.'

She pushed slowly through the crowd, looking out for the easy clues – Max's heavy-rimmed 'nerd' glasses, Hanna's bright hair, Elise's shouts. There were dozens of other children running about; it was a child's paradise, with apple bobbing, horseshoe tossing, potato-and-spoon races, a tug of war . . .

'Nope. They're not here,' she said as she met up with Tove again several minutes later. 'I don't get it.'

'Well, don't let it ruin *your* day,' Tove mumbled, still filming the boys. 'You've got the weekend off, remember? Stop worrying about work for once. They've probably had a better offer to go . . . potato printing, or something.'

'You're right. That's highly likely,' Bell quipped, swigging her beer.

Tove brought her phone down from her face and squinted at something. Then she put it back up again. 'Babe, I think your luck might be in.'

'Huh?'

'No, don't look at me – don't look over there –'

'Where the hell can I look, then?' Bell chuckled. 'And what am I *not* supposed to be looking at?'

'Not what. Who. Now act natural. I've just watched some guy watch you go all the way round the crowd just now, and now he's looking right over again . . .' She applied the zoom. 'Oh my God, and he's shit-hot!'

'Who? Where? Lemme see him,' Bell laughed, scanning the crowd opposite out of curiosity rather than any real interest.

But for all the faces over there, none of them appeared to be looking in her direction.

'He's over – oh. Oh no, wait . . . scratch that.' Tove gave a disappointed sigh. 'Dude's married. Kids too, it looks like.'

'What? How'd you know?'

Tove pointed. 'See him? Guy in the cap?'

Bell looked over. The only man in a cap she could see had his face turned away as he listened to something a very sleek, very sharp-looking brunette was saying in his ear. 'Oh God,' she said with a groan, looking away immediately. 'Him? Ugh!'

'What do you mean, *ugh*? He is very definitely not ugh. Who is he?'

'The guy I told you about last night? The one who made a right bloody fuss about letting me use the trike, until I almost had to beg him for it?'

Tove pulled a face. 'Oh. Jerk.'

'Yeah.'

She carried on staring at him. 'Ugh. Hot but married, *and* an asshole. Shame.'

'I thought your man-radar was better than that, to be honest.'

Tove made a disappointed tut. 'I know. I just got distracted by his jaw. That's a good jaw.'

'With a bad personality. And a wedding ring.'

The song ended and Kris and Marc staggered over, arms slung round each other's shoulders, both out of breath. 'That was so great!' Marc gushed, reaching over and slapping a huge kiss on Kris's cheek.

Bell looked back at them both, loving their happiness but sensing something too. Their unusual exuberance, the way they kept sharing loaded looks . . .

'What's . . . going on with you two?' she asked them slowly with a curious grin.

'What do you mean?' Kris was all innocence, but she knew him too well.

She gasped. 'You're up to something, I can tell.' She pointed a finger playfully at them.

'Us? No.'

'Come on, tell. You know I won't shut up until you do!'

Tove was looking between the three of them, equal parts excited and intrigued.

'It's true, she won't,' Marc shrugged to Kris, who gave a tiny shrug back, his eyes on Bell.

'Well . . .' Marc said slowly. 'We weren't going to tell anyone yet, because we wanted a little time to just keep it as our secret. But seeing as you're, like, a damn spy or something . . .'

Both girls' hands flew to their mouths, already knowing what was coming.

'. . . Kris and I have decided to move in together.'

'Oh my God!' Tove yelled, shooting her arms in the air jubilantly, unwittingly spraying beer everywhere, before flinging her arms around the boys' necks. The three of them began excitedly jumping up and down in a circle, but Kris pulled away seeing Bell's expression.

He held out his arms to her and she stepped in for the bear hug, the same thought running through both their heads. Because if Marc was gaining a live-in partner, she was losing a flatmate. Everything was changing again, Life shifting its cogs beneath her feet.

'I didn't want to tell you like this, I'm sorry. The whole thing took me by surprise too.'

'I'm so pleased for you,' she whispered into his neck.

'I know you are. But I'm going to miss you, Hell.'

'Not as much as I'll miss you. You'll have Marc.'

'You'll always have me,' he said, clasping her head between his hands and kissing her right between the eyes.

'Oh god, I'm so drunk,' she laughed, as happy tears began to trickle down her cheeks.

'And about to get drunker!' he cried, just as the fiddles started up again. 'But first –' His eyes widened with devilish glee as they heard and recognized the first few chords.

'Oh no!' she cried, as they all circled around her and hustled her into the centre of the dancing ring. 'No, no no!'

'Yes! First, we're gonna dance like frogs!'

It was midnight but still the sky burned, a red smoulder that looked like the heavens were on fire. Trees and houses were silhouetted into inky shapes, but by the water's edge, all the way round the island, small fires flickered on the beaches, and the marina glowed with cabin lights as people held parties on their boats. The bass of distant music was stippled with groups bursting into rousing choruses, shouts of laughter rising into the night like vixens' barks.

Bell staggered out of the Yacht Hotel, where the dancing was only just really getting going, and tried to get her breath back. She was hot and sticky, her heart pounding, the flowers on her crown wilting but somehow still on her head.

She turned her face to the sky and breathed in deeply. The longest day of the year. The shortest night. She could never decide which was the more optimistic description. Either way, these were the times – day or night – when she missed him most, when it felt most unbelievable that Jack was no longer a part of this. Her loneliness had been a shadow chasing her all day, especially with Kris and Marc's happy news, and so far she had outrun it, but there were moments when she turned the wrong way and walked straight into it. Like now. As she looked back through the many windows of the grand hotel, watching the people inside dancing and laughing and bloody *living*, it shrouded her like a veil.

She turned away, needing more than air now, but space too. She wouldn't be missed. Tove was getting hot and heavy on the dance floor with a guy who had introduced himself by pouring a drink over his head to cool down; Marc and Kris had gone home, no doubt to make their own noise. She didn't want to go back in there, but she couldn't go to bed either; she felt caught between worlds, as she so often did, present but somehow not fully involved. An observer, perhaps, doomed to watch from the other side of the glass.

The boardwalk was sandy, grains kicking up and rubbing painfully against her sweaty feet as she walked, and she took off her Vans, holding them in one hand as she rubbed her neck with the other. The wooden planks rattled softly underfoot as she padded along in silence, listening to everyone else's fun and glancing across at the people dancing on deck, demurring with a smile as various drunken invitations were issued for her to join them. It wasn't the Cannes super-yacht league, by any stretch, but the boat party scene tonight could have rivalled any of the European hotspots. No one would be getting much sleep, whether they wanted to party or not.

The lights were on in almost every berth, except the last two moorings of the final jetty before the ferry docks. Down there, in that one small pocket, the boats sat in darkness and relative – very relative – seclusion. She turned in and walked to the end, peering down into the dark water for a moment before sitting down and swinging her legs off the edge.

She sighed heavily. Sometimes, in moments of dislocation

like these, she wondered where she would be right now, if things hadn't unfolded the way they had. Was she supposed to be somewhere else? Or had she always been destined to end up here?

She wondered what Jack would make of her life now, so different to theirs together – suburban city life, looking after other people's children, her new friends, nights like these . . . He would be surprised, she imagined, possibly even disappointed. She certainly couldn't imagine him in this version of her life being lived here. He would have called this 'settling' and maybe he'd have been right, but settling was precisely what she had needed when she found herself in the gaping hole of losing him. He hadn't been the one who'd been left; *she* had. Not once, but twice now, and there had even been times when she'd felt he'd been the lucky one . . .

She sniffed and pressed her index finger to her nose, trying to stop the tears from falling. She knew what was happening. She was drunk and getting emotional, feeling lonely. It wasn't an unfamiliar scenario to her, although she hid it well from her friends and she knew perfectly well what she had to do – go back to the hotel and start dancing again, hide the tears with laughter, blot out the pain with booze. Tomorrow would be a new day and she'd feel brighter about things again, once the hangover had passed. She just needed a few more minutes here first, alone, in the darkest, quietest spot on the island –

'Would a beer help?'

She gasped, almost screamed, her body immediately tense and primed to run as she looked in the direction from which the disembodied voice had come. It took her a moment to find its source – a man, lying on his back on the bench of the boat to her left. All the lights were off, no signs of occupancy. She had just assumed no one was on board.

She stared down at him. He didn't look threatening. His ankles were crossed and he had one hand clasped behind his head, the other resting a beer on his stomach.

'Oh my *God*!' she whispered, mainly to herself, her hand pressed over her heart as though to still it. 'I nearly died of fright. I didn't know you were there.'

'Well, clearly. I wasn't going to say anything, but you looked upset, so I thought . . . beer's often the answer.'

'Or in my case, the problem right now.' She rolled her eyes. 'I'm a bit of a maudlin drunk.'

'You looked to be having a high time earlier.'

'Earlier?' She frowned, peering to try to see him better, but he was largely in shadow. 'Sorry, do I know you?'

There was a hesitation and then he slowly swung himself up to sitting. She felt herself take a shallow breath as the borrowed light from the other boats revealed his face. His bone structure spoke to a type – finely carved, well bred, privileged – but there was something particularly singular about his gaze. His eyes were a thick, almost creamy, pale green, circled with a darker ring and fringed with thick lashes. The effect was startling.

'I don't think we've –' she murmured, knowing she would have remembered that face. In fact, it would be a problem to forget it. He was mesmerizing to look at.

He reached to his side and held up a battered, sun-bleached baseball cap.

'Oh.' Oh *no*.

'Yes,' he said after a moment. 'Hello again.'

'I . . . I'm sorry, I didn't recognize you without the cap.'

'Generally I prefer it when people don't recognize me *with* the cap.'

She smiled politely. It was clearly a joke, although she didn't quite get it, unless he fancied himself as a bit of celebrity (which, given those looks, was fair enough really).

'I almost didn't recognize *you* with your hair down. I wasn't sure. I saw you earlier at the maypole.'

'That's right. You were with your family.'

'Yes, it was fun.'

'Yes.' Confirmation he was married then. In spite of the fact that she disliked him on a personal level, the reflexive twinge of disappointment in her gut told her she'd still been rather hoping he was single. She didn't need to like the guy; one night staring into those eyes would have been just the kind of comfort she needed. '*Midsommar's* for families really, isn't it?'

He paused. 'Yes, I suppose it is.'

'If ever there's a time to be with the ones you love, it's tonight,' she murmured, feeling her loneliness wash over her again, taking her away from him, here . . .

He was quiet for a moment. 'So, do you want that beer?'

She looked back to find him holding out a bottle for her. 'Oh, I should probably be getting back . . .' But her gaze met those eyes again. Even if she could only look at him . . . 'But I don't suppose one would hurt.'

She took it, and self-consciously adjusted her floral crown. Suddenly it seemed a ridiculous thing to wear, even though she'd had it on all day with no embarrassment at all.

'Are those the flowers you had in the basket yesterday? They look good.'

She touched the crown uncertainly again. 'Oh, well . . . it all seems a bit silly when you're nowhere near the maypole.' She swigged the beer and felt him watch her.

'I'm Emil, by the way.'

'Oh. Bell.'

He arched an eyebrow. 'As in . . . ding-dong?'

'Yes,' she chuckled. 'As in that. It's short for Isobel. With an "o".'

'Boll.'

She laughed at the joke, feeling the awkwardness of yesterday's encounter begin to dissipate. He might have been a reluctant hero, but she supposed she'd hardly been the sympathetic damsel in distress either, indignantly demanding he give up the trike as her arms almost gave out.

A breeze rippled over her and she shivered, her little sundress not such a great idea after midnight.

'You can come and sit in here if you like,' he offered, nodding towards the bench opposite his. 'I promise I'm not a serial killer. It's a lot warmer down here, out of the wind.'

'Is that why you're here?' she asked, deliberating for only a moment before getting up and jumping onto the boat. It was one of the less glamorous ones in the marina. Most were navy-bellied gin palaces with white leather and drinks cabinets. This was an early eighties cabin boat with yellowing paint, upholstered in a shocking green-and-white zig-zag cloth that seemed to have been inspired by Culture Club, and it would be good going if it had a first aid kit on board. 'Keeping down, out of the wind?'

'I'm keeping my head down in every sense.' He drank some more of his beer.

'Oh dear. Did you upset your wife or something?'

His gaze was direct, flashing on her like a torch beam. 'My wife?'

'Yeah, the dark-haired lady I saw you with earlier . . . ? You said you were with your family.'

'I was.' A small smile flickered on his lips. 'She's my sister.'

'Aaah!' She couldn't quite contain the happy relief that

117

statement brought her – he wasn't married! – and she quickly drank some more. There was nothing else to do, and she needed to distract herself from that face.

He watched her fidget nervously. 'You're not from here.'

'Nope. I'm English.'

'Your Swedish is excellent.'

'Thank you. Swedish grandmother.'

He nodded.

'Do you speak English?' she asked.

'Only when I'm trying to impress beautiful English girls,' he said in faultless English, no trace of an accent.

'Oh my God, you speak it better than most of the English!' she laughed.

'As I understand it, so do most Swedes . . .'

She laughed. 'Hmm. You're not afraid to be controversial, I see.'

'It would be very dull to be otherwise, don't you think?'

Her eyes met his for a moment, and she felt a charge between them. There was definitely something there, a chemical attraction that seemed to have ignited a spark. 'So have you ever been to England?'

'Yes.'

'Where?'

'Cambridge. I worked there for a short time.'

'Doing what?'

'Oh, a bit of this and that. Some bio-engineering.'

'*Some* bio-engineering. Huh.' It didn't sound like something people would dip in and out of. 'Did you like it there?'

'Cambridge? Sure. The university's so beautiful.'

'It is, isn't it?'

'Did you go there?'

'Who, me?' she laughed. 'Oh no. I didn't go to uni full-stop.'

She shook her head, a large dot of pink staining her cheeks. 'I didn't get the grades, sadly. I had a place to read geography at Manchester.' She forced a smile, not wanting to remember any of that time now, either. 'But it just wasn't to be. Not the path for me.'

'You believe that? You don't think you determine where you end up in your own life?'

'*Definitely* not that,' she spluttered. 'I honestly think you end up where you're supposed to be, one way or the other.'

There was a short pause. 'So you think it was pre-destined that you should end up drinking beer on a boat on a tiny island in the Swedish archipelago on the longest day of the year with a perfect stranger?'

She laughed, her head tipping back slightly so that her profile curved at the sky. He really was a perfect stranger. Quite perfect. She tucked a wisp of hair behind her ear, sensing their acquaintance make a small shift from stiff, formal politeness to something more unguarded and relaxed. More shapeless. Or maybe that was just the beer thinking for her. 'Well, clearly this is but a *moment* in the bigger picture,' she conceded. 'But was I supposed to end up in Sweden?' She sighed. 'I think I was.'

He kept watching her, the weight of his stare like hands on her shoulders. 'So, what did you do then, if not university?' He took a swig of his beer.

'I sailed round the world.'

He paused, the bottle at his lips. 'What?'

'Yeah. We had a boat and we just . . . headed off. No particular plans, we just went with the wind.'

He stared at her as though she was a changeling, shifting in front of his very eyes. 'Who's we?'

'Me and my fiancé, Jack.' She swallowed. There always

seemed to be a ring around his name when she said it out loud; like an audible force field. 'We did that for a couple of years. And then after that, well, I found myself in Sweden and I've ended up staying here ever since,' she went on quickly.

He stared at her with narrowed eyes, and she knew he'd picked up on what she hadn't said. 'And what is it you do here, then?'

'I'm a nanny.'

'And your fiancé . . . ?'

Oh God. 'Died.'

The word was like a bullet, stopping everything in its tracks, stopping his bottle mid-arc from reaching his lips again. His hand dropped down. '. . . I'm sorry.'

'No, it's fine.' She gave a too-bright smile and shook her head. 'Well, I don't mean it's *fine*. Obviously.' Her breath came like a gasp, tension in the muscles around her mouth. 'Clearly it isn't. But it . . .' Her leg was jigging, she realized, and she put a hand on her thigh to stop it. 'It just is what it is.'

He watched her, seeing the physical accompaniments that came with the words. 'When did he die?'

'Nearly four years ago.' She nodded, swigging her beer a little too deeply, her movements suddenly wide-ranging and spasmodic.

'The loss is still fresh.'

'Yes, it is.' It struck her as a surprisingly open thing to say. Most people looked the other way and changed the subject if it came up. She felt an expectation to be over it by now.

'And it's why you were sad up there just now?'

She shrugged, biting her lip. 'Sometimes it just hits me. Times like this, really – celebrations, anniversaries, Christmas . . . Most of the time I'm okay.'

He stared at his beer. 'I'm sorry. You seem very young to have gone through something like that.'

'So was Jack.' She glanced at him, but something in his eyes made her hold his gaze. What was she seeing? Sympathy? Compassion? Understanding? Empathy? There was something intangible about him that went beyond the solitary, something 'held back', an invisible cloak of vulnerability draped over his shoulders. '. . . Have you ever lost someone?'

It was a long moment before he answered and she realized what it was that she saw in him. *Pain.* 'Everyone. There was an accident and . . . my wife, child, father . . . I lost them all.'

She stared at him, open-mouthed, words stoppered in her throat. None would do. 'Oh my God,' she whispered finally. 'Emil, that's –'

His eyes flashed to her again as he heard his name in her voice.

'I just don't know what to say.'

'No one ever does,' he said, shrugging his eyebrows with a tired smile, and she saw how the loss curled up in him like a sleeping mouse. She felt a swipe of guilt, for his was surely the greater: his wife, child, father . . . it was as multi-layered as a peony, a blade on every petal. 'Words aren't enough.'

He was right – they weren't. Words didn't bring back souls that had taken flight; they weren't arms that could hold her in the night.

They let a silence envelop them, the distant beat from the Yacht Hotel dance floor drifting over like mist on the water. Time was beginning to lose its edges. It was well after midnight now, the sky still a brilliant red as though set to pause on a dazzling sunset, a perpetual dusk.

'Flares,' he murmured, looking at a point beyond her head.

She looked back over her shoulder, just as a burst of red

smoke painted the sky. It was too light for fireworks to work their magic, but it was something, a last spectacle to keep the party spirit going. 'Oh wow.'

'You can see them better from here, if you want,' he said, shifting up the bench seat slightly as explosion after explosion rocked the archipelago. Red, purple, green.

His gaze was fixed on the sky as she came over and sat down beside him, wordlessly. Still, she immediately felt the shift at the new proximity. They weren't touching but she could feel his body heat as they watched the light show, two strangers, alone together on the shortest night of the year – both sad, both broken, both a bit drunk.

She had finished her beer, the bottle sitting empty and light in her hands. It was her cue to go, soon.

'I love *Midsommar*,' he murmured, before she could stir, as though sensing her thoughts. 'As a boy, I thought it was better than Christmas.'

'Mmm, it's not a patch on St George's Day,' she murmured back, prompting him to look over at her quizzically – until he saw her deadpan expression.

He grinned at her quip. 'Now who's being controversial?'

They continued to look into the sky, but, too soon, the show was coming to an end, the punk colours and intermittent bangs dwindling.

'What is it you like about *Midsommar* so much?' she asked, not wanting to leave yet.

'Growing up, my mother used to tell me it was our consolation for all the months of darkness we had to endure –'

Consolation . . . She looked at him and found he was already watching her.

'– And now, as an adult, I hate the darkness. I would happily never sleep again. I want the shortest night, every night.'

Time contracted in on itself as she looked into those eyes. She was drunk, but they both knew what he was saying. They'd had their dark days; tonight was about grabbing the light . . . Their consolations . . .

She realized something suddenly.

'You're speaking in English,' she whispered, seeing that his gaze was on her lips and feeling the indefinable *something* that hovered between them – an instinctive locking of spirits – bloom into being.

'I know. Are you impressed yet?'

Slowly, so slowly, she leaned towards him, stopping with her face just inches from his, his eyes roaming hers for an answer to a question she didn't yet know. His hand cupped the back of her head, holding her, before his lips pressed gently on hers – softly at first, then firmer – and she sensed the world shifting around them, changing by a single degree.

Chapter Ten

'Where have *you* been?' Tove asked, almost falling out of the chair as Bell opened the squeaky gate, her crown lopsided on her head, her hair particularly bed-headed this morning.

Bell winked as she closed it behind her and stretched her arms high above her head. She felt like she was floating on air.

'You did not! *Who?*' Tove gasped with deep melodrama. 'You weren't even dancing with anyone.'

Bell flopped down into the other chair and let her arms and legs splay in straight lines like a stick doll. 'His name's Emil, and he's possibly the most beautiful man I've ever seen. Ever.' She arched an eyebrow, suspicious that it was so quiet – and tidy. 'Where are the boys?'

Tove groaned. 'Running,' she said, batting her hand dismissively. 'Bodies, temples, all that jazz. But forget them. Emil. Emil. Tell me everything. Who is he? Where is he? And when am I gonna meet him?'

'I don't know, I don't know and I don't know,' Bell grinned. 'He just took off in his boat. Could have gone anywhere,' she sighed with an easy shrug.

'And you don't know where?'

Bell shook her head with a happy sigh. 'Nope.'

Tove stared at her like she was delirious. 'What is wrong

with you? Why would you let the most beautiful man you ever saw take off in his boat, without knowing where he was going?'

Bell ignored the question, smiling happily, tipping her head back and reliving the memories. She sighed, remembering his hands, his mouth on her neck . . .

'Oh my God, just look at you! I don't even need to ask.'

Bell rolled her head to the side. 'Best sex of my life, Tove. I swear to God, it was like . . .' She narrowed her eyes, trying to put it into words. 'It was like it was his first time, almost. But in a good way! I mean, the way he looked at me, and touched me . . . I felt like a goddess.'

Tove's jaw dropped down. 'And yet, I refer you to my previous question.'

Bell arched an eyebrow. 'Well, I don't want to fall in love with him Tove.'

'Yeah, that would be bad. It'll inevitably end and then your life will be shit again. Sure, I see that,' she drawled.

'Says you.' Tove never mentioned it, but Bell knew perfectly well that her friend liked to be the one to do the leaving ever since she had discovered that her long-term boyfriend had bedded all her friends.

'Yeah, but you're not me. You've actually got a heart.'

'Well, thanks, but I'm perfectly happy with current arrangements. Hot man on a boat? Hell yes. Thank you, next.'

Tove reached an arm over and squeezed her hand affectionately. 'Babe, not every guy you love is going to die on you.'

'You don't know that,' Bell said, throwing her the side-eye. 'And besides, you think *I'm* not ready? He is nowhere close. Believe me. His wife, child and father all died in an accident. He lost them all.'

'Fuck!' Tove whispered.

'I know. It's so awful.'

'What happened to them?'

'He didn't say, and I didn't like to ask.'

'God, so he's beautiful *and* vulnerable?' Tove mumbled. 'No wonder you got with him.'

'Mmm.' She sighed, remembering how he'd been staring into space as she woke up this morning, a look of unbearable sadness on his face. She didn't know if he'd ever recover from it, but if he did, it wouldn't be any time soon. He was damaged, like her, a fatal crack running through them both.

'And he had a boat too?'

Bell laughed. 'Oh, trust me, that was the least beautiful thing about it! This was not some fancy-pants gin palace. I was just grateful it wasn't taking on water.'

'I'll say, with all that rocking that must have been going on –'

They cackled with laughter together.

'How about you?' Bell asked, looking over at her friend.

'Agh, you know. My usual.' She shrugged. 'Wham-bam-thank-you-dude. I didn't stay over. But he was fun. It was a good *Midsommar*'s.'

They lapsed into silence, both of them tired. Bell let her head drop back onto the headrest, her fingers interlacing across her stomach. 'Shame we can't go back and do it all again, really,' she murmured, thinking back to Friday and her inauspicious first meeting with Emil – the terse nod in the store, his reluctant chivalry, the sight of him unsmiling and stiff in the crowd. She'd had absolutely *no* inkling then of what was going to happen between them. If her Self of right now could have gone up to her Self of yesterday and told her what was going to happen, she would not have believed it. Nothing would have made her believe she was going to turn the shortest night into the longest one, staying awake all night in *his* arms . . . And yet, it had all happened, been so natural. With his baseball cap off so she could see his eyes, when her dress had come off and he could see her curves . . . it had been like they'd devoured each other, both frantic, as though they hadn't realized they were starving.

She got goosebumps just thinking about it again, and gave an involuntary shudder.

'Oh my God,' Tove groaned beside her, her eyes closed and enjoying the peace as the birds trilled around them. 'Get a room.'

'Sorry,' she whispered.

'. . . You don't think you might have made a mistake not getting his number?'

'Yes. And that's precisely why I'm glad I didn't. This way, it just is what it is. One incredible night.'

They heard the pounding of feet, and heavy breathing.

'You're back,' Tove said, still with her eyes closed, as the squeaky gate was opened.

'Yeah,' Kris panted, his hands on his hips. He shot an enquiring glance Bell's way, and she replied with a confiding smile. He winked at her, understanding; it didn't need to be said. There was a dark arrow of sweat down the front of his top, his hair was pulled into his man-bun, and for the thousandth time she wondered why her soulmate had to be gay. He came over and kissed her on the forehead as Marc pulled to a stop a moment later, looking wrecked.

'What took you so long?' Kris asked, sitting on the arm of her chair like he'd been there for hours.

Marc chucked a twig at him.

'So – lunch,' Tove announced, as the guys began stretching.

'I don't mind where we go so long as they serve stuff starting with carb- and ending in -ohydrates.'

'Vardshus, then?' Kris chuckled, getting up. 'Let me have a shower and then we can go.'

'Me too,' Marc said, following after him.

'Not together, please!' Tove called after them as they stepped into the little yellow house. 'I know what you two are like, and we've got a ferry to catch, remember.'

Bell groaned. 'Oh bugger. It's Sunday already? I forgot.'

'He really did fuck you stupid, didn't he?' Tove chuckled. 'Yes, it's Sunday. All day. Almost time to ship back to real life and our most excellent jobs again.'

Bell felt her good mood get a crazy-glaze. She hadn't seen the Mogerts at all yesterday, which was just weird. And she had to face Hanna tomorrow. The conversation she'd been dreading was almost here. How to *not* get fired? She still couldn't work it out.

'I think this thing has surgically attached to me,' she muttered, reaching up and trying to disentangle the floral wreath from her hair. With a sharp tug, she pulled it free, staring at the battered, misshapen garland, the flowers wilted and limp. For some reason, it felt totemic, her first and last remaining link to him.

'Going to keep it for posterity?' Tove teased, seeing her hesitation.

'No. I'm going to get changed,' she said, getting up and tossing it in the bin, hoping Tove didn't see her wince.

The pub was rammed, every table taken and a queue snaking down the lane. 'Looks like we're not the only ones needing to carb-load,' Marc muttered as they waited in line, looking as longingly at the shade of the apple tree as at the cold beers.

'And guess what? They're *all* going to be getting the same ferry back with us,' Tove groaned.

'Forget to take your happy pills, you two?' Kris asked, looping his arm through his fiancé's.

'Ugh, it's just the Sunday blues,' Marc groaned. 'Why does the weekend have to pass so quickly? I want to stay out a few more days. I *need* to.'

'Well, we can't all be as lucky as Bell, getting to spend the summer here and being paid for it.'

'Excuse me! I'd like to see you keep two three-year-olds and a ten-year-old occupied simultaneously, when there are hazards *at every turn*. I'm living on my nerves from the moment I leave my bed till I'm back in it again. You have no idea how hard it is.'

'And to think in my job, I only have to keep them alive,' Marc quipped.

'That's nothing. I've got to do that *and* keep them happy!'

Kris laughed. 'I'd only know how to keep them fed, but if Tove could do "the birds and the bees" chats, vet their boyfriends, show them how not to get their drinks spiked –' He raised his hands in the air triumphantly. 'Between the four of us, we'd be the ideal parents.'

A table came free and they settled at it gratefully, ordering a round of beers. It wasn't quite in full shade and they played a game of musical chairs for a few minutes as Marc and Tove fussed about the dangers of 'being in the sun' and kept switching seats with the others, who didn't care.

Their drinks came quickly and they ordered what they always had here – Tove, a quiche; Bell, a burger; and the boys, large salads with steak.

Bell fussed distractedly with her dress, a flippy red gingham with fluttery short sleeves. It clashed with her yellow chequerboard Vans, but she quite liked that. Her hair was still wet from the shower but she'd piled it into her usual topknot to get it off her shoulders. She'd got a tune stuck in her head – *If you can't be with the one you love . . .* – and it was beginning to drive her nuts. She didn't even particularly like the song.

'– don't want anything big. Town Hall and a room at the back of a pub would do me fine,' Marc was saying.

'Oh, you can do better than that,' Tove chided. 'This is your wedding we're talking about.' She placed her hands on the table. 'Have you considered holding it at the *Vasa*?'

They all laughed.

'I can't think of anything more tacky!'

Tove looked hurt. 'But it's got history there. A sense of scale. This is a huge deal, guys. You're getting married.'

'It's not an epic occasion in Swedish history, though,' Kris said carefully. 'Although we do love your enthusiasm.' He patted her hand on the table.

'Ugh, I'm so tired,' Bell groaned, leaning over and resting her head on Marc's shoulder. 'I'm just going to go to sleep here. Don't move, okay?'

'Poor baby. Not getting enough sleep last night,' he teased. Tove had of course wasted no time in telling him and Kris all about her athletic night as they were walking over here.

She stuck her tongue out but her eyes were still closed as she rested on his shoulder, happily listening to her friends' weary, hungover chatter, the gentle clatter of ice cubes as drinks were lifted and set down, other people's laughs, bird song around them all . . . his salt-crusted dark hair, sun-bleached clothes, puttering about on that paint-flaked, under-powered boat.

She opened her eyes, sensing something.

The others were deep in conversation about the festival they had booked tickets for in Croatia next month, but she had an instinct she was being watched. She swung her gaze round the garden, looking at all the other people enjoying their Sundays, until –

He gazed back at her. He had his baseball cap and sunglasses back on; it was almost like he was hiding himself away. His arms were folded on the table, a pint in front of him as the dark-haired woman – his sister – talked animatedly with two teenagers sitting opposite, neither of whom was remotely animated in return.

She felt her stomach do a flip. When he had left the jetty today she had assumed he was *leaving* leaving; that he'd come here only for the *Midsommar* celebrations and would disappear to wherever it was he lived, never to see him again. But she realized now – she'd seen him in the shop on Friday, stocking up on essentials. Even if he didn't live on Sandhamn, he was nearby. She was going to keep bumping into him like this . . .

She swallowed, her body saying one thing about it, her head quite another.

He inclined his head in the slightest of nods, a movement so slow and tiny, no one watching him would even see it as such, not unless they saw how he had tethered her with his stare, how she couldn't look away . . .

They had finished eating, she saw, the waitress coming over to clear the plates. He glanced up at her and sat back slightly to allow her more room, but his gaze came straight back to Bell.

She felt paralyzed. After everything they had done, it seemed ludicrous that she couldn't get up and walk over and say hello; to even smile. But they were separated by three tables, a patch of grass and whole other lives. Only last night united them, two perfect strangers looking to lose themselves for a few hours, to keep the darkness away. And this morning, as she had prepared to leave, he hadn't asked for her number or where she was staying, or even her last name. He had pulled away from the jetty with burning eyes but an air of finality, no more wanting to shape a future from one night than she did.

All of which was completely achievable, so long as she didn't ever see him again.

His sister got up beside him, all thin limbs and blow-dried hair. She was wearing skinny cropped jeans and red-soled ballerina pumps, a cotton shirt and pearls; she was understated in her style, yet still somehow screamed 'rich husband'. He, by contrast, was in another faded t-shirt, a hole at the neck, navy cargos, battered boat shoes that looked the same vintage as his actual boat.

She felt her heart constrict as he got up to leave too, his niece and nephew shuffling with bored torpor, fiddling with their headphones. She tried to think of something, a reason to make him stay, an excuse to talk to him; but there was nothing. It was done. He stood by his table and stared at her openly for a moment, before giving a smile as tiny as the nod, hidden in plain sight. No one else was watching. No one else cared. But as he turned away and followed his family out of the garden, she knew she did.

Sandhamn, 27 July 2009

He stared at his untouched lunch, not reading the paper open before him, his hand spread in a tense claw. Their laughter dominated the space, heads turning towards their vibrant group. They were young and beautiful, poised on the cusp of taking on the world.

Though his head was down, the brim of his baseball cap allowed him to sneak furtive glances in her direction. He could see her friends joking about, the conversation open and buoyant – yet always somehow coming back to her, everyone's eyes settling on her face like bees returning to a flower. Her fingers tapped against her glass as she talked, her bright hair worn up in a sleek ponytail and showing off her slender neck. Under the table, he could see she had kicked off her shoes and was scrunching the grass between her pink-varnished toes, her laughter tickling the air as the guy beside her cracked a joke. She clutched his arm, weak with amusement.

She was with him. His friend. He remembered the contents of her basket . . .

He looked away as she threw a casual, queenly glance around the garden. Was she aware of the way everyone watched her? Was it what she wanted? She had to have known what she was doing in the shop earlier, her impact upon people. Men.

His fingers drummed the wooden table, his sandwich beginning to curl in the midday sun, but he still couldn't stomach it. He felt tied up in knots. Anxious. Sick. He took a sip of his beer, feeling it slide down his throat. He reminded himself it was cool, refreshing, relaxing . . .

He looked back up at her again, and perhaps it was the abrupt movement of his head that caught her attention too, because their eyes met in the next moment. She looked straight at him – startled, but something else too. Intrigued? Interested? The smile faded on her mouth, but not in her eyes.

Not in her eyes.

Chapter Eleven

Bell walked over the soft carpet of pine needles, the sun glancing through the trees and heralding another thumping hot day. The air was ominously still, no trace of a breeze, sooty terns gliding effortlessly on the thermoclines. She wished she had some of their early-morning grace but she had woken with a distracted, nagging feeling, unable to fall into the deep and dreamless oblivion she had craved. She had kayaked back over here last night after the others had caught the ferry back to the city; it had felt too sad to be the only one left in the little yellow house, so she had put the key back in the Croc and crept into her cabin. Perhaps it was that extra day off on Friday, the holiday weekend a little too good, but she wasn't ready for reality yet. She already knew it was going to bite.

She stood in the shadow of the trees and watched the twins play in the shallows as memories played insistently through her mind, refusing to let her go just yet. They were abbreviated flashes, like a black-and-white cine film – the shock of those startling eyes he preferred to keep hidden, the reserve that had quickly become abandon, the low groans as their hands had roamed, his sadness in profile in the dawn light, his quiet acceptance of what must be in the pub garden . . . It had been a lapse of reason, a kink in the time continuum when they had briefly stepped out of their own lives and become different, other people. Rationally, she knew that. It was just a one-night stand. A hook-up. She couldn't make this into more than it was.

She watched as Hanna came out of the cabin, clasping a coffee between her hands, her gaze on the horizon. She was wearing her white linen shorts and favourite blue blouse, her hair drawn back in a sleek ponytail – a vision of composed femininity, impossible to link to the drunken wreck who had stumbled in, dishevelled, on Thursday night.

She had left a posy of wildflowers in a glass beside the bed and a box of Bell's favourite biscuits from the bakery on the table, along with a yellow post-it on the top with 'so sorry' written in neat script and a sad-face emoji drawn beside it. Bell had sighed at the sight of the apology. It was something, she supposed, to make their reunion less awkward; but there still needed to be an explanation, some reason that 'justified' Hanna abandoning her children in their beds. It couldn't be left unexplained.

Hanna turned and went back into the house again and Bell, knowing she couldn't hide out forever, stepped out of the trees with a sigh and onto the gentle curve of the tiny beach. The girls were as bare as babies and digging a trench with long-handled spades. Their high-note chatter carried like burbling water, and she found herself smiling as she approached. Their fine blonde hair was worn in matching French plaits, but the gentle fuzz around their heads suggested those styles had been put in one, or even two days before. The same ones she had done before she'd left?

'And what do we have here?' she asked them, her shoes in her hands as she kicked through the sand.

They looked up at her with excited gasps. 'We're digging for treasure!'

'Treasure! Oh well, please continue – I could definitely do with some of that,' she ribbed. 'Can you find me some gold, please? I really do need to get rich.'

'Okay. But Mamma lost her ring, so we've got to find that for her first!'

Bell felt her own smile fade. Were they joking? Was Hanna? Perhaps it was a ploy to amuse them for several hours. 'Well . . . keep looking, then. Be Mamma's heroes. I'll come back in just a minute. Have you got suncream on?' She reached down and tapped their little shoulders; they were tacky to the touch. 'Okay, good girls. I'll be right back.'

She walked up the sand with a frown, and – dropping her shoes in the basket on the deck – stepped through the fully slid-back glass doors and into the cabin. The coffee cup Hanna had been drinking from was on the counter and she was juicing oranges, her back to the room.

'Hey!' Bell said brightly. Too brightly. It sounded forced.

Her employer turned. 'Bell, hi!' She gave an equally fake smile, but up close Bell could see that her complexion was pale beneath the tanned, puffy pillows under her eyes.

There was a half-moment of tension as they looked at one another for the first time since they had met here on Thursday night. Bell instinctively understood that now wasn't the best time for accusations. Her boss, though no longer drunk, though outwardly composed, seemed hardly more held together than she had been then. 'Good weekend?'

Hanna pushed her immaculate hair back from her face. 'Great! Oh my God, the weather! I mean . . .' She shook her head in disbelieving gratitude, but her hand was shaking a little.

'I know, right?' Bell agreed, walking in and automatically scooping up the girls' discarded pyjamas from the floor, eager for the distraction. 'Did you enjoy *Midsommar*?'

'Oh yes. Absolutely.'

'I didn't see you there. I thought I'd catch you all dancing. It's the girls' favourite bit.'

'Oh, yes.' Hanna grabbed the coffee cup again. 'Well, we decided just to keep it small this year, so we stayed here.'

Bell was shocked. 'You mean you didn't go to Sandhamn at all?'

'No. Max is under the weather, and the girls were just overtired. You know what they're like – it always takes them a while to sleep well out here. Tilde complains the silence is too loud.'

Bell smiled, but it hadn't been a problem last year.

'Did we miss much?' Hanna asked.

Well, my *life changed*, Bell didn't reply. 'Oh, you know, the usual. Floral crowns, frog dances, too much strawberry cake.'

'And too much schnapps, I hope?'

'Of course,' Bell smiled, folding the clothes and plumping the sofa cushions too, shuffling the weekend papers into a neat pile and getting down on her knees to put the stray Sylvanian Family figurines back into their box. She was aware they were both at pains to be *very* busy and *very* jolly. She looked up. Hanna was pouring the fresh juice into a jug. 'So Max got out here okay?'

'Oh yeah, you know what he's like – this is his happy place. Nothing can stop him coming out here.'

'Did you go anywhere?'

'We took the boat round to Swan Lake on Saturday and had a picnic there. We gathered the greenery for the girls' garlands. It's a good spot – lots of cotton grass and hare's tail to put in with the flowers.'

'I hope you took photographs.'

'Of course.'

Bell watched as Hanna went to the freezer and shuffled ice

cubes from a tray into the jug. 'The girls mentioned you've lost your ring. Please say that was a ploy to get them to –' But her eyes fell to her boss's hands and the conspicuous tan line around her index finger.

'I'm afraid not.' Hanna wrung her hand anxiously.

'Oh, Hanna,' she said quietly, knowing what it meant. Hanna's ring had been designed with two pear-cut aquamarines, set side by side but facing in opposite directions so that they appeared to nestle together. Max had given it to her when the twins were born. Hanna always laughed that it was her 'push' ring, but – with the benefit of full disclosure about her first husband, now – it was clearly a substitute engagement, wedding and eternity ring in one.

'I know. I'm beside myself about it. And Max is . . . well, he's just so upset. It had huge sentimental significance.'

'I know it did.' Not to mention, it must have cost a bomb. 'God, I'm gutted for you. Do you know what happened?'

Hanna swallowed. 'I don't, really.'

'You didn't see it come off?'

'No.'

'Feel it?'

She shook her head.

'When was the last time you remember seeing it?'

'A few days ago? I can't be sure. I never take it off, so I don't notice it in the way I might something else.'

'No, of course. But you think you might have lost it on the beach?' Bell looked out at the twins still digging, still chatting happily.

'Maybe.' She shrugged, seemingly giving up. 'It could be anywhere.'

'Well, you have lost weight recently,' Bell said lightly, sensing the observation trod on dangerous territory somehow.

She stood up and crossed the room with the piles of clothes and toys, setting them down on the island. 'It must have slipped off your finger.'

'Yes.' Hanna stared at the offending hand, her brow furrowed. 'I knew it was getting too big. I should have . . . I should have taken it off when I had the chance.' Her voice sounded strained, bitterness inflecting the words.

'You mustn't blame yourself. These things happen. Is it insured?'

'Yes, but . . .' She trailed into silence.

'I know, it's not about the money,' Bell murmured. 'God, I'm so sorry, I really am.'

The sound of bare feet, sounding sticky on the wooden floors, made them both look up as Linus walked through, his hair a deliciously wild tangle that told Bell he hadn't brushed it once since she'd left before the weekend either. His sleepy eyes brightened somewhat at the sight of her.

'Hey, champ,' she grinned, ruffling his hair as he leaned in to her briefly by way of greeting.

'Hey.'

'You look like you were hibernating, not sleeping!'

He grinned as he shook his cereal, already on the counter, into a bowl. 'It's 'cos it's so quiet here.'

'I know. Good, huh?' She squinted at him suspiciously. 'Have you *grown*?'

His mouth turned up in a lopsided smile at the tease. 'You've only been gone three days.'

'Yeah, well, I missed you,' she said, ruffling his head again as she picked up the pyjamas and toys. 'Now, I'm going to put these away. Have you made your bed?'

He rolled his eyes. 'Not yet. I only just got out of it.'

'Okay, well, when you're finished eating, do that and we

can make a plan for the day. I think we should let Mamma have a day to herself, don't you?'

She looked to Hanna for clarification that was okay, to find her boss looking back at her with a grateful stare that bordered on desperate.

'Great. Well then, get your thinking cap on for where to go.'

'I want to find the hidden beach.'

Bell rolled her eyes. The great, apocryphal hidden beach of the archipelago. An off-the-cuff comment made by Max once – that he'd played there as a child – had led to endless quests by the children (Linus, really) ever since, to try to locate it. Max had long since forgotten which island his parents had taken him to, and Bell was personally convinced no such thing existed; just a little boy's imagination and a grown man's nostalgia. 'Okay. Well, you can lead the way. I appoint you chief orienteer.'

She wandered down the corridor and tidied away, pulling the duvets up on the girls' cot beds, opening their blinds and folding their pyjamas. Linus's room looked like it had been hit by a meteor. She stood at the door for a moment, staring in with weary despair.

A blue asthma inhaler was on the floor, and she went to pick it up. He and the girls sometimes became wheezy in the cold or when they had chest colds and because they only had one, Hanna always liked to keep it in the same place so that they would know where it was in case of an emergency.

She walked through to Hanna's room and slipped it back into the bedside drawer, automatically going to close it again when something caught her eye, a glint of ice winking from beneath an old photograph. She reached for it and gasped – almost screamed with happy delight, in fact. But something made her catch the words in her mouth and hold them there. She stood, staring for a moment at the long, narrow box beside it and all that it implied . . . Then she closed the drawer again softly, walked back out of the bedroom and through the cabin to the kitchen. 'Hanna, I found the ring.'

Hanna and Linus both looked up at her in astonishment.

'*What?*' She looked stunned as Bell held it out to her.

Linus dropped his spoon in his cereal bowl excitedly. 'Mamma's been looking for that all weekend!'

'Where was it?' Hanna croaked.

'In your bedside drawer. I was just returning the inhaler, and –' She shrugged.

'It was never lost at all, Mamma!' Linus laughed.

Hanna blinked at him as though she couldn't quite understand his words. 'Oh my goodness,' she managed. 'I'm so silly. I must have put it there and forgotten all about it.' She slapped a hand to her forehead. 'I must be getting old! How could I be so forgetful?'

'Wait till we tell Pappa.' Linus began eating again.

'Bell, thank you. I can't believe I did that. I've worried myself stupid all weekend, for no good reason.'

'I'm just glad it's found,' Bell smiled, although technically, it had never been lost. Merely forgotten. It was a funny thing to forget, though.

She watched as Hanna slid it onto her finger again – *I never take it off* – a question running through her mind.

So why *had* she?

Sandhamn, 3 August 2009

It had been a long day and his feet burned as he jumped onto the old boat, already late for dinner. The stock-take had taken twice as long as it should have done when the bakery's cat had leapt from its sleeping perch on the very top box and sent the whole tower crashing to the floor. Some of the tin cans were dented but otherwise fine, but half the tubs of herring had exploded on impact and he'd had to mop three times to get rid of every last speck, else the smell would quickly become unbearable once the temperatures rose again tomorrow.

He couldn't wait to get back home and swim. The stench of fish sat on his skin and his whole body ached from shifting boxes all day; his lower back was stiff from manning the tills, which were set too low down for someone of his height.

All around him, the marina hummed to the low buzz of life as the boat owners went about enjoying their summer on the high sea – some catching the last of the sun on deck, or sitting chatting in foldaway cabin chairs with a glass of rosé; others hosing the waterproof cushions, polishing the bowlines or checking the sails. He unwound the mooring rope from the low bollard, ready to sink onto the bench and putter out of the marina and into the sound. Another day done . . .

A pair of soft, pretty feet with pink-painted toenails stopped in front of him, and he looked up. But there was no surprise in his face. He already knew to whom they belonged.

They stood in silence, as though they already knew each other well, and he had a strange sense of time collapsing in on it itself in her presence – the future; the past. It all dovetailed into the present. This moment right now. Nothing else mattered.

'You haven't called,' she said, but there was no smile in her eyes today, and doubt chimed through her voice. She wasn't used to being resisted, he could tell.

'No.' He blinked, but kept his gaze steady, hating the visceral shock that came with connection with her.

'Why?'

'You know why.'

'Do I?'

'. . . Your boyfriend is my friend.'

Her eyes narrowed, not liking the reply. Sensing judgement? 'We've only been together a few weeks. It's not like I've married the guy.'

He shrugged. 'He's my friend,' he repeated.

She scuffed the ground with one of those pretty pink toes. 'Is that why you wouldn't sit with us?' She could be tart when it suited her.

'I told you, I had to get back to work.'

She took in the old, patched-up boat: the blue baling bucket with string on the handle pushed under the bench seat; his father's yellow oilskin rolled up at the back, home-made mackerel nets slumped in a heap. 'And have you finished work now?' She looked back at him with open interest, dazzling him with the full wattage of her sparkling blue eyes.

'Yes. But I'm late.'

She gave a disbelieving laugh. 'For what?'

'Dinner.'

Her mouth parted. '. . . With your family?' Her eyes gleamed mockingly but he could see the hurt she was trying to hide. She kept dangling bait, but he just wouldn't bite. 'You are just so very . . . good, aren't you?'

He inhaled, wishing he wasn't, not understanding what this was between them. They had barely shared five minutes of conversation together and yet they agitated something in the other, something restless.

'Bye, Hanna.' He unwound the final coil of rope and tossed it onto the jetty, letting the boat glide away from her and everything she promised.

And everything that that threatened.

Chapter Twelve

'Bell, can we talk?'

Bell hesitated at the door, hearing the tension in Hanna's voice. '. . . Sure.' They'd been tiptoeing around one another for the past few days, with cringing politeness and bright smiles that bordered on lunacy.

It was late and yet again, the children had only just gone to bed. Another day that had started early and finished way past their bedtimes had left them all feeling exhausted, the unsetting sun less of a friend to her mid-week.

'Here.'

Hanna was holding out a glass of red wine to her. 'Oh. Thanks.' She wandered over and took it, sitting politely on the edge of the sofa seat.

'Fun day today.'

'Yeah.'

Hanna curled up on the armchair beside the sofa, tucking her legs up, her scarlet nail polish winking in the shadows of the cushions. 'The girls are *loving* that water pistol you bought them!'

'Oh, it was just a cheapie; they had them on offer in Westerbergs when I went to get the milk.'

'Well, anyway, it was thoughtful of you – as usual.'

Bell gave a stiff smile. Compliments and wine were nice, but she would rather have been enjoying what remained of her evening in solitude. By contrast, she suspected Hanna was lonely without Max here, that she craved some adult company.

Hanna stared out into the night: the sun was bouncing along the horizon like a golden balloon, darkness a slow bleed that trickled like a stain from the higher reaches of the sky. She smacked her lips together and looked back over. 'Bell . . . I hope you know how much you mean to us all. Not just the children, but . . . to Max and me, too.'

Odd thing to say. 'I think so,' Bell nodded, waiting for a 'but'.

'And you know you are absolutely pivotal to how we . . .' She frowned, straining for the right word. 'Well, how our family *works*.'

'Thank you.'

'And I'm very aware that you go above and beyond in helping us, really I am. Far beyond what your contract stipulates, and I probably don't tell you enough how much your flexibility and . . . *forbearance* helps us –'

Bell held her breath. Whatever the hell was coming, it surely couldn't be good if she was being this nice.

'– especially when we've had so much change to deal with lately.'

Where was the damned 'but'?

'As you are no doubt very aware – but far too polite to mention – we've had a difficult few months. You saw at first hand how the, uh . . . miraculous news about my husband's recovery and our subsequently disastrous visit to Uppsala threw me into a tailspin.'

Had it? Yes, Hanna had lost some weight, and she and Max had been more snappy with one another recently. But apart from last Thursday night's freak events, everything had been business as usual. No mention of the Uppsala trip was ever made; the family seemed to have unilaterally agreed to a pact of silence on the incident, and it hadn't been raised (at least in her earshot) since. Bell was a little ashamed to admit that she'd all but forgotten the poor man. Life had carried on for the Mogerts, with only a tiny stumble on their otherwise smooth path.

Hanna gripped her wine glass with both hands, the aquamarine ring gleaming under the lights. 'I'll be the first to admit I haven't handled things very well. And I know I haven't been . . . the easiest person to be around lately.' She looked away again, embarrassment and something else – guilt? shame? – forcing her to avert her eyes. 'I've been under a lot of strain, you see, trying to do the right thing by my ex – as you can probably imagine, there's a lot of admin and practicalities, as well as all sorts of legalities that we need to sort out now that he's recovering so well.'

'Oh. Yes, well, I assumed –' She wasn't sure what to say. 'But it's great that he's getting better.'

'Oh, you wouldn't recognize him as the same man,' Hanna said, with what seemed like reluctant admiration. 'He went to a specialist clinic in Switzerland and they've worked miracles with him. Honestly, he's almost back to normal again.'

'Almost?'

'Well, the physical recovery is surprisingly quick, all things considered. It's the mental and emotional aspects that are hardest to conquer. He's not always . . . rational.'

'Oh.'

'Which makes negotiating with him tricky.'

Bell watched her. 'What do you have to negotiate?'

'Our divorce, for one thing.'

'He must have known it was coming, surely?'

'No. He didn't know about Max and the girls.'

146

'Oh.' Bell bit her lip, thinking back. It had been, what, six months months since he'd woken up? Six months that Hanna had kept her new family a secret?

'Yes. I only told him last week. I kept putting it off, you see; I could never find the words to tell him.'

Bell blinked. Much the same as she hadn't been able to find the words to tell Linus, either. 'How did he take it?'

'Terribly.' Hanna scrunched her eyes tightly at the memory. 'That was what Thursday was about. I had had a few glasses of wine here, and I suddenly screwed up the courage to go and see him and just *do* it.'

'But it didn't go to plan?'

She shook her head. 'I think he could tell I'd had a few drinks to steady my nerves; he offered me some more, and I accepted – I wanted it to be a civilized discussion, I thought we could deal with it as friends. We ended up wandering down memory lane, reminiscing about the good times – about Linus as a baby, our honeymoon, how we met. But then . . . then he kissed me.'

'Oh!'

'Yes.'

Bell stared back at her, hearing what she wasn't saying. 'And you kissed him back?'

'At first, yes.' Hanna nodded, biting her lip. 'It's just all so difficult and confusing.'

Bell felt a bolt of concern for Max. '. . . Well, it's understandable,' she managed. 'You were married to him, there's bound to be lots of deep emotions between you both still. And as you said, you don't have to be enemies just because you're not together any more.'

'That was what I hoped. But when I stopped . . . it,' Hanna stammered. 'And I blurted out the truth about Max . . . I think he was so shocked and hurt; I think he felt humiliated.' She sighed, pressing a hand to her forehead. 'It was the hardest thing I've ever had to do. He's a good man who had a bad thing happen to him, and then I had to sit there and explain to him what he's really woken up to – that the life he left behind no longer exists. The *wife* he left no longer exists.'

'His shock must have been immense.'

'I don't think I'll ever forget the look in his eyes.' Hanna splayed her hands questioningly. 'I tried telling him that I had had to make the best decisions as things were presented to me at the time. The doctors had said there was almost no hope that he would recover, so, for Linus's sake, I had to move on with our lives. But he just won't accept that I'm with Max now, that we have the girls. He refuses to even hear their names.'

Bell winced. 'God, Hanna, I'm sorry, that's awful.'

Hanna looked back at her with a hopeless shrug. 'Awful for me, but worse for him. He's not a bad man, he's a sad one. He's been through so much and suffered so unfairly. It feels like the ultimate betrayal for him to endure all that, only to come through it and find we'd left him behind.'

Bell nodded sympathetically. 'I can see that, but there's no villain in this. You are not a bad person, Hanna. You made the best choices you could, in incredibly difficult circum-stances. You're *all* in an impossible situation. You, Max and him.'

Hanna looked back at her gratefully. 'You know, I travelled up to that clinic every single month for those seven years. I'd tell him about how Linus was doing at school, and I would read his school reports. I'd tell him about how tall he was getting and how lucky we'd got finding *you*. And in all that time, there was never once a sign that he heard any of it. Nothing. Not a finger twitch or a flutter of an eyelid.' A sob escaped her suddenly. 'I tried to do my best by him, but now . . . now I think it would have been better if he *hadn't* woken up!'

'Oh Hanna, you don't mean that,' Bell hushed.

'I do, Bell, I do. He won't accept our marriage is over. Even after I told him the truth, he kept saying things could get back to how they used to be now that he's back. Like Max and the girls don't even exist! He said he had based his entire recovery on getting back to being the man he was before, for our sakes, and he won't give up on us now, even if I have.'

'Well, that's . . . just the shock talking. It's a blow for him, clearly, if you have been his main motivation to recover; but he'll come to terms with the new reality, painful though it may be. You did the right thing telling him. He had to know sooner or later.'

'You don't understand. He's angry and hurt, so now he's lashing out.' Hanna looked back at her, eyes red-rimmed and watery, and Bell suddenly knew this wasn't the first time she had cried today, or even in the past hour. 'When he finally realized I was serious about staying with Max, he turned on me. He's saying he wants joint custody.'

'Of Linus?' Now it was Bell's turn to be shocked.

'Yes.' The word came out as a sob.

'But he . . . he can't! He's been in a coma for seven years. Even if he knew his son – which he doesn't – how would he be fit to look after him?'

Hanna fixed her with a steady stare, and something in her eyes made Bell feel a tremor of alarm. 'Because his family are powerful, Bell, and incredibly wealthy. Even in the coma, he had the best care money could buy – all the best surgeons, experimental treatments, pioneering drugs. And from the moment he woke up, they threw another fortune at his re-habilitation – he spent eight weeks at that specialist clinic in

Switzerland basically being . . . rebuilt.' She stared bleakly into space. 'He's normal now – he can walk, talk, run, lift, carry, you name it, there are no physical impediments to block his claim . . . And there isn't a judge in the land that would deny him access, or even dare to try.' She sank further back into the chair, as though there was safety in the cushions.

'Oh my God,' Bell murmured, feeling waves of panic beginning to slap against her insides. 'Does Linus know about this?'

'Nothing.' Hanna shook her head wildly. 'I've been trying to keep it from him till I had, I don't know, *control* of the situation? After the hospital visit went so badly, and that stupid doctor –' Her voice snagged on the words, tearing and becoming ragged. 'I could have had her licence for that.'

Bell swallowed, remembering the immediate fallout only too well. She could see why Hanna hadn't gone near the subject with her son again.

'But I'm going to have to tell him now. Tell him everything,' she sobbed, pinching the bridge of her nose. 'I have no choice. His father wants access and if I don't grant it, he's said he'll take it to court. He'll have the top family lawyers in Europe, and I won't stand a chance. It'll all get into the press.'

'Surely if his family are that powerful, they'd get some super-injunction or something?'

'On the contrary, he'll want it out there. He's the victim in all of this. Imagine how the narrative will read – the scion to Sweden's Camelot wakes from a tragic accident and coma to find his wife shacked up with another man. They'll dig up my life with Max, go through our tax returns, our bins, our social media . . . They'll paint me as the bitch who didn't wait.'

Bell winced. It was an intimidating prospect. She closed her eyes, thinking fast, remembering Linus's terror at the hospital. How would he react to being told that the wild man he'd seen raging and screaming obscenities in that hospital bed was his real father? That that same stranger wanted Linus to go and live with him for half the time? 'Okay, well then, you need to find a compromise. Clearly, as his father, he does have rights – so Linus needs to be told the truth, and they need to be reintroduced to each other. Properly.'

'That was my plan too, and I thought he was on side with that. He knew that after the hospital visit went so badly, it was going to need to be handled better the next time he met Linus. *He* was the one putting off their meeting; he said he wanted to be strong for him when they met properly. He wanted to be the father Linus might remember.'

'But Linus doesn't remember him, does he?'

'No. But he doesn't believe that.' Hanna looked straight at her. 'But then, I don't know – something's changed this weekend – *Midsommar* got him all revved up. He texted me this morning saying he's been deprived of his son for long enough. He's lost over seven years already. He wants him with immediate effect.'

'What?'

Hanna inhaled deeply, swelling herself up with disbelief and despair as she shook her head. 'He wants Linus to go and stay with him – from tomorrow.'

Bell gasped in horror. '*Tomorrow?* But he can't do that! No way! The man's a stranger to him!'

'I know. I know. That's what I told him, but he won't listen to me. He says he may not have rights over me, but he does over his son.'

'But –' Bell spluttered, the thoughts rushing too fast to form words. 'He's only thinking about himself, not what's best for Linus.'

'*I* know that, *you* know that – but *he* doesn't! He thinks because he can walk and talk again, that that's enough. I've told him it takes more than that to be a father to a child who doesn't remember him – who, who doesn't even know about him.' She began sobbing again. 'Oh God, how am I going to tell Linus about all of this? What can I say? I panicked that day in the hospital, and I lied.'

Bell looked down, remembering her own anger with Hanna that day. She'd handled it badly, made every mistake, and now – now she was having to it face again, telling her son a truth that couldn't be denied any longer. Would he forgive her the lies and deliberate duplicity? Was 'panic' a justifiable excuse to a little boy who had just been unwittingly reintroduced to his own father? Back then, telling that truth had seemed like an impossibility, but things were very different now. They were worse. Now it wasn't revealing the identity of his true father that was the main problem, but the reality of Linus having to stay with the stranger who had terrified him.

She stared out into the night, trying to calm her own panicky thoughts. Two swans were swimming past on the inky water, dazzling in their bright relief; but all she could see was the young boy sleeping down the hall, with no idea of the volte-face his life was about to take with the dawn. 'Okay, look,' she said slowly. 'We don't want to antagonize him. We can all totally understand how . . . desperate he must be to get his life back in some way. He knows he can't have you, but Linus is still his son and as his father, he has rights. No one's disputing that – this is just a timing issue. You need to get him to see that you're not saying you're denying him access, just that you want to delay the timing of it so that Linus can adapt to the news. It's for Linus's sake, not yours. He's the child and his needs must come first. As a parent, he'll understand that, surely?'

Hanna shook her head despondently. 'He's adamant it'll be harder for him to rebuild their relationship once we're back in the city and school's back. He wants the summer block to give them time to get to know each other, before we start discussing formal living arrangements within a shared custody agreement.'

'You mean, moving between his place and yours?'

Hanna nodded.

'Is he in Stockholm?'

Hanna gave a scornful laugh. 'He's got places everywhere. But yes, Stockholm is their base.'

'So then, we're all going back to the city tomorrow?'

Hanna's eyes fluttered up to her, and back down again. 'No. He's out here for the summer.'

Of course he was. The entire city was out here. And last Thursday, when Hanna had gone to see him, taking the boat . . . That meant he had to be somewhere relatively nearby.

'Well then, that's something, I guess,' she said finally, trying to find the bright side. 'At least Linus will still get to have his summer on the islands. And with you beside him every step of the way, perhaps it won't be so bad.'

'You don't understand.' Hanna's voice was flat and toneless. '*I* can't be there. Not unless I leave the girls. And Max, clearly.' She swallowed. 'He wants me to choose – but the twins are three. They'd never understand.'

'You mean Linus would be there *alone*?' Bell's mouth formed a perfect, aghast 'o'. She reached forward – urgent, desperate. 'Hanna, you can't do that.'

'I have no choice.'

'Yes, you do! Go to court, take your chances. You *cannot* let

Linus go and live with a perfect stranger, even if he is biologically his father.' She stopped to draw breath, seeing Hanna's
defeated expression. 'Shit. What does Max say?'

'Exactly that. He's with you. He's enraged, been shouting
down the phone at me all day. He says let the bastard take
us to court.'

'So *do* that.'

Hanna shook her head. 'Believe me, I know my husband.
I've gone over this from every angle and I have no choice – I
have to let him see Linus. If I refuse, he'll not just take me to
court – there's every chance he could go for full custody, not
just joint, and I can't risk that. He's so angry with me right
now that . . . I have to do what I can to keep him on side.
Perhaps with time, and giving him something he wants, I can
show him we can make this work and that he can still have
a happy life *alongside* us. Playing along is my only hope. I
know exactly what hell he could unleash if he gives his lawyers
the green light. They'd destroy me.'

Bell was confused. 'But . . . how? I mean, with what ammo?
You're Linus's mother, an excellent mother. You have a great
career, you live in a beautiful house, with a loving partner
and family. What could they possibly use against you to take
him away?'

'They'd find something.' Hanna looked away, staring into
space.

Bell watched her, feeling her panic rise at Hanna's acquies-
cence. She was defeated. She was going to let this happen.
'Hanna, look, I can understand why you're worried about a
possible worst-case scenario of full custody, but there's an
actual disaster scenario looming if you let this happen. We
both saw the state Linus was in when he came out of that
room. This could damage him emotionally, being taken away

154

from you like this, he'd be terrified,' she said in a low, calm voice, the best she could manage. 'Forget your husband's threats – he's just trying to intimidate you. As his mother, you can't allow this. Linus cannot go and live alone with that man.'

'I know.' Hanna looked straight at her.

Bell looked back, waiting for more. So then, what?

'That's why I wanted to talk to you, Bell. Linus loves you. He adores you. He feels safe with you –'

Oh God – she realized it suddenly – this was the 'but'. 'You want me to go with him?'

'As a chaperone. As someone he loves and trusts deeply.' Hanna nodded, desperation in her eyes, her mouth a narrow slash of bitter regret. 'You are the only person I can ask, Bell. The only one we trust.'

Bell swallowed, hating even the idea of this, hating the very idea of this man and what he wanted. He was a victim here too, she understood that, but he was risking his son's well-being with this demand, and putting himself first. Couldn't he see that?

'It would mean . . .' Hanna sounded hesitant again and Bell braced, wondering what else was coming. What could possibly make this situation worse? 'I'm afraid it would also mean staying out here for the entire summer. No trips back to the city at the weekend. Linus would need you there at all times.'

No time off at all? Bell was going to have to put her entire life on hold for the summer? She could already hear her friends' reactions to that.

Hanna gave a small cry as she saw her expression. 'Bell, I'm so sorry to ask it! But I've already negotiated a new salary for you – triple what you're on. Money means nothing to him. He'll pay anything, just so long as he has Linus.'

'It's not about the money,' Bell mumbled, looking away, feeling conflicted. She had plans booked in – the festival in Croatia, a mini-break to Copenhagen booked with Tove –

'I know it's not. And I know I have no right asking you to give up your entire summer for us. But he's my son.' Her voice cracked again, the words splintered and hoarse. 'And I know you love him too. If you don't help us, I don't know what else I can do. Please, Bell.'

Bell looked at her, experiencing up close the full force of a mother's desperation. She'd never been good at saying 'no' at the best of times.

Now was hardly the time to start.

Chapter Thirteen

He opened the shutters and looked down the wide tranche of lawn, able to just make out the sea twinkling through the narrow-legged alders. It was a midnight-blue this morning, the breeze a gentle south-westerly breath. The flowers swayed and nodded in their beds, a nuthatch singing from the aspen tree. Ingarso, his island refuge, had never looked more beautiful and he felt a quiver of anticipation, as though it was a sign that nature, the universe, was on his side today.

He turned away, catching sight of his own shadow cast in the sunny rectangle on the wooden floor. It was elongated and thin, something of the hermit still in its harsh lines and angles. Was he changed *enough*? Did he still look like the wild man in that hospital bed? Was his son going to run from him again? He closed his eyes, remembering the boy's golden hair – he had his mother's colouring, but the curls were his. And those eyes – green, clear, so close to his own –

'Good morning, sir.'

He looked round. Måns was carrying his breakfast in on the tray. The grey hair was now snowy white, the upright deportment softened to a slumped stoop in the seven years he had been 'away' – as it was referred to by the family – a slight tremor in the hands these days; but he remained the man he had known all his life, quiet but indomitable.

Dependable. Always in his corner. Seeing everything, but saying nothing. The living embodiment of discretion being the greater part of valour. Their first words to one another, after he'd come home, had been about whether he still wanted sugar in his coffee.

'Another beautiful day, sir.'

'Yes, isn't it?' he replied, walking out of the sunny patch and back into the cool of the room. Unlike everything else in this house, he and Måns were the only things changing in it. The walls were panelled and still painted the same soft pearl grey of his boyhood, the reed-legged brick-red linen settle still pushed against the end of the bed, the moody August Strindberg oils – which his teenage self had wanted to replace with Green Day posters – still hanging between simple crystal wall chandeliers. He stared at Måns's polished shoes on the rug as he set down the tray; there was a tiny red mark in the linen fibres; it looked like a bloodstain, but he knew it wasn't that. He knew precisely what it was and how it had come to be there – a lingonberry unwittingly transported in on the knee of his jeans after playing in the garden when he was seven. His eyes roamed the pale, striped rug, finding other marks of long-forgotten moments – the splash of coffee after his father trod on a Lego brick and stumbled, the small ash burn from his mother's cigarette as she kissed him goodnight before a party, Nina's make-up from where she would sit cross-legged on the floor and doll herself up as he watched from his bed, planning her midnight escape from his window (because unlike her, he had the veranda below), her own bed expertly stuffed with pillows; she had had a leather jacket that year: grey, with buckles. It was a curious thing, he marvelled, staring at the innocuous stains beneath their manservant's feet, how great swathes of his memories remained defiantly blank, and yet others were as fresh and sparkling as this morning's dew.

He watched Måns set down the tray in what had always been the usual place, when this had been his room – on the desk, now cleared of childish scribbles and notes. He stared at the platter: ham, honey, bread, apricot compote. As a boy, he had only ever been allowed to eat in his room if he was sick, and it still felt vaguely itinerant to be eating in here now, *just because*. But he had wanted to soak up the energy of this space once more before his child got here. He had missed out on so much of his son's childhood – how could he connect except by remembering the boy he had been, living in this room?

His mouth was dry, and he crossed the room to gulp down the hand-squeezed orange juice. He felt sick with nerves and had scarcely slept. Was this the right thing?

'I think he will love it here, sir,' Måns said, reading his mind as he pushed one of the shutters back fully so that it sat flat to the wall.

'Do you think so?'

'Certainly.'

'I'm worried there aren't enough . . . gadgets.' His gaze swung over the bookcases, the shelves stacked with puzzles, board games, craft projects . . . An old balsa wood aeroplane, hand-painted with red bullseyes, rested on one wing on top of the bookcase; a leather backgammon board was set out with the counters in play, as though a game had been momentarily interrupted. Wifi appeared to have become the world's greatest commodity during his absence. Not oil, nor water. But bandwidth, 4G, download speeds . . . None of these things were easy to install on a glorified rock in the yawn of the Baltic. When he had made enquiries, mention had been made of laying cables along the sea bed, which sounded . . . excessive.

'Perhaps not, but even ten-year-old boys don't summer in the archipelago expecting gadgets.'

He picked up the red Nintendo that had been his own most treasured possession. 'God, I loved this at his age. I think if I'd had to choose between this and the dog –' His fingers ran over the buttons, muscle memory making the digits move quickly. 'Does it still work?'

Måns came over with his hand out and took it from him. He pressed the buttons once, twice, but the screen stayed dark. 'I'll make sure it does.'

He stiffened, feeling the anxiety rise again. 'He's arriving in two hours. Ten o'clock, she said. I need everything to be perfect.'

'Absolutely, sir. I'll see to this right away.'

Måns's feet were quiet even on the wide, aged boards, and he sank into the hard desk chair, wishing the wait was over. He felt perpetually on hold, always waiting for someone else to respond obligingly to a decision or to appear before him. He was at the universe's mercy, a slave to its whims. For seven years, he hadn't even been able to control his body, his own *eyelids*. How was he going to control his stranger son? What would they do? Say?

He was the parent; it would be up to him to lead. He ran over the itinerary for the day in his mind again, rehearsing his role, the things they would do, the words he would say: nothing had been left to chance. Måns had been thorough even by his high standards. He gazed around his old bedroom again, trying to glimpse the ghost of his own boyish self, trying to feel what he had once felt, to see once more, through the curious and open-hearted gaze that came with a child's blank, unfounded optimism, that good things happened to good people.

But the room remained empty and still. Vacated. Long ago abandoned. To reach for otherwise was a futile exercise in hope over experience, because if Life had taught him anything, it was that anything could happen. That fate was capricious and cruel. And no one could be trusted.

They were ominously silent on the boat over, Hanna at the tiller, Bell and Linus on the bench seats, packed bags at their feet, the twins bundled in life jackets. Usually Linus sat by the edge, chin on one hand as the other trailed down in the silky water, but this morning he was holding his small body closed and still, as though he was a robin's egg in a giant's fist.

He had heard the truth only two hours ago, broken over the 'special breakfast' his mother had prepared for him. Bell had been in the laundry room, discreetly out of the way, folding the bed sheets as Hanna had haltingly explained that it wasn't Max who was his father, but the man in the hospital bed. Yes, the crazy one. But he was better now, and that not-crazy-any-more man wanted Linus to live with him for a few weeks over the summer. And that those few weeks over the summer were starting now. In two hours.

A tear had slid down her cheek as she'd heard his stunned responses: 'What?'; 'Why?'; 'Do I have to?'; 'I don't want to.' But worse had been his silences, each of them distinct, as though painted in different colours: shocked. Aghast. Frightened. Angry. Bitter. Defeated.

Bell felt much the same herself, but she at least was an adult; she had a choice whether to do this or not. It was only the fact that Linus so patently *didn't* that persuaded her to be there too. How could she let him go through this alone?

Their three erect bodies looked as stiff as chess pieces as they glided in silence. The water in the lagoon was mill-pond-calm, ribbon scraps of a tentative mist hovering just above the surface. The islands in the constellation curled around them in a ragged frill, the pine forests a sharp emerald-green in the midsummer light, the splash of kayakers' oars splintering the silence, bodies already lying on the rocks.

Bell saw a few ringed seals basking on the bleached rocks of Dead Man's Bones off to their right-hand side, 007 up ahead. She peered, as she always did, through the narrow gaps of the wooded shore, hoping for a glimpse of the palatial property supposedly set at its heart, hidden from prying eyes. But all she could see was a stony path winding through the mossy hummocks, and besides, she had no appetite for gossip or intrigue today anyway. Instead, she fastened her listless gaze on a heron standing motionless in the shallows, wings tucked in, its pointed bill like a golden dagger, waiting to deliver the death blow. She saw how the rocks on the beach were covered with yellow sedum flowers, like thousands of fallen stars. She didn't notice they were in the lee of the island until Hanna cut the engine on the approach to the jetty.

Here? He lived *here*? The island directly opposite theirs? Was that some kind of joke? She looked back at Hanna for confirmation – surely this couldn't be right? – but her boss was looking far beyond her as she prepared to dock. She looked at Linus instead and thought his expression must match hers – open-mouthed and incredulous. His father lived here, on 007? *He* was Dr No?

She gave what she hoped was her best, most encouraging smile, even though what Hanna had told her about his threats to take Linus from her had already confirmed he was every inch the villain Bell and the children had role-played all last summer.

She felt her doubts rear up again. This was wrong. Forcing a child to live with a complete stranger, just to satisfy the whims of a wronged rich man? Whatever sympathies she might have had for him were now gone.

Hanna docked the boat, throwing the rope over the bollards and winding it around several times, her body moving with a rigid, grim efficiency. She could scarcely look at her son, avoiding the silent plea in his eyes as he willed her to look back at him and change her mind.

They stepped up onto the jetty, just as legs appeared through the shadows of the glade, fast-moving and purposeful. Was this him? She watched Hanna straighten up, Linus's suitcase in her hand, waiting patiently for him to reach them as though she was merely in line for a taxi.

'Mrs Mogert?' The man stopped in front of her. He appeared to be in his late thirties to mid-forties, and was wearing dark-green heavy-duty waterproof trousers and a matching polo shirt. He looked more like a gardener than a . . . whatever he was. Security guard? 'Allow me to take that for you. Would you follow me, please?'

And with the suitcase in his hand, he headed back into the trees again, without even so much as a glance Linus's way. Hanna stared at his retreating back with an expression Bell couldn't explain, only feel, but after a moment's hesitation, she took the girls' hands and followed on the path too. Linus came after, walking with the stiffly swinging arms of a toy soldier, the resigned fate of the prisoner.

Bell reached for him as he passed and took his hand in hers. 'Ready for an adventure?' she winked, forcing a jollity she didn't feel. For his sake, she had to somehow find some positives in this perverse situation.

He nodded uncertainly. 'You won't leave me here?'

'Hope to die,' she said, crossing her heart. 'Now, look out for the rottweilers, okay?'

He looked surprised, then managed a small smile. 'If you keep a lookout for the sniper rifles and camouflaged man-traps.'

'Deal,' she said with a sharp nod, beginning to walk.

They strode through the woodland, moving through deep shade into sudden puddles of sunlight, the sun flashing over their faces like a playful sprite as they wove between the trees. Ahead, the twins were chattering like busy birds, stopping every few metres to admire a flower or pick up a particularly straight stick that might pass for a fairy wand. Hanna walked in silence behind them, oblivious to their games, her pale legs scissoring over the stones, slender as the birches, until after a few minutes, she stepped out of the wood and stood with the girls, bathed in a fierce light. Bell and Linus caught up with them a moment later, all of them taking in the view.

It was sensational, but not at all what she had expected of 007. It wasn't a show space – all clipped box and clever topiary – but rather an old-fashioned garden, the sort that seemed to have fallen out of style. A real-life chintz, somewhat scruffy and overblown, it was as unlikely a thing to find in this landscape as a giraffe on an iceberg. Clover and daisies and buttercups speckled the grass, a few mature specimen trees dotted around, old flowerbeds a riotous jumble of colour with butterflies flocking to agapanthus and buddleia stems, towers of frothy pale blue delphiniums nodding in the breeze, pink and yellow roses rambling wildly up arched trellises, an old oak swing dangling from a four-metre length of thick nautical hemp rope.

The long, gently sloping lawn was fringed by the dense wood, hiding this garden and home from the curious gazes on passing boats. The house itself matched the garden, like a glove to a coat – wide and two storeys high, with a columned portico in the centre and a mansard roof, a row of seven large rectangular windows winking back at them. It was grand, but nonetheless stamped as an island house by the vertically grooved wooden walls that were the vernacular of properties in the archipelago. Those were usually a brownish-red (and significantly smaller) but this was a bold, juicy tangerine. A Bond villain's lair it was not. Dr No wouldn't have been seen dead in an orange house. It was far too . . . cheery.

Bell wished she didn't like it. She wished she hated all of it – the gracious, somewhat tired-looking house, the enchanting, overgrown, blowsy gardens. 'It's going to be a nightmare playing football on that lawn,' she muttered to Linus.

'Yeah, I know,' he breathed back.

'Dibs I get to play downhill.'

'That's not fair!'

'Yes it is. I'm way older than you. You've got youth on your side.'

He looked at her through narrowed eyes, wanting to lose himself in their game, but she could see the glint of fear in them and knew he was faking it as much as her.

Hanna looked across at them both, seeming baffled by their role-play as a tiny frown puckered her brow. She turned to Linus and crouched down so that her knees dipped into the cool grass. 'Do you see how lovely it is, darling?'

Linus hesitated, then nodded.

'This is your daddy's home. Which means it's yours too. All this is yours, isn't that wonderful?' He stared at her. 'You can play in this garden – there's not another island in the archipelago with a garden like this, did you know that? Not a single one. You're going to have so much fun. And you can climb on the rocks, find the hidden beach –'

'The hidden beach is *here*?' he gasped.

'I want to go to the hidden beach!' Elise interjected, but Bell silenced her with a reproving look that seemed to work for once. The girls instinctively understood that nothing today was quite as it seemed. This wasn't just any boat ride, any island, any garden . . .

Hanna nodded slowly. 'Pappa pretended he forgot, because this island is privately owned, so you wouldn't have been allowed over to play. But now you can.'

'How will I find it?'

She smiled. 'Trust me, you will. The Soviets accidentally dropped a bomb here on their way to a missile test site during the Second World War and – pow! – the hidden beach was created. It's completely invisible from the sea. That's why no one else knows about it. Only the people lucky enough to get to stay here.'

His interest was piqued – *that* was worthy of a Bond lair – and Hanna's face brightened momentarily in response to his expression. 'The fun is in finding it.'

Bell wasn't so sure. How could a beach be hidden? They weren't like socks kicked under the bed.

'Trust me, you'll love it here,' Hanna went on, her voice thickening suddenly. 'You were always supposed to play in this garden, darling. When you were a baby, I would think about how exciting it would be for you when you were a big boy of ten, able to go exploring. You're so *lucky*.'

Had it not been for the way her voice splintered on the last word, her proclamations might have been convincing. Instead, Linus threw his arms around her neck. 'I don't want to be lucky. I want to be with you.'

There was an anguished silence as they gripped each other with tightly squeezed shut eyes. 'And you will be, darling. Very, very soon. I promise.'

Bell saw the tears begin to stream, and watched as Hanna quickly pulled down her sunglasses from the top of her head as she pulled back from him. She tried to gather herself, glancing up at the house again and falling still as she saw someone standing there, watching them. Bell followed her gaze. A white-haired man was standing there, Linus's suitcase positioned by his legs.

She watched Hanna turn back to her son again. There was something different in her expression now. 'In the meantime, you've got Bell. She'll be with you *all* the time. You won't ever be alone here. Bell will look after you, as she always does.'

Linus nodded, his green eyes flashing between their two faces, but it was to his mother's that his gaze returned. 'You promise you'll come back?'

'Nothing can stop me.' She forced a smile that fooled no one. 'Now go up to the house and Måns will look after you.'

'Who's Måns?'

'A very kind man who'll help take care of you.'

'Aren't you coming?' This time, it was Linus's voice that shook.

'It's better if I leave you here today. But I'll visit, I promise. I'm just across the water, remember that.' Hanna rose to standing again. 'Now off you go. Be a good boy for Mamma. And your father.'

Linus stared up at her, his shoulders heaving like an ocean swell, unformed emotions rolling through him like a storm. '. . . What if he screams again?'

Hanna's mouth parted at the question, but no words came.

'Then we'll scream back,' Bell said firmly, taking his hand in hers again and giving him one of her signature wry looks.

Linus looked shocked. 'We can't do that.' He looked at his mother. 'Can we?'

'You won't need to. Your father was sick then, but he's much better now. You'll see.'

Bell tugged his arm affectionately, pulling him away. 'Come on. I want to see what our rooms are like.'

'Do you?'

No. 'Absolutely,' she said, sticking her chin in the air. 'I hope I've got a revolving bed.'

He nodded, as though that seemed like a good thing to have. 'I want an observatory in mine.'

'You might well have one,' she sighed. 'Have you seen the size of this place?'

'The mirrors had better be two-way.'

'They'd *better* be,' she agreed. They trod over the grass, crushing daisies underfoot, the ground springy beneath their feet. 'D'you reckon they keep cheetahs here?'

He looked up at her. 'Why cheetahs?'

'Why not?' she shrugged. 'Perhaps your dad's a fast runner.'

'He was in a coma for seven years.'

'All the more reason to run now he's awake, then.'

Linus chuckled. 'I think you're the crazy one, Bell.'

'You could very well be right, Linus,' she grinned.

They were at the top of the lawn now, just a few metres from the feet of the white-haired man. He hadn't moved a muscle in all that time. The suitcase was still standing on its side, beside him.

Linus gave a little startle at the sudden nearness of him and turned back, realizing he had distractedly left his mother and sisters by the trees. But they were not there now. Only a rabbit, hopping lazily through the longer grass, ears pinned back as it began to nibble on a dandelion.

Bell squeezed his hand and made him look at her. She gave him the slow blink they sometimes shared in the playground when he didn't want to hug her in front of his friends.

'You must be Isobel?' the man said to her, after a moment.

She turned to face him, gripping Linus's hand more tightly in hers, though whether that was for his benefit or her own, she couldn't tell. All she knew was, she had to protect this child against these people. 'Yes. But please call me Bell.' Her voice was polite but firm, her eyes steely.

To her surprise, the blue eyes looking back at her were kindly. 'I am Måns, Mr Von Greyer's valet. And this must be Master Linus?'

Linus stared back at him, anachronistic against the grand orange house and the valet's crisp suit, in his cut-off jean shorts and trainers. 'Pleased to meet you.' His voice was robotic and he looked ready to run.

'I'm very pleased to meet *you*, young sir. Everyone is very excited that you have come to stay with us. Won't you please follow me?'

They both stared after him for a moment, wrong-footed by the warm welcome. Bond villains weren't supposed to have friendly old men as their sidekicks. Nor orange lairs.

They followed him into the building. It was immediately cool and shaded inside, the brightness of the day falling in long strips through the large windows. They both looked left and then right. The house was a series of interconnecting, open airy salons, high-ceilinged with old, worn strip-wood floors. There didn't seem to be much furniture but what there was – stickback chairs, diamond-doored cabinets, curvy long-case clocks – was very old and seemed to be largely pale and peeling, in the old Gustavian style, a baroque fashion that was very different to the Mogerts' modern, minimal aesthetic. Bell had the impression of peering through bright light and dust, even though the place was clearly spotless; everything was muted, hushed, as though a veil of silence had been hung over the roof, in distinct contrast to the bright, almost shouty exterior. She tried to imagine Linus haring about in here, and couldn't. It wasn't that it was grand *per se*, just that it was somehow disapproving of frivolity.

They caught up with Måns on the stairs – which wasn't hard – treading slowly behind him, their eyes casting nervously around at the dark oil paintings on the walls, up at the crystal lights, hands gliding over the polished elliptical handrail. They swapped glances in silence, noticing every creak of the floorboards, the sheer scale of the house dwarfing them. Bell felt like it was swallowing them whole.

Upstairs, the house felt a little cosier, but it was a matter of mere degrees – maybe half a metre off the ceiling heights? There was more furniture, though, dressing the spaces and making it feel like a home rather than a museum – rugs at spaced intervals on the floors, an antique smiling wooden horse on bows.

Måns walked towards a closed door at the end of the corridor, furthest from the stairs. 'Master Linus, you will be sleeping in the room that your father had when he was a child. He was most insistent it should now be yours. Everything has been kept exactly as it was, including all his old toys.'

Bell arched a quizzical eyebrow, but said nothing. Clearly neither Måns nor his employer knew the first thing about kids. They wanted new and they wanted tech; old Action Man figures – or whatever the guy had played with as a boy himself – weren't going to cut it with his press-ganged son.

'Your father is waiting for you in here.' Måns paused, as though about to say something else, but he appeared to think better of it, and turned away and knocked on the door instead.

There was no reply, but he opened the door anyway and entered. 'Your guests, sir.'

Bell and Linus looked at one another as they stood on the threshold. 'You okay?' she mouthed to him.

He nodded, but she could see the tension in the downward pull at the corners of his mouth. The man they were about to meet had threatened this poor child's mother with a ruinous court case, public shaming and loss of custody. How could she put a positive spin on that?

She dipped her head closer to him, speaking in a hushed tone. 'Remember, he's your dad and he loves you. A very sad thing happened to him and he was poorly for a long time, but all he wants is to get to know you. That's all this is. And I'll be here the whole time.'

'Promise?' Linus breathed.

'Hope to die,' she mouthed, crossing her heart again. She gripped his hand harder and, taking a long, deep breath, they walked in together.

Måns was standing motionless in the centre of the room, his long shadow in the window frame flattering his stooped stature.

'Where is he?' she asked him, more snappily than she had intended.

The old man looked back at her with a look of fluster and bewilderment. She suspected it wasn't a familiar feeling for him; he seemed to ooze capability. 'I'm sorry, Miss Bell. I have absolutely no idea.'

Chapter Fourteen

The day passed quietly. Literally. Though Bell and Linus crept and whispered, not wanting to make an imprint on this new place of residence, the house seemed to breathe around them; other people's stories were held in abeyance in every picture, table-top, chair. There were few photographs to identify the family who had built this house and inhabited it for five generations, but those that were around were old black-and-whites of long-ago scenes. The two of them peered at unrecognizable faces, trying to find Linus's features in a young girl's muddy squint into the sunlight, his gait in a boy's stride as he walked away from the camera, the stern frown, caught off guard, of an older man fishing from a boat.

Måns's embarrassed beseeching that they should make themselves at home whilst he located the absent host – and father – didn't extend, they were sure, to skateboarding down the long, smooth corridors, though both she and Linus had caught each other's eye and thought about it.

For a while, they had sat quietly in the bedroom – hers was next door to Linus's, though not interconnecting – pretending to be interested in the old wooden and tin toys which had a retro charm to them, but little beyond that. Bell had flicked idly through the paperbacks in the bookcase whilst Linus dutifully sat on the floor, playing with an old red Corvette

Matchbox car and building with the Lego bricks he'd found in a box – both of them waiting, braced, any second for the sound of footsteps on the boards and the door to open . . . But as the minutes turned to hours, their stiff manners had softened, both of them curling up on the bed for a quick nap, the emotional anticipation of the day having drained them.

Finally, boredom had propelled them into leaving the room and exploring the house. Timidly, they had crept from room to room, always knocking on the closed doors before peering in. There were eight bedrooms upstairs, and it was almost impossible to tell which were inhabited and which were for guests; all were sparsely decorated and restrained in content, as though to own anything more than was strictly necessary was infra dig.

Her own room was frustratingly charming. It had hand-painted hessian wallpaper, with drawn tendrils of ivy dangling and creeping down from the ceiling in varying lengths. Her bed was a pale grey sleigh-style with a green-and-pink padded eiderdown and there was a vast, peeling painted armoire against one wall which she felt sure must provide passage to Narnia. Everything felt weighty, substantial and grandiose.

Her room overlooked the 'back' garden, although given all approaches to the house were by water, she wasn't sure there was any such thing as front or back; guests simply arrived wherever they docked, surely? The lawn swept around the property like a green velvet cape, flowerbeds dotted whimsically, stray linden trees looking statuesque and dramatic – like eight-pointer stags – compared to the huddled and slender modesty of the birches and pines in the woods.

Downstairs, they had found a dining room with a beautiful whitewashed oval table that looked like it could seat thirty people, a library, a drawing room with some very formal, uncomfortable-looking wooden settles, an exceptionally well-equipped modern gym, an office, the kitchen, a laundry room and behind that, in the darkest corner of the house, a tiny snug with two squashy sofas and a pile of sailing magazines that suggested more life in this space than the whole rest of the building.

Their curious faces at the kitchen door had been taken as proof of hunger – as well as proof of life – and lunch was served on the terrace shortly afterwards by a middle-aged lady who stuck a strawberry on the side of Linus's fruit juice and extra jam on his waffles. Afterwards, aware they were on show to the various staff who flitted in and out of the house like swifts, they had lazed on the lawn, playing Would You Rather and knocking a ball about with wooden beach bats. Occasionally, Måns would step out onto the terrace with a tray of juice or fruit, but his placid smile couldn't quite suppress the anxious gleam in his eyes, his gaze constantly darting to the shaded woods at the fringes of the garden. It was the only way in and the only way out. Where was he? It was the question they all wanted answered.

Finally, they told him they were going for an exploration of the island, to 'get their bearings' before dusk. It had been an exhausting, anticlimactic day, and although everyone had been kind, Bell knew they both needed some time away from strangers' eyes before the ritual of going to bed in this foreign house. Linus's mood was beginning to deteriorate, and who could blame him? He was frustrated and angry about his father's unexplained disappearance – as was she. It was bad enough for him to be dragged here against his will, but to then find his father wasn't even here . . . it wasn't just arrogant, it was insulting.

They left the garden at the front of the house, dipping into the trees and onto the narrow pebble path that seemed to trickle in curving loops around the property. After a day in the sun, with no swimming, it felt good to wander in the shade, and they walked at a slow pace through the trees, ears pricked as tiny creatures rustled in the undergrowth, both of them lost in their own thoughts.

The sea glinted through the trees, growing ever bluer as they ambled, pushing away branches from their heads until eventually they were at the shore again. They were looking east, having crossed the width of the island; Krokso was visible beyond the body of water, and behind that, Sandhamn – her only point of contact with the outside world. It seemed hard to believe that over there ferries were arriving and departing, taking people back to the capital, selling newspapers, boasting wifi, serving porn star martinis and beers, having sex on boats . . . It felt like a whole other world, not a mere ten-minute boat ride away, and she felt a sudden, fierce pang of longing for the carefree summer that was going on without her. She hadn't even had a chance to contact Tove and the others yet and apprise them of her changed circumstances.

They carried on walking in silence, Linus's anger growing as he beat a stick against the tree trunks and kicked out at nodding flowers. The landmass curved away, bearing right. They had only been walking for fifteen minutes or thereabouts, but they were facing the lagoon again now. They stopped on the rocks and watched a man dive from the prow of his boat, which had dropped anchor in front of Dead Man's Bones. They could hear the splash clearly across the water, watching as he surfaced and tossed his head back with a joyous shout. But it wasn't him Linus was watching. Behind the boat lay Summer Isle and, somewhere on it, his family.

'Fancy a swim?' she asked him, laying a hand gently on his shoulder.

He shook his head fiercely. '. . . No.'

He moved off again and continued stepping over the smooth, humped grey rocks with angry, silent, gigantic strides. The ground was generally flattish with various dips and rises, but there was a steeper slope on the lagoon side, taking them high enough to get something of an aerial perspective. She stopped to take in the view, but Linus sank to his haunches on the warm rock once again and looked back towards Summer Isle, like an old lost dog trying to get home.

It broke her heart to see it.

'Wow!' she breathed, trying to engage some interest. At this height, maybe seventy feet up, they were above the canopy of most of the trees. The roof of the orange house could be clearly seen from up here, and the clearing for the garden was like a dimple. The shape of the island was just about discernible as well – it was a ragged, almost rectangular sheet of land, with numerous nips and pleats, tucks and inlets, like a rag that had been burned. She calculated the perimeter had to be about a mile and a half, maybe two miles long. Positively gargantuan! She pivoted on the spot, taking it all in, her –

'. . . Linus, come look at this.'

Her tone was enough to stir Linus from his resentful reverie. 'What is it?'

'Come and see.'

'Why can't you just tell me?'

'Because I think you'll like it.'

He got up, giving an exasperated sigh that would have made any self-respecting teenager proud. 'What is it?' he asked, standing by her. His expression changed as he caught sight of what she was staring at. Perhaps a hundred feet inland, a crescent of blue could be glimpsed through a crater. 'That's the sea.'

'Right?' She grinned.

'Do you think that's . . . ?' He looked up at her, mouth agape. 'The hidden beach?'

She winked at him. In all their miserable resentment, they had both completely forgotten about it. 'There's only one way to find out. Come on, let's find the way in.'

Together they scrambled down the incline.

'Right, you go first,' she said, pushing him ahead of her.

'Why me?'

'Because you're faster, and if this *is* where Dr No keeps his sub-atomic testing facility, then I'm going to need a head start for getting out of here.'

Linus laughed, shooting her a look that wouldn't have been quite so wry a year ago. He was growing up.

They climbed, ran and scrambled over the rocks and through the trees, the sea at their backs, until the crater suddenly opened up at their feet. Absolutely huge, perhaps fifty metres across, it was an almost perfect circle blown in the rocks. The force of the bomb had set the beach ten metres below ground, the grooved granite walls scooping away beneath them. Three quarters of the basin floor was covered by sea, with a shallow beach that could only catch the sun through the middle of the day.

'How do we get down there?' Linus asked in amazement.

'Maybe we don't,' Bell said, puzzled. 'Your mamma didn't say anything about swimming down there. Only that it was there.'

'But I want to swim down there.'

Bell rolled her eyes. Of course he did. *Now* he wanted to swim. 'Well, it's too far to jump down, and we're definitely not going down if we don't know if we can get back up again,' she said, seeing the sharp concave angle at which the rocks were cut away.

'There has to be a way down,' Linus murmured, beginning to walk around the perimeter. 'Maybe there's a rope.'

'Oh yeah, because I could definitely get myself back up again on that!' Bell guffawed.

'Look!' He pointed to something halfway round. In one spot, perhaps a seam of thicker rock, the wall hadn't been blown back quite as far as elsewhere and the cliff kicked into the basin, like a stray pleat. A narrow channel ran down the centre of it, rainwater running through like a rill. It was about a foot's width – depending on the foot.

'Linus, those are not steps,' she protested as he tore ahead and skittered down it like a mountain goat. 'Linus!' she called, seeing how he held his arms out wide, stepping confidently, jumping onto the sand a moment later.

'Bugger,' she muttered, knowing she'd have to follow suit. Carefully she scrambled down, with significantly less stealth and flair, cursing under her breath. And then, as her feet touched the sand, not under her breath, 'Holy shit!'

If looking down upon it had been impressive, standing down and looking back up again was awe-inspiring. The cliff walls swooped around them like a vaulted hall, the walls scooped back as if by a melon baller, the late sun a smear down the far side and throwing a golden sunspot onto the calm, shallow body of water that rocked and shushed gently onto the beach.

'This can't be for real,' she whispered. 'Linus, are you remembering to breathe?' she asked him, perfectly serious. It wouldn't be the first time he'd forgotten to inhale and exhale when he'd been surprised. He'd once fainted when he'd thought he'd seen Lionel Messi walking past his school window. '. . . Linus?'

But if he was breathing, he certainly wasn't listening; he

was staring at something. She followed his gaze to find a man sitting on a rock at the far end of the beach, staring back at them.

No one spoke. It was perfectly obvious who he was. Hanna's husband. Linus's father.

She felt her heart rate trip and quicken as he got up and began walking towards them.

The man who had screamed from that hospital bed. The villain of the piece, putting his needs first.

Silhouetted, he raked a hand through his hair. The hair that her own fingers had combed. A baseball cap in his hand.

He stopped in front of them. The very last person she had wanted to see again. To see here.

Here.

Bell realized she was the one forgetting to breathe, her body reacting to the sight of him with a visceral shock. This was a disaster – it couldn't be him. He couldn't be Hanna's ex. Linus's father.

His eyes cast lightly over her with the same surprised zip of recognition, but then something else too, something she couldn't quite grasp . . . But he looked away in the next instant; this moment wasn't about her, or their stolen night together. His gaze settled heavily on Linus, weighted like an anchor.

She felt the moment swell and tighten as father and son looked at one another, both so changed and grown even from their last, disastrous meeting. She saw Linus's shock at his father's altered appearance. Gone were the shaved head and withered limbs, the sunken eyes and papery skin. The man before him now was tall and lithe; he had muscles and a suntan; he even had a few freckles on the bridge of his nose – like Linus. His trousers were rolled up at the ankles, but they were still wet, showing off brown feet. He looked well. He looked *normal*, nothing like the half-man, half-beast in that hospital bed.

A look that could only be described as wonder bloomed on his face. His eyes were shining, his mouth parted as he scanned his child almost like a robot, taking in all the changes, developments, likenesses, differences . . . His right hand was hovering forwards slightly and she knew he wanted to reach out and touch him. That he did not dare.

'You've grown, Linus.' His voice was hoarse.

'Yes, sir.' Linus sounded almost apologetic for the fact. Was it a betrayal to have grown – grown up – whilst this man, his father, had been sleeping? '. . . So have you.'

A half-smile cocked Emil's mouth. 'I've been trying.' He gave a shrug. 'I heard you were a fast runner, so I thought I should train.'

'Who told you that?'

'Your mamma. Is it true?'

Linus gave an embarrassed shrug and kicked at the sand.

'Absolutely it is,' Bell interjected, putting a hand on Linus's shoulder and squeezing it. She could tell he was overwhelmed, now that the initial adrenaline burst was diffusing. 'He's the fastest boy in his year.'

Emil's eyes narrowed with pride, never lifting off his boy as she spoke. As though she wasn't really there. 'You must get it from me, then. I was always the fastest boy in my year too.'

Linus glanced up at him, but instinctively stepped back. His interest was piqued, but Bell knew it was still far too soon, too hard for him to fathom that he 'got anything' from him, was biological kin to this stranger; that it was this man here that was his father and not Max, the only one he had ever known. The child had had only a day to absorb that fact, thanks to Emil's bullying tactic to be reunited as soon as possible, whatever the fallout. They all needed to remember that. *She* did. Behind those good looks and that diffident, reserved charisma was a man who Hanna had warned her always got what he wanted.

'Do you remember me?'

Linus nodded, looking even more uncertain. 'In the hospital.'

'Oh.' Emil frowned. 'I'm afraid . . . I don't remember much after I woke up. No, I meant . . . do you remember me from *before*?'

Linus shook his head. 'No, sir.' He looked anxious again, as though his negative answer was the wrong one.

There was a pause and Emil seemed to shrink a little, as though he'd been pushed.

'Well, you were very little,' he said after a moment, staring at his own feet half buried in the sand. He looked up suddenly with a lit expression. 'You were obsessed with Thomas the Tank Engine. Remember that?'

'A little bit.' From his tone of voice, Bell knew that meant 'no'. He just didn't want to say it again.

'Gordon was your favourite engine. He was the fastest one on the island. Maybe that's why you liked him so much. You were both speed machines.'

'Yes, sir.'

Bell saw the excitement leave Emil's body, the conversation dwindling in the face of his son's evident wariness of him. Emil glanced at her, as if for help, and she forced a smile; but he surely couldn't be surprised that things were playing out this way? What had he expected? That Linus would run into his arms and they'd start making sandcastles? He had rushed things, forced this meeting by beating down his child's mother to impose his will, no less.

Even so, as their eyes met, she felt that strange invisible pull towards him pick up the slack again, and she looked quickly away. He seemed to snag on something deep inside her, catching on a tiny hook buried away that she hadn't even known was there.

He looked away too, his attention back on his son. 'Did Måns tell you I was here?'

'No, sir. He didn't know where you were.'

'Oh. Was he kind to you?'

'Yes.'

'Måns is very kind. He has worked for our family for a very long time now. Since before I was born.'

Bell saw again how Linus flinched at the words 'our family', and how Emil seemed oblivious to the impact it had upon his son.

'Do you know what we call this place?'

'The hidden beach.'

Emil arched an eyebrow. 'Your mamma told you?'

'Yes.'

He shoved his hands into his pockets. 'Mmm. She's one of the very few people to have been here. It is a rare privilege, you understand?'

'Yes, sir.'

'People around here, they talk about the Hidden Beach – is it real, isn't it?' A hint of a smile climbed into his eyes. 'We never tell, and you, now you've found it, you mustn't either. Can you imagine how many people would sneak onto the island to come and see it otherwise?'

Linus shook his head, awed. 'No, sir.'

'It would be a *lot*. And obviously for our family, that could be a security risk and we wouldn't want to have to get to a situation where we had to have guards and dogs, or electric fences, or anything like that.'

'No, sir.'

'That's why we try to dispel the rumours about this place. No one can see it from the water, and we don't even take our guests here.' He looked up and around at the open-topped vaulted cavern. 'It's for family only.' He blinked. 'And you are family, Linus.'

Bell stepped forward slightly, resting a hand on Linus' shoulder. Emil looked back at her, sensing a warning in the gesture even though she had slapped a bland smile on her face. He bristled, not getting it at all, not understanding his words were threatening to his son – each comment attacking and dismantling the notion of the only family unit Linus had ever known. How could he not see this was too much, too soon?

'Are there any pebbles in the water?' she asked, throwing him further off guard.

Emil frowned. '. . . Why?'

'We could do some stone skimming. Linus loves that. He's insanely good.' She looked down at Linus. 'Do you want to see if there are any good ones?'

'Okay,' he nodded, eager for something to do, and for an excuse to get away.

Emil watched his son run down to the water's edge, out of earshot, before looking back at her. His eyes were cold. 'Is this some kind of joke?'

'What?' She looked back at him, confused.

'You're my child's nanny?' he hissed. 'Don't tell me you didn't know!'

'How could I possibly have known who you were? *You*

told me you were a widower!' she hissed back. 'That you had lost your wife and child!'

'No, I never said I was a widower. I told you there'd been an accident and that I lost them! But *I* was the one in the accident – and when I woke up, they had moved on.'

She stared at him. 'Well, you didn't exactly make that clear, did you!'

'Because I didn't want to get into it with you!'

'No, you just wanted to get into my pants!' she hissed furiously.

He blinked but didn't deny it. 'What happened to me now defines me. It's all people see when they see me. I didn't want that, just for once.'

'Yeah? Well, it worked, because I *didn't* know. I had no idea! Do you really think I would have slept with my boss's ex-husband if I'd had the faintest clue?'

'Well, what the hell am I supposed to think, when I find you standing here with my son?'

'Oh, I don't know, probably the same as I thought watching you walk towards me just now! It's just a peachy situation for us both!'

His eyes narrowed, the two of them back to the scratchy antagonism of their first meeting. '. . . And I'm her husband, by the way, not her ex. We're not divorced.'

She arched an eyebrow. 'Yet.'

'That won't be happening. Hanna still loves me.'

'She loves Max.' She saw the words strike him and she could see, then, how hard it must have been for Hanna to tell him the truth. His expression changed, hardening, and she saw all their former passion and playfulness of that *Midsommar* night curdle and sour. 'And besides, what was the other night with me, if you're still so in love with Hanna?'

He glowered at her. 'Opportunity? Lust? Relief? Take your pick.' Her mouth opened in outrage, but he stopped her. 'And don't say it wasn't the same for you too. You're still in love with your fiancé, and you didn't want any more from me than I wanted from you. We were consenting adults, both lonely and drunk on *Midsommar*'s night. That was it.'

His words might be true, but they were still like body blows, leaving her breathless. Her world had just turned inside out in the space of five minutes.

He frowned again, as though just her presence, the mere sight of her, upset him. 'Why are you even *here*? I told my wife, he's a ten-year-old boy. He doesn't need a nanny.'

'Maybe not, but he needs a chaperone. Someone to protect him.'

'From what?' he scoffed. 'He's got me.'

Bell looked back at him evenly. 'It's you he needs protecting from.'

It was her words that drew blood this time. He visibly paled, looking wounded by the suggestion. 'I would never hurt him.'

'Maybe not intentionally,' she agreed. 'But given you thought threatening a court case was the right way to go about getting to see him, I'd say your judgement's off.'

'It was you who said people should be with the people they love on *Midsommar*'s!' he retorted furiously.

'Oh! So this is *my* fault?'

'You know what I mean! I've already lost out on too much with him.'

'Bell?' Linus's voice carried over to them and they turned to find him walking hesitatingly back towards them, his hands filled with pebbles.

'It's fine, Linus, we're just coming!' she called back with

false cheer, beginning to walk too. He couldn't see them fighting like this.

Emil matched her stride. 'This won't work!' he insisted through gritted teeth.

'Well, it's going to have to.'

They marched in silence, arms swinging angrily in time, and she could sense his anger and resentment growing beside her.

'Well, don't think that what happened between us is—'

She stopped walking with a scoffing laugh. 'Oh, I don't. As far as I'm concerned, it's already forgotten.' She stared at him with mutinous eyes. 'It was a terrible mistake – let's just leave it at that.'

Chapter Fifteen

'There. That wasn't so bad, was it?' she asked, tucking the thick linen sheets back into the side of the bed, holding him firmly. The little red Corvette car was on his bedside table; he'd put it in his pocket whilst they went exploring, his fingers running over it nervously like a lucky charm as he and his father exchanged their first words.

Linus stared back at her, his hair splaying on the pillow. 'Not as bad as last time.'

'Exactly.' She sat on the side of the bed and smiled down at him. 'So what do you think about him now?'

He shrugged.

'I think he seems nice enough,' she said lightly, still aware of the small vibration in her bones at the way he'd talked to her earlier. But it wasn't up to her to make this relationship work, only to allow it space to grow – safely. 'He found that nice-shaped stone on the way back for you.'

'He thought it looked like a mammoth's tooth.'

She heard the wry note in his voice. 'Didn't you?'

'No. Anyway, it's babyish looking for stones. I'm ten, not two.'

'Well,' she sighed. 'Give him a chance. At least he's trying. It's bound to take him a while to get used to how big you are. Remember, for him, you were only two when he saw you last.'

They were both quiet, the enormity of what had happened – what had been taken, from both father and son – settling upon them.

'I – I don't know what to call him.' Linus's voice was hesitant. 'I don't care what Mamma says. He's not my pappa and he never will be.'

She smoothed a hand over his hairline again. 'No, of course not. No one's expecting you to let him take Max's place.' She gave a sad smile, looking into those anxious green eyes which were usually so clear. 'Don't worry, little man, it will all become apparent in the fullness of time. Just do what feels right for you. Emil is a grown-up. He knows this can't be rushed.'

She leaned down and kissed him on the cheek, smoothing his hair gently. 'Sleep tight, okay? I'm just on the other side of that wall if you need me.'

'You won't leave me here?' he asked as she got to the door.

'Never. We're a team, dude.' She winked. 'Where you go, I go. No exceptions.'

She closed the door with a soft click and hesitated on the landing, not sure where to go next. She wasn't a guest in this house, but staff. She wasn't expected to dine with him, although frankly, after the things he'd said to her earlier, she'd rather choke on her dinner than eat it with him, anyway.

There was no wifi on the island, so she'd have to go old-school. There had been books in the library, although they were the gilt-edged sort no one ever read. She'd spotted paperbacks in the snug, though, that tiny room off the kitchen corridor at the back.

She moved downstairs and through the house quickly, silent in her bare feet. She could hear a voice coming from one of the larger salons, the door closed, and nipped into the small room. It felt so completely different in there, like an apartment contained within the house.

A jumper lay strewn over the navy sofa; a pair of boat shoes with the backs pushed down were under the coffee table. The room had a curious feeling to it, like it was backdated. The TV was an old floor-standing set, with a DVD player below it, and in the corner was a stacked hi-fi system with a radio, CD player, and even a turntable.

She headed straight for the bookcase and scanned the titles quickly. Swedish, English, she didn't care, she just needed something to absorb her mind and help her forget that she was stranded here, trapped in a waking nightmare with the man she had hoped – and now truly wanted – to never see again.

'Oh.'

She turned with surprise at the exclamation and saw him standing by the door, looking equally shocked, as though it was impossible to believe they should both be here.

'Oh,' she said back, struggling like him to regain her composure. 'I wasn't prying, I was . . . looking for something to read. Måns had said I could come in here.'

'. . . Yes, it's fine. Of course.' He gave a nod and after another hesitation, walked in, sinking down into the sofa. 'Feel free to go wherever you wish.' His stiff manners now were in heightened contrast to their bitter argument earlier.

'Thank you.' She stood awkwardly, feeling the blood rush to her head and reaching for the first book her hand came to. '. . . Well,' she said after another silence, 'I've found something, so I'll leave you in peace. I didn't mean to disturb you.'

His eyes fell to the book in her hands. '*The Art of Angling.* Really?'

'Huh?' She looked at it in dismay. Unbelievable.

'A favourite of my father's, to be sure,' he said wryly, his head lolling against the back cushion. He looked drained. 'But I'm sure there must be something there that's more interesting to you than that.'

'I . . . well . . .' A large part of her wanted to insist that she liked angling, *actually*, just to naysay against him, but the reality of spending an evening looking at maggot-flies, carp and dogfish was too much to bear. She turned back to the bookcase again and replaced the volume hurriedly, her fingers tracing across spines for a suitable replacement. Anything. Anything at all that wasn't angling . . .

'Is he in bed?' he asked to her back as she stood on tiptoe to read the titles on the higher shelves.

'Yes.'

'It seems early for a ten-year-old.'

'He was exhausted. It's been a very draining day for him.' She desperately hoped he heard the barbs in her words. He should be ashamed of himself for the way he'd acted in the past twenty-four hours to Hanna, Linus. Her.

'I wanted to go in and say goodnight, but I wasn't sure if—'

'No, he'll be asleep already,' she said tersely. 'He could scarcely keep his eyes open.' Couldn't he see it was far too soon for fatherly kisses?

'. . . Right.'

'Your evening snack, sir.' She looked over her shoulder as Måns came in with a tray. 'Ah, Miss Bell, good evening.'

'Good evening,' she replied, looking at the contents of the tray: a thick shake, a ramekin of pills and a plate of Toast Skagen.

'I don't want it,' Emil said in a low voice.

Måns lowered his chin as he dropped his voice too, innately

understanding that they were trying to keep the conversation from her earshot. 'You're seven hundred calories down on your daily tally, owing to your missed lunch.'

'I said, I don't want it.' He was speaking through clenched teeth, his gaze hard on the floor.

'It's doctor's orders, I'm afraid, sir.' Måns was equally firm within his signature deference.

Bell listened in embarrassment, but also interest. This wasn't a usual staff–boss relationship. Måns was elderly and slow, but he was somehow also everywhere at the right moment, and implacably right.

With an angry sigh, Emil picked up the toast and began to eat, giving his valet a sarcastic 'happy now?' look as he chewed.

Måns nodded gratefully. 'A drink, Miss Bell?'

'No, thank you. I'm about to go to bed.'

'Very good.' He looked back at Emil. 'Christer will be ready for you in ten minutes, sir.'

Emil just nodded, swallowing every mouthful with resentment.

Måns left the room as silently as he'd entered, and Bell hovered for a moment.

'He seems very good.'

'My father's valet,' he muttered. 'He's been with us for fifty-three years.'

So Måns had watched Emil grow up, then? He didn't appear to want to talk about it. She changed the subject, feeling his hostility prickle through the room. 'That's a lot of CDs you've got there,' she said, casting a bemused gaze over the multitude of discs set into a stacking tower.

'Is it? It seems a normal amount to me.'

'Yeah, I mean if . . . if that's what you . . .' He appeared to have missed the point. 'Don't you stream?'

He looked at her blankly. '. . . Oh yes, right. I keep forgetting. *Streaming*.' The way he shook his head wearily, the wry note in his voice . . . she realized this was a new technology for him, one of the changes the world had shifted to whilst he'd been in the coma.

'Yes, Spotify. Have you heard of it? It's a Swedish company.'

'I know. I think we own it.' He tore off another bite of toast.

She gave an astonished laugh. 'You think? You don't even know?'

'There's been a lot . . . a lot to catch up on,' he muttered. 'Quite a lot happened while I was "away". Instagram was a niche photo filter app when I left, and now it's a global publishing phenomenon with content curated to every individual on the planet.' He shrugged.

'And are you going to buy that too?' she asked, folding her arms across her chest.

He didn't look at her. 'We're considering it.'

She laughed. 'My God, who are you people?' She shook her head as he looked over. 'Don't answer that. I don't care.'

He frowned. 'Not the usual response,' he mumbled.

She leaned against the bookcase, intrigued. 'So what else changed whilst you were "away", then?' She made speech marks in the air.

He thought about it as he chewed. 'Well, let's see . . . When I was hit, Obama was president. No one had heard about Islamic State . . . I was using an iPhone 5. Messi had just won the Ballon d'Or for the fourth time . . . Mandela was still alive. Prince was still alive.' He looked down. 'A lot of people were still alive when I went under.'

She remembered what he'd said about his father. Him too? 'I can't imagine what it's been like for you, coming back and finding the world so changed.'

'It was just one of the things I had to adapt to, like muscular atrophy,' he said shortly, clearly not wanting her pity; not wanting any connection at all. He drank the shake in one long gulp, grimacing as he swallowed the last bit, staring at the empty glass like it owed him one.

'Christer is ready.' Måns was back at the door again.

'Right.' He sighed, handing back the empty plate. 'Happy?'

'Delighted, sir.'

He looked back at Bell stiffly, his green eyes still low-simmering with anger and resentment. 'Well, goodnight.'

'Goodnight.' She felt herself loosen as he left the room, taking all the air with him. She felt jarred and dislocated, rattled not just by his presence but by his absence too, her eyes lingering on the space he had just occupied as though he had warmed the air. She looked away abruptly, feeling a tangled knot of emotions in her stomach. Why him? Why did it have to be him? Would he still have an effect on her if *Midsommar*'s had never happened? She had hardly fallen at his feet outside Westerbergs, after all.

Then again, he had kept himself largely hidden behind his cap and glasses then, and she wasn't sure she could ever be unmoved by his eyes and the depths she saw in them. There was a hairline fracture that drew a jagged line all the way through him, and she recognized it because there was one running through her too. They were both haunted by their own pasts, hollowed out by loss, and that made them kindred spirits on one level – even if on this one, they were bitterly opposed.

She remembered his face at her words, the flash of pain

amid the anger. '*It was a mistake.*' They had been the right words to say, because they were true – it was a mistake.

Unfortunately, just not one she regretted.

She awoke with a start, glancing round the room in a panic, trying to get her bearings. It took a moment to remember where she was. She was lying on top of the bed, still dressed, and the paperback thriller was still in her hand; she had fallen asleep mid-sentence. Linus wasn't the only one who'd been drained by the day's revelations.

She closed the book and stretched, her neck feeling stiff from the odd angle, seeing her phone flash with notifications. She picked it up – eight messages from Hanna checking on their day, a barely subdued note of panic in each one.

Quickly Bell replied, doing her best to reassure her boss, which meant omitting the fact that Emil had – unbelievably – not even bothered to be there to greet them. '*Sorry, been a busy day. Lots of exploring the island, found the hidden beach. Initial meeting with E was fine. L quiet and shy but to be expected tbh. E didn't push it and was quite light touch, thankfully. L now fast asleep after a good dinner. Shall I get him to text you in the morning? Bx*'

All the lights were still on in the room, her windows open, and she saw moths were fluttering in, the ceiling speckled with dozens of tiny thunder bugs. She got up and closed the shutters, keeping the windows open to allow for a breeze. It was a sticky night.

What had disturbed her? she wondered. Was Linus awake? She stood still for a moment and listened for a sound coming through the wall. She could hear something, like voices whispering, but it was coming from the hallway. Was he going to the bathroom? Sleepwalking?

She opened the door and peered out through the crack. Linus's door beside hers was still closed, everything silent and dark behind it, but down the far end of the corridor she could make out shapes. She opened the door a little wider and frowned as she saw someone being half walked, half dragged. His legs kept buckling, his head dropping down, and the man with him was struggling to hold his arm around his neck.

'Come on, Emil. We're nearly there,' the man was panting. 'Lock those knees, buddy.'

She watched as he bent forward awkwardly to open the door at the farthest end of the hall, and they staggered in together.

Bell closed her door again, her heart racing; she had a sense she had seen something she shouldn't have. Had Emil collapsed? Was he physically frail? He was lean for his frame, but he'd seemed strong enough to her that night they'd spent together. More than strong –

Her phone beeped and she went back to check the message, already knowing it was Hanna.

'Thank God! Been desperate all day. Hardest part is done then, hopefully. Yes, please get him to text when he's awake. Send photo too if data will permit. Thanks Bell, for everything. Hx'

Bell scrolled quickly through the photos she had taken that day, mainly of Linus playing in the room as they had waited for Emil's arrival, their exploration through the gardens. There had been none taken at the hidden beach, of course . . . She was sending one of Linus playing with the red Corvette when the sound of footsteps on the treads again made her lift her head. She ran back and peered out just in time to see the same man jogging back down the stairs. She hesitated, then followed after. She was here to protect Linus, after all; she needed to know if there was anything happening that might affect him. Emil couldn't collapse if they were all out together, not in front of Linus . . .

The man had disappeared into one of the smaller rooms at the back of the house, opposite the grand spaces of the formal salons.

'Excuse me?' She stopped outside the door of the room, the gym. The man was inside, rolling up some mats. Weights and kettlebells were scattered everywhere; a heavy-looking battle rope lay, anaconda-like, on the floor.

'Hmm? Oh, hi!' He got up with an athletic bounce and came over, his muscular arm outstretched. 'You must be the nanny? I'm Christer, the physio.'

'Yes, I'm Bell. Pleased to meet you.'

He had his hands on his hips. 'I heard you guys were coming today.' He gave a grin. 'It's been a big deal, all he's talked about for months. How did it go? He was pretty quiet tonight.'

'Oh. Well. Yes, very well, I think. Under the circumstances.' She bit her lip. 'It's not an easy thing, for anyone.' Did he pick up on the serrated edge of her words?

'You're telling me. I don't know how he's got through all this.' Christer shook his head in admiration. 'Every time he was told he couldn't do something, he went and did it. When the docs said he'd walk with a limp, he trained his left side twice as hard to counteract it. And in the weights room, when we were trying to reverse the physical atrophy and spasticity, he went longer and harder than anyone there had ever seen. You'd never be able to tell it now.'

'No?'

'Uh-huh. He's got grit, I'll give him that. I only wish my

other clients would take a leaf out of his book. He's the miracle, I keep telling him. He's the One Guy, you know, the one in a million chance. He's the One.'

'And is he okay? Now, I mean?' She gave a worried smile as he looked at her, a little confused. 'It's just that I was in my room just now and thought I heard something, and I saw him being carried –'

'Ah yeah,' Christer grinned, batting away her concern with a bear paw. 'Don't worry about that. Looks worse than it is. He often does that – works himself to his absolute limits.'

'To the point of *collapse*?'

'Yep. He just won't stop.'

'But surely you can make him?'

'I can tell you're new here,' Christer laughed. 'Listen, if there's one thing you'll find, it's that no one can make Emil Von Greyers do anything he doesn't want to do. He's a stubborn bastard when he wants to be; but people need to understand that what might make him difficult to be around at times is also what helped him recover to this point. You can't have one without the other.' He shrugged.

'He's difficult – how?'

'Well, not sleeping doesn't help his general mood, for starters,' he commented, rolling elastic bands around the mats to hold them in place as tubes.

'He doesn't sleep?'

'Barely. Well, would you want to, after what he's been through?'

She pulled a face. Maybe not.

'And it would sure help if he could just eat something he can taste. He keeps losing weight because he doesn't want to eat.'

'He's lost his sense of taste?'

'And smell.'

'Oh.'

He glanced across at her as he replaced the dumbbells onto the racks in weight order. 'You didn't know all this?'

She shook her head. 'Not much beyond he was hit by a car and in a coma for seven years, to be honest.'

'Pfft.' Christer frowned. 'Well, the poor guy's had a lot more to deal with than just learning to get strong again, I can tell you that.'

'Like what else?' she prodded, and then, seeing his expression, added, 'This isn't nosiness. I'm Linus's chaperone. I need to know what to expect so I can prepare Linus for it. The hospital visit immediately after Emil woke up went really badly. It did a lot of damage.'

'Oh yeah, I heard about that incident from the nursing team.'

'It was awful. He was shouting obscenities and thrashing and screaming.'

Christer watched her, hearing the judgement in her voice. 'You know that's an actual condition, right? Like, a medical thing, for people recovering from traumatic brain injuries?'

'. . . No.'

'Sure. Post-traumatic amnesia, it's called. It's common in post-coma patients waking up. They get very agitated, violent even, although they're mainly a danger to themselves, of course. They don't remember anything about it.'

'Nothing?'

'Usually the last couple of weeks before the injury, and the first few days of coming to, are completely wiped. Gone. No memory.'

'And is that the case for Emil? He doesn't remember any of it?'

''Fraid so. It's a protective thing, I think. The brain protecting the body from the horror of those moments.'

She didn't know what to say.

'So what else can I tell you?' he asked himself rhetorically. 'Well, the headaches are pretty consistent, so that can make him grouchy. Bright light can be a problem sometimes, although hopefully that'll improve.'

She nodded, remembering his cap, the sunglasses . . .

'He's pretty strong on balance now; we've been working on that a lot. Oh, but forgetfulness – remembering dates and things, but also struggling to find the right words sometimes, particularly if he's stressed. On the other hand, he can also have no filter and be very direct. He'll say things he probably shouldn't, so warn his boy not to take offence.'

She nodded. *Opportunity? Lust? Relief? . . . Both lonely and drunk on* Midsommar's *night . . . That was it.* Did they count?

'I know he's pretty normal to look at, and that's what confuses people. They think because he's walking and talking, it's all done, that's he's better. But it's a long road ahead for him still. He's had to fight so hard just to get here.' He threw a smile her way. 'Which is why it's so great his boy's come to stay. He was motivated before, but I reckon he'll be bionic now, if tonight was anything to go by.'

'Great,' she said, chewing on her cheek, realizing now why it had taken Hanna so long to work up the courage to tell him about Max, taking his dream – and motivation – away. How hard it must have been for him to hear it. 'Well, thanks. I'll . . . bear all of that in mind.'

'No problem,' he shrugged. 'And good luck with your side of things. I hope the next few days go well. This place needs some life to it. A kid running about is exactly what's been missing from here.'

Grand Hotel, Stockholm, May 2010

'You're hiding from me.'

He looked back from his position on the balcony, hands clasped as he stared out over the city. Her hair was swept up, pearls at her throat. 'Well, I'm afraid you're far too beautiful to look at today. It's like staring at the sun.'

She laughed, swishing her dress, oblivious to the cool night air. 'So you really like it? You're not just saying that?'

'You look sensational.'

She stared at him and he felt his heart click into the gallop that came with meeting those eyes – but a shadow flashed behind them, almost immediately. 'What is it?' he asked.

'You do think we've done the right thing, don't you?'

He swallowed. '. . . Of course. There's not a doubt in my mind. Why would you even ask it?'

She stared at him, swollen silences pushing her words apart. 'You . . . you don't think we've rushed into it? I mean, people don't have to marry now, just because they're having a baby. It's not the Dark Ages.'

He smiled, sliding his hands into his pockets so that she couldn't see them tremble. 'This is only the beginning, Hanna. Just you wait and see.'

She smiled, her body relaxing at his words. Soothed. Comforted. Reassured.

Behind them, the band struck up the first notes of 'You're Beautiful', prompting cheers from the dance floor.

'Dance with me,' she said, stepping forward, her hands reaching out. He straightened and put his hands on her waist, feeling her still-slender narrowness. She laced her arms round his neck as they moved softly to the music, the city lights winking beneath them, the sea dark and sleek beneath the night sky.

They moved away from the doors, away from the lights, the music diffusing through the thick walls as the guests caroused without them. They wouldn't be missed for a while yet; there were so many people here, far more than he cared to count.

He closed his eyes, feeling the gentle sway of her body against his, the strictures of her corset beneath his fingers. Her skin smelled of gardenia and orange blossom. 'Are you having fun?' she murmured, her voice low and sweet against his ear.

'Best day of my life.'

She pulled back to look at him, knowing it was a lie. He looked down into those eyes again. Smiling and questioning all at once; always.

'Too many people,' he conceded, giving a conciliatory shrug.

'I know. I wish it could always be like this,' she murmured, sliding in closer to him again, her breath warm against his neck. 'This moment.'

He closed his eyes, wishing the same, as they danced in the moonlight, cheek to cheek.

Chapter Sixteen

Her eyes opened but did not see, a vestige of her troubled dreams hovering, then landing on her again. He had been lying on his back, on a bed, and she had been staring down at him, as if she were a spider on the ceiling. His arms had been folded behind his head, and he was stretched out in just his favourite jeans, tanned, relaxed, a soft smile on his lips as though listening to music, light brown hair splayed on the pillow. She watched his foot tap, his eyes closing for long moments but then opening again and fastening directly upon her, as though watching her back, knowing she was there. He looked so quiet, so happy. It had been . . . soothing, seeing him like that, how he had really been before the cancer achieved critical mass, a new image to overlay her last memories of him and the usual dreams, where he was whittled back to sinew and bone, green-tinged, hairless . . .

She had allowed herself to believe, in the dream, that there was a happy ending, but no matter how much she tried to keep her gaze on his face – the curve of his lips, the first bloom of stubble – she saw the water seeping across the floor, making it shine. Slippery. She refused to look, to acknowledge it, but then it began inching up the walls, getting deeper and deeper, and soon it was trickling over the mattress where he lay. She tried to speak, to tell him he was getting wet, but she couldn't speak, couldn't get him to hear her, and he made no sign of having noticed the creeping danger as the water gradually traced around his shape, then over it, closing over his legs, his chest, his arms, his face . . . submerging him.

It was the sight of him, underwater, staring back at her, refusing to move or do anything to save himself, that had made her wake up, she realized now, and she pressed a hand to her throat; it was still tingling from her shout. Too late to help.

Heart pounding, she curled back under the sheets, the unfamiliar sounds of the melancholic house coming to her ear – footsteps on the terrace outside her window, the *swoosh* of a window opening, a whistle in the pipes . . . From the blade of light escaping past the solid shutters and drawing a line across the floor, she could tell it was another beautiful day. But her spirits still sank at the prospect of spending it here.

Dreams about Jack always tokened a bad day, she knew that. Experience was a hard master, and she breathed deeply for a few moments, trying to articulate her affirmations for why she should get out of bed: it was it was a beautiful day. A beautiful summer's day on a stunning private island in the Swedish archipelago. She was in one of the most beautiful places on earth. She was alive. She had so much to be thankful for –

A sudden sound, something smashing, made her gasp and look at the far wall.

And Linus. She had Linus to look after.

She threw the sheets back and leapt out of bed, darting out of her door and peering in through his. 'Okay, buddy?' she asked, trying not to look wild-eyed, but the sight that greeted her was alarming – he was sitting fully dressed on the bed, the bed so expertly made with hospital corners that either Måns had already been in and made it, or Linus hadn't slept in it. But she had tucked him in herself last night.

Linus was staring at the floor. She cast an apprehensive gaze around the room and, in the pristine simplicity, easily caught sight of the remains of the Lego truck he had been working on after arriving here yesterday, now smashed into hundreds of pieces against their dividing wall.

She stepped into the room and shut the door behind her. She ruffled his hair as she sat on the bed beside him. 'What's up, dude? Bad night?'

He shook his head. His eyes weren't puffy, and he didn't look pale.

'How come you're dressed already? I was just about to come and wake you. Are you that hungry for breakfast already?'

'I've already had breakfast.'

'Oh.' Bell was taken aback. 'Oh. Well, you should have woken me, then. We could have gone down toge—'

'He told me not to tell you.'

She frowned, puzzled. 'Who did?'

'Emil. He woke me up early and said it was our secret.'

'. . . What?'

'We went out on his boat for breakfast and—'

'You went on a boat with him? Just him? My God, are you okay?' Now she was on her knees, kneeling in front of him and looking him over as though scanning for signs of injury.

He nodded, but he was visibly upset.

'What did he do? What did he say?' Her voice was frantic, heart clattering and making the blood roar through her ears so that she could barely hear his responses anyway. 'Linus, tell me. What happened?'

'He said . . .' A sob escaped him, one bitter tear squeezing itself out and wending a defiant trail down his cheek. 'He said Pappa and Elise and Tilde aren't my real family.'

Bell rocked back on her heels, scarcely able to believe this was happening. She'd been awake all of five minutes, emerging from one nightmare straight into another. 'He said that to you?' she whispered, feeling the adrenaline pump.

Linus nodded.

She was up again. 'Wait here,' she said grimly.

'Where are you going?' he cried as she ran to the door.

'Stay right here, Linus, and don't leave this room. I'll come straight back.'

'But –'

She tore down the hall, past the closed bedroom doors and watchful eyes of dark portraits, her bare feet almost silent on the worn boards as her hair streamed behind her. The polished, ebonized banister glided seamlessly beneath her hand as she took the stairs two at a time, and began charging from one room to the next.

Where was he? Where the hell was he?

She ran to the snug first, but he wasn't there. She looked into the kitchen too, startling the cook, who nearly dropped a dish at the sight of her. She darted out again, lightning fast, cheeks flushed.

'Miss Bell?'

She whipped round to see Måns walking towards her, coming from the direction of the drawing room and looking alarmed by her fluster.

'Where is he?' she demanded, her head still flashing left and right as she passed by open doorways. One to her right led onto the terrace, the round table and chairs at the top of the steps conspicuously empty.

'Where is who?'

She had no time for mannered games and procrastination right now. 'You know who.'

'The boy is in his room, Miss Bell.'

'Not –' She ran straight past him, towards the drawing room. The double doors were open and it was like running into a daydream: the hemp and silk cushions on the settle plumped, fresh white ranunculus roses arranged in a heaped dome on the low coffee table; sunlight pouring through the tall windows like it was painting the room a fresh new colour, and everything smelling of cut grass.

The doors leading off to the left, to the dining room as she recalled, were closed and she was about to turn away – why would he be in there, alone in a room to seat thirty? – when the low timbre of a male voice made her stop in her tracks.

'Miss Bell –' Måns said, reaching the threshold of the drawing room.

But she wouldn't be stopped. She flew across the space like she was on strings and flung the door open with a burst of indignation and rage, so hard it banged against the walls. 'How dare you!'

Emil stared back at her with a look of utter astonishment. 'Bell—'

'You woke a sleeping child and made him get up in the dark and go out on a *boat* with you? With *you*?'

He put down the sheet of paper in his hand and placed it very carefully on the table. 'Not just any child,' he said slowly. Carefully. 'My child. My son.'

'You're a stranger to him! He doesn't know you!' She felt herself quiver with fury and realized her hands were bunched into tight fists, her head pushed forwards like an aggressive gander.

Emil stared at her for another moment, then looked to the men sitting at the table with him. Bell felt her anger dissipate as she noticed them suddenly too, remembering she was dressed in just an AC/DC t-shirt and knickers. Her fingers found the hem and pulled it downwards as Emil cleared his throat. 'I think we had better pick this up another day, gentlemen.'

Bell watched in horror as the *one-two-three-oh-God-four* men in suits shuffled and put away the paperwork on the oval table before them. An awkward silence settled over the group as they scraped their chairs back and murmured their farewells to him, looking at her critically as they passed by.

Bell had never felt more humiliated and she bit her lip hard, staring at the floor as the last one left, the leather on his shoes so highly polished that she could almost see up her own t-shirt in their surface. She waited for the sound of his footsteps to fade before she looked up again. Emil was leaning against the vast oval table, watching her, his arms folded across his chest. Unlike his lackeys, he wasn't suited, but was wearing a pair of faded grey cargo shorts, a raspberry t-shirt and those boat shoes that were on the point of collapse. His seemingly beloved baseball cap sat on the table beside a water glass.

They stared at one another in silence for a moment and she felt her heat was matched by his freeze. He was angry too. She'd embarrassed him in front of his . . . *team*, or whoever they were.

'He doesn't know you,' she said again, quietly, through clenched teeth, trying to retain some dignity.

His eyebrow arched fractionally, barely perceptible across the room. 'That was the point of the exercise. I'm trying to get to know him. How else can I do that, if not by spending time with him?'

'You can do it by showing a little *patience*,' she said. 'He's a ten-year-old boy who had never heard of you before breakfast yesterday morning.'

'That's not true.'

'Yes. It is.'

He shook his head. 'Actually, he's known about me for months. He came to see me in the hospital after I woke up. His mother brought him.'

'I know,' she scoffed. 'I was there, and I saw the look on his face as you screamed obscenities after him. He was terrified of you.'

Emil's expression changed at her words, his froideur faltering, and he looked away quickly, a ripple of pain passing over his features. 'That's not fair. I wasn't myself back then.'

'I know. But it doesn't change the fact that you frightened him. And he *didn't* know who you were – Hanna had told him you were just an old friend. His godfather.' She shook her head bitterly. 'You should have seen his face when she told him the truth yesterday morning, and said you were making him come here to spend the summer with you. All the way over here, I expected him to just leap from the boat.'

Emil paled visibly and turned away, raking his hands through his hair. She could see the muscles in his back beneath the thin fabric of his t-shirt, but also the bones too. Despite herself, she felt another pang of guilt as she remembered Christer's words. 'Look, I appreciate you've been through a lot –'

'Oh, you don't know the first thing about what I've been through,' he snapped.

She recoiled from the fury in his voice. 'What I was going to say was that no matter what you have been through – awful though it was – *this* is not about you now. Not this bit. It's about Linus.' She saw the surprise in his eyes at her words, and she suddenly understood that every single thing that had been said to him since he had emerged from the coma *had* been about him. His accident, his trauma, his loss, his coma, his recovery, his family . . . He had no concept of what it meant to put someone else first. His entire existence since waking up had revolved solely around himself.

'Yes, he's your son – but only biologically, at the moment, and you need to recognize and respect that distinction. He doesn't know you yet. You frighten him. You've taken him away from his mother after you *threatened* her, you've told him the only family he's ever known isn't his *proper* family – and then you just expect him to see you as the Great I Am?' She threw her arms up in the air. 'It doesn't work like that. *You* need to show the understanding and compassion and emotional intelligence, because you are the adult and he is the child. That's what being a parent is – putting the child's needs before your own. And let me tell you something: right now, you are failing at that. You're failing big time. My God, you couldn't even bother to be here when he arrived yesterday.'

His eyes flashed, pain and anger a constant swirling torrent. 'You don't understand. I felt . . . overwhelmed.'

'*You* did? Try being ten and going through this.' She shook her head, staring at him coldly. 'You hurt your little boy over and over yesterday. And now you've started today on the same footing.'

'I was doing something nice!'

'That wasn't nice! You keep stepping over his boundaries and pushing too hard.' She stepped forward herself. 'But I won't let you, do you understand? You will not go anywhere with him without me, not unless Linus himself explicitly tells me he is happy with it.'

'You don't get to speak to me like that! I'm his –!' Emil stopped himself, Bell's words of what he was and what he wasn't still hanging in the air. He stared at her with a frustration that was beginning to feel palpable. 'You're not his mother.'

'No, I'm not. But I'm the next best thing, and I'm her

representative here. Every decision you make has to be in his best interests, and if it's not, then it's not happening. I'm not here as decoration! There's a point to me being here – where he goes, I go. And if you try to sneak off without me again, or ask him to keep secrets, I'll take him straight back to his mother.' She heard the courage waver in her own voice – she knew she didn't have the right to make that call and worsen things for Hanna.

He picked up on her hesitation. He had an instinct for weakness, it seemed. 'You want me to take it to the courts? That wouldn't be in Hanna's best interests.'

The threat was cold, like a trickle of ice down her spine and she knew he must make a formidable enemy. Hot, angry tears pressed at her throat as they squared off against one another, but she refused to look away. She would not be bullied by this man. His wealth, power and contacts couldn't affect her. Unlike Hanna, she didn't need anything from him. Bell drew herself up to her full, unimpressive height. 'I only care about Linus's best interests, and if you were any father at all, so would you—'

A sudden sound made them both start, a rumbling roll of thunder that made the antique white tureens on a demi-lune table begin to vibrate.

'What's that?' she whispered.

'Oh great,' Emil said, turning away, his hands on his hips as the roar grew. He looked back at her, then past her. 'Did she even bother to call this time?'

'No, sir,' replied Måns, who Bell now saw was standing in the doorway.

'Did who call? What's going on?' Bell said, almost having to shout. For that was no thunder, she realized now.

Emil didn't bother to reply. He just walked over to the long, tall windows and stood staring into the garden. The tops of the trees were being flattened by the considerable downdraft of a large blue helicopter, petals scattering across the lawn, the gardener who had met them down by the jetty yesterday standing with one foot resting on a spade, all the thunder now on *his* face as his months of hard work were undone in mere moments.

They all watched as the helicopter hovered slowly downwards, landing in a clear spot of lawn, free of trees and beds.

'Who is that?' she asked Måns, stepping towards him.

'That will be Mrs Stenbock,' Måns said, just as the door slid back and the lithe, dark-haired woman she'd seen before jumped out, wearing white trousers and a coral linen knit camisole. She was promptly followed by two very tall, lanky teenagers in jeans and headphones. '. . . And Master Frederik and Miss Sophia.'

'Your sister?' she asked, feeling a burst of panic as she went to the window too and watched them begin to walk slowly up the grass.

'I shall go to greet them, sir,' Måns said sombrely, slipping from the room.

'You never mentioned anyone was coming.'

He glanced across. 'I didn't know. I guess she thought it would be nice for Linus to meet his cousins.'

'Shit,' she hissed, remembering again her just-out-of-bed look as the unexpected visitors began ascending the terrace steps; a few seconds more and they'd be through the garden doors and standing in the hall . . . Without another word, she ran down the corridor as fast as she could, knowing that whatever righteous indignation she had struck at Emil's presumptions was now wholly undermined by the flashing of her butt cheeks. She took the stairs two at a time again, and was almost halfway up when she heard the woman's strident tones.

'Emil, are my eyes deceiving me, or did I just see a half-naked woman streaking down your hall?'

Chapter Seventeen

'She is the nanny.'

'Is she any good?'

'She's got ideas above her station. She keeps overstepping the mark.'

'Do you mean to say she doesn't kowtow to you? Goodness, that'd be a first.'

'She doesn't understand boundaries,' he snapped.

Nina turned away from the window with a smile. 'Oh, is *that* why she was streaking down your hallway, then?'

He shot her a look. Sarcasm was his sister's default setting. 'Don't be rid—'

'Emil, relax,' she laughed. 'I'm messing with you. Honestly, what's got you so wound up today?'

He didn't reply.

She went and sat down on the wooden settle. It was more comfortable than it looked, the proportions highly considered and the wooden arms almost silky to the touch after hundreds of years of absent-minded stroking. 'Come and sit down. I want to hear everything. How's it gone so far?'

Emil stared at her, too many emotions rushing at once. He couldn't pick one, couldn't settle on it. '. . . I don't know.'

'What do you mean, you don't know?'

He shrugged, just as Måns stepped into the room with his

usual innate timing, setting down a tea tray and beginning
to pour.

'Well, did he recognize you?'

'No.'

'Not at all?'

He shook his head, looking away from her and out of the
window again. It was a moment before he realized Måns was
holding out his cup of tea. 'Thank you.'

'Well, we shouldn't be surprised. He was, what, three?'

'Two years and four months.'

'. . . Right,' she said slowly. 'So that's only to be expected,
then. Especially given Hanna didn't see fit to keep you in his
life, with hospital visits or photographs –'

'She was trying to protect him.'

She arched an eyebrow, one of her finest features. They
brought something fierce and elegant to her face, like sleeping
panthers – silky and muscular. 'Oh. We're on her side now,
are we?'

He sighed and Nina looked at him through narrowed eyes,
scrutinizing him with that X-ray vision she'd had since childhood. 'Just for the record, little brother, I'm on yours, okay?'
She winked again and sat back. 'So how's he been since getting
here then? He must love it, surely?'

'He's quiet. He only speaks to answer a question. And he
barely looks at me.'

'Well, you are pretty tough to look at . . . Oh dear God, that
was a joke!' she sighed, peering at him over her cup. He could
tell she was determined to tease, jolly and poke him out of his
bad mood. She, and she alone, had had that ability since they
were little; but he was in no mood for jokes right now.

'It's all her fault.'

'Whose? Hanna's? Oh, you mean the *nanny's*?'

'She's deliberately getting in the way. I get no time alone with him. How can I be expected to . . . f-ford a relationship –'

'Forge.'

He frowned. 'What?'

'It's forge a relationship. Not ford.'

'Oh.' He digested the information for a moment, reprocessing the word. 'Well, how can I if she's always around? Of course he likes her better. He knows her.'

Nina sighed. 'Please sit down, Emil. You're agitated, and you know that's no good for you.'

He sat down, despair making him obedient.

'How are the headaches?' she asked with a frown.

'Better. They've got me on some new pills.'

'And your sleep? Please tell me you're managing more than three hours at a stretch?'

'What would I want to sleep for?'

'Emil, you were not *sleeping* whilst you were in a coma. It's an entirely different thing. You need to sleep.'

He looked up at the ceiling, noticing the delicate tendrils of cut-leaf plasterwork as if for the first time. 'I'll sleep when I've got my family back. Then I can rest.'

He felt Nina watching him. It was like being stared at by a witch's cat; there was intensity to the gaze. Weight.

'Hmm. And how is it going with Hanna?'

'You mean, now I know she's got another family? How d'you think?' Nina didn't reply, but he saw the pity in her eyes, and he looked away quickly. 'I was able to get my point across to her about rebuilding my relationship with my son. She understood that.'

'*Did* she? And did the words "custody" or "court" come up at all, or was she just entirely obliging, acting from the goodness of her heart?'

214

'Don't be a bitch, Nina.'

She sucked in through her teeth. 'I don't know why you're so determined to defend her. *You* didn't have to sit by and watch on for seven years as she got on with playing happy families with another guy, whilst your favourite brother was lying comatose in a bed.'

'No, because I was the lucky bugger lying comatose in the bed . . . And I'm your only brother, by the way.'

She winked at him again, and this time he smiled.

'You never liked her. Even before the coma.'

'That's not true. I just don't trust a woman who moves on to her boyfriend's friends.'

He rolled his eyes. 'That was all a very long time ago, and they were never serious.'

'Hmm, I wonder if that's how he saw it? What was his name again?'

'Liam. And he was cool. He came to our wedding, for chrissakes.'

'A lot of people went to that wedding,' Nina groaned. 'I was surprised not to see my old maths teacher there.'

He grinned in spite of himself. 'Just admit it, Nina – you never liked her.'

'I will not.'

'Name one thing, then, that you liked about her. One thing.'

'Oof.' It was Nina's turn to stare up at the ceiling, her eyes tracing the delicate whorls of plasterwork relief. She was quiet for a long time. 'Well, she dresses well. She has good taste,' she said finally.

'You don't care about taste. You said people who care about fashion are cretinous husks with no souls.'

'*When* did I say that?' she gasped.

'After the couture shows, when Mamma took you to Paris

for a dress for your eighteenth and you were stuck next to that woman at dinner who had frozen her face and kept asking for champagne for her pug.'

She threw her head back and laughed at the memory, her shoulder-length dark hair shining in the sunlight. 'Oh yes! I did say that, didn't I? How on earth do you remember these things?'

'The one good thing about a traumatic brain injury – long-term memory recall. They never broadcast these things, you know. They only ever present the downsides of comas, giving them a bad rap, but things from years ago feel to me like they happened yesterday.'

Nina laughed harder, and he chuckled with her. He had to laugh or he'd cry.

'And things that happened yesterday?' she asked, when she'd recovered. It was a serious question, they both knew.

He shrugged. 'Touch and go. But getting better, I think. The doc's suggestion of keeping a journal has helped.'

'But you haven't remembered anything about the ac—?'

'No.' He cut her off quickly. 'Nothing.'

She nodded, staring at him as she took another sip of her tea, her eyes roaming over him like a sniper's rifle dot.

'What? Why are you looking at me like that?'

'Nothing. It's just always nice to see you . . . awake. Something of a novelty still.' She smiled and gave him another wink. 'You'll have to indulge me, little brother.'

They finished their tea and returned the cups to the tray.

'So are you ready, then?' she asked, getting up.

'For what?'

'Introducing me to my long-lost nephew and your wild, half-naked nanny who doesn't know her boundaries.'

'It's not funny.'

Nina pointed to her deadpan, severe expression. 'Do you see me laughing?'

Old-fashioned games: they never failed. They could turn adults – and worse, teenagers – back into kids again. The cereal game had helped break the ice first off. As Linus and his big, cool cousins had eyed each other in wary silence, she had asked the kitchen staff for a box and proceeded to set it on the ground.

'Pick it up with no hands,' she had instructed, watching as the teenagers, bored and having seen it all, casually dipped and picked it up with their teeth instead. They hadn't looked quite so cocky when she'd torn a strip off the top and asked them to do it again. Five rounds later and it was a flat disc on the floor, and they were all splitting their sides laughing.

Now, as Bell sat crouched against the shed wall, waiting to be found, she burrowed her feet into the soft earth. There was no need to bother with shoes out here; the grass was so springy and soft, it was almost like walking on fur.

She closed her eyes and waited as she heard Linus counting up to fifty in English; she was never one to miss a teaching opportunity, plus it bought her a little extra time. He could have counted to eighty in Swedish in the time it took. She dropped her head down, her arms loosely on her knees, glad of the rest. She could have killed for a coffee. They'd been playing flat-out for an hour now and she hadn't had any breakfast yet.

'Found you!'

Her eyes flew open as she looked up into the dark, beady eyes of Emil's terrifying sister.

'I thought Linus was seeking?' she spluttered.

'Oh. Is he?' Nina shrugged. 'Well, we can hide together, then. Mind if I join you?'

In those white jeans? Bell wondered as Nina sat down on the cool earth beside her. Hiding in the narrow crack between the potting shed and a rusting lawnmower had seemed like a safe bet for a few minutes' peace, but now it felt like the most dangerous place on earth. 'How did you find me?'

'I saw you disappear into the bushes there. I always used to hide here too, when Emil and I played this game as kids.'

'Oh. The mower was here back then?'

'Oh yes,' Nina nodded, pulling out a pack of cigarettes from her Chanel bag. 'Nothing ever changes here, although I guess you could already tell that by the decor in the bathrooms.' She offered Bell a cigarette.

'No. Thanks. I don't smoke.'

'No, neither do I. Well, not officially, anyway,' Nina said, casting her a sideways look and a sly grin. 'I suppose it doesn't look good on the CV, does it? Nanny, smoker.'

'No. Not really.'

'D'you mind?' Nina hesitated before lighting up, the cigarette already perched between her lips. The question was clearly rhetorical, but Bell shook her head anyway. 'So . . .' She exhaled a plume of grey smoke. 'You seem to like your job.'

'I do.'

'How long have you been doing it for?'

'Three years. The Mogerts are the only family I've worked for.' She noticed Nina flinch at the sound of Max's surname.

Nina's eyes narrowed, assessing her. 'But you're, what – late twenties?'

'Twenty-six. Before that, I was travelling,' she said, anticipating the next question.

'Ah yes. Everyone's so . . . free-spirited and rootless these days.'

There was bite to the words, and Bell looked away. She didn't need to explain her life history to this woman. What did she know about life choices or career paths? She was a spoiled, rich stranger who had clearly never had to work a day in her life.

'And my brother,' she said, taking a deep drag, holding it for a moment before exhaling with a sigh. 'How are you finding him?'

What had he said? she wondered. 'He's not playing too, is he?' she replied coolly.

Nina laughed loudly, displaying a set of perfect teeth. 'Ha! My God, no! Ha, you're hilarious.' She had that rich person's way of showing amusement by speaking her laughter, rather than actually laughing it. She took another drag, enjoying her cigarette, playing with the smoke with her lips and blowing rings; it seemed a somewhat subversive, teenage act for such an elegant woman. 'I meant . . . is he behaving himself?'

'We're not . . . He hasn't tried anything on, if that's what you mean.'

Nina laughed harder. 'Ha! It wasn't, but –' She began coughing, she was laughing so hard. 'Ha! Oh God, honestly? I'd ask you to do him a favour and jump his poor bones, but I'm not sure one can say that sort of thing these days, even as a joke.' Her smile faded and she sighed, looking suddenly sad. She was quiet for another moment, seeming to sink into her thoughts. 'You've been filled in on the accident, I'm assuming.'

'Of course.' Only thanks to Christer, though. Hanna had effectively let her come here blind.

'So then you know that he's still not fully recovered, in spite of appearances?'

'I do, yes.'

'Good. Because he could do with a little kindness right now. God knows he won't show any to himself. He's picking at old wounds, trying to get *her* back.'

Bell hitched an eyebrow at her tone. Was she not a fan? 'If it's any consolation, I don't think he'll succeed. Hanna's happy with Max.'

Nina gave a snort. 'Sadly it's not. God knows I never liked the woman, but he's pinned his flag to that mast; he's convinced she's the happy ending and he'll get her, you see if he doesn't.'

Bell didn't reply and they were quiet for a moment – Nina still blowing smoke rings, Bell burrowing her toes even deeper into the earth, the two of them like truants hiding from a teacher.

'Still, you know what they say: where there's life, there's hope –'

Bell bit her lip. Her hope had long gone, been snuffed out like a candle in a storm.

'– And perhaps I should just be grateful that he's still here to make shitty choices.' Nina blew a stream of smoke through flattened lips. 'He died, you know, before he arrived at the hospital. He was in full cardiac arrest when they got to him . . . I'll never know how they got him back.'

'I didn't know that,' Bell murmured, feeling stricken by the thought. He had *died*? 'My God.'

'Mmm. And just when you think he got the happy ending and woke up, he discovered his son was calling another man Pappa, and found out that our father had died.'

'Were they close?'

She nodded. 'He was everything to Emil, and vice versa. Very much the favourite,' she added with a shrug. 'Everything he did was to make our father proud.'

'That's so sad.'

'Sad's what he is, though he hides it by being angry instead. Of course, he gets terribly cross with me always checking up on him. He doesn't like it at all, says I'm fussing.' Nina splayed her hands wide as if she couldn't understand it. 'Well, wouldn't you?'

Bell smiled.

'I should go.' She took a final, deep drag of the beloved cigarette before grinding it out in the earth. She gathered her feet in and levered up to standing. 'Just do me a favour, okay? Cut him some slack. He loves his boy and just wants to be a father again. God only knows, he's an optimist in a glass that's half empty. A foolhardy romantic with all the plans and only half the facts . . . It was nice meeting you, Bell.'

'It – it was nice meeting you.'

Nina gave another of her amused barks. 'Ha! Was it?' She disappeared through the trees as quickly as she had come, Bell staring after her in puzzlement.

Only half the facts?

They left after lunch – a fresh but extravagant spread of crispbreads, eggs and smoked fish roe served on the terrace, the view down the garden somewhat blighted by the giant blue helicopter sitting dormant on the lawn. The gardener had spent all morning draping the flowerbeds with lightweight muslins and tethering them to the ground with tent pegs, in the hope of saving them from further decimation when the chopper inevitably took off again. Emil had noticed a pointedness in his endeavours as he stomped around, but Nina remained oblivious, and as she got up to depart there was a look of triumph about her.

'Well, that was a very pleasant morning,' she said, looking first at him and then at the children. 'It's good to see you cousins reunited at last. We have missed you, Linus.'

'Thank you, Aunt Nina,' his son replied obediently, looking terrified.

'Ha! Such manners. He's far too polite, you know,' she said to Emil, kissing him on each cheek. 'You'll need to stamp that out of him.' She shot him one of her sharp-eyed smiles.

'Well, it's lovely to see you, but next time, please ring.' He stuffed his hands in his pockets lackadaisically. 'We might have been out today and your trip would have been wasted –'

Nina laughed as though that idea was hysterical.

'– And next time, come by boat. It's obnoxious bringing that thing.'

'It's efficient, darling. I've got dinner in Copenhagen tonight, and I can't spend an entire day travelling on the water just to check in on my baby brother, now, can I?'

'You don't need to check in on me,' he said in a low voice.

Nina responded with a silent arched eyebrow, and he was aware of Bell looking on with apparent bemusement. He and his sister switched seamlessly between insults and affection with no friction at all; they always had. It had been one of the few constants he had come back to. Her and Måns.

Hanna and Linus, on the other hand . . .

It was apparent his son was terrified of him, or couldn't abide him – possibly even both. Every response was a 'yes' or 'no', and on the boat, having their picnic breakfast that morning, he'd said barely a word and eaten even less. It had been an unmitigated disaster from start to finish, and had left him feeling low even before the forgotten meeting with his lawyers – and especially before *she* had flown down the stairs in a state of wildness and undress to castigate him.

He closed his eyes, struggling for the strength to remain patient. Remain calm. Everyone had warned him it would take time for the bonds to be renewed, but he had under-estimated the pain that would bring. It was a physical ache – along with all the others he had to endure – constantly having to hold himself back. He wanted to squeeze his son in a hug, ruffle his hair, pinch those cheeks, hold his hand, kiss his temple as he had as a sleeping toddler . . . But he couldn't. These privileges were forbidden to him. Aside from their initial handshake, there had been no physical contact between them. Nothing at all. Another man – another father – got to love his son; even *she*, the nanny, was allowed to touch him in ways he couldn't – squeezing his shoulder, bedtime cuddles – while he was nothing more than a remote stranger with long-ago memories no one else remembered.

That was the hardest part of it all: the dislocation between how it was for him and everyone else. In the seven years he had been under, they had all moved on without him. He had been, ultimately, disposable, and it was a hard fact to accept, especially because he had woken with the same love and same bonds as seven years prior. For him, it had been but the blink of an eye. One long night's sleep. Nothing altered, nothing changed. And now, he had to somehow win them all back – like it was a competition. He had to prove himself worthy, better, *more* than the other guy.

All under *her* watchful gaze. Something about her unnerved him – her honest, probing stares made him feel nervous, like she could shine a light into his darkest corners.

He glanced over, seeing how Bell and Linus waved politely – obediently – as the helicopter rose into the air like a giant dragonfly, the cousins giving bored-again nods through the windows, their phones already back in their hands. The gardener stood by the side of the garden like a touchline referee, racing down the lines any time it looked like a bolt of muslin was going to wrench free; but his system held strong, and no sooner was the helicopter safely clear than he started pulling up the tent pegs and rolling back the cloth again, bringing colour and texture back to the garden scene.

'Well,' Bell said, into the fresh settling calm. 'That was an . . . unexpected surprise.'

'You have to expect the unexpected with Nina.'

She looked back at him with guarded eyes, their argument this morning still unresolved and lingering in the air between them like coloured smoke.

'So . . .' he murmured, at a loss as to what to do next. He couldn't do right for doing wrong, it seemed, and his confidence felt battered. 'It's a nice day. What shall we do with it?'

He directed the question at Bell. She had made it perfectly plain nothing would happen without her say-so, and to be honest, he didn't trust himself to get it right on his own now anyway.

She looked surprised by the deferral, her mouth parting in a pretty 'o'. She looked back at Linus. 'We could kayak? Or go for a swim?'

Linus shrugged. The idea clearly didn't thrill him, but the look on his face asked the question, what else were they going to do? He looked bored.

'I know some high rocks we could jump from,' Emil said.

Linus's head snapped up. 'You do?'

'Yes, but they're about an hour's sail from here. They're about ten metres high, though –'

His little face brightened. 'Cliff jumping?'

'Well, I'm not sure cliff is quite the word,' he smiled. 'But they're better than anything else you'll find around here.'

From the look in Linus's eyes, it was apparent they had a plan.

Half an hour later, they were on the water, lifejackets buckled and the old sail boat's patched sails bellying and flapping as they slipped their mooring and drifted across the lagoon. They passed the smaller day-trip sailboats bobbing along the coastlines, moored in coves and bays for family days out, the tinny sound of music playing on radios drifting over the waves, children's shrieks as they jumped and splashed from the rocks carrying to the ear and making heads – even his – instinctively turn. He felt a burst of intense emotion as he realized he was part of that scene too – sailing with his son.

He looked across at Linus, staring down into the water. Its surface was a rich, glossy peacock-blue, occasional flashes of dazzling light catching on the seam of a ripple. The water was so clear, Linus could see a school of tiny silver fish flicking one way, then the other, far down below the boat, his arm dangling over the side and trailing in the water as though he might touch them. Bell, by contrast, was enjoying the warmth on her skin and kept automatically angling her face upwards, like a daisy trying to find the sunlight. Emil tried not to look at her at all.

They approached Summer Isle, on their starboard side, and he saw how Linus looked up as they passed, his body tensing as he scanned the shoreline for sight of his mother, his sisters, Max, getting ready to wave, to shout . . . The happy expansive feeling in his chest contracted violently and in one sharp movement, he turned the boat away, snatching the view from sight, seeing how his son's head turned instinctively towards him, unformed protest stoppered in his throat. They sailed clear of the lagoon's claustrophobic embrace and pointed towards a horizon that stretched out – endless, empty, clear. Almost immediately, he felt released from the archipelago's rhythms of normality, from home and the long lonely hours, where the mundane imposed itself – what to eat, what to wear, what to do . . . He felt himself breathe more easily again, the immediate threats quenched.

The horizon was sharp and precise, as though painted around the earth's waist with a fine nib, and he felt a distinct pride in knowing – without being able to see it – that an equally fine white vein marbled the water behind them too, like a physical marker of his presence back in the world. It was an endeavour the doubters had continually told him could never be, but they had underestimated him. He had already disproved every fact they laid at his feet, he had already beaten every target they set – and still it wasn't enough for the naysayers who said he could never claim back what he had lost. He wasn't a fool. He knew he couldn't claw back time, nor the past. But to say his family was denied to him forever . . . No. They weren't out of reach. They were tantalizingly close, and growing ever closer . . . He just had to keep believing, keep showing them he was the man they used to love. He wasn't *less* now. He was the man he had been before.

He felt his spirits begin to soar as they sailed for miles in contented quiet through the beautiful desolation of the Baltic, cutting and sluicing, tacking and gybing beneath a soundless symphony of blues. He felt warily happy. It was an alien emotion these days, where pain and loneliness and frustration defined his days. But out here, he was in his element. In the rest of his life, he had to pitch himself against the odds, but out on the water, he merely had to do battle with the elements. It was an arena where he rarely won, of course, and yet he wished he could stay there for days, escape into the solace of an empty sea and feel his hair fly back and his eyes stream, the spray on his face. This was where he felt most alive. Most awake.

In front and above him, the mainsail was bellied out, taut and curved into a perfect half-ellipse as the keel tore through the water, slicing the sea as though skating over glass, until ahead, creeping into view, came the fractured embrace of the next group of skerries. He approached the ragged scraps of land with masterly ease, the specks of rock breaking up the pristine perfection of the horizon, gulls wheeling far above in scattered flocks and chasing after distant fishing boats as they piloted towards the city. He remembered the route in with dazzling clarity. His own father had always taken him here as a boy. It was one of his 'quiet pleasures' – isolation as luxury, when they needed to escape the Board, the press, and even the Sandhamn scene – and he knew exactly which markers to navigate by.

The rocks here were wild and ragged, jutting high out of the sea like shards of glass. No one lived here and few came this way. The inlet was narrow and only smaller boats with experienced skippers could navigate through safely, but Emil had loved it precisely because of its wildness and isolation, its air of abandonment and danger.

He turned in at precisely the point his father had taught him to – between the humped rock and the one they called the 'jagged tooth' – his mouth already open to announce their joyous arrival. But the words stuck in his throat at what he saw there.

Linus and Bell sat up as they drifted into the lee of the island cluster, all straightening as they saw it too – a wall of sea mist ahead of them, rising like a steam above the water, perfectly caught within the walls of the lagoon.

It was a common enough sight out here – the sky could be a cloudless, singing blue overhead, but the scattered dots of land would be all but lost to view as the marine mists rolled and billowed, smothering and obscuring even nearby isles from sight. They usually passed quickly enough, sometimes in just a few minutes, others in an hour, or several.

Still, this one was dense. The islands' feathery green-black silhouettes quickly faded from sight, becoming shadowy and crepuscular. Emil took off his sunglasses as the murk enveloped them, his hand hovering lightly on the tiller as they edged in, cutting the speed further as even the warning sticks became difficult to spot. The mist was gauzy and diaphanous from a distance but inside the mass, it was as dense and opaque as a cumulo nimbus; the endless sun was finally blotted out and everything seemed to slide forward a notch, like a car shifting gear – day became evening, summer became autumn. It felt impossible to recall the open brightness and warmth of even a few moments earlier, for it was cool in the gloom, the only sound the boat sluicing through the eerily calm waters of the inlet.

Bell looked across at him worriedly – possibly even accusingly; perhaps she would say he should have known this was a possibility – but he was oblivious to her censure, his jaw set in a rigid lock, his eyes moving fast as he scanned for the markers that would tell them where they were. Ripping the bottom off the boat out here was a distinctly dangerous prospect. In the space of mere minutes, the over-reaching, buttery sky had dimmed and closed down around them, blotting out the rest of the world so that nothing existed beyond the confines of this boat. Had they been in a bigger vessel, they would have had radar equipment to guide them through, but the two oars on the floor by their feet were the only back-up system on board here.

No one spoke. Shapes emerged from the gloom, receding again in the next breath: a bird flapped its wings in a nearby tree, startling Bell so that she gave a little gasp; a ripple creased the water as a fish surfaced, then sank back into the depths. To their left, a vague mass drifted past. Or rather, they drifted past it. Emil could just make out the spiny points of pine trees, higher in the skyline than anywhere else. They were in the right place, at least, and he pushed on the tiller lightly, guiding the boat closer towards the landmass, remembering there were no rocks in front of the island's apex.

He glanced overboard, but the dim light made it impossible to gauge depth. He threw the small anchor overboard anyway. If it was too deep, they would drift, albeit slowly, for the currents were gentle inside the lagoon. If not, they could wait here until the mist rolled back and he could get his bearings.

They all stared out into the miasma. It had fallen as thickly as a velvet curtain, its approach silent as a cat. It almost seemed to dance for them, a living thing that swayed and rolled and breathed. There were no edges to it, no signs of it furling or peeling back to expose the blue beyond. Instead it kept on rolling in in plumes of changing density, a totemic warning stick in the shallows occasionally winking back into focus momentarily, then disappearing again. Even to him, the sense of isolation was eerie. There were no passing boats, no sounds of shrieking children skating across the water, and it could have easily been the middle of November, deserted and abject.

'Should we . . . go back?' Bell asked him cautiously, her voice low. He knew she was trying not to alarm Linus, who kept looking back at them both, but she, too, was like a doe, all big eyes and run instinct.

'No. We need to just sit tight,' he replied. 'It will pass.'

She turned away again, biting her lip, and he noticed the mist's dampness was like a sheen on her skin, the wispy tendrils at the base of her neck beginning to darken, the fluttery sleeves at her shoulder beginning to droop.

He looked quickly away, finding Linus already watching him. He smiled reassuringly. 'It's okay, Linus, we're perfectly safe here.'

'But what if it doesn't go?'

'It will. We just need to be patient. My father used to say to me birds fly not into our mouths ready roasted.' They sat in silence on the still water, all waiting. Waiting. The sense of expectation – of something having to happen – settled heavily upon him. This had been his idea after all. It was his fault. Fifteen minutes passed. Twenty . . . His eyes fell on something beyond his son's shoulder.

Linus turned and saw a dot of blue begin to grow, the mist beginning to thin and peel back. Emil saw his son's body soften with relief, a small laugh escaping him now that the worst of the danger was seemingly past. 'That was so cool!'

Bell laughed too as the landscape became less hostile and more friendly by the moment, the reasserted sunlight high-lighting now caramel-coloured rocks covered with yellow sedum and violet beach pea, wild bilberry and lingonberry bushes, fir and alder trees – and a sheer ten-metre escarpment that had Linus almost leaping from the boat in excitement and Bell grabbing him by the arm.

Within minutes the sea mist had gone without trace, as insubstantial as candyfloss, and both Linus and Bell were stripping off their clothes and leaping in without hesitation, both of them joyous. So ready to be happy. He looked away as she leapt, refusing to look again at the last body he had touched, the only woman he had known in eight years. He refused to remember the yielding feel of her in his hands . . . They surfaced laughing, enjoying the cool as they trod water and looked around them again, before doing some playful duck dives and backward rolls.

Emil looked on, feeling a stab of envy at their closeness. He could see how Linus's gaze always tracked back to Bell like a safety buoy, and he felt his position as the third wheel keenly again, his confidence having disappeared like that mist . . .

'Aren't you coming in?' Bell asked, as though it was that easy. As though happiness could be grabbed with a single leap.

'I thought I'd film Linus doing some jumps first.'

'Oh. Okay.' She gave an easy shrug.

'Cool!' Linus exclaimed, looking more lively than Emil had ever seen him. It was clear neither one of them was bothered whether he joined them or not.

'So is there a path up there?' she asked, straining to see.

'Yes. Climb out below the bushes and you'll see it runs behind. It's narrow, though, in places, so –'

'Okay, I'll go first and he can follow me,' she said, hardly able to wait. 'Come on, Liney.'

He watched them swim off, their wet, darkened heads like seals' as they moved further away. Their voices carried as they got to the rocks and he watched their limbs scramble and climb as they hauled themselves from the water. Within minutes they were standing on the shallow ledge that had always been his jumping-off point as a boy. This was his place; he had brought them here; and yet he felt shut out from it. An observer of a private moment.

He held up his phone and watched them through the zoom lens. They were holding hands, peering over the edge – checking for rocks, no doubt – and chatting away. She was wearing a black bikini, her wet dark hair slicked back. Her body looked soft, relaxed, in the sunshine but he still remembered the way she had tensed like a stray cat as she talked about her dead fiancé . . . It was a strange thing to know something so intimate about a near-stranger, to see a beautiful woman in a bikini, a child by her side, and to understand that despite this distant image of seemingly perfect happiness, she was hollow inside too. Like him.

He watched them jump together, heels kicking back, arms outstretched, hair flying upwards, their shrieks carrying over to him. They were everything he wanted to be, everything he wanted . . .

But no. That evening with her had been but a glancing flash of light in both their lives. Though it had held a quiet importance for him – reminding him he was alive, that he was a flesh-and-blood man, still – she could never know it. They must remain, fundamentally, strangers who had once shared a night under the midnight sun. Nothing more. She could never be more than that. Now, she was just the nanny.

'Did you get it?' Linus yelled, triumph in his still-high voice.

Emil caught his breath, realizing he had forgotten to click.

Chapter Eighteen

'So what shall we do today?' Emil asked as they finished breakfast. It had mostly been taken in silence, the overnight sleep somehow setting them all back a step from yesterday's adventures, formality restored again.

Bell inwardly groaned, feeling like she was trapped in a groundhog day. Was it going to be like this every day for the rest of the summer? Did she have to plan every step of Emil getting to know his son? She had expected he would take the lead yesterday but he had seemed reluctant to get into the water, in spite of the fact it had been his idea. He had seemed almost shy. He had eventually done a few jumps with Linus (although they hadn't held hands on the rocks. Perhaps he thought it wasn't acceptable for a ten-year-old boy to hold hands with his father?), but she must have scrambled up and jumped off that rock with Linus thirty times. Each time she had felt a spike of fear at the drop below her feet; she had never been good with heights, and it had taken all her courage to make herself do it, for Linus's sake. Her body was complaining today, though. She was stiff, and had a few scrapes and bruises from where she'd knocked herself on the rocks.

She looked at Linus, trying to gauge his mood. He had bags under his eyes, and she could tell from his sullen silence that he hadn't slept well, that he didn't want to be here. Was this going to be groundhog day for him too? Would Linus reset every morning to his default resentment at being made to be here, no matter how fun or exciting the day before?

She felt exhausted, caught between them both. 'Fancy a kayak?' she asked as brightly as she could manage.

'No,' Linus muttered.

'We could go fishing?'

He shook his head.

'Cycling? We could go to Sandhamn and you could take your board instead if you like?'

'No!'

She was shocked by the suddenness of his snap. 'But Linus, you love—'

'I don't want to!' he cried. 'I'm *tired*, why can't you just let me be?' She knew it wasn't the activities he was resisting, but the person he had to do them with. His plea to her to be left alone was, in fact, a plea to Emil. She glanced over at him to see whether he understood that, but on the contrary, he seemed almost pleased by Linus's bad mood, because it was ostensibly being directed towards her.

'Well, we could just chill out and watch a film,' Emil suggested, playing the good cop to her bad.

Bell arched an eyebrow. She had seen his DVD collection, and *The Flight of the Condor* and *Dambusters* weren't going to cut it. Linus had never even seen an actual DVD before, much less those films.

'We can go over to Sandhamn,' he shrugged, seeming to get her point.

'There isn't a cinema there, is there?' she puzzled.

'No. But there's a screen at the hotel, in the conference room. I can get them to set it up for us.'

'Just the three of us?' she queried.

'Well, is there anyone else you'd like to bring?'

She and Linus swapped hopeful glances. It was obvious, surely? But one look at Emil's face . . . There was a long silence, and Bell's heart ached as his mother's and sisters' names didn't fill it. Linus swallowed. 'No, sir.'

'Okay. And what film shall we watch? Anything you want.'

'Anything?' Linus queried.

'Anything at all. New. Old.'

Linus looked overwhelmed by the seemingly unlimited scope of choice. 'Umm . . .'

'Hey, has the new Avengers one come out yet?' she asked him.

'No. September twelfth,' he said with certainty. He took his superheroes very seriously.

'Oh.'

'Okay, you want to see that one?' Emil asked.

'Yes, sir,' Linus said hesitantly.

'Okay then. Avengers it is.'

'You don't understand. It's not out y—' she faltered.

He stopped her with a look. 'It is for him.' He looked back at Linus and gave him a wink. 'Shall we say be ready in an hour?'

'Yes, sir,' Linus said uncertainly, a faint excitement blooming in the words and in his eyes. Emil smiled, somehow growing, becoming bigger before them.

'Good. Then I'll see you down at the dock.'

Linus bolted from the table excitedly to brush his teeth and find his shoes as Emil half glanced over his shoulder. 'Måns?'

'Absolutely, sir.' And the valet slipped from the room to make the necessary arrangements.

Bell watched on. Surely he couldn't just . . . rig up a private cinema for an unreleased film, within the hour?

Emil got up at the table, stopping just by her. 'I assume you'll be coming with us. Where he goes, you go, wasn't that it?'

'Of course.'

He nodded, the resentment in his green eyes like a cold wind upon her. She was still unforgiven for yesterday's show-down. Unwelcome. 'Yes. Of course.'

Docking at Sandhamn again after a couple of days on 007 was like touching down in LAX after a year in Alaska, or emerging into the Mardi Gras after a long sleep: the noises, the colours, the aromas of barbecues on the beaches . . . Everything felt dialled up to the max after the gentle, sleepy tranquillity of private island life. *Midsommar* was over, but the holiday fever continued – every berth in the marina was still rammed with yachts, and all the guest moorings were taken in the sound too, sails wound tightly around masts, rigging clinking in the breeze. Boats were coming and going like trains in a station, people calling across decks to one another. Holidaymakers were sashaying slowly in bikinis and flip-flops from boats to beaches and bars, joggers running in just shorts with towels tucked into their waistbands, kids choosing ice creams, locals walking their dogs or pushing wheelbarrows loaded up with pot plants, towels and the other tokens of city life that had come in with the ferries.

Emil jumped off first, reaching down for Linus and helping pull him up onto the jetty. He held a hand out for Bell too, and she managed not to react as his hand closed around her wrist.

They walked along the rattling gangplanks, long since bleached grey by the lashing winters and beating summers on the Baltic's edge. No one had to be anywhere in a hurry, it seemed. A quartet of girls on bikes dawdled past, ringing their bells lazily, tennis racquets slung across their backs, brown legs levering up and down in micro-skirts, ponytails swinging.

Linus had brought his skateboard with him – excited by the prospect of dirt roads and makeshift pavements again – and began weaving expertly through the crowds. She saw Emil's mouth open as he sped past and instinctively his arm went out – but too late; his son was already out of reach. Emil glanced back at her, as though for help, but when he saw her looking back at him, snapped around again, chin down.

She stared at the back of his head; he was pointedly walking two strides ahead of her, his baseball cap back on so that his face was obscured from casual, enquiring glances; nonetheless, she noticed he still somehow drew the eye, women looking over with latent interest, oblivious to the complicated history of the man. Too late, she remembered she hadn't yet managed to get Linus to send his mother an email. After yesterday morning's breakfast ruckus and Nina's unannounced arrival . . . She picked up her phone and took some shots of Linus skateboarding ahead of them.

'Bell!'

The shout made her jump and she wheeled round to find someone running towards her, jumping over a couple of kayaks that had been laid out on the ground.

'Kris!' She threw her arms up in delight as he picked her up and swung her around. 'What are you doing here mid-week?'

'I got a last-minute gig catering for a dinner on one of the bigger boats tonight,' he said proudly, jerking his chin towards the sound.

'No way!' she gasped.

'I'm just on my way to get the fish. Wanna hang for ten minutes? I could murder a beer.'

'Oh.' Her smile faded. 'I can't. I'm working.' She looked over to where Emil and Linus had stopped, further ahead, looking back and watching them with curious stares.

'Oh. I didn't realize you were all together.'

'No, well, I think that was the intention,' she said under her breath.

'Right.' He frowned. 'You okay, Hell? You look a little . . . wonky.'

'Wonky?'

'Out of sorts. Not quite right.'

She shook her head. 'All good. Just working hard, around the bloody clock.' She couldn't help but groan.

'You don't mean that, I hope.' He gave her a quizzical smile.

She twitched her nose. 'Things have changed quite dramatically in the last few days,' she sighed. 'But it's a long story. I'll have to tell you properly when there's time.'

'At the weekend, then? Marc and Tove are coming back tomorrow night.'

'No, I'll be working this weekend, sadly. And the one after that. And the one after that.'

'Hell, Bell, that's crazy,' Kris said sternly. 'And it's certainly not legal.'

'It's a very complicated situa—'

'Hi.'

She jumped as Emil came back and stood beside them both.

Kris stared back at him, not looking his friendliest, although even unfriendly, he was still traffic-stoppingly handsome. From Emil's assertive, questioning body language, an introduction appeared to be required. 'Hi?'

'I'm Emil. Bell's boss.'

Bell inwardly flinched. Last weekend he'd been the best sex she'd ever had; her mystery lover. Now he was her boss.

'Hi. Kris,' he replied, deliberately not supplying any further information, like who he might be to her.

Both men shook hands, but there was a passive-aggressiveness to it, as though they had decided they didn't like each other.

A brief pause followed, with Emil looking as though he was waiting for something further – for her to stop talking to Kris, perhaps? Then he said, 'Linus and I will go ahead. We'll see you in there.'

Had he really come over just to say that? 'Okay. I'll be right there.'

Kris watched him go, his eyes narrowing. 'He seems easy-going,' he muttered under his breath.

'Yeah,' she sighed.

'Emil . . . Emil . . . He looks familiar . . .' Kris murmured as they watched him catch up with Linus and go to pat a hand on his shoulder; but the boy ducked and pushed away on his board, out of reach again. 'That's not . . . oh, holy shit, that's not Emil Von Greyers, is it?'

She blinked her reply.

His eyes widened. 'You know who he is, right?'

'Yes. My boss.'

'*And* scion of one of the biggest industrialist families in the country.'

'Bully for him,' she muttered. 'Trust me, you'd never know it from the state of his boat. Or shoes,' she added, watching him go.

'How come you're working for him?' But the answer came even as he asked the question. '*He's* coma guy? Hanna's ex?'

'Technically not ex, they're still married. But yeah – and he's now my new boss for the rest of the summer. Long story short – he wants to bond with Linus. I'm the chaperone.'

'I can't believe you never said!'

'I didn't know myself until a few days ago. But look, it's probably best if you don't say anything to anyone. They're very private.'

'Not that private. Everyone on the island saw the helicopter arriving yesterday.'

'Oh.' She could already imagine what Emil's reaction would be to that.

'*You* weren't on it, were you?'

'God, no.'

'Shame.' His eyes twinkled with mischief. Kris had a taste for the finer things in life.

'Look, I'd better go,' she said, standing on tiptoe and kissing his cheek. 'We're watching the new Avengers movie.'

'I didn't think that was out yet?'

'It isn't, apparently,' she shrugged, beginning to walk away backwards. 'Give my love to the others. I'll let you know when I can get away. I'd better dash.'

She hurried along the boardwalk, hopping out of the way of a cyclist and running up the steps into the dark-timbered cool of the hotel lobby. She stood at the door for a moment, trying to get her bearings. Emil had said 'conference room', hadn't he?

There was a man with an extravagant blonde moustache working at the reception desk and she walked over, composing herself with a deep breath. 'Hello. I'm with Mr Von Greyers and his son. Could you tell me where they are, please?'

The man's eyes narrowed at the sight of her – was there a dress code here? Was her dress too short? Her hair too scruffy? – and he stopped typing. 'May I see some ID confirming that?'

Her smile faded. 'What?'

'ID, miss.'

240

'I don't have any *ID*. What would I need that for?'

He looked away and around the room, as though checking he wasn't going to offend any neighbours with his words. 'Well, I'm afraid you wouldn't be the first young lady to purport to be one of Mr Von Greyers' employees.'

She stared at him, incredulous. 'I'm his son's *nanny*.'

'Yes, madam. That's what they tend to say.'

She gave a short bark of laughter that would have made Nina proud. 'Oh my God! Are you seriously—'

'It's okay, Lennart, she's with me.'

She turned to find Emil walking towards her. He must have been sitting in one of the chairs by the window. Had he been waiting for her? Watching her with Kris?

Why?

'Where's Linus?' she asked, hot-cheeked that he must have overheard this pompous man's ridiculous intimations that she was some sort of . . . *groupie*.

He regarded her coolly, his cap still on. 'Already in the cinema. I thought I'd wait for you. The room can be hard to find if you don't know where to look.'

'Oh. Thank you.' A reluctant hero again?

A moment pulsed, silent and tense, the two of them ever at odds.

'Lennart, please remember her for future reference,' he said, not taking his eyes off her. 'Her name is Bell Appleshaw.'

'Certainly, sir. And I'll make a note that she's your son's nanny?'

Emil began walking briskly away. 'That's correct. She's just the nanny.'

Chapter Nineteen

'Linus?' She sat up, the dim light playing tricks on her as she squinted into the gloom, her heart pounding deeply in her chest. 'Is that you, sweetie?'

Her ears strained for a sound, but the silence was as enveloping as the darkness. It was a cloudy night and the moon was hiding behind tufted clouds, the resident owl silent in his tree. But someone had been in here, she could feel it – the trace of their presence like a heat, a scent left behind, her sixth sense twitching, lifting her from sleep.

Was her mind playing tricks, or had she simply been roused by something outside? A fox catching a mouse? She waited another moment, still listening hard, before she threw back the covers and walked to the windows, folding back one of the shutters. She looked out over the treetops. The dusky sky vaulted above her; the pine wood was an inky blot, the lawn silvered and . . . studded with footprints in the dew. She peered more closely into the black mass of trees, hearing now branches snapping, the flash of something pale suddenly catching the eye like quicksilver. She stared harder, her heart beating strongly again. It could have been a white hart.

But there were no deer on these islands. Everyone knew that.

She dashed across the floor and out into the long corridor,

glancing down to Emil's door at the far end; it was closed, no light shining through beneath the crack as it often did. She looked in to Linus's room, willing herself to see what she always saw when she checked on him – Linus fast asleep and lying on his side, his body tucked up in a caterpillar curl, thumb in his mouth – a babyhood habit he had outgrown during the day but not, as yet, at night. But the scene that greeted her was unequivocal. His bed was empty, the alarm beeping on his clock again as it came off snooze . . .

'Oh God,' she gasped, knowing exactly what was happening. He was running away, taking the boat back to Summer Isle. But though there was no breeze, though the water would be flat, he didn't know how to navigate the lagoon by night. He wouldn't see the spar markers warning of the rocks that could tear the bottom of a boat . . .

She flew down the landing and stairs, neither knowing nor caring if she made any sound, stuffing her feet into a pair of wellingtons left by the back door. They were several sizes too big but she ran anyway, hearing them wallow and flap around her bare legs as she sprinted down the lawn in her t-shirt.

It felt eerie running through the trees in the dead of night. Although the sun and moon both hung in the sky like dimmed chandeliers, the fabric of the air felt different – thicker, dense, populated with tiny shining, watchful eyes and the myriad sounds of the nocturnal world. Still she ran, weaving a warp thread through the pines until the pewter sea glimmered in flashes, growing ever larger . . .

She heard something behind her, she was sure. Footsteps? Breathing, too?

No. She couldn't stop. She wouldn't. Her imagination was playing tricks, her childish fright rearing in scant breaths, and she could see now that Linus was on the jetty. His slight figure was a silhouette against the glimmering water as he carried an oar down the gangplanks towards the rowing boat, slack-tied to the ladder.

She went to call out, to stop him as she reached the beach, but the word caught in her throat like a sleeve on a nail. She watched in silence as he lifted the oar – which was not an oar at all.

'Bell –' The word was a whisper, a pant, the hand on her shoulder a pull-back, and she turned in fright to find Emil behind her. He too was in his bedclothes – pyjama trousers only, no shirt, nor even any shoes – a wild look in his eyes, like hers. 'What are you doing? Where are you going?'

But the questions didn't need an answer, because his gaze fell on the boy behind her, waving a white flag. And across the water, a white flag was waving back. A silent communication in the dead of night. The forlorn attempts of a son to reach his mother.

Bell looked back at him with angry tears in her eyes, seeing how he shrank before her. 'Now do you see what you've done?'

Emil watched in splintered pain as his child waved the giant flag. It was tattered with age, holes worn through where the sun had broken down the fibres, the former tent-pole heavy on his still-little arms. After several minutes, the movements slowed, becoming jerky, and his every instinct was to go over there and help him, be his father and take the weight for him. But Bell was right. It was *because* of him that his son even needed to do this. He could see from the strong rhythmic waves coming from Summer Isle just how much Hanna was missing him, trying to convey her love and longing through a consistent, unfailing stroke. None of them – not Hanna,

Linus nor Bell – wanted him here, and to intrude, even to help, would bring their moment of connection to an abrupt stop.

He heard a sound coming from the jetty. Linus was groaning as the weight in his arms became too much. He couldn't wave the flag now, only hold it, and after another few moments he was forced to lay it down.

'Mamma!' Linus called, waving his arms frantically and jumping so that the boards rattled. 'I'm still here, Mamma!'

But across the water, the waving stopped, the flag becoming almost instantly invisible in stillness. It was impossible to see Hanna from here, not from this distance in the crepuscular light, a tendril of sea mist winding its way into the lagoon.

'Mamma!'

His heart twitched at the anguish in his child's voice. For the thousandth time, he questioned what he was doing – dragging Linus here and holding him, to all intents and purposes, against his will.

He saw Bell flinch too, her shoulders hitched high, as Linus jumped higher, his calls becoming more frantic, desperate, pleading – but Hanna had gone, and Linus began to weep at the prospect of facing another night and day here without her. Would he be back on the jetty tomorrow night? Had he been doing this every night since they'd arrived?

Emil felt the rejection like a blow to his chest. He loved that child with every fibre of his being, but his attempts to bond, to connect . . . What he was doing wasn't enough. *He* wasn't enough, and he never would be. He'd missed out on everything – his son's first day at school, learning to ride his bike, skiing together for the first time, Christmases, birthdays . . . and now nothing could make up for the time lost. His son was a stranger to him, and he called another man 'Pappa'.

Those were the facts. That was the hand Fate had dealt him. He was 'lucky' to be alive, everyone kept telling him, as though that should be enough. But what was the point of it all, if he'd lost the only thing worth living for?

When he lay in bed at night, he could remember certain memories so strongly, it was like he could step back into them – taking Linus to his baby swimming class when he turned eight months and the open, trusting way his baby son had gazed at him underwater as he swooped him down with strong hands, Linus's dive reflex kicking in as the instructor had said it would, before scooping him up again onto his chest. Father and son, skin on skin, cheek to cheek . . . It felt like an unimaginable luxury now, when his son had still only touched him once since their visit began, and that had been to shake his hand, a politeness to a stranger.

Bell took a sudden breath, pushing him back into the trees, her hands cool on his bare skin, both of them hiding behind a fir as Linus finally turned and made his way back up the jetty, sobbing and lurching onto the stony path and back towards the house.

He could smell her shampoo as she stood just inches away, and he watched her watch his son. She loved him, he could see; it was more than a job for her. She'd lost sight of the boundaries – or perhaps she'd never had them in the first place? Perhaps she too, like him, wanted his family as her own.

He remembered again his first sighting of her – her indignation by the porter's bike, overloaded and overwhelmed. At first glance, he'd only been able to see her legs, arms and topknot, her angry, pretty face angled around a box of beer. But then, by the maypole, when she'd been laughing and dancing with her friends, she'd seemed to him to be the very embodiment of what it was to be young and free and alive, so different to the girl who'd ended up sitting on her own by the water later that night . . .

The memories ran unbidden then, unspooling quickly like a dropped reel . . . her long hair down and spread beneath him, the midnight sun on her skin, the light in her eyes as . . .

He caught his breath as she turned, just inches away, looking up at him . . . with contempt. 'Don't mention a word of this to him. I'll deal with it,' she hissed, and without another word she stepped around him, following Linus at a distance, making sure he was safe and that he thought his secret – his lifeline – was still his.

Emil watched her go, feeling the despair seep through him like an ink stain. When he had heard her on the stairs and seen her flying down the lawn, his own feet had instinctively moved too. Not because he feared his son was leaving in the dead of the night – but because he feared she was.

Bell slipped on her bikini and lathered on the suncream, as she did every morning. The days had begun to acquire a rhythm now that the hoarfrost had thawed between father and son. Linus's excitement at discovering the hotel conference room transformed into a private cinema – with leather sofas brought in, balloons, buckets of popcorn and, of course, his idols on screen five weeks before the 'entire rest of the world' got to see them – had changed the prism through which he saw the man who claimed to be his father. Linus no longer saw the wounded beast hauling himself back from a seven-year-long brain injury. He had forgiven him the abrupt entrance into his world, and then the no-show when they stood at his door. He had brought the Avengers to a tiny island in the Baltic, leapfrogging premieres and celebrities and studio heads. Now he knew two things: his father was rich. His father was powerful.

Bell knew it too, watching with silent apprehension as she saw Linus's excitement begin to grow each day for their next 'adventure'. It had used to mean 'snorkelling safaris' in new coves, or gathering the mackerel nets at sunset, but now they were going on jetbikes, swimming with Seabobs, having McDonald's flown over from the city as a treat. They had only been here a week, but so much had changed already.

Partly it was down to her and Emil keeping a wary distance from one another. Their showdown in the dining room and then the middle-of-the-night confrontation by the beach had burned them both. *Midsommar*'s night now belonged to another lifetime, other people even, and they had settled into an uneasy truce as co-workers on a project. He didn't try to elbow her out of plans or winkle his son away without her permission; and she was stepping back to allow father and son to interact more naturally, without running interference or acting as a referee.

Emil was spoiling Linus, she could see, but her job was only to make sure the boy was happy and protected and felt safe – it wasn't her job to teach Emil how to parent. He was entitled to be the father he wanted to be, and Linus certainly wasn't complaining. They were becoming relaxed in each other's company, and although Linus's twilight visits to the jetty continued unbroken – Bell always setting her alarm and following at a safe distance now – he had been happy to do an early breakfast run over to Sandhamn for the papers with Emil yesterday, without her.

By all accounts, today was going to be a big day. Emil had promised Linus an 'extra special surprise', but Bell didn't feel excited; she had woken with a gnawing feeling in the pit of her stomach that she couldn't explain. There was something in the air, something was off – a nervous energy, a delicate tension that felt at breaking point. Things were happening so quickly with all these perpetual adventures, Emil's desperate need for every moment to be perfect . . . It made her feel as though something *had* to fall apart.

She and Linus took breakfast on their own, texting Hanna in between courses. Måns informed them in his mellifluous voice that Emil had already left to make the final preparations, and would they please meet him by the jetty? They tried to guess what extraordinary plans Emil might have for them today. Cave diving? Swimming with dolphins? Hover jetpacks?

'I hope it's kiteboarding,' Linus said as they strode down the lawn together, ducking into the trees and meandering along the pebbly path, their hands trailing along the slender tree trunks. 'Think about it – I'm an expert skateboarder, *and* it's going to be windy today. It's got to be kiteboarding.'

'God, I hope not,' she muttered. Though it would explain her jitters.

They reached the island's edge and saw Emil sitting at the edge of the jetty, silhouetted like a Huckleberry Finn figure, his back propped against an upright as he waited for them. He was perfectly positioned to see Linus's mouth drop fully open as they stepped from the trees and onto the pine-dropped beach. Bell stopped in her tracks too as she caught her first sight of the black-sailed trimaran, motionless on the mid-morning water.

She knew enough about boats to know it was state-of-the-art, world-class, America's Cup-worthy: 220ft wing sail, shrink-wrapped Clysar skin, carbon-fibre hull . . . 'Holy shit,' she whispered, forgetting her prime rule of never swearing in front of the children.

'Holy shit,' Linus echoed, taking full advantage of the moment.

They walked slowly down the rattling gangplanks, unable to tear their eyes off the boat. It was transfixing: sleek, powerful, a billionaire's plaything.

'Is that really yours?' Linus whispered as they reached Emil, both of them able to see from here the black-clad crew running through final checks on board, scrambling up and down the masts, racing over the webbing like it was a bouncy castle.

'Well, look closer. Do you see what I called her?' He pointed to the grand red lettering along the hull: *Linea*.

Linus gasped.

'I had to use the feminized version of your name, obviously. I hope that's okay? Boats don't have boy names.'

Linus stared at Emil, then at the boat, then at Emil again – throwing his arms around Emil's neck so suddenly that his father almost lost his balance and they both would have gone flying off the jetty.

Bell's own hands flew to her mouth as she saw Linus bury his face into his father's neck, tears flowing down his father's face. It was their first touch beyond a handshake and she knew it was more than a hug – it was a wall coming down, a breakthrough, the first step in their new relationship.

'I'm so pleased you like it,' Emil said, his voice choked, his face partially obscured as ever by his cap.

'I love it!'

'I love you, Linus.' A gasp of shock followed as the words escaped before he could stop them, blood rushing behind a dislodged clot. Was it too soon?

Bell saw Linus looked shocked too for a moment, his little body instinctively stiffening as he pulled away. But then he forced a bright smile again. 'I can't believe you bought me a boat!'

What? No –

Bell automatically stepped forward, catching sight of Emil's expression too. He was taken off guard, his tears suddenly staunched, his mouth shaping soundless words.

'Well,' he faltered, seeing her horror, then recovering himself. 'I wanted to show you just how much you mean to me – so that meant it had to be something *big*.'

'I love sailing!' Linus cried, jumping up and down at the sight of the machine.

Emil laughed. 'You get that from me. As soon as I was able to, once I got out of the hospital, I came out here just so I could be on the water every day. And then I waited and waited and waited for you. It's the thing that made me better – the thought of sharing this with you.'

'Are we going to go out on it?'

'Of course we are. The crew's got everything ready for you. The conditions are perfect. How fast do you want to go?'

'*Really* fast!' Linus shouted, almost overcome with excitement, and Bell instinctively stepped forward again and placed a hand on his shoulder, a silent command to settle down.

Emil looked down at her hand accusingly. She removed it again. She was interfering. In the way.

'Well, you'd better hop in the dinghy then, and we'll go out to her. She can't get in here, the water's too shallow.'

'Me first!' And Linus clambered down the small ladder at the side and hopped easily into the boat.

Emil turned back to face her, blocking her path. 'You look unhappy.' He stared at her levelly, confrontational. 'Is there a problem?'

She glanced down at Linus to check he wasn't listening. 'You can't just *give* him a boat,' she said in a low voice.

'I haven't. It's entirely notional. If he wants to believe it's his, that's fine. Where's the harm?'

She stared back at him, unable to find the words – few enough to make her point, low enough to remain out of earshot. 'Fine,' she sighed, conceding defeat on this. Linus couldn't see them at odds with one another. He was putting his trust in them both; it was only fair for him to believe they were doing the same. 'Whatever you say. He's your son.'

Emil smiled at the comment, looking down lovingly at the excitable boy in the boat. 'Yes. Yes, he is.'

Chapter Twenty

Not here, she told herself. *Not here.*

But as she sat clipped to the railings with her head tipped back, her hair streaming, screaming with exhilaration, the tears flowed uncontrollably. It was all too beautiful, too perfect, too pure. She had made herself forget this feeling, spent four years suppressing the residual sensation of skating over the surface of the world, but now with the briny spray against her face and the wind tangling her hair into little whipsnakes once more, she was straight back there – in time. With him. In another life . . .

'Are you crying?' Linus asked, his hand warm on her arm.

She looked down at him, the wind whipping away her tears. 'No, it's just the wind,' she fibbed, pushing down her heartache with a bright smile, knowing just how much Jack would have loved this moment. This had been their life together – well, not *this* rarefied echelon, clearly, but the world gliding beneath their feet as they rigged the sail and set the boom. This was what he had lived for. But the truth was brutal and simple and unavoidable – he wasn't here, and he never would be again. He was gone.

She made herself say it in her head. *He's gone . . .*

She saw Emil, clipped to Linus's other side, watching her as though he detected the lie, and she looked away with a defiant chin-thrust to the air, her eyes closed, willing the past to leave her alone.

'Hold on!' Mats, the skipper, suddenly yelled as the boat turned, catching the wind, and in an instant they were aloft, up on the hydrofoils, a metre above the waves. She screamed with shocked delight as she looked down to find they were slicing across the water's surface as if on a blade. Linus met her widened eyes, screaming and laughing too like they were on a rollercoaster, then looking over at Emil, who was the same, all of them caught in a shared bubble of euphoria. She had never seen him laugh before, she realized, and it changed him completely, lifting away the grim mask of endurance that he so often wore.

She had never experienced anything like it as the boat sliced along, ever faster, the crew slick and professional, oblivious to the spray that soused them as they worked. They looked almost menacing in their all-black *Linea* kit, working together intuitively. There was no doubt this boat was an eye-wateringly expensive piece of kit, an international player on the professional scene – and a mere toy for a family like his.

She still harboured strong doubts about the ethics of allowing a ten-year-old to believe he owned a multimillion-kroner boat, but she couldn't deny this was fast shaping into a perfect day. The forecast storms were still nowhere to be seen, but the vanguard winds were playing to their advantage as the crew skilfully manoeuvred the super-vessel into catching it, billowing out the sails and skimming them for miles across the glassy ocean's surface. They went so fast and so far, she half expected to see the coast of Finland.

Watching the crew in action was a masterclass in elite sailing, the men running full-pelt from one side to the other trying to catch the wind, winching in and out the sails from the grinding stations, leaping across the nets. They were both athletes and commandos, all being dunked repeatedly in the bracing water, the sea breaking over them with relentless force as the boat carved too sharply and deeply on some of the turns; without being clipped on, they would have been overboard, no question.

'Keeping the platform stable on this boat is more complex than flying a helicopter,' Emil shouted over the wind to Linus. 'How many knots?' he yelled over to Mats.

'Fifty-two!'

Bell's mouth opened. That couldn't be right, could it? Could a sailing boat do those speeds? It would be fast for a speedboat!

'Remember there's a child on board!' she hollered, unable to stop herself, her nerves getting the better of her again. Was this what it was going to be? An accident with Linus on board?

Mats turned back and winked at her. He was a stocky Australian, with a butter-blonde beard and hair tied back in a ponytail, the skin on his broad, planed face pleating thinly as he grinned. He probably wasn't that much older than her, but life on the ocean didn't just weather boats. 'Don't worry,' he grinned. 'I've got you.'

It was true, he did make it look easy as he handled the boat with instinctive skill. He was both powerful and light on his feet, issuing orders, hauling the giant helm, making tactical decisions . . . She didn't notice the minutes clip by. There was too much to watch, always the expectation and then the thrill when the men got the boat exactly where they wanted her and she flew along on her rails again, making them all scream with delight. But eventually, Mats turned to

Emil with an enquiring glance and, at his nod, the crew began winding in the sails, the boat dropping back into the water again, it's speed falling from a sprint to a crawl, and eventually a stop.

It was like coming off a rollercoaster, all of them panting and beaten about by the wind. They bobbed on the water, no land in sight, just deep blue above and below.

'Oh my God, that was incredible!' she sighed happily as the crew unloaded the lunches and they were able to unclip themselves and stretch their legs.

'My butt's gone numb,' Linus cried, seeming somewhat delighted by it.

'Yeah, mine too,' Emil agreed, copying his son in a strange glute-squeezing dance clearly intended to improve blood flow. Bell grinned, amused as she watched them both. There was a physical echo between them as they jiggled about, trying to outdo each other with their silliness. She thought they probably didn't see that they had the same walk, or that they both tipped their heads to the side, just a little, when listening, or that they pulsed their index fingers and thumbs together as an impatient tic.

'Not the most deluxe lunch you'll ever have,' Mats said, breaking her attention and handing her a baguette and bottle of water.

'Oh, thanks.'

'But weight's crucial to performance, so we can only bring a minimal load on board.'

'Especially when you've got three bodies sitting as dead weights behind the helm,' she said self-deprecatingly.

'Emil's the boss. He's no dead weight,' Mats laughed, as the man himself wandered over.

Linus – having watched the crew running back and forth

over the trampolines all morning – followed suit, running with a bandy-legged gait between the cross-members like he was in a soft play centre.

'Did we bring the, uh . . . ?'

'Yeah, sure,' Mats said, reaching down and pulling out a magnum of Bollinger. Chilled.

'Hey, Linus –' Emil took it from him and shook it up, letting the cork pop in a perfect arc through the air, plumes of champagne streaming out so that Linus was running through mists of effervescence, arms outstretched to the sky. Bell sighed. Any hopes of preventing him from becoming overexcited were well and truly dashed for the day.

'So a bottle of champagne isn't considered a detriment to the weight–drag performance ratio, then?' she asked, as Mats presented a couple of plastic wine glasses too.

'Of course not. The bubbles keep it light,' Mats quipped as Emil poured.

Bell laughed.

'Do the guys want some too?' Emil asked Mats.

Mats looked back at his team, their lifejackets off now that the boat wasn't moving, all of them tucking in ravenously to their lunch. 'Best not. They'll need clear heads in case we meet those storms later.'

Bell looked at the huge bottle. Surely she and Emil weren't expected to drink all that on their own?

'They're not due till evening, I thought,' Emil said.

'Nope. But that wind's gustier than I'd expected at this point,' Mats said, thoughtfully casting his gaze over the horizon. It was still bright, but the distinct, sharp seam between sea and air had become blurred, atmospheric conditions beginning to change. 'I'll buy them all a beer back at base.'

'Well, buy them from me,' Emil said. 'Put it on the account.

You've all worked hard for us this morning. We appreciate it, don't we, Linus?'

'Huh?' Linus called, still playing on the nets.

'Thanks, boss,' Mats said, echoed by a broken rumble of appreciative voices from the men behind. 'That's very generous.'

'You must be exhausted,' Bell said as Mats began to eat, tearing at his baguette like a lion devouring an antelope.

'All in a day's work,' he shrugged.

'You didn't stop.'

'Can't afford to. In a twenty-minute competition, I can make up to 1,100 adjustments to the foils and rudders.' He smiled at the shocked expression on her face. 'Did I hear that you're a sailor?'

She was further taken aback. 'I don't know, did you?'

His eyes slid over questioningly to a wide-eyed Linus, who was dangling from the boom. 'Hmm.'

She gave a small groan and smiled. 'I was, once. A lifetime ago.'

'Ah, you know what they say – once a sailor, always a sailor.'

'Well, I never did anything at this level. The speeds you can reach, the tech you've got . . . it's an entirely different beast to what I knew.'

'Different, but still the same,' he shrugged. 'You don't miss it?'

She froze, not wanting to think about how much she missed it. Missed him. A silence stretched, but she didn't notice.

'Bell had been sailing the world with her fiancé, but then he died,' Emil said bluntly, stepping in for her.

Mats' expression changed from curiosity to shock. 'Oh jeez, I'm sorry, I had no idea!'

'Well, of course not. Don't worry, it's fine,' she said in a wobbly voice, forcing a smile as she glanced angrily at Emil, drinking his champagne like nothing had passed. She knew he hadn't intended to be cruel, but he had delivered the statement so clinically – just facts, no emotion. No filter.

'Can I . . . ask what happened?' Mats enquired, his face a picture of concern.

She looked back at him. 'Cancer. Pancreatic.'

His face fell. 'Oh God. That's the worst. My best mate's brother was diagnosed three weeks after the birth of his daughter; the poor bugger died nine months later. By the time they found it, it had spread too far . . .' He shrugged hopelessly.

'That was the same with Jack. He died within four months.'

'No symptoms either?'

She hesitated, feeling the pinch of blame in the words she must say. '. . . Actually, there were some. But he ignored them. We both did.'

Her face must have registered some of her all-consuming guilt because Mats leaned forward. 'Hey, don't do that. Don't make it your fault. I know what it's like when you're on open water, normal life seems so . . . improbable. You're out there, free, seeing the world, and life feels beautiful and limitless; but it can also be really hard and distracting on the waves; there's no mercy out there. Things get missed or put off. And what the hell can you do in the middle of the Pacific anyway, you know?'

She nodded; she would never forgive herself but she could hear the kindness in his message, the empathy. Something his boss was incapable of. 'He was only twenty-four. I think we both just thought he was too young and fit to be that sick.'

The pity spread across Mats' face. 'Where were you when he was diagnosed?'

'Here. Sweden. We'd been sailing the Barents, intending to get over to the Caribbean for the winter months. We stopped at Malmö for a few days to stock up; there were these sweets he always liked that you couldn't get anywhere else.' She gave a small smile at the memory before it faded again, rubbed out by a harsher one. 'He collapsed in the street. They took him in to hospital and he never left again.'

'Jesus,' Mats murmured, reaching over and squeezing her arm warmly. 'I'm really sorry. That's rough.'

'Yeah.' She realized her sandwich was sitting, untouched, in her hand. She forced herself to take a bite, but it was like chewing cardboard.

'So that's why you're here, then? In Sweden?'

'Basically. I couldn't physically have sailed the boat alone, even if I'd wanted to, and I definitely didn't want to sail with anyone else.' She shrugged. 'Besides, I was in shock for a long time; it had all happened so fast. I sold the boat and bought an apartment in Stockholm with the money and spent a year just staring at the walls. I didn't work, didn't go out, barely ate . . .' She sighed. 'Until one day, it was raining, absolutely pouring, and I decided to go for a walk. It was the first time I'd been outside in weeks.'

'You wanted to walk – in the pouring rain?' Emil asked.

'Exactly! Those are the best walks!' she said, seeing his scepticism. 'It woke something in me, that feeling of the rain on my face.'

'It reminded you that *you* were still alive,' Mats said, getting it.

'Yeah, exactly. So I began walking every day, even when it was sunny.'

He chuckled at her contrariness. Emil looked confused.

'Then I advertised for a roommate and got Kris, who's become my best friend; he's the brother I never had.' She glanced at Emil. Did he remember the name, the handsome face? Did he care? 'He introduced me to his friends, and I started hanging out with them all. And one day I looked around me and realized I'd put down roots, and my life was in Sweden, and that was that.'

'What about your family back home?'

'There isn't one. I was an only child and my father was much older – his marriage to my mum was his second; he died when I was thirteen and my mother died six years later.'

Emil was staring at her. 'When you were nineteen.'

Good maths, she wanted to quip, but she bit her tongue. 'Yes.'

'That's why you flunked your exams and didn't go to uni.'

She swallowed. Tact really wasn't his thing. '. . . Yes.'

'So you went sailing round the world instead.' It was as though he was putting together a picture in his mind, arranging her life story to a sense of order. Good luck with that . . .

'There's no greater escape,' Mats said, nodding. 'I reckon I'd have done the same.'

Bell smiled at him, grateful for the affinity, and he winked back.

'So then, the question is – we know how you got to Sweden, but how exactly did you end up here, on a shabby boat like this with us reprobates?' Mats joked. Still, he shot an enquiring glance in the direction of his boss in case he took umbrage at either 'shabby' or 'reprobates'. Emil's sense of humour could be unpredictable – it didn't always show up.

'I met Hanna in a cafe one day after my walk. The twins were babies and she was struggling to feed them *and* keep this chicken amused,' she said, ruffling Linus's hair lovingly. He had finally finished with his exertions and was sitting beside her, picking the filling out of his baguette. 'So I offered to help and the next thing I knew, I had a job.'

She saw Emil had stopped eating, his baguette barely touched in his hands, listening to the story of how she came to be here – on his boat, in his family's life – the conversation an echo of the one they'd had that night on the little boat about Destiny. 'Funny, isn't it, how you end up in places? Never in a million years would I have predicted *this*.' She motioned to their simple champagne lunch, the sleek carbon hulk of the vessel.

'Tell me about it,' Mats said. 'I'm the proverbial wanderer. I don't do more than a season anywhere.'

'No? Where's next for you?'

'New Zealand. I'm part of the team for the America's Cup next Spring.'

'Oh wow! That's incredible.'

'Yep. Living the dream. I'm leaving in a few weeks, actually. Sailing myself down to Auckland to start getting things in order.' He looked at her. 'Are you going to stay in Sweden, do you reckon?'

Bell patted Linus on the head. 'Well, certainly until this one becomes a teenager and refuses to sit on the naughty step any more,' she joked. At least, she had intended it as such, but the words tapped a wellspring of deep emotion she hadn't known was there. Talking about this wasn't in the least bit funny.

'And when you've outlived your usefulness? Go travelling again?'

'Yeah, maybe,' she shrugged lackadaisically, trying not to acknowledge the sense of panic that idea stoked in her. The thought of leaving her life here – her friends, her little apartment, the Mogerts, Linus especially . . . He blinked back at her, his green eyes deep and soulful, so like his father's.

It was impossible to imagine it, not having him or any of them in her life any more. It was true, she hadn't envisaged this version she was living without Jack; but she had found perfect strangers and moulded them into a family of her own. They were all she had. They were all she was. They were her life now.

She looked over at Emil, seeing his sense of separateness like a cloak upon his shoulders. She got it, suddenly. She understood why he was so intent upon getting his family back, and why he couldn't move on; his dogged refusal to let Hanna go or to concede defeat to Max. It wasn't down to ego or will or a rich man's spoiled whim. It was simple. Without them, the man who had everything, had nothing.

'Okay, is it clear?' she yelled down.

Emil looked back at her. 'We're in three-hundred-metre depth! What do you think could possibly be in your way?'

The crew laughed, whether from obedience or genuine amusement she wasn't sure.

She cringed. 'A whale?'

They all laughed harder, even Emil. 'It's fine.'

'Okay then, I'm ready,' she said, facing the horizon, her gaze high, arms by her sides.

'Wait! This better not just be *a dive*. You said this was going to be good!' Mats hollered. 'Unless you're going to do a penguin dive?'

'Oi!' she grinned. 'Just you wait. And don't give *him* here ideas!' She winked down at Linus, standing behind her, then took a deep breath. 'Right, count me in.'

'Three – two – one!' they all cried, and she walked forward two steps, raised her arms up and leapt . . .

The men were cheering when she surfaced a moment later.

263

'A reverse pike?' Emil asked, looking shocked as she swam over to him, away from the diving point.

'Agh, I was a fraction out on the entry. But you know, it's been four years, so . . .'

'Where did you learn to do that?'

'I lived on a boat for three years. Getting into the water elaborately becomes a *vital* source of amusement, believe me.'

They were treading water, his eyes looking particularly startling against his tan and slicked-back hair and she realized it was a good thing he wore his shades so much. He might have dismissed their night together, but she hadn't. Couldn't. 'Well, I guess you really have raised the stakes,' he said, looking impressed.

'My turn!' Linus hollered, and they turned to see him standing on the edge of the boat.

'What are you going to do?' she called up.

'The penguin!'

'No!' she said quickly. 'It's too high from there, you'll hurt your head!' But she was too late. With his arms pinned to his sides, he dived in head first. 'Linus!' she chided, as he surfaced seconds later with a triumphant look. 'You could have hurt yourself!'

'But I didn't!'

'But you could have done.' Her nerves were frayed again. One moment dormant, the next tingling.

'But I *didn't*. I'm okay.'

'You did a great job, bud,' Emil said, interrupting them, playing good cop again, overruling her. 'Right, my turn. You can decide what I do this time.' He turned away and swam over to the boat, hauling himself onto the ladder, muscles taut as he heaved himself out of the water.

'Do the penguin!' Linus cried. 'See if you can do it as good as me.'

'Okay then.' Emil walked across to their diving-off point.

'. . . Is that a good idea?' she called, as he positioned himself at the edge, peering down into the endless blue.

He gave her a quizzical glance. '*I'm* not ten.'

The crew, sprawled on the nets, chuckled. They were resting, some of them napping, before the inevitable exertions of the journey home.

'No, but – I mean . . .' She didn't want to say it out loud, to make a big thing of it in front of the other men. 'You don't want to get a headache.'

'I've already got a headache. I *always* have a headache.'

For some reason, this prompted another laugh, and before she could protest further he sprang forward, his body like a blade. It was a good dive, and he popped up seconds later to cheers, but she thought she saw the minute tightening of the muscles across his face.

'Let's do it together!' Linus cried, fast crawling back to the boat.

'Okay, sure.'

'Do you think that's a good idea?' she asked again, quietly, as he went to swim past.

'Bell, what are you, the fun police? I'm having fun with my son. Could you let it be?'

'I'm just worried –'

'Well, don't be. I'm not your concern.' He blinked at her, droplets on his face.

'All right. Whatever,' she mumbled, kicking away and watching as he swam to catch up with his son. He was right. She was overreacting to everything, as jumpy as a cat.

She watched as they went again and again, trying different

combinations of dives and jumps – screwdrivers, penguins, backward dives, bombs, side dives, tucks, pikes, bellyflops . . . She knew the impacts were making Emil's head ring, she could see it on his face every time he surfaced, in that split second as he gasped for air before he could ready a smile. But he was right. She wasn't his keeper. He was a grown man who could manage the risks to himself, a father going to any lengths to bond with his son.

It was working, too. She saw it in the way Linus maintained eye contact as he talked now, his laugh was readier, he was *hungrier*; crucially, he was getting a bit cheekier as he became more relaxed.

'Bell!' They were both looking at her. 'Jump with us.'

'Really?' she asked sceptically. She'd been treading water for ages and was a little chilled, her skin wrinkling quickly. But she swam over and climbed out. 'So what are we doing?'

'You choose,' Linus said. 'We can't think of any more.'

She thought for a moment. 'Well, I guess we could try the spinning top.'

'The what?' Emil frowned.

'I've only done it as a two before, but I'm sure it'll work as a three. We just need to make sure we jump out far enough. We jump in as a circle, but spinning.'

His frown deepened. 'Spinning?'

'It's important to hold on tight or it'll break up when we enter the water. So hold your arms out and clasp mine, at the elbow there –' She held hers out and felt his hand grip her upper forearm. 'Linus?' She looked across to join up on the other side, but she had only a split second to process his mischievous face as his hands shot forward and pushed both of them off the boat.

There wasn't even time to scream as she and Emil landed

side-on in the water, instantly surrounded by millions of tiny bubbles hissing and fizzing around them that cleared as quickly as they'd come. For a moment – just one – his face was all she could see in the deep blue sea, his sad eyes not hidden for once by the armour of his shades. Away from the crew's chatter and Linus's over-excitement and the billionaire boat, there was just peace and stillness as they looked at each other underwater. No distraction, no filters, no hiding.

The air in their lungs made them buoyant and they popped up to the surface, the real world coming back into full colour and sound.

'Linus!' she hollered, remembering her indignation. 'You are a cheeky monkey!'

The weather was fully on the turn. It was still bright and warm, but the wind had picked up and the clear skies had become heavier through the afternoon, the razor-line of the horizon now blurred into indistinction.

Mats didn't like the look of it and had ordered the crew to get ready to set sail again. Bell was sunbathing on a towel; she didn't need to tan, but it gave her an excuse to be out of the way – both of the crew, and Linus and Emil beside her, who were now deep in conversation. Or rather, Linus was machine-gunning Emil with question after question about the boat: 'What's a Code Zero spinnaker?'; 'Can it tip over?'; '*Has* it tipped over?'; 'Have any men gone overboard? Have any men been lost at sea?'; 'Have any drowned?'; 'Why aren't you skipper?'

Bell was listening with one ear open, and heard Emil stall at that last one.

'Can't you sail any more?' Linus pressed.

'I can sail, of course, but a craft like this is technical and highly physical.'

'So you're not strong enough?'

There was another pause. 'It's not just a question of strength, Linus.'

'What, then?'

'. . . Well, obviously I *could* do it.'

She heard the sound of footsteps.

'Your dad's right, little man,' said the Aussie voice. 'I know it might look easy, but trust me, this isn't for amateurs. This is an expensive boat. It can go four times faster than the wind. It's best to leave it to professionals, and you guys just clip on and enjoy the ride.'

There was a small silence and then Emil spoke. 'Well, *I* don't have to do that, clearly.'

Bell heard the silence and turned her head, seeing Mats frozen in a crouch in front of Linus, holding out his bespoke, all-black *Linea* life jacket. 'Well, no, I didn't mean you . . .' But his hesitation betrayed evident uncertainty.

'Will you skipper us home, then?' Linus asked him, green eyes shining with the wonderment that accompanied his new-found father's every move.

Bell felt her stomach tighten. Linus wasn't challenging his father; he was investing his hopes in him, which was worse. She sat up, her dread growing again.

Emil smiled tightly. '. . . Sure. Why not?'

Mats looked back at Bell for help – as though *she* had any influence over him! Several of the crew stopped what they were doing and looked up with sceptical expressions, low hisses as they whispered below their breath. But if Emil heard their doubts, it only served to make him more determined.

'Yes, that's a great idea, in fact,' he said, warming to the idea. 'Well done, Linus. Will you be my first mate?'

Linus gasped so deeply, Bell thought he was going to sneeze. 'Oh, can—?'

'No!' she said, so quickly, she was sitting up and positioning herself between the two of them, her hands automatically outstretched onto his shoulders and holding him firmly. Emil's gaze went to them as before, but this time she didn't remove them. 'No.'

A moment passed in which she thought he was going to berate her again, defy her in front of all these men, but then – either because he saw the madness of what he was suggesting, or he clocked the unwavering defiance in her eyes – he relented. 'On second thoughts, you're probably too light, bud; the wind's got up.'

They all looked up at the darkening sky. The clouds were gathering quickly, and she'd sailed through enough storms to know they wouldn't outpace this one. They had overstayed their time here. 'You'd best stay clipped by the rails with Bell. I don't know what your mother would do to me if I told her we'd lost you at sea. She's pretty scary when she gets mad.'

He winked and Linus laughed, and Bell could see he seemed to revel in the familial intimacy implied in such a scenario. His father and mother, together in a story; together in real life? Was this the first time such a thought had occurred to him? Even with the excitement and novelty that Emil had brought to his life, Bell knew he had still only ever seen Max as his father. Until now.

'Let's go,' Emil said, looking first at Mats and then casting pointed looks at the crew, who all nodded reluctantly at this management takeover.

The atmosphere was different on the way back: the dizzying joy that had accompanied their playful, boastful, 'faster, faster' sortie on the way out had become muted and tense. The crew seemed to be working twice as hard as they had on the outbound leg, and several times, Bell saw Emil shout an order that made them stop in their tracks and look at one another quizzically, before Mats would countermand it with either a tiny shake of his head or give another under his breath.

Emil didn't seem to notice, his gaze pinned to the horizon. He had planted his legs in a wide-legged stance, but as the swell grew, it became harder and harder for him to remain stable. He didn't have either Mats' strength or his balance. Linus was clipped in beside her and she threw urgent glances Mats' way, but he could only shrug, feeling as helpless as she did. Emil was the boss. This was his boat.

They cut a jagged path over the sea, turning erratically as Emil struggled with the power required to work against winds of this force. The men were repeatedly knocked off their feet, jumping up again and trying to undo mistakes; they were sailing upwind now, and Emil was just performing a gybe when the boom swung round with dangerous force and almost caught one of the men. He ducked, only just in time.

It was a near miss, but there was no time to count any blessings as another gust caught the sails violently. It was the kind Mats had been able to harness on the way out, lifting them onto the hydrofoils and out of the water – but they weren't yet out of the turn, and the sail was instead forced leewards, towards the water. Immediately, the far side of the boat began to lift.

They were going to capsize.

Bell screamed, hooking one arm around the rail and grabbing Linus with her other. They were clipped on – that was keeping them safe. But if the boat went over, they'd be tethered underwater. Not safe.

'Hike out!' Mats yelled and the crew raced, as one, across

the width of the boat. They were like marines on a commando course, powerful and hunched, hands and feet scrabbling over the nets before they clipped onto the rails in a seamless leaping movement and stretched their bodies at full lengths over the side of the boat, leaning out as counterbalances. Bell saw them strain as the sail's tip skimmed the very surface of the water on the opposite side. If it dipped below even for a second, the speed and torque would drive the sail deeper downwards and they would go over.

Linus screamed and she grabbed him as tightly as she could, the deck now like a wall below them, anything loose skittering over the surface and down into the churning water, as for several agonizing seconds, the boat glided on its side in a terrifying, perfectly held balance – the sail flat on the water, the men straining as they arched back as far as they possibly could.

And then, suddenly, it gave. The men won out and the boat crashed back down onto both keels, making Bell cry out again. She had known this was going to happen, something bad. She had felt it coming. But there was still no time for recriminations. The crew were instantly moving again, dispersing and grinding in the jib.

'Emil!' Mats hollered over the wind, racing over to Emil at the helm and gripping the column as he tried to balance. Standing in the middle of the boat like this, he was unclipped and vulnerable. 'Let me take over, man. That was too close. This swell is pretty big now.'

But Emil stayed staring at the horizon, making no move that he had heard.

'Emil? Did you hear me? Let me take over! I can take it from here!'

Emil glanced at him. 'No!'

Mats looked aghast. 'Look, man, fire me when we get back if you want, but this is a technical ride –'

'I said no! I told my son I would skipper us back, and that's what I'm going to do!'

'Dude, it's *because* of your son I'm taking over! He's ten, for chrissakes! Look at him!'

Emil turned around, taking in the expression on Linus's face. The wonderment and awe of even twenty minutes earlier had gone, and he was now rigid with terror.

Emil's face went slack, his hands lifting off the helm. 'Linus!'

Mats moved fast, stepping in and clipping himself on. 'Go and sit down!' he yelled, before his eyes widened so that they were more white than brown. 'Look out!'

He grabbed Emil's lifejacket, trying to pull him down as he lunged for the floor, but Emil saw nothing but his son's terror. He didn't see the boom coming, and it caught him above the left ear. He crumpled like an autumn leaf.

'Emil!' Bell screamed, scrabbling on her hands and knees to try to reach him as Mats staggered up again and got a hand to the wheel. He was standing in a wide straddle above Emil's limp body as he struggled to gain control of the boat. The wind tossed them both about like they were paper bags.

'Have you got him?' Mats yelled, checking she had a hand on Emil's lifejacket before he freed his harness from the steering column. Linus was crying now. Bell tried to drag Emil towards her, out of Mats' way, but he was out cold and a dead weight. He was unsecured to the boat except by her left hand. One large wave would be enough to wrench him from her grip, free-falling in the boat, overboard . . . She looked up desperately. The crew were leaping across the nets again, in full defence mode as the swell grew. There was no one to help.

'Look out!' Mats yelled, and she tightened her grip as hard

as she could while a large wave rocked them, the forward
momentum pitching the boat – and Emil – forward. She
strained to hold on to him, giving a cry as his full body weight
was held in place by her one hand – then, in the next instant,
the wave passed and the boat rocked back, sliding him straight
towards her, limp and inert.

'Oh my God!' she gasped, immediately clipping him to
their rails and stretching out her legs so that she could lay
his head in her lap, to protect him from any further impacts.
She checked him for signs of injury. He wasn't bleeding, that
she could see. No open wounds. But he was unconscious
again, from a head injury. *Oh God. Oh God.*

Linus was sobbing.

'Emil, can you hear me?' She shook his shoulders. 'Emil?
Wake up. You've *got* to wake up. You hear me? Linus is here.
You son needs you.' She looked across at him. 'Linus, talk to
him. Let him hear your voice. He needs to hear your voice.'

Linus stared down at the unconscious man. 'Em–' He
stopped. 'Dad? Can you hear me?'

Emil groaned, his eyes flickering.

Linus gasped. It had worked? He was coming round? 'Dad!'

'Emil?' Bell asked. He looked up at her, clearly stunned.
'What's my name, Emil? Tell me my name.'

He hesitated, seconds ticking past as nothing came. Then:
'. . . Ding-dong.'

It wasn't supposed to be a joke, clearly, but a laugh escaped
her anyway, the relief tangible. 'Yes, that's right. Ding-dong
Bell.' What he'd called her that first night together. He remembered that?

Linus was gripping her arm, and she looked into his frightened eyes. 'Is he going to be okay?'

'Yes, he's going to be okay. It's probably just a concussion.'

'But –'

She knew what he couldn't say – that this had to be worse than that. He'd only just emerged from a seven-year coma; he couldn't sustain another traumatic head injury without devastating consequences, surely?

'I know, but he'll be okay,' she lied; she knew nothing of the sort. 'He's only just got you back, Linus. He won't leave you now.' She looked at Mats' back, seeing the strain in his shoulders as he struggled against the wind. It was beginning to rain now, the deck becoming slippery. 'How long?' she called over to him.

Mats turned, seeing the patient dazed on the ground. He shrugged, helpless to do more. 'An hour?'

An hour before he could see a doctor. She looked down at Emil – his head in her lap, staring back at her with a bewildered blankness – and tried to smile.

Chapter Twenty-One

The helicopter had well and truly destroyed what remained of the flowerbeds, the gardener given no time again to deploy his defensive measures. Bell watched as he went round the garden, muttering to himself while he stooped to stake the heavier-headed blooms, sweeping up the petals bellowing around like confetti. She thought it looked rather pretty.

She turned away from the window and back into the hall, her eyes returning to the closed bedroom door. They had been in there for at least forty minutes now. What could be taking so long?

She sank into the beige gingham settle and pulled the towel closer round her shoulders. She kept shivering, the chill having set into her bones. She knew she should run to her room and get out of these wet clothes – and yet she couldn't leave, not even for a minute, in case they came out with word on how he was doing.

Linus was in his bedroom at the far end of the corridor. His door was open, and she could see his legs as he lay on the bed, the little red Corvette car beside him. Poor child; he had fallen into an exhausted sleep, the rough journey back depleting him on top of the afternoon's emotional stresses. She didn't think she would ever forget the look on his face as Emil had been carried off the boat – limp and helpless again, everything he'd been trying to prove he wasn't – and taken to shore in the dinghy, where the paramedics were waiting with a stretcher. Mats had managed to get a call through to the coast guard, who had contacted Måns, who in turn had contacted Doctor Sorensen and arranged for the helicopter to bring her straight here to assess him.

She heard footsteps coming up the stairs, and turned to see Mats. 'Hey,' he said with a nod. 'No news?'

'Not yet. I'm still waiting. They've been in there for ages now.'

He came and sat beside her, his weight pushing her cushion upwards slightly.

She looked at him curiously. 'I didn't expect to see you here. I thought you were taking the boat back to Stockholm?'

'I was going to, but the crew are dealing with it. We've just gone through a debrief and they're heading back now. I thought I should stay here and check everything's okay.'

She sighed. 'I wish someone would just tell us something, at least. This waiting around is agony.'

'Yeah.' He glanced at her. 'Listen, Bell, I'll get fired for this, no question. I take full responsibility for what happened. But I just want you to know I'm so sorry.'

She looked at him in confusion. 'Why will *you* be fired? It wasn't your fault.'

'Of course it was. I'm the skipper. I should never have let him take the helm. And I should have been checking the conditions more closely. I just allowed myself to have a nice afternoon, instead of –'

The bedroom door opened, and she instinctively stood up as Måns stepped through. Bell felt her heart lurch at his expression. *Oh God.*

'He would like to see the boy,' Måns said gravely. 'I'll just go and g—' But Linus was already sprinting barefoot down the corridor. Bell wasn't the only one who could sleep with one ear open, it seemed.

'Is he going to be okay?' he panted.

'Your father wishes to see you, young man.' Måns glanced at her, and Mats too. 'You are welcome to come in.'

Glancing at one another, Bell and Mats filed in after Linus. Emil was lying on a bed and looking almost . . . robotic: tens of wires were attached to his head, a chin strap around his jaw.

Linus froze.

'It's okay, Linus,' Doctor Sorensen said, seeing his fear. 'I know it looks alarming, but I've just been performing an EEG – it measures brain waves, shows us electrical activity in the brain. And I'm very glad to tell you, your father's is showing as normal.'

'It is?' Linus murmured, looking unconvinced.

'I'm fine,' Emil said, holding out a hand towards him, though his voice was slightly slurred still. Linus walked towards the bed and obediently took his hand. 'Don't worry, I'm okay.'

'We'll need to run an MRI in the next few days just to be absolutely sure, but all the signs are that this is a concussion, nothing more sinister than that.'

'Thank God,' Bell whispered, her hands to her lips. He looked so vulnerable lying in that bed, rigged up like the national grid. 'I thought . . . I mean, we all thought . . .'

'I know. And you did well to raise the alarm and get him back as quickly as you did.' She nodded her appreciation at Mats. 'Emil's been very lucky in this instance.' She looked back sternly at her patient. 'Although he had been warned that he couldn't take *any* sort of risks – no skiing, water-skiing, snowboarding, paragliding, parachuting, hockey, ice hockey.'

'You never said sailing,' Emil shrugged.

'Leisure sailing is fine, on the condition you wear a helmet. Race sailing, however? No. This sort of injury *cannot be repeated.*'

'Yes, doctor,' Emil sighed, but rolling his eyes behind her back and making a face at Linus, who gave a surprised laugh.

'He's going to need rigorous supervision,' Dr Sorensen said, turning to Bell and talking in a low voice – as though she was *his* nanny. 'I'm afraid he isn't taking the potential risks seriously. His physical recovery has been impressive to this point, and I fear he thinks he's indomitable now.'

'Okay. But –' Bell wanted to explain that she wasn't his carer.

Mats stepped towards the bed. 'It's good to see you looking okay, boss. You had us worried there for a moment.'

Emil looked at him. '. . . Thanks. And, look, I'm sorry.'

Mats shook his head. '*I'm* the one that got us into this mess, and if you're going to fire me, I completely understand –'

'I made it impossible for you,' Emil said slowly, sounding almost reasonable. 'Don't quit. You promised me this season.'

'Well, if you're sure . . .' Mats said, with a very relieved laugh. 'I don't know how you do it, mate, fighting back these knocks. Is there anything I can do to help?'

'You could help him by not letting him take these risks,' Dr Sorensen said, stepping in. 'Even a cat only has nine lives. I'd appreciate it if you would personally ensure he doesn't step foot back on that boat.'

Mats pulled a rueful face and held his hands up in surrender. 'I can certainly stop him taking the helm again, doctor, but stop him sailing at all? It'd take a stronger man than me.' Bell watched as he walked over and gave Emil a handshake, his loyalty still with the man who paid his salary.

Money talked; it always did. 'Anyway, look, I only stopped by to check you're okay. I'll pass the good news on to the crew, and we'll speak when you're back on your feet again, boss.'

Emil nodded.

'Uh, Bell –' Mats murmured, pausing as he passed. He was holding out a folded piece of paper.

'What's this?' she asked, taking it. But he simply winked at her and walked on.

She opened it, to find his phone number and a message. *'If ever you fancy a drink . . .'*

She turned back, but he'd already gone.

'What does it say?' Linus asked her nosily.

'Oh, it's just . . . I just asked him for . . .' she stammered, unable to immediately conjure a lie. 'The name of a dentist.'

'A dentist?' Linus squinted quizzically. 'Why'd you ask *him*?'

'Well, h-he's got nice teeth, hasn't he?'

'Pfft.' Linus looked back at her like she was crazy. She shrugged, not daring to look up, knowing Emil was staring at her too. She hoped, with his concussion, it would sound entirely plausible to him.

'*I* can recommend a good dentist if you need one,' Dr Sorensen quipped, a lively humour dancing in her eyes, and it was quite clear she wasn't buying the cover story.

Bell felt her cheeks flame, just as the sound of footsteps running down the corridor made them all turn. Mats, coming back?

'I came as quickly as I could! Is he okay?'

Bell blinked in surprise as Linus gave a yell of delight and tore across the room into his mother's arms. 'Mamma!'

Sandhamn, 23 June 2011

'Hey! Why aren't you celebrating? It's the longest day of the year,' he said, joining her on the deck. 'Our favourite day.'

She glanced behind her as he approached, but there was no smile this time to greet him. 'All the days are long,' she sighed, looking out to sea. 'And the nights.'

He watched her, pale hair blowing in the breeze, her gaze distant as it so often was these days. 'Hanna . . .' His hands on her shoulders, he turned her to him.

She looked back at him, her beautiful face pale in the dusk. They understood each other at a molecular level. It was instinctive, innate. There were never any lies between them, not when their eyes met. He pushed a wisp of hair back from her face, seeing the dark circles below her eyes, the hollow dip of her cheeks. 'You're exhausted.'

'Yeah, well, babies will do that to you,' she murmured, almost too tired to shape the words. 'I don't know why we should all be so surprised. It does say so on the box.'

He smiled. 'You need a decent night's sleep.'

'That's just about the one luxury we can't afford.'

'So get a nanny.'

She shook her head. 'No. He's my child. I'm his mother. I want to do it myself.' It wasn't up for discussion. She looked away again and back at the boats on the water, their lights spilling small pools.

He stared out into the night with her, hearing the parties go on without them. In truth, he hadn't felt like celebrating anyway.

'. . . Things are different now, aren't they?' she said quietly. 'Between us, I mean.'

He looked across at her and down again, feeling his heart thud heavily. He swallowed, knowing he couldn't show her . . . 'Perhaps it was to be expected. They say babies always change things.'

'It's been harder than I thought it would.' She fell quiet and when she spoke again, her voice was choked. 'The way everything happened . . . so fast . . . falling pregnant, getting married . . . There was hardly time to think –'

'I know,' he nodded. There had been a ferocious momentum to it all. One event triggering the next, making it hard for him to breathe.

She turned to face him. 'I could never regret him. Linus.'

'Of course not.'

'. . . But I can feel you slipping further and further away from me, and it makes me feel . . . it makes me feel that the world could end.'

He looked back at her, reaching out an arm and stroking her hair. 'You'll always have me, Hanna.'

'Do you promise?' she whispered.

'I promise. For richer or poorer. In sickness and in health.'

Hanna stood in the door frame, tanned, flushed and very beautiful in a soaked-through navy cotton sundress. She had crossed the lagoon in the storm to get here, her hair dripping puddles onto the floor. She hugged her son back, but her gaze was firmly fixed on her ex.

'Don't worry, Hanna,' Dr Sorensen said calmly, seeing her concern. She walked over to the bedside and began carefully removing the sensors attached to Emil's scalp. 'I was just running an EEG. It's a concussion.'

'But Cathy, for him –' She was in panic mode, her eyes darting every which way.

'I know – the potential complications are far more worrisome. We need to monitor him very carefully over the next few days.' She shot another stern look his way again. 'But I'm cautiously optimistic he's going to get away with this one.'

'Oh thank God,' Hanna gasped, seeming to fold in on herself, crouching down further over Linus and holding him even closer. Relaxing, finally.

Bell watched Emil observe the scene – his family gathered in one room, for him, frantic with worry – and she knew that whatever realities kept them apart now – Max, the twins – there was still love here.

She wondered briefly who had called Hanna – Måns? – and she felt bad that it hadn't even crossed her mind. After what Hanna had told her about their bitter last meeting, she had thought she'd be the last person who'd want to hear.

She watched as Linus tightened his arms around his mother's waist and she kissed the top of his head. 'I've missed you *so* much,' Hanna whispered into his hair, before returning her gaze to Emil again, silent on the bed.

Bell sensed a pause between them, as though they were gauging one another first. As though something was shifting. And then a silent agreement was understood.

Tenderly, Hanna extricated herself from her son's grasp, ruffling his hair softly. 'Let me go and say hello to your father.' She crossed the room, an expression on her face that Bell couldn't quite place. 'You're okay?' she asked, hesitating for a moment and then reaching for his hand.

Emil looked at it, and Bell saw him squeeze her fingers lightly. Hanna sank onto the edge of the bed, as though something strong had left her body.

'I'm fine. This fuss is embarrassing. Anyone else would be told to take some paracetamol and have a lie down.'

'Well, you're not just anyone,' Hanna chided softly, her eyes roaming over him looking for wounds as Bell's had, watching as Dr Sorensen removed the last of the sensors from his scalp and packed them into a case. Gently, Hanna reached forward and rearranged his hair, rustling it affectionately too, as she had just done for their son. 'There. Better.'

He stared back at her, immobile but for his eyes, which burned.

'You gave us all such a fright,' she said after a moment, staring from his hands to his face again. She sounded like she might cry, her voice choked.

His eyebrow cocked. '. . . Us?'

'Me. Linus.' Hanna pressed her lips together, as Bell knew she always did when worried about saying the wrong thing. 'We've only just got you back.'

His fingers squeezed hers again. 'And I've told you – I don't intend to leave either one of you again.' There was hidden weight, double meaning, in the words and Hanna dropped her gaze, nodding.

Bell frowned, confused by their apparent closeness. Hanna had told her Emil couldn't bear to look at her, that he had threatened to take her son from her, to drag her to court and the world's press; but sitting here, holding hands and whispering assurances to one another, they seemed far from sworn enemies.

Linus was watching them closely too, his face impassive but his gaze intense as he saw every look and gesture pass between his parents. They had the familiarity of old lovers, at ease physically, anticipating words, their body language a shared dance.

Dr Sorensen stepped back into the vignette. 'I'll leave you now, but I'll be calling in regularly for updates, and I'll come back on Monday afternoon to run some more tests.'

'That's fine,' Hanna nodded. Her tone implied she would be there, and it drew Emil's gaze again; he traced her face, as though committing her to memory.

Bell watched on until he glanced across at her suddenly, as though remembering her presence, and she quickly looked at the floor. An intruder, again.

'Good,' Dr Sorensen nodded. 'In the meantime, call me if there's any deterioration in his behaviour at all – vomiting, double vision, hallucination, sensitivity to light, seizures, sudden anger or change in mood, clear fluid coming from the nose or ears, abnormal eye movement –'

'What a catch I am,' Emil quipped, and Hanna laughed at the joke.

'You always knew it,' she replied, giving him a lingering gaze.

Bell was stunned. They were definitely flirting.

'I've already warned him he'll need to be woken up in the middle of the night.' Dr Sorensen had put her stern voice on again. 'It's very important you wake up, Emil.'

'You're telling me,' he drawled, looking over at Linus again and giving him a wink.

'I'll wake him,' Linus offered excitedly.

'You'll have a proper night's sleep, thank you,' Bell said quickly, the words out before she could stop them. She gave an awkward smile as his parents both looked at her.

'Goodbye for now, then,' the doctor said to the room. 'Emil. Everyone.' She cast a glance over Bell and Linus.

'I'll see you out,' Hanna said, the lady of the house again. 'I'll be right back,' she whispered to Emil.

Linus trotted out with them, barely half a step behind his mother – not wanting to let her out of his sight again – as she and the medic made their way down the hall, their footsteps and low conversation gradually fading into silence.

Bell looked back at Emil, feeling awkward. 'Well, I'll let you get some rest.'

'Bell –' She was at the door when he called.

She turned. 'Yes?'

'. . . Would you mind bringing some water over?' He pointed towards the carafe on a table by the window. 'My balance is off.'

'Sure.' She crossed the room, noticing it for the first time as she went. In all the worried activity, she had seen only people – only him – but now she saw that the walls were lined with old hessian paper panels, trompe l'oeils of gentle arches drawn on in dark-grey surrounds, the centre panels left white; the wooden bed was made up with vintage mono-grammed sheets and a duck-egg-blue blanket folded across the end. A vast mirror with mottled, foxed glass dominated one wall and twin lampshades with faded red shades sat on the bedside chests. It had a gracious, cultured feel to it but, like all the other rooms in the house, there was almost nothing personal in it – hardly any books, magazines, pictures – as though everything had been packed away. But there were photographs on the table with the water jug.

She couldn't help but glance at them as she poured. Several were of Linus as a baby; one showed Hanna in her wedding dress, classically beautiful and poised. She was wearing a minimal gown – sculptural satin column, bare arms – her hair twisted into a chignon, pearls at her throat, white roses in her hands . . . She seemed to be listening to someone talking just out of shot, her mouth parted in interest, the light catching on her eyes and making them sparkle. The largest photograph showed her and Emil running through a shower of confetti, Hanna pinching the skirt of her dress as she ran, her new groom holding her hand and gazing back at her, both of them laughing. Emil had looked bigger back then, more muscular, his hair worn shorter. He didn't look, in this image, like the man she knew, who seemed to choose his clothes on the basis of how close they were to collapse.

'Nine years ago next month,' he said, seeing her staring at them.

'They're beautiful. What a couple you –' She hesitated, not sure of which tense to use: were? Are? Were they a couple again? Was Hanna having secret meetings with her own husband? Was *that* why she'd taken off her eternity ring from her other partner? She was the woman who had two eternities to choose between?

'Best day of your life, was it?' she asked lightly, retreating to cliché.

'Just us, and a thousand of our closest friends.' He made a disapproving tut as she came over. 'No. I'd have been happy with the town hall, a bottle of champagne and a hotel room.'

'Said every male ever,' Bell murmured, handing him the glass.

'Thanks.' His fingers brushed hers as he took it from her and drank slowly. '. . . So, was it you who called her?'

'Hanna?' She shook her head, feeling guilty. 'I'm afraid not. I wasn't thinking that clearly. I wasn't thinking that far ahead.' She remembered the panic she had felt that he was gone too, the weight of his head in her lap the whole journey back, Mats and the crew working like devils to find the fastest way home; the way he'd stared up at her as they'd cut through the waves, the look on his face, unfiltered . . .

Concussed. She blinked it away. 'It must have been Måns.'

He shrugged. 'Or Cathy.' And when she frowned, he added, 'Dr Sorensen. She would have known Hanna's my next of kin. She was always the point of contact when I was in the hospital. Apparently.'

'Right. Well, either way, it's great she's here and can look after you for the next few days.'

'Mmm. Maybe I'll pretend to be sicker than I am.' A dark gleam came into his eyes. 'It's nice to see she cares.'

She looked away, not wanting to be his confidante. She couldn't pretend to be his friend. 'Of course she does.'

She felt his stare become more focused upon her. 'I suppose this means *you'll* be leaving, then. For a while, at least.' She looked back at him quizzically. 'Well, if Hanna's here to look after me and . . . chaperone Linus, you can escape this place at last.'

A residue of sarcasm traced the word 'chaperone', reminding her of their fight – that her very presence here offended him, that she was a necessary burden to tolerate whilst he rebuilt his relationship with his son.

'Yeah, I guess I can,' she said with a spark of defiance. 'Someone will have to look after the girls. Unless of course Max is over.'

She saw the anger flash through his eyes at the casual mention of Max's name, but she refused to look away. She was allowed to speak the truth, wasn't she? Max's existence couldn't be hidden or ignored, no matter what Emil might wish. If he was going to win his wife – his family – back, then he was going to have to go through Max first.

His eyes narrowed, the mood between them changing, becoming darker again. 'You like him.'

'You would too. He's a good man,' she shrugged. 'And a great father. He loves his kids.'

'And I don't?'

'I didn't say that.'

'But you don't think I'm a good father.'

'I didn't say that either.'

'But you think it.'

She sighed, taking the empty glass from him and turning away. 'I should go—'

He caught her by the wrist, and she felt how cold her skin was in comparison to his hand. She needed to get out of her wet clothes. She was shivering. 'I've seen it in your eyes. You disapprove of how I'm trying to win back my son.'

'It's not my place to disapprove. I'm just the nanny.'

'No you're not. You're not "just" anything, and we both know it. You're everywhere, all the time.' Bitterness and a hot anger spiked every word. Doctor Sorensen had warned that volatility was one of the signs of concussion, but this felt more than just that.

She swallowed, feeling a lump form in her throat at his continuing anger at her. She felt brow-beaten by it. 'I'm sorry that you feel I'm in your way, but I'm only trying to do my job,' she said in a quiet voice, trying not to agitate him further. Clearly this was no time for another of their disagreements. 'I care for Linus very much and want him to be happy.' She looked back at him with steady eyes, refusing to let them tear up. '. . . So could I have my wrist back, please?'

He looked at her wrist as if in surprise to find it in his grip, dropping it just as Hanna walked back in.

'How's the patient?'

Bell nodded, trying to compose herself, unsure of why she felt so upset. Simmering contempt seemed to be their new normal. 'All good here. He's just had some water.' She walked across the room and returned the empty glass to the carafe on the table.

'Great. It's important to keep hydrated.' Hanna pressed her hand to his forehead gently and Bell noticed – sure enough

– she wasn't wearing her aquamarine ring again, the shape of the band picked out by a bright tan line.

'Hanna, I was thinking . . .' Hanna sank onto the bed and turned to face her with a smile. 'If you're going to be staying here this weekend, should I . . . go back to Strommskar? Give you all some . . . family time alone?'

Emil's hand reached for Hanna's. 'Family time. Just us. That sounds good.'

Hanna smiled back at him, considering for a moment. 'Well, my mother's at the cabin this weekend,' she said obliquely, not saying, or having to say, that she was therefore babysitting the girls. Bell wondered where Max was, or if, in fact, he was there too, livid that his partner had been dragged over here for the weekend on account of another of her ex's medical emergencies. 'So listen, if you want to take the weekend off . . . ?'

Bell brightened instantly. 'Really?'

'Of course! Don't you agree, Emil? The poor girl needs a break. She's worked straight through since *Midsommar*.'

Emil stared back at her with an inscrutable stare. 'Absolutely. It's been awful for her being stuck here with us.'

If Hanna picked up on the sardonic tone in his voice, she made no sign of it.

'Can I take the boat?'

'Of course. But listen, can we start from the morning? I could really do with the help tonight. Dr Sorensen says we have to wake him every two hours through the night and ask him some questions, and I'm not sure I can do that on my own.'

'Måns can do it,' Emil said, sounding terse.

'We can't ask him to do that!' Hanna chided. 'He's in his mid-eighties.'

They really did sound like the proverbial married couple,

Bell marvelled, seemingly slipping straight back into old patterns, bickering lightly. 'What sort of questions?'

Hanna looked back at her. 'Oh, nothing much. Chit-chat – what's your name? Favourite song? What year is it?' She shrugged. 'I thought we could do every other shift, starting from, say, eleven? That way we'll get four hours' sleep each.'

Oh, great, Bell thought to herself as she gave an obliging smile. Her day off would only come after a night of utterly broken sleep. *Excellent.* 'Sure.'

'I'll do eleven and three, if you can do one and five?'

'One and five, got it.' Bell walked towards the door. 'Where's Linus?'

'He stayed down to have some supper. And then I've told him it's off to bed early tonight. I think everyone's had an exhausting day.'

'Okay, I'll go check on him.'

'I'd get to bed early yourself, if I were you.' Hanna turned back to Emil with a look. 'It's going to be a long night.'

Chapter Twenty-Two

What?

She blinked, her eyes fixed and unseeing upon the moonlight puddling on her floor as her hand flailed and scrabbled for the alarm. She had left the shutters open deliberately, hoping it would make this middle-of-the-night obligation easier to endure, but in spite of the full moon and open windows – the owl calling from a nearby tree – she had slept heavily the moment her head had hit the pillow. The day's dramas had left her feeling drained, and the anticipation of some time off had set her tingling with relief. She needed to get away from here, off this island and away from this toxic situation. *Him.*

She had already messaged Tove and Kris, desperate for friendly company. It was exhausting being Enemy Number One. Both Tove and Marc were working shifts tonight, but they'd all be taking the early ferry in the morning, arriving at Sandhamn in time for lunch.

With a deep breath and a yawn, she pushed herself up to sitting and planted her feet on the floor, head hanging low, hair falling forwards. She could do this. She could. She didn't even have to wake up fully herself. The man was clearly perfectly fine; he'd been more than lucid earlier, needling her into another argument. All she had to do was go down the hall, shake him awake, ask him a question, and then they could all go back to sleep again. She could be back in this bed within the minute, the sheets still warm . . .

Scarcely conscious of her surroundings, but subliminally knowing there was nothing to walk into – the advantages of a minimally furnished house – she carefully opened her door and trod quietly down the landing. Moonlight fell in through the tall windows that gave onto the lawn, the world cast in ghostly shades of grey and white.

She paused at his door with a sigh. Nearly there. Twenty more seconds and she could be back in bed . . .

She opened it and looked in. He was lying on his stomach, arms up by his head, one leg bent beneath the sheet. He was wearing just boxers, and she could tell from the soft set of his muscles and the rhythm of his breathing that he was soundly off. She tiptoed across the floor, knowing it was ridiculous to make efforts to be quiet when she was going to have to wake him up anyway.

She stopped by the edge of the bed and looked down at him, one hand poised to tap his bare shoulder. But she paused, her hand hovering in mid-air before slowly, silently, she crouched down, level with the mattress. Face to face, she stared at him in a way that was impossible when he was awake. Without the resentment in his jaw, without the anger in his eyes whenever he looked her way, he was probably the most beautiful man she had ever seen. She could see Linus in his profile, that darling child.

Her eyes grazed him, remembering how she had reached over that night on the boat and how his cheek had curved beneath her palm, how his lips had felt as she'd kissed him first . . . How easy it had been in that aberrant moment when, simply strangers, they had succumbed to a momentary temptation because it felt so good. So right. So natural.

His eyes flickered open, the pupils dilated, sleep like a veil upon him still, and it struck her suddenly how cruel it was that those eyes had remained closed for seven years. How much had he missed? The world had carried on turning without him, his family's lives had continued –

'Bell.' The word was an exhalation, a sigh, a fragile sound giving shape to a wish.

'I'm . . . sorry,' she whispered, trying to pull herself back. She was delirious, sleep-addled herself. 'It's one o'clock. I have to . . . I have to check you're okay.'

His eyes had closed again and her gaze skimmed him once more with a voracious freedom never normally hers. She remembered how it had felt to lie beneath him, his weight pinning her down, his mouth on her neck . . . Her heart rate quickened and without even knowing she was going to do it, she leaned in, kissing his temple as lightly as a feather falling onto snow.

She pulled back and saw he was looking at her. The sleep was lifting and there was recognition now, eye to eye in the moonlight. There was truth. They had started something that wasn't yet finished, lighted a flame that wouldn't go out until they let it burn.

'Bell.' There was heat in the word, shape to a need, and his arm reached out, snaking around the back of her neck, gripping it tightly, cupping her head. Instinctively, she leaned into it, eyes half closing as his fingers worked in her hair. A groan escaped her as she rubbed her neck against his hand, wanting more –

He pulled her to him, his lips so close she could feel their warmth, and her body ached for that first primal touch between them again, the touchpaper that would send them both up in flames. She waited for it.

And waited.

She opened her eyes and stared straight into his. But it

wasn't desire she saw – but despair. He didn't want to want her.

She felt her breathing grow shallow, as though the air in the room had thinned. His arm retracted, the hotspot on her flushed skin cooling instantly.

'Bell . . .' The word held apology, regret. Conviction.

They were both wide awake now.

She tore her gaze away, humiliated, as she rose in her t-shirt and stepped away from the bed. Without a word, she walked towards the door and closed it behind her softly as the tears began to stream down her cheeks. Not a question had been asked. No need. They both had their answer.

She blinked, her eyes fixed and unseeing upon the moonlight puddling on her floor as her hand automatically switched off the alarm. The moon had moved round, long shadows slanting on the floorboards, the owl still hunting.

It was five o'clock already and sleep hadn't come. Though her bed had still been warm, her own impression still visible on the sheets as she fell back in, she had lain stiff and wretched, trying to make sense of what had happened: her ready capitulation, his unequivocal rejection. Had she imagined what had pulsed between them in those few moments? It had felt as real and alive as her thumping heart. And yet, could she deny that almost every day he had treated her with scorn and resentment? That he had told her plainly it had meant nothing?

She felt the tears fall again, hot on her cheeks, the pillow and her hair damp. She would have sworn, in that room, by that bed, the raw emotion in those few moments of swollen silence had been more real than any cruel word or askance look. But she was mistaken, clearly. In just her t-shirt, sloughed of sleep, she had revealed her longing to him, only to be dangled like a mouse by its tail. He had toyed with her, that was the truth. It was a power play, designed to humiliate. He couldn't kick her off his island, he couldn't keep her out of his son's life, so he had brought her to her knees instead. Literally, put her on her knees.

Five o'clock and already it was bright outside, the impatient sun rising even though the moon still floated through the sky. She needed to get away from here. Her friends would be here in a few hours; she could wait for them at the hotel. Treat herself to an early breakfast, lie by the pool, read a book, forget she'd ever met Emil Von Greyers.

She pushed herself up to sitting and planted her feet on the floor, head hanging low, hair falling forwards. She could do this. She could. All she had to do was tap him on the shoulder, ask him his name, leave again. Job done.

Heart pounding, she carefully opened her door and walked silently down the hall. The first pale dawn rays fell in through the tall windows that gave onto the lawn, casting the world in shades of peach and white.

She paused at his door and took a deep breath. Nearly there. Twenty more seconds and this would be over . . . She could leave.

She opened it and looked in. He was lying on his back, one arm bent behind his head, one leg folded beneath the sheet. His boxers were on the floor and she could tell from the hard set of his muscles and the rhythm of his breathing that he was awake.

Bell felt herself freeze as Hanna stirred beside him and gave a small moan. Her blonde hair was draped across his chest, her lithe body pale in the moonlight, scarcely covered by the sheet. Emil looked down at her, then back at Bell, desire spent, despair in his eyes.

His voice was flat when he spoke. 'It's okay. I'm awake.'

Chapter Twenty-Three

'Well, *some* of us are living the life!' Tove laughed, dropping a heavy bag on the sunbed and jolting her awake with a loving prod to the backside.

'Ugh.' Bell pushed her sunglasses up and squinted up at her. 'I was sleeping!'

'Billionaire lifestyle getting too much for you, is it?' Tove threw out a towel and pulled off her sundress in one fluid movement. She was wearing a purple bandeau bikini that immediately made Bell's yellow string one look basic.

'How did you . . . ? Oh, Kris.'

'Oh, babe, please. I already worked it out. How many rich dudes coming out of seven-year comas do you think there are in Sweden?'

'Oh.' She rested her cheek on her hands and sighed wearily, watching as Tove flopped down beside her with a sigh, her lean body gleaming in the already fierce sun. 'Where are the boys?'

'Coming in a bit. They wanted to do a hike first before we kick off in style. You know what they're like. Puritans. Can't enjoy themselves without a bit of punishment first.' She spied Bell's Coke on the table beside her. 'Oooh, I hope there's rum in that thing,' she winked, taking a long sip through the straw. 'Fuck, there actually is!' she spluttered a moment later, coughing and kicking her long legs about. 'Why didn't you warn me?'

'I would have if you'd given me a chance.'

Tove stared at her. '*You* don't drink rum and Coke at lunchtime. You're a lightweight.'

Bell pushed her sunglasses back down, hoping to hide the bags under her eyes. 'It is summer, is it not?'

'Hmm.' Tove regarded her suspiciously as she continued to drink.

Bell gave a sigh and hoisted herself back up to a sitting position, taking it before her wayward friend finished it off. 'I was enjoying that, thanks. Get your own.'

'How many of those have you had?'

'None.' Bell hoped she wouldn't clock the two glasses on the ground beneath her sunbed. 'And anyway, it's party time, or hadn't you noticed?' She indicated the bunting that had been strung up all around the pool and bar area, every chair and table taken. Kids were playing in the pool at the moment, but that would change as the day wore on and the adults came out to play in force. The prestigious Royal Yacht Club's Round Gotland four-day race was in full swing and the lead boats were expected to sail past the island this evening on their way back to Skeppsholmen, just outside the city. 'It was lucky I got here so early, or we'd never have got these beds.'

'When *did* you get here?'

'Seven.'

'In the morning?' Tove spluttered. 'What were you here that early for?'

She gave a weary sigh. 'This is a circular argument, Tove. Gotland. Biggest weekend of the year. Sunbeds . . . ?'

'You're being weird.' Tove shrugged, reaching into her bag and pulling out a stack of gossip magazines. 'I got you some reading material. Figured you're probably going *insane* without wifi. Got to keep up with what's going on in the world.'

'Because *Hänt* mag is really hot on current affairs?' Bell quipped, picking it up anyway and flicking through it idly. 'Thanks, babe.' A moment later, she tipped her head back, not remotely interested in the newest moisturizer or Enrique Iglesias's twins. 'So tell me everything. What have I missed?'

Tove looked around them furtively, before leaning in. It was the clear sign that whatever gossip she was about to spill was going to be good. 'Well, I'd better tell you this before they get back here. I mean, they'll tell you themselves, no doubt, but just to give you the heads-up – Kris and Marc almost split. Well, actually they did split. But they're back together again.'

'*What?*' Bell gasped. 'But they just announced they are moving in together!'

'I know, but Kris found some messages on Marc's phone, some junior doctor dude, and –' She shrugged. 'It all sort of blew up. Kris got absolutely wrecked and needed to be carried home.'

'But he hardly drinks.'

'And Marc doesn't usually stand in the street, shouting up at windows in the middle of the night either, but he did. It was all pretty bad.'

'I can't believe this,' Bell said, aghast. 'I've been gone for two weeks and the whole world's gone mad! I saw Kris last week and he was fine.'

Tove gave her freckled shoulders a shrug. 'I don't know, maybe it was some sort of reflex to the enormity of what they are doing? Moving in together's a big deal. Marc must have just freaked, panicked, had a brain fart? But they're good now. They've talked, for like fricking *days* – I think they've worked through it.' She wagged a finger at her. 'But don't say I told you, and look surprised if they bring it up. Kris'll talk to you when he's ready, but I think they both just want things to get back to normal.'

Bell nodded, but she felt upset that she hadn't been there for her flatmate. She knew better than anyone that Kris had the looks of a god and the heart of a marshmallow. Her own life had been yoked to someone else's itinerary and agenda – and where had it got her?

Tove swung her legs off the bed and got up. 'More of the same?'

'Sure. Make them doubles.'

Tove's eyebrows shot up as she shoved her feet into a pair of fake Hermes slides. 'Don't look so worried, Bell. They'll be okay. And the timing of your text was perfect; a massive blowout this weekend is exactly what they need.'

'A massive blowout this weekend is exactly what *I* need,' she murmured under her breath, as Tove walked over to the pool bar. She flicked through the magazine, stopping at the social diary spread, her gaze snagging for some reason on a picture of a royal couple in tiaras and sashes. They were in full white tie regalia in some red and gilded room, and beside them was another couple, minus the crowns. It was another few moments before she realized the erect, sharp-gazed woman staring back through the lens was Nina. *We're having dinner in Copenhagen tonight*, she'd said. She just hadn't mentioned it was with the King and Queen of Denmark.

She remembered Nina's audacious entrance, turning up unexpectedly, her helicopter just appearing suddenly in the sky. Emil had seemed bemused, if somewhat resigned, to his sister's forthright attitude and entitled manner – so different from his own. She certainly never would have guessed, from his scruffy appearance in the marina, that he was the scion of an industrialist dynasty, or that he might be the kind of man to consort with kings. Or that he might seduce his own wife.

'Drink up,' Tove said, returning with a tray loaded with drinks. 'Double the doubles.'

'Great.' She was going to get drunk. So very, very drunk . . .

'And tell me – how's Hanna?' Tove asked. 'How are things with our Mogerts' very chic, oh-so modern family?'

'Ummm . . .' Bell hesitated. 'Well, it's all rather *old*-school, since you ask.' Her voice sounded thick.

'Old-school?' Tove was intrigued, peering over her cat's-eye sunglasses at her. 'What does that mean?'

Bell swallowed, forcing herself to say the words. 'Hanna's having an affair. With her husband.'

Tove's jaw dropped open completely. 'The slut!'

'Sshhhh!' Bell hushed her furiously, glancing around at their neighbours as heads turned at the commotion. 'Keep it down! There are kids about.'

'Sorry,' Tove squeaked, not sorry at all. Her body was suddenly tense with excitement. 'But what the actual fuck?' she stage-whispered. 'What about Max?'

Bell sighed. 'Quite.'

'Are you sure? I mean, how do you know?'

Bell swallowed, feeling the enormity of it all hit her again. 'Because I saw them in bed together last night.'

Tove's face crumpled. 'Oh my God, poor Max!'

Poor Max. 'Yes, I know.'

'Does he –?'

'No.' Bell shook her head. 'I don't think anyone does.'

'Except you.'

'Yeah, except me.'

Tove frowned. 'And how come you saw them in bed together?'

Bell swallowed, tipping her head back on the headrest, not

wanting to go back there. 'Oh, long story,' she said as dismissively as she could. Her voice was strangled, tears were threatening.

'You weren't hiding in his closet, were you?' Tove asked devilishly. 'Because let's be honest, I would – the guy is *hot*.'

'Nothing so exciting, I'm afraid,' Bell said quickly, cutting her off before she could start to extol Emil Von Greyer's physical virtues. 'He was concussed, and –' In spite of herself, she felt the tears begin to slide out of the corners of her eyes, and she thanked God for the gigantic Chanels she had picked up years back in duty free. 'Hanna and I had to check on him throughout the night, and that's when I found them together.' The words ran into each other like children on a slide.

Tove was quiet for a moment, staring at her. Then she leaned over and pulled off her glasses entirely.

'Tove!' Bell gasped, reacting just that bit too late. 'Don't.'

'Why are you crying?' Tove asked, concern softening her. '. . . Oh God, babe, what have you done?'

'We are going to be her pimps.' Tove looked round at them all seriously. 'All of us. We are getting this woman a man tonight.'

It was the kind of Tove comment that they might have shouted down when sober, but after a day of drinking in the sun, it sounded almost reasonable. Kris and Marc had returned midway through her story about Emil, and with every new tray of drinks that came back from the bar, she had revealed more about what had passed between them – he was her *Midsommar* lover, the confrontations she had won, the insults he had, yesterday's perfection blighted by his accident on the boat, his cruel rejection in the middle of the night, flaunting the seduction of his own wife to her . . .

'Yes! Do it. Let's get me a man,' Bell slurred, as Kris, sitting at the end of her sunbed, gave her a foot rub. At some point they had switched from rum and Coke to mojitos. 'Lighter,' Tove had said earnestly, as though it was the Coke they had to watch out for.

'I can't . . . I can't choose properly,' Bell went on. 'My man radar is completely broken. Pimp me out. I don't even care.'

'This makes me sad,' Kris sighed. He rarely drank to excess, but when he did, he was usually a sorrowful drunk. 'You deserve someone who *cares* about you.'

'No. That's the worst thing I could do,' she protested, shaking her head vehemently. 'I don't want love.'

'Yes, you do,' Marc said, his skin looking tight after an intense tanning session followed by a competitive volleyball match in the pool. 'It's all you want.'

Music was pumping loudly through the speakers; coloured lights were on around the bar area as the sun bumped along the horizon, unable to sink. It was approaching ten and all the families had long since gone home; the sea club was filled to capacity, with partygoers overflowing onto the gangplanks, beers in their hands and the ambient noise levels of laughter and conversation rising rapidly. Every boat in the marina had people on it, deck parties and dinners adding to the carnival atmosphere as others stood on the rocks with binoculars, watching the lead race boats clip past. It was party time again on Sandhamn.

'Love and good sex very often don't go hand in hand,' Tove said, with a gravity that suggested she was passing on divine wisdom. 'I mean, I get it when people bang on about intimacy adding to it, blah-blah-blah, but sometimes, with a stranger, it's actually better.'

Bell closed her eyes, remembering again the moment she had leaned across and kissed him –

'Stop it!' Kris wiggled her foot, knowing exactly what she was thinking. 'Not him.'

'No,' she sighed again. 'I wasn't. I –' She didn't have the energy to lie.

She gave a small shiver as a sea breeze rippled over her bare skin. She was still in her bikini, having just pulled on a pair of denim shorts, and she tried to remember what she had worn here this morning. It was so long ago now. Fourteen hours spent lying and drinking and crying on this sun lounger.

'Bell?'

They all turned as one to find a blonde-bearded guy smiling down at her, several beer bottles precariously held between his splayed fingers.

'Mats?' She saw Kris and Marc give him the once-over. He was an attractive guy – athletic physique, twinkly eyes, ready smile. 'Mats!' she cried, scrambling to stand and accidentally delivering a glancing blow to Kris's nether regions in the process.

'Oof!'

'Guys, this is Mats. He's Emil's skipper.'

'Emil's skipper?' Marc repeated, as though this counted against him. Guilty by assocation?

She reached over the lounger and greeted him like an old friend, giving him an enthusiastic kiss on each cheek. 'What are you doing here?' she asked excitedly. 'I thought you went back to the city.'

He hesitated. Could he tell she was tipsy? Perhaps she wasn't doing a terribly good job of hiding it. 'I did, but I just got back in time. I always like to watch the race from here.'

'From the bar?' she laughed, looking down at his beers.

He gave a rueful shrug, as though busted. 'That was the plan, anyway. You want one?'

'Oh, I shouldn't, I've had so much already,' she demurred, before taking it in the next instant anyway. 'Oh okay then.' She took a swig. 'So what are you doing here?' She winced, catching herself as he laughed; she'd already asked that. God, she was drunk. 'I mean, I mean, who are you here with?'

'Those guys over there.' He jerked his thumb to show a group of eight or so, standing on the other side of the pool. There were five guys and three women, all talking in a group.

'Oh.'

He looked back at her quickly. 'But they're not, I mean, I'm not –'

'You're not . . . ?'

His gaze fell to her mouth, then back to her eyes. 'I'm not *with* them.'

Did he mean the women? 'Oh.' She put her lips to the bottle and watched him as she drank. Everything seemed to slow down a little.

'And you?' His eyes grazed over Marc and Kris questioningly, as they stood protectively a step behind.

'Oh. Oh, no,' she laughed. 'We're not a . . . four. They're a two, in fact,' she said, taking both Kris and Marc's chins in her hands and squeezing their handsome faces together like chipmunks. The two men blinked back obligingly.

'Right,' Mats grinned, looking relieved.

'Yes, this is Kris and I'm Marc,' Marc said as they all shook hands. 'We're her pimps.'

'And me. I'm Tove,' Tove said, leaning in. 'I'm her pimp too.'

'Actually, I'd say you're the *chief* pimp, Tove,' Marc deadpanned.

They all looked back at Mats, who was motionless and open-mouthed, before collapsing into fits of hysterics. 'Uh . . .'

'They're messing with you,' Bell laughed, slapping a hand on his chest and leaving it there. He looked down at it – and back at her again. 'It's just an inside joke.'

'Right. Well *good*,' he smiled. He stepped in closer to her, encouraged by her initiation of body contact, and she sensed the others draw back as their conversation became more intimate. '. . . So, it's funny running into you like this. I was really hoping I'd see you again,' he said quietly. 'Did you read my note?'

'Of course.'

'And were you going to call me?'

'. . . Of course.'

He gave a mock-outraged gasp. 'You weren't!'

She laughed. 'I was! I was!'

'I don't believe you!' he protested, grinning anyway.

She leaned into him slightly, pressing her curves gently against him. 'Does it matter? We're here now, aren't we?'

The question was coquettish, and he stared down at her for a moment, a question in his eyes that she answered with a look in her own. She was wildly drunk and she didn't care who knew it. Him, the whole bar . . . Nothing mattered anyway. Not really. She had made the first move and it was his call whether to respond or not.

He bent his head and kissed her – just like that. It was that easy. His lips were chapped and a little rough, but she didn't mind; it was better than being kept hanging in mid-air.

'Attagirl!' she heard Tove yell, and someone – Kris – gave a two-fingered whistle.

'Pimps or cheerleaders?' Mats grinned as they pulled apart.

'Both!' she giggled, feeling woozy and silly and like she was on an unstoppable train.

He kissed her again, emboldened now. 'I wanted to do that all day yesterday.'

'Did you?' she breathed, remembering how Emil had stared up at her from her lap all the way back, her hands stroking and cradling his face as she told him it would all be okay . . . What a joke.

She could still see him so clearly, even now, like he was right there –

He *was* right there.

'Boss!' She felt Mats stiffen with the surprise, his hands falling from her waist.

Hanna, Emil and Linus were standing on the other side of the fencing that partitioned off the sea bar from the boardwalk. Judging by their collared shirts, she could tell they had come from having dinner in the hotel.

'Mats,' Emil said back, staring at them evenly – before remembering his manners. 'This is Hanna, my w– . . . Linus's mother.'

'Pleased to meet you,' Hanna said quickly, her eyes darting to her son like a dragonfly on the river. 'I think we passed by each other in the house yesterday? I'm sorry if I was rude, rushing like that. I've heard a lot about you.'

'All good, I hope.'

'Of course. I understand it was thanks to you he received medical aid so quickly. Not to mention, the hit from the boom would have been a lot worse if you hadn't pulled him down.'

'Not quite fast enough, though,' Mats said ruefully, looking back at the boss again. 'How are you now, honestly? I didn't think you'd be up and about so quickly.'

'I'm fine, really.'

Mats looked sceptical. 'Yeah? You took a proper wallop there.'

'Just some headaches. They'll pass. I've been well looked after.' He draped an arm over Hanna's shoulder, as if to prove she was his Florence Nightingale. Bell looked away. Was she going to get any credit at all – she had clipped him back to safety again, protected his head from further blows, held him all the way back – or had he erased her completely from his version of events?

She realized that Hanna hadn't greeted her. And that in fact, although friendly to Mats, she was seemingly unable to even meet her eyes? She must have realized that she had fallen asleep in the bed, that Bell would have seen her there.

'Uh, Hanna, about that –' She pulled a face, hoping she could pull off the lie. 'Listen, I'm really sorry about this morning. I was going to text you. I'm afraid I slept right through the alarm for the five o'clock check.'

She felt Emil's stare spring on her like a cat as she watched Hanna's expression change, relief suffusing her like a spring bloom. 'You did?'

She shrugged, not sure why she was rushing to save her boss's blushes. 'Yes, I'm so sorry. I mean, clearly everything's worked out well, but still, I feel terrible about it.'

'No, no, not at all,' Hanna said quickly, glancing at Emil with a secret look. 'It's fine. He's fine. Aren't you?'

Emil nodded, his eyes meeting hers finally and scorching her. He was looking smarter than at any other point since she'd met him, a pale-blue Oxford shirt making the most of his eyes, white chino shorts with Tods, shoes with actual backs. He looked a step closer already to the man in the wedding photo. The Hanna Effect. He was getting what he wanted – his old life back. First his son, now his wife.

'Bell,' Linus said excitedly, interrupting now that the first round of pleasantries was over. 'You should have been there today. We went skateboarding down the halls and had a picnic at the hidden beach!'

'Oh!' she nodded, trying to see only one of him and trying not to look as drunk as she actually was, hanging off a handsome sailor in just her bikini at ten o'clock at night. 'I *wish* I'd been there.'

'Where did you go? You were already gone when I woke up.'

Her smile set in place. 'I came here.'

'What? All day?'

'Yep.' She nodded. 'All day.' Drinking from that bar . . .

'Well, it's *good* to see you letting your hair down, Bell,' Hanna said, smiling warmly, relaxed now that her indiscretion had gone unseen, generous now that it was Bell – and not her – who was wrecked. 'It looks like you've had a great day.'

'Oh, the best. *So* much fun. Very . . . needed.' She refused to look Emil's way, even though his stare was like a hot needle dragging over her skin.

Linus looked between her and Mats with open curiosity. 'I didn't know he was your boyfriend.'

'Oh! He's my . . .' A silence opened up. Her brain wasn't working fast enough to work out what to say.

'Special friend?' Mats supplied for her, looking bemused.

'Yes!' she said, pointing a finger at him. 'Very good.'

'We're special friends, mate,' Mats said with a wink.

'So does that mean you're going to New Zealand too?' Panic lit in his eyes.

'What?' she asked, bewildered.

'Mats is racing in the America's Cup. He's going to go over there soon. You're not leaving too, are you?'

She stared at him, a little boy with two fathers and a mother who couldn't choose. 'Oh Liney –' She went to put a hand to his cheek, as she so often did, but before she could make contact, Hanna pulled him back.

'Now, Linus, we've discussed this. Bell has her own life

too. We can't keep expecting her to give up everything just for us.' Hanna looked back at Bell and Mats with a smile. 'Apologies. We should let you lovebirds get back to the party.'

'Okay, sure,' Mats said, clearly relieved. 'Well, good seeing you all. Sleep tight, champ.' He gave Linus a high five. 'Nice to meet you at long last, Hanna. Emil, stay strong, man.' Mats held out his hand, but there was a noticeable hesitation before his boss took it.

'See you Monday, Bell,' Linus said reluctantly, as he was led off by his mother.

'Yes, Monday, dude,' Bell said quietly, feeling Emil's stare lift off her finally. Her gaze lingered on the trio as they walked down the gangplanks to the berth where the paint-flaked, underpowered boat was moored. To the unwitting, they looked just like a regular, highly photogenic, small family. There was nothing to indicate they were anything but.

'Shit,' Mats hissed under his breath, raking his hands through his hair as soon as they were out of earshot.

'What?' she asked, watching them become silhouetted in the harbour lights, Emil jumping into the boat first and holding out a hand for Hanna. She looked more beautiful than ever in a red silk dress. It was a dress that said she would be sleeping in his bed again tonight.

'Did you see Emil's face? He looked like he was ready to explode.'

'Did he?' she asked, swaying slightly and feeling an unexpected surge of triumph.

'You didn't notice?'

'I wasn't looking.'

'You don't think he had a problem with . . . *us*, do you?'

She shrugged angrily. 'Why should he? You're his boat's

skipper and I'm his kid's nanny. What does he care if he we hook up? It's none of his business what we do in our own time. We're employed by him. Not owned by him.'

A surprised chuckle escaped him. 'Feisty, aren't you?'

She shrugged again, feeling the adrenaline pump through her now that the crisis was over. So what if he'd seen her here with Mats? She owed him nothing – he'd made that perfectly clear. He'd won Hanna back and got exactly what he wanted.

Mats pulled her closer to him again, seeing the dark gleam in her eyes. 'So, we're hooking up, are we?'

She looked up at him and smiled. 'We are now.'

Chapter Twenty-Four

The darkness claimed him and his body jolted into sleep like he'd been pushed from a cliff. There was never complete refuge to be found for him here; a part of his brain – perhaps the only part that had remained alert enough to classify him as alive for all those years – always refused to surrender, a lone night-light burning in an empty house.

But the tension in his body softened, his fisted hands curling open like autumn leaves, the headaches that strapped around his brain unbuckling for the night. It would not be for long, this fitful oblivion – the irony of emerging from a coma an insomniac never failed to amuse him – but it would be enough to quieten the hounds that snapped at his heels, their relentless shadows crossing over him like blades in the sunlight. The accident might have passed, the trauma healed, but danger persisted, he knew. For a man who could neither taste nor smell well, he had an acute sense that it was still here, close at hand.

He moved through the blackness, wading through its different textures and shades, always searching for the speck of light that would grow if he turned towards it. And she would be there, as she always was, held within the brightness, her pale hair and lambent skin like beacons showing him the way. She had saved him, brought him back to life . . .

And now she was here. Far away, pressed against his body, he felt the silken slip of her against his flesh, the tickle of her breath, the warmth of her limbs tangled with his, and he fell deeper into the velvet where nothing existed. No light, no taste, no touch, no smell. Just a sound.

A . . .

Bell.

'Knock, knock.'

She peered through the open door as Max looked up. He was sitting at the table, a coffee mug still steaming in front of him, reading yesterday's paper. 'Hey, Bell!'

He seemed pleased – and surprised – to see her, standing up as she came in and giving her a kiss on each cheek. 'Long time no see.'

'I know! Wow, you've really been looking after the place,' she marvelled, looking around the spotless cabin like she'd been gone for ten years rather than two weeks.

He gave her a bemused look and she remembered what Hanna had said about her mother coming out this weekend. 'All by my own hand, naturally. Coffee?'

'Yes. Don't worry, I'll get it,' she said, walking over to the espresso machine.

'Have you lost weight?' he asked her, sitting back down again.

'Funny, I was going to ask you the same,' she smiled, glancing over her shoulder.

'Maybe.' He gave a hapless shrug. 'Probably.'

'You look tired. Did you meet that client deadline?' she asked, popping in a capsule and speaking over the gurgling machine.

'Only at the expense of my sanity and two members of staff,' he sighed, sitting back in the chair, looking exhausted.

His skin was sallow beneath the tan, and he hadn't shaved in days. Bell thought his dark hair looked noticeably more salted, too. 'They kept making changes after everything was signed off.'

'Well, it must be great to have it done, at least.'

'Honestly, it's been so much hassle, I'm not even sure we want the client now.'

'Oh dear.' She brought her coffee back to the table and sat opposite him, interlacing her fingers around the hot mug and letting the steam rise in her face for a moment. Anything to purify . . . It had taken a full day in bed – her own bed – to recover yesterday. 'And the girls? Where are they? I've missed them.'

'Still sleeping.'

Her eyebrows shot up. *'Really?'*

'Yeah, Ebba thinks they're having a growth spurt.'

'Is she still here?' She hoped not. Hanna's mother was an exacting woman to be around. Nothing was ever quite right.

'No, she went back last night. Bridge tournament this week.' He rolled his eyes. 'Thank God,' he mouthed, lest she should in fact be hiding behind the sofa, listening.

She grinned into the mug, feeling something unspoken creep into the room and sit down beside them. A baby elephant.

'So . . .' Max tapped his fingers lightly on the table. 'How are things over at Ingarso?'

'Where?' Her brow puckered quizzically.

'Also known as 007.' His tone aimed for levity, but his eyes could play no such game.

'Ah, of course.' Bell smiled vaguely at the family's dramatic nickname for the island. She wondered if he knew the 'villain's lair' was in fact a tired but genteel bright-orange manor house.

'They are . . .' she paused, wondering what on earth she could say. 'They are okay.'

'Okay?' He looked underwhelmed.

'Yeah. It was a pretty sketchy start. Linus was very quiet and reserved to begin with. Understandably.'

Max nodded, looking pained. It couldn't be easy for him to hear about the boy he had raised and loved as his own son bonding with his biological father.

'I think he was so wary, after the hospital visit.'

Max winced. 'I told her it was a mistake. She never should have taken him.'

'No, I agree,' Bell murmured. 'But I guess it's just so hard to know what the right thing is in a situation like this. There's not exactly a handbook, is there?'

'Christ, if only.' He dropped his head into one hand and raked it through his hair. 'And now? Is he calling him Pappa?'

'No, that's you and it always will be, Max.' She took a breath. 'But he is beginning to call him Dad.'

'In the English?'

'Yeah. I guess it feels . . . a step removed? It's warmer than Father, but not *you*.'

His face flinched, and she reached out and touched his hand lightly. 'He loves you, Max – you'll always be his pappa. This is not about replacing you.'

'Isn't it? I replaced Emil.' There was a brutality to his words; they almost had a self-flagellating quality to them.

She watched him. 'How are you bearing up?' She sensed that out of all of them caught up in this web – him, Emil, Linus, Hanna – he was the one most overlooked. He didn't have a blood link here, nor even a legal or religious one. Emil was Hanna's legal husband and Linus's legal father. He had all the rights, all the sympathy, all the money, all the power . . .

'Me? Oh, I'm just . . . waking up every morning wondering if this will be the day Hanna finally leaves me.'

Bell looked back at him in astonishment. Did he know? How could he possibly? Had he seen them out on Saturday night, or heard about it? They'd hardly been discreet.

'What?' he asked, reading her face. 'You can't be surprised, surely?'

'M-Max, Hanna loves you,' she said, stumbling over the words.

'Yes. But more than him? Ever since that bastard phone call that he'd woken up, she's been . . . different. Distant.'

'She's in an impossible situation.'

'We *all* are, Bell. Believe me, I've got sympathy for the poor guy. What he's been through . . . No one should have to endure that . . . He was my friend too. Christ, he was my friend first.'

'What?'

'Yeah. Before he met Hanna, before I did, we were childhood friends. Out here.' He shrugged, motioning to the cabin, the island.

'No one's ever mentioned that before.'

He shrugged. 'I guess it's not important. But it's also pretty obvious, isn't it? His place is across the pond. His family built on that island five generations ago, and my grandparents bought this plot. We've both been coming to the lagoon our entire lives. I've never really *not* known him . . . Well, until recently.'

'Were you close?' She shifted position, hardly able to believe she hadn't heard about this before now. Hanna hadn't said anything, nor Emil . . .

He gave a reflective smile. 'When we were about eight or nine, he and I used to row our boats to the middle of the lagoon and tie them together at the oar hooks and sit fishing all day.'

'That's so sweet.'

'I'm not sure you'd have thought it was sweet if you saw the contraband we smuggled out.' He chuckled. 'Chocolates and sweets when we were younger, but then as we got older – *Penthouse* magazine, cigarettes, weed, booze. We would smuggle out bottles of schnapps and drink ourselves stupid. It was perfect. No one ever came out to bother us; the only rule was, we had to return home when either of our families waved a white flag.'

The white flag . . . She remembered the ones both Linus and Hanna had waved at each other in the night.

'It sounds idyllic,' Bell murmured, watching the memories flit across his face like sunbeams. 'It sounds like you were best friends.'

'Oh, in the summer we were,' he said, glancing at her and away again. 'Everyone is equal out here on these little islands and skerries.' He chewed on his lip. 'But it's a different matter back in the city, of course. His family owned – still own, in fact – the Grand Hotel; they had an apartment that covered the entire top two floors. Whereas we lived in a cramped duplex in Tensta.'

'Tensta? I don't know it.'

He gave a wry smile. 'No, it's a suburb in the north-west of the city.'

'And you didn't see each other then?'

'He was at a boarding school in Switzerland, and his family travelled a lot. He was only really around in the summers. I used to feel like I spent all year waiting to see him.' He gave an embarrassed smile and looked away.

'Max, if you were such good friends, why haven't you gone to see him?'

'Because . . . how can I, Bell? I'm the bastard sleeping with his wife!'

And now he's the bastard sleeping with yours, she thought, watching as he dragged a hand through his hair again. She hated that she was stuck in the middle of this and being forced to lie, but this wasn't her secret to tell. 'So, if you were his friend, then you were Hanna's too, I assume?'

'Of course. I went to their wedding.'

Bell nodded. She could see how it had played out – Hanna in a tailspin after the doctors' prognosis; old friends consoling each other, comfort turning into refuge, into something more . . . But was it guilt, or rekindled love, that had sent her spinning back into her husband's arms again?

'So then Emil must understand how it would have happened between you and her, even if he doesn't want to admit it to himself.'

He was silent for a moment, watching her. '. . . You'd tell me if you knew anything, wouldn't you, Bell?'

'Max –'

'Please don't tell me I'm being paranoid. I'm not a fool. When Hanna heard about the accident, she rushed out in the middle of a storm to be with him. And now she's been there all weekend, just her and Emil and Linus, playing happy families. *You* got given the weekend off –'

She swallowed, wishing she had never set foot in that room that night and seen what she'd seen. Ignorance would have been bliss. 'For the record, *I* asked for that time off. But they're not alone, if that's what you're thinking. Måns is there too.'

'The old guy's still going?'

'He's still going – slowly, but going.' She smiled. 'Plus, there's cooks, gardeners, a physio . . . . Look, she's *only* there because Emil was concussed, and I think she was terrified he was going to slip back into a coma again.'

He shot her a sceptical look. 'Statistically, that wasn't likely to happen.'

'Statistically, Emil was never supposed to wake up.'

'Touché.' With a mirthless smile he sat back in the chair again, staring into space. They sat in easy silence, Bell drinking her coffee as his fingers tapped absently on the crossword.

He glanced over at her again. 'So back to you – why *have* you lost weight? You didn't answer before.'

'Oh.' She gave a groan, trying to make light of it, find a reason. 'You know – boy trouble. The usual.'

'Ah.' Sympathetic nod. 'Anyone I know?'

She shook her head. 'No. He's . . . uh, a sailor, skippers a megaboat. Leaving for New Zealand soon, just my luck.'

'New Zealand?' he grimaced. 'That really is unfortunate.'

'Yeah. He couldn't get further away.'

'Well, I'm sorry to hear that – but don't cry too many tears over him. In my experience, The One appears whether you're looking for them or not.' He shot her a wry look. 'Clearly, I was *not*.'

She gave a sympathetic smile.

'Anyway,' he said, changing the subject. 'Enough of our respective heartbreaks. What's the plan for today? When are you going back? I've packed a bag for Linus, just some little things he forgot –'

'Back?' She got up, taking their empty cups over to the sink. 'To 007.'

'Oh. I'm not,' she said over her shoulder, rinsing them.

'You're not going back?' he echoed, as though he hadn't heard correctly.

'No.'

He came over and joined her by the sink. 'But Hanna hasn't mentioned you *not* staying there.'

'Well, I was only needed to help Linus settle in and get to know his father. Emil I mean,' she corrected, flashing an apologetic smile. 'Which he's now done.'

'But it's only been two weeks.'

'I know, but it's going well. They're certainly relaxed together. You know, Emil's like the cool uncle.' She shot another apologetic smile. 'Not that you're not cool.'

'But doesn't Linus need you still?'

'No. He's having fun now and I was getting in the way of that, somewhat.'

Max stared at her. '*Were* you? Or was that just Emil trying to make you feel that way?'

She shot him a blank smile. 'Well, either way, I'm not going back.'

'Bell, I'm sorry to have to say this, but I don't think you've got any choice in the matter. As far as I'm aware, Hanna wants you over there with Linus.'

She turned the cups upside down on the draining board and reached for a tea towel, drying her hands. 'Max, I love Linus, you know I do. And I wouldn't leave him there with his father if I didn't genuinely believe he will be absolutely fine. But I've made my decision. I can continue working for you here, with the girls.'

'Or?' He stared at her, incredulous.

'Or I can quit.'

Chapter Twenty-Five

'That's it. Now keep your chins down,' she said as Tilde and Elise kicked frantically, their tiny bare bottoms peeking up through the water like little islands. Their breathing sounded Darth Vader-esque through the snorkels as they excitedly scanned the bottom of the sandy shallows, most likely seeing nothing more exciting than her fluorescent-orange-painted toenails. 'Can you see the fishes?'

The twins nodded their heads underwater, in unison, as she walked them slowly along the edge of the curved beach, holding a hand in each of hers, the water clear and cool. She stretched her neck as she walked, feeling the sun beat on her shoulders, and knew she ought to reapply some sunscreen. The weather had settled again after the storm at the end of last week, clear skies stretching tightly overhead. She checked her skin for signs of burning. Her tan was growing deep, and caramel highlights streaked the wispy front sections of her hair so that her eyes looked especially fiery and bright in the mirror.

The sound of a boat made her glance up and she saw Max coming round the headland with Hanna beside him, in the twin stroke; she had been stranded at Emil's when Bell had left in *Nymphea* and not returned.

The girls heard the engine too underwater and lifted their

heads quizzically, forcing Bell to grab them around the waists as they kicked about excitedly, almost sinking themselves.

'Mamma!' Tilde yelled, the mouthpiece still in her mouth so that her voice trumpeted. 'We're snorkelleers!'

Bell smiled at her description as Hanna just waved, unable to either hear or understand their garbled shouts. Max let the boat glide in to the shore, nudging the sand just enough for her to jump out onto the sand, before he circled back to the buoy where he would tether up and swim back in himself.

'Mamma! Mamma!'

Bell waded back to the beach, a twin on each hip, putting the girls down when it was shallow enough for them to stand again. They ran ahead comically through the water, arms lifted to their heads and hair tangled in their mask straps, running into their mother's arms as though she had been gone three months and not just for the weekend.

A lot could happen in that time, though. So much *had*. Families could be unpicked in mere moments. Had theirs? She watched as Hanna grabbed her daughters to her, the doting mother. The unfaithful wife.

'My babies!' she was laughing, holding them close to her, eyes closed in bliss as she sank down in the sand with them, not caring that her shorts were getting wet.

'Hanna, I'm really sorry, I totally forgot about the boat,' Bell said as she approached. 'I should have brought it over for you. I could easily have kayaked back here.'

'No,' Hanna said quickly. 'It's perfectly fine. It was no problem for Max to collect me.'

Bell caught something in her voice – an obligingness that seemed almost too ready, an eagerness to please. Appease.

'And how's Emil?' she asked dutifully, refusing to let her voice or face betray how even just his name made her feel.

Max had backed off as soon as she had mentioned quitting: she would look after the girls for the rest of the summer, and then they would be back in the city. Normal life would resume, Emil would be forgotten.

'He would be fine, except for those headaches. Cathy's coming back later to give him another once-over.'

'Right.' Bell nodded briskly. 'Well, hopefully it'll all settle down soon enough.'

'Yes.'

She heard splashes behind her, and turned to see Max wading in. 'I'll make some coffees, shall I?' he asked as he passed, not stopping, his mouth set in a grim line.

'Sure.' Hanna watched him go, her gaze cautious, and Bell wondered what had happened when he'd glided up to the jetty to collect her just now. Had Emil been waiting there too? His old friend, his new foe.

Bell felt a knot of tension tighten in the pit of her stomach just at the thought of it all – the chaos Emil had shaken loose from the fibres of this family crossing the lagoon and following them back here, the lies and secrets pinned to them like shadows.

'Well, it's been non-stop here all morning,' she said with forced brightness, refusing to get drawn in again. Their problems weren't hers. They weren't her family and this wasn't her life. She had sympathy with them all – it was an impossible situation to be in – but it was a job, nothing more. She had to remember that. She was just the nanny, here for the kids. 'These two have become expert snorkellers—'

'Snorkell*eers*,' Elise corrected her, sitting between her mother's legs now and letting wet sand drizzle through her fingers.

'Sorry, snorkell*eers*, in the space of one morning. If I didn't know better, I'd say they have mermaid genes.'

'*I* want to be a mermaid,' Tilde said sadly.

'I know, honey, we all do,' Hanna said, kissing her head and speaking into her hair.

Bell thought their shoulders looked pink. 'I'd better get more cream on them,' she said, wading out of the shallows. The sand was hot underfoot and she jogged lightly up onto the deck, rifling through the beach bag for the bottle.

'Girls, go and rinse off the sand first,' she heard Hanna saying behind her and moments later, the squeak of the pipes started up as the twins stood under the outdoor shower, just past the steps.

Hanna grabbed a beach towel and came and sat beside her on the chairs, both of them watching the girls shriek and play, droplets of water catching the sun's rays and sparkling like crystals. It made for an idyllic image. The radiance of summer. The innocence of childhood.

'Just look at them. So close . . .' Hanna murmured wistfully.

'Yeah . . .' Bell felt herself stiffen at Hanna's proximity. She didn't want to be this close to her, the woman who – unwittingly – had what she herself wanted, even though Bell knew she had no rights here. This was Hanna's family, her life, her mess, her husband . . . She couldn't imagine how Hanna would react to learning that Bell had fallen for him, been with him too. Not that she ever would; that secret, at least, would be safe. Emil had far more to lose than she if the truth came out. God, what a mess though. She and Hanna had both trodden on each other's toes without even knowing it and it occurred to her that this was how Max must feel – caught in the web of someone else's story, an unwitting bystander become collateral.

'How was Linus when you left?' she asked, stepping onto safe ground.

Hanna's mouth turned downwards and she lifted her gaze

off her daughters, staring out to sea, a flock of scolder ducks coming in to land on the water in a riotous chain of splashes. 'So-so. I think he would have liked to come back here with me. But then Emil offered to take him on a helicopter ride around the archipelago later, so . . .' She shrugged.

'Wow.'

'Mmm . . . He's spoiling him, of course.'

'Yes.'

'I knew he would.' She clicked her tongue against the top of her mouth, still watching the girls. 'I don't suppose I can blame him, though. I would do the same. I would do whatever it took to make my child love me again.'

Bell didn't comment. She would not be drawn. She was the nanny. This was a job.

Hanna sighed, clasping her hands together between her knees and dropping her head. 'Listen, Bell, Max told me what you'd said, about not going back there. You don't want to deal with Emil.' She pinned Bell with her customary cool stare. 'And I think I know why.'

Bell felt her blood freeze, her cheeks burn. *Oh God. Oh God. Oh God.* Emil *had* told her the truth about them?

Hanna glanced around, checking they were still alone. 'You know, don't you?' she whispered. 'About the other night.'

What? Bell blinked back, heart thudding as the confusion cleared. Her secret was still just that? He hadn't said anything about them? '. . . Yes.'

'That's why you didn't want to go back – your loyalty is with Max.'

Bell looked down at the deck. 'Yes,' she lied.

Hanna leaned in to her, urgency in the movements. 'Bell, it was *never* my intention to drag you into this. I would never knowingly put you in a position where you had to lie for me, or felt like you had to choose.' Hanna glanced at her askance. 'You must think I'm a terrible person.'

'Of course I don't. I . . . I don't know what I'd do if I was in your shoes.'

'I love Max. You have to believe that.'

Bell looked sidelong at her, sensing a 'but'.

Hanna dropped her head, nodding ashamedly. 'But, yes, I love Emil too. As much as I wish I didn't. As much as he doesn't deserve it after the things he's said and done.' She sighed. 'Maybe part of it is guilt, I don't know.'

Bell looked at her. 'Why would *you* feel guilty? He's treated you appallingly.'

'But he doesn't deserve what's happened to him. No one does. No matter how vile his behaviour, he's still lost more and suffered more than the rest of us put together. I can understand his rage, even if I don't like it. He's a desperate man.'

They watched the girls together in pensive silence, both knowing there was no easy answer, no compromise, no kind solution to their problem. Someone had to lose. Someone had to get hurt.

'You know you will have to choose, though,' Bell murmured. 'Sooner or later. Everyone's suffering this way.'

'I know, but *how*?' Hanna asked, her voice a desperate whisper. 'How do I choose between the father of my son and the father of my daughters?'

Again, it was a question with no answer. 'Does Max know?' Bell asked instead, keeping her voice down, glancing back to check he was still in the kitchen. She could see him through the glass door, scrubbing the perfectly clean worktop, his muscles flexed and tense.

'He hasn't said anything outright, but I think . . . I think he suspects there's *something*.' She gave an unhappy laugh, rubbing her face in her hands. 'He's feared it from the first day.'

Bell well remembered his haunted look when she'd come into the kitchen that early winter's morning. He had looked . . . not defeated, but somehow resigned to that eventuality, as though he expected to always lose out to Emil.

'But it *wasn't* from the first day, was it?' Bell hardly dared ask, a quaver in her voice. She didn't want to hear the details and yet, perversely, it was all she wanted to know. Whatever else had happened between her and Emil, there had been no lies between them; he had never deceived her. He had been upfront and direct about his plans to win his family back from the start.

'God, no. It's been a long, slippery slope.' Hanna sighed and gave a weary shrug, looking worn down. 'I tried hard, so hard, to keep the boundaries clear, but . . . there's history there, you know? And as Linus's father, we had to create some sort of new partnership together; I couldn't cut him out of our lives . . . I just never realized how difficult it would be – to be together but apart.'

'I'm sure,' Bell murmured. Together but apart was precisely what she'd had to navigate with Emil for the last two weeks, too. 'You took vows together, and he's still your husband at the end of the day.'

'He is, yes,' Hanna said slowly. 'But he's not the man I married, if that makes any sense.'

Bell glanced at her, confused.

'The accident has changed him . . . The Emil I married was . . . different. Repressed, I guess you'd say.' She rolled her eyes. 'His family are so prominent, their views can change the stock market fortunes of companies, alter careers of politicians . . . so he learned never to speak his mind, never to really show how he was feeling – which didn't always make him the world's best husband.' She sighed. 'But now, he's different. He's more quick-tempered, volatile . . .'

'And that worries you?'

'If I'm being honest . . . it sort of excites me,' Hanna whispered confidingly, eyes shining with her guilty admission. 'He's passionate now. Unpredictable. If anything could ever be said to be a positive outcome of a traumatic brain injury – it's that he has no filter.'

'That's not necessarily a good thing,' Bell murmured, having been on the wrong end of it herself. *Opportunity. Lust. Relief . . . Just the nanny . . .*

'I know. But now he just says what he feels, and when a man wants you and tells you like that –'

His hand in her hair. 'Bell.' A fragile sound giving shape to a wish.

Hanna gave an involuntary shudder, and Bell knew she was right. She clearly remembered how he had looked at her in the moonlight too, that same night; the same way he had looked at her on *Midsommar*'s . . . It had been the abandonment in his eyes that had undone her.

'Bell.' A shape to a need.

'When I went to check on him, he was already waiting for me –'

'Bell.' An apology, regret. Conviction.

'– I knew the moment I walked in . . . All those months, I've been trying so hard to resist what we both knew was there, circling around it, trying to deny it . . . I just couldn't pretend any more.'

'I'm awake.'

Bell felt a hollow in the pit of her stomach, every word a knife to her heart. She had confused his feelings for Hanna as feelings for her. Or he had. She wasn't sure – everything was so tangled, pulled and tugged into a tight, hard knot. 'Well,' she managed, her words little more than a mumble. 'You'd both had another scare. You thought you might have lost him again. That's bound to focus the mind.'

'It did. I've been living on my nerves for months and I've been so frightened, so confused—'

'Coffees, as promised.' Max's voice startled them both, and they looked round to see him coming through with the mugs on a tray. 'Apologies if you've been waiting for it, but I thought I'd give you both time to talk through the happy news.'

'Happy news?' Bell asked after a beat, hearing his wry tone as Hanna physically straightened, composing herself back into his capable, loving wife.

'Thank you, darling,' she said with a tight smile as he handed her a mug. 'I was actually just about to get to that bit.'

Happy news? After being 'frightened' and 'confused'?

Max frowned as he set the tray down on the wooden cube block that served as an outdoor table. 'You mean you haven't told her yet? What on earth have you been talking about for all this time then?'

There was a startled silence, and then –

'Linus,' both she and Hanna said together.

'Oh.' He sat down on Hanna's other side, one ankle resting on the opposite knee, and lifted the binoculars he had brought out with the drinks. 'Think I just saw some eider ducks,' he murmured.

The women exchanged looks.

'Anyway, Bell,' Hanna said after a moment, her tone lapsing back into the brisk efficiency Bell knew so well; the mask was back on, the actors were on the stage. 'You made it perfectly clear to Max you don't want to have to stay at Emil's going forward, and we respect that. Linus is bonding well with his father and, as you say, there's no need for you to be there when you can be more valuable here, with the girls.'

Bell gave a wary smile. 'But . . . ?' she prompted, looking between them both. She had an instinct for provisos.

Hanna inflated herself with a nervous intake of breath. 'Well, it's Emil's birthday tomorrow, and clearly . . . well, clearly he's had a rough time. It'll be the first birthday he's celebrated since he was . . . God . . . since he was twenty-four –' Her voice broke suddenly, and she pressed a hand to her mouth as a sob escaped her.

Max leaned forward, rubbing her shoulder. 'Hey,' he shushed.

'I'm sorry,' she whispered, a single tear wiggling down her cheek. 'Sometimes it just hits me.'

'It's bound to,' Max murmured, glancing at Bell apprehensively.

Bell gave a worried smile back, but it was clear Hanna was buckling under the strain of pretence. She was mired in lies. Living two lives. This couldn't carry on . . . It wouldn't.

Hanna sniffed and tried to straighten up. 'Sorry. Sorry.'

Bell waited, feeling her own nerves fray. She didn't care if it was Emil's birthday tomorrow. As long as what Hanna was about to tell her didn't involve her in any way . . . She didn't want to see him again; she couldn't. The expression in his eyes as he'd looked at her across the bedroom, Hanna beside him . . . *I'm awake.* She never wanted to see him again.

Hanna composed herself. 'Anyway, it's his birthday tomorrow, and it's only right it should be celebrated with his family. That's what he wants, and . . .' Hanna nodded, glancing at Max. 'I don't feel we can disoblige.'

'Of course not,' Max mumbled, patting her hand.

'So you're going back there tomorrow?' Bell asked with relief. 'Well, that's okay. I can stay here with the girls –'

'No, that's the thing. He wants *everyone* there – including Max, including the girls.'

'Good news, huh?' Max said drily, his expression one of grim resignation.

'But . . . I thought you said he wouldn't even acknowledge their existence?' Only the other week Emil had said to Linus that they weren't his 'proper' family. How much had really changed since then?

'He wouldn't – back then. But he's had time to adapt, and I think he appreciates now that Max has been a wonderful father figure to Linus –'

Father *figure*? Not father? Bell saw how Max flinched at the small distinction.

'– and Tilde and Elise are Linus's little sisters and, therefore, an inescapable part of his life. I think he's finally accepting the reality of the life he's come back to.'

Bell looked between her employers as Max gave a small snort and looked away. She knew he suspected what was really behind this new beneficence – if he'd won Hanna back, Emil could afford to be magnanimous in victory.

Hanna didn't seem to notice their mental scepticism. 'Please, Bell, we are going to need you there too. I know you don't like him. Emil told me you were very protective of Linus, and that you think he's spoiling him –'

That might be true but it wasn't his bloody parenting style that made it so impossible for her to return, she thought, looking down at her own hands, the fingers tightly interlaced, worried that she might betray herself in some way. They were, all three of them, balancing on the edge of a precipice.

'– You're right, of course, and it's something I'll have to

address with him at some point. But tomorrow is going to be a huge test for our family. It's going to be the first step forward with all six of us involved, and there's no question it'll be fraught. It's taken eight months to get to this point, and we really need you there to keep a hand on the tiller – take the kids away if things start getting fractious, distract them with a game if he's got one of his headaches.'

She suppressed the urge to roll her eyes. Hadn't Emil had suggested to her he was playing up the headaches for Hanna's sympathy vote?

'It's just tomorrow we need to get through. Please, Bell, help us over this next hurdle, and then I promise, I won't ask for another thing. Ever.'

Bell sincerely doubted that.

'The children are going to need a friendly face, someone they can escape to if everything goes sour.'

They're not the only ones, she thought, looking at Max's bitter expression and sorrowful eyes. Somehow, she sensed they both knew tomorrow was going to be the day he woke up and Hanna finally left him.

Ingarso, Stockholm archipelago, 15 June 2012

'He's so fast!' he laughed, standing at the door and watching Linus proudly totter down the long corridor, scarcely bending at the knees, arms held out to bounce off the walls. The old oak floors gleamed in the early evening light, all valuables removed from the consoles, lest he should charge into them.

'He's the fastest in kindergarten,' she said, and he heard the pride in her voice, saw how her eyes shone, her hands pressed to her mouth, a wince already hovering at the corners of her eyes as she braced and waited for the topple.

It didn't come. One length safely navigated, Linus turned and headed back again.

'I'm beginning to see your mother in him, I think,' he said.

'On account of the walk?' Her eyes shone with amusement at her own joke. 'What are you trying to say?'

He laughed. 'Around the mouth!'

She watched him with a rapt expression. 'Thank God you're back. We've missed you.' She kissed him, squeezing him in her embrace too. She was still slim, but her body was softer since having the baby. Everything about her was softer. Motherhood had, if not quite tamed her, certainly muted her somewhat.

'I've missed you too. Fill me in on everything.' He shrugged off his jacket, feeling his cares roll back. This was his first trip out here of the summer, having been caught in a roster of weeks of back-to-back travel, and already he could feel the archipelago's calm push down on him like a weighted blanket.

She set down a glass of rosé in front of him, and it caught the light. His eyes fell to the pretty flesh tone, the promise of summer. 'Well, there was a fright last week with Jakob, the harbourmaster – did you hear about his accident?'

His brow furrowed. 'No. What happened?'

'He tripped and fell in the water when the ferry was docking.'

His eyebrows shot up in alarm. 'No!'

'It's okay. He'll live. The bow thrusters were on, but not the engines. But he could have been crushed against the walls, of course.'

'Is he all right?'

'He's in hospital with a badly broken leg. They had to put

in metal plates and pins. He's in a bad way, poor man; his wife says he can't tolerate the morphine.'

He winced. 'Talk about kicking a guy when he's down.'

'I know,' she agreed. 'He's being very brave, though. Apparently he's loving all the fuss. The entire island's been to visit him, just about.'

'It'll make a change him being the subject of gossip for once, and not just the bearer.'

'Indeed.'

They clinked glasses, eyes meeting momentarily in a soft embrace, and he felt that sense of ease descend over him that he got any time she was near. It felt so good to be back; he had long ago realized she was his home. Linus waddled back into the room, falling inelegantly onto his bottom as he tried to pick up his favourite toy, a vintage matchbox car – a red Corvette, by the looks of it.

He looked back at her, seeing how her gaze dipped and skipped away from him as the small talk dwindled. She was flighty and nervous. 'And you? How are you? Really? You sounded down last time I called. I've been worried.'

'Oh, I'm fine.' She bit her lip, her body language changing. 'I shouldn't have thrown it all at you, like that, I'm sorry. You're so busy and—'

'Hanna.' He stopped her short. 'You don't ever need to apologize to me. You know that.'

She bit her lip and nodded. 'I know. And I know it's just hormones, the doctor keeps telling me that.' Her brow furrowed quizzically. 'I just thought it would have passed by now. I mean, he's walking! You'd think I'd be through it by now . . . I want to get back to feeling like my old self again, you know?'

He nodded. Her hand was lying flat on the table, and he

reached over and held it in his. 'We all want that too. Because you do know how very loved you are, don't you?'

For a moment, a flash of her old playfulness tripped over her like a sunbeam and she tossed her head haughtily. 'No, I'm not sure I do. How loved am I, exactly?'

Their eyes met, the connection vibrating like a gold thread between them. 'Only to the stars and back, and for all of eternity.'

He had never meant a word more, but he waited for one of her more waspish remarks. But though her mouth opened, she looked away, something unsaid residing in her profile. He frowned as her silence lengthened. 'Hanna . . . ?'

She looked back at him, tears shining in her eyes. Her lips were quivering as she tried to hold back emotions she didn't want to show. But it was no good. A single tear slid down her cheek, utterly perfect and pure on her pale, velvety skin. Without even thinking, he reached over and rubbed it with his thumb. 'Talk to me. What's going on?'

'. . . What if it's not the baby blues?' she whispered. 'What if it's . . . actually about something else that's wrong? What if it's about . . .' She swallowed. 'Us?'

His heart pounded faster as he realized what she was saying to him, the desperation in her eyes for him to acknowledge the truth.

'I don't think it's going to get better.' She shook her head more quickly now, her conviction beginning to harden. 'No matter how much I try, I don't think I can keep pretending with things the way they are. I'm not happy. You know I'm not.'

'I know, of course I do, but –'

A familiar beating sound suddenly made them both look up, descending upon the house like a thundercloud. They looked back at each other, the helicopter's downdraft already flattening the flowers outside the windows.

She gave an unhappy laugh at the timing, but he could see her devastated look was already being bitten back. 'Always so damned prompt,' she said with a single shake of her head, but below the withering top notes, he heard despair.

'Hanna, we need to talk about this –' He reached for her hand again, but she withdrew it quickly and began patting her eyes dry with her fingertips. Several moments later, she was remade again – no trace left of her distress – and she looked back at him with her usual composure. It was an incredible thing to witness, to see the mask being put back on.

'It's fine, honestly. There's really nothing to say, anyway. My mind is made up.' She pushed back her chair and rose, her meaning clear – the rest of the dinner party was arriving; their precious time alone together was already up. 'I'm leaving him.'

Chapter Twenty-Six

'You've got to keep it together,' Nina said, watching from her spot on the armchair as he criss-crossed the room.

'I am.'

'No. You're like a tiger in one of those zoos – pacing, pacing, pacing. You're setting me on edge, and I'm already one gin and tonic into my afternoon.' She watched as he tracked a figure of eight around the settle and past the ottoman. 'At least take those sunglasses off. It's quite disturbing looking at you wearing those things in the house.'

'It's not a fashion statement, Nina,' he said through gritted teeth, wishing she would stop telling him what to do. 'It's helping with my –' He suddenly grimaced and doubled over, clutching his head between his hands. The room had gone black, but his mind was alive with colour, images flashing past in an incomprehensible flash – faces, noises, pain. And Hanna. Always Hanna. Her clear eyes, a streak of her pale hair, the dazzling whiteness of her perfect teeth. And then the darkness enfolding him like a mother's arms, taking him away, keeping him safe . . .

He came to. Still standing, albeit stooped, Nina with her arm around him, a look he'd never seen in her eyes before.

Fear.

'I'm calling Cathy,' she said, guiding him over to a chair. He sank into it without protest, feeling his body slowly start to relax again, nerve ending by nerve ending. He knew the rhythm now. The pain built up in waves, whipping to a crescendo before dropping him like a body from a plane, no parachute.

'I'm fine.'

'Clearly not.'

'She was here yesterday,' he mumbled. 'Just before you arrived. She ran the usual tests and there's nothing more sinister at play. It's just the concussion. It'll pass. She's told Måns what to watch out for, don't worry.'

'Well, I do. It's irksome, but there you have it. It's not like I've not got enough to think about, without worrying your head is going to explode at any moment.' She sniffed. 'God, that would *ruin* the rugs.'

Even through his pain, he managed a smile. 'I'll do my best to avoid the rugs, then.'

She rewarded him with a half-smile as she retrieved her drink from the side table and sank back into her chair, watching him. 'What time is everyone coming?'

'From now. Linus is down there, waiting for them.'

'Hmph. Anyone would think he's missed them. Sentimental little thing, isn't he?'

'If by sentimental you mean loving, then yes.'

Nina took a sip of her drink, staring at the ice cubes as they clattered gently. 'It's funny that the nanny didn't come back.'

He looked at her, hearing the slice in her tone. 'Funny ha-ha?'

'A shame,' she said. 'I rather liked her. Thought she had spirit.'

'She certainly has energy,' he muttered.

'What did you do to scare her off?'

'I didn't do anything.' That was the truth, at least. He had done nothing. Let her go. Made her leave –

Nina arched an eyebrow. 'Emil, please. I am not a fool,' she drawled. 'She clearly had an impact on you.'

'How?' he snapped. 'In what way? What was the *impact* she had on me?'

'Well, she seemed to bring up your . . . what's the word? . . . anima.'

'My what?'

'You know, your life force. You seemed more alive whenever she was around.'

'Nina, you can't be *more* alive. You're either alive or dead. There's no –' He stopped short. He was the living proof that there was a middle ground. 'Look, if I seemed more lively, it was because Linus was here. She's just the nanny. She was only ever supposed to be here for a few days to help Linus settle in, until he and I got to know one another.'

Her eyes narrowed interestedly. 'You know, you always say that about her.'

'What do I say?'

'That's she's The Nanny. Just the nanny. Like it's a spell, or something. As though reducing her to just her job will somehow diminish her. You're not trying to lessen her *impact* on you, are you?' She gave a contented smile, pleased to have circled her argument. 'You forget I know you too well, little brother. You never could keep any secrets from me.'

He was too tired to argue, the pain draining him. 'I know what you're doing, you know.'

'Do you? What am I doing, then?'

'You're trying to divert me from Hanna, but I'm afraid you're too late. We're back together.'

Nina stared at him, for once lost for words. '. . . Does Hanna know?' she asked eventually.

'What do you –?' he blustered. 'Of course she knows! I'm not delusional!'

'Well, you are concussed.'

'I haven't imagined this. She was very definitely in my bed a few nights ago.'

'I see.' She took a slow sip of her drink, watching him, assessing for the micro-movements that would supposedly tell her whether he was lying.

'It can't be that surprising, surely?' he asked, offended by her evident disbelief. 'She is my wife and the mother of my child.'

'Mmm, but someone else's too, though. That's the bugger.'

He looked away, the words like razors, drawing blood.

'Does Max know?'

'He's no fool. He must suspect. Hanna and I weren't exactly discreet at the weekend. We went to the hotel for dinner; plenty of people saw us there together.' An image of Bell at the sea club – all languid curves and drunken laughs, hanging off Mats – flashed through his mind and he physically shook his head, casting her out.

Nina frowned as she watched him. 'But she hasn't had the decency to tell him yet?'

'It's a difficult thing to do, Nina. She's waiting for the right moment.'

'Or she's keeping her options open.'

He shot her a sharp look, refusing to go down this path. Nina loved to argue the way most women liked to shop. 'She knows we can't maintain this charade forever. It's time the truth was out.'

There was a small pause as Nina absorbed the information. 'Oh, so *that's* why you've got them all coming here. This is your birthday present to yourself,' she murmured, sipping her drink again.

'I –' He felt another spasm ricochet through his skull and he winced, emitting an involuntary gasp. 'I'm fine,' he whispered as soon as he could speak, knowing she would be looking at him with fright again. It was a minute before he had recovered enough to look back at her. 'I'm fine.'

She watched him, knowing he was lying, knowing he wouldn't let her help. She looked away, back into the ice cubes of her drink. 'So how do you feel about seeing Max again?' she asked, picking up the interrogation like it was a glove she had dropped.

'I haven't thought about it.'

'That seems rather disingenuous. You two were like brothers when you were little. I used to feel quite jealous.'

'I'm not interested in Max. Hanna and Linus are my only concerns. We can come to some arrangement, I'm sure.' Bitterness inflected the words, his patience worn thin by the pain. He needed to lie down before they got here.

'Pay him off, you mean?' Nina gave one of her staccato laughs. 'Ha! The apple really didn't fall from the tree, did it? Daddy would be *so* proud.'

His head jerked up at her barbs. 'Well, how do you think I feel, Nina? He was the closest thing I ever had to a true friend, and I woke up to find he's got with my wife and taken my family as his own! I thought he was different; I thought he didn't care about who we were and what we had; but he's just like all the rest, trying to get a slice of the pie. He might not be able to get the penthouse or the boat, but my wife? My sad, frightened wife, told by the doctors she's a half-widow? He wasted no time moving in, did he?' His eyes glowed like night flares. 'So don't ask me how I feel about seeing him, or tell me he's my brother. I owe him nothing. He took the best things in my life and made them his own. And now, when I take them back, it'll be *his* life that's destroyed. What's coming, he knew would someday come. He's always known it.'

Bell kept her eyes on the jetty, feeling her pulse quicken as they drew ever closer over the water. Bunting, strung along the handrails, was flapping noisily, and bunches of brightly coloured balloons bobbed manically from the trees, announcing a celebration to the rest of the lagoon. The weather was forecast to change, a spell of low pressure moving in from Finland, and gusty winds were already whipping and skimming over the lagoon, the water a desolate grey. The tideline was higher up the beach than she recalled, too, almost to the grass.

Tilde was sitting to her right, Elise to her left, their little bodies awkward in the lifejackets. Max was driving the boat and Hanna was up towards the front, ready to jump off and secure the lines as they docked. There was a strange, proprioceptive mood on board, and even the girls were sitting quietly (for once) and peering up at the adults with enquiring expressions.

They could already see Linus waving to them. Long before he was visible, they could see the white flag in his hand, the one he waved at night to Hanna across the water, a silent communication between mother and son. It was ragged and faded with time. She remembered what Max had told her about their boyhood jaunts on the water, and how their parents had gathered them home with exactly that system. It was intended as a welcome, but today it looked just as much like a warning.

She saw Max see it too and stiffen, his movements thrusting and abrupt as he manoeuvred the boat towards the shore, no hint of his usual relaxed manner.

'Did you see me?' Linus yelled, as the boat nudged against the dock and he grabbed the ropes with the instincts of someone raised on the water.

They all jumped off, the girls running to him for hugs. He submitted, but with a look of almost comical distaste.

'You look funny!' Elise exclaimed. 'What are they?' She pointed to his trainers – box fresh with chunky soles, and red and black detailing on them.

'They're Nikes. You can't buy them in Europe. My dad got them for me.'

His initials – his birthright initials – had been embroidered across the back – LVG. It was an aggressive move. Bell glanced at Max, and saw from his ashen expression that he had spotted it too.

'Did he indeed?' Hanna asked in a bemused, indulgent tone, kissing the top of his head. 'Well, I shall have to speak to him about that. That's far too extravagant for a boy of ten.'

'I want some!' Tilde cried.

'Well, you can't. My dad's rich, that's why he can get them, but I already told you – they're not available in Sweden.' Linus shrugged, beginning to walk ahead, leading the way.

Hanna and Max stared after him, mouths agape. Hanna went to run after him, but Max caught her by the arm and shook his head. 'Let it be. He's had a lot to deal with.'

He had. But was this how it was going to be? Bell felt a kernel of dread settle in her gut. She had been gone only four days, Hanna only one. How much could the child have been altered – spoiled – in that time? What else had Emil done to buy back his love?

They followed after him, into the trees. The shade was a welcome respite from the muggy heat as they trod the path in silence, single file; it was a chance for them not only to escape the glare and pounding heat, but to collect their thoughts before a meeting that was inevitably going to be fractious.

She reminded herself this was not her family; theirs were not her dramas. She was merely a bystander, a paid agent for the welfare of the children. *She* had nothing to worry about. But as they emerged from the trees and she saw the blue helicopter sitting on the lawn, blades drooping like a resting dragonfly, she felt her heart leap like a bucking horse.

Hanna too, seemingly. 'Fuck,' she muttered, stopping dead at the sight of it. 'He never said *she* was going to be here.'

'Nina,' Max said under his breath, with the weariness of a parent saying 'teenagers'.

The girls ran straight towards it, led by Linus, who couldn't stop himself from boasting. 'We went out on that last night. We went really high. You'd have been terrified.'

'No I wouldn't! I want to go on it,' Elise hollered, suddenly close to tears, and Bell ran forward, scooping her into her arms. She knew the toddler sensed Linus's hostility, his anger and defiance, and she felt a stab of remorse that she had left him here alone. This was her fault. She had indulged her own feelings of humiliation, and put her own need to get away above his need to have her stay.

'Linus, that wasn't kind,' she said firmly. 'Apologize to your sister, please.'

'No! She's not my sister! I don't have to be nice to her, and you can't make me. You're just the nanny.' And he suddenly sprinted away, up the lawn and into the house, his arms pounding like pistons.

Bell felt like she'd been punched.

'Oh my God,' Hanna whispered, watching him go.

'He'll settle,' Max said unconvincingly. 'He's just

overwhelmed. His emotions are too big to process just now, but he'll get there. Give him time.'

'I don't understand how you can be so calm about this,' Hanna cried, scooping up Tilde, who had started to cry too. 'He's rejecting us. You!'

'Yes. And we have to show him that no matter what he says or does, we love him and we're not leaving him. He needs to see we won't abandon him. Okay?' He smoothed a hand through her hair, calming her.

Bell watched, knowing their easy intimacy was invisible to them both. Hanna had been captivated by Emil's reckless, nothing-to-lose passion for her. Did this cosy familiarity feel boring by comparison? Was she going to give it up for the excitement – and glamour – of life as Emil Von Greyer's wife again?

They walked on. Max, looking stiff and paler than ever, still had that air of resignation about him; but she saw now that it wasn't a defeated position, but an accepting one. Perhaps the guilt of falling in love with his old friend's wife was too much, whatever the mitigating circumstances? Maybe he saw himself as the villain in this tragedy?

'Look, Pappa, it's orange!' Elise pointed excitedly at the house, forgetting her tears as they moved past the large helicopter and stopped in their tracks again.

'So it is,' Max murmured, taking in the sight. A carousel had been set up on the lawn, a bouncy castle and helter-skelter beside it; at the sight of the children, there were suddenly jugglers, fire-breathers, stilt-walkers and a marching band, all advancing across the lawn from the wooded fringes. Balloons had been tied to every single tree, so that it felt the entire island might be lifted out of the sea at any moment and drift heavenwards.

Both girls shrieked with utter delight, wriggling from the

women's arms and heading straight for the carousel. Bell saw the gardener standing to attention beside it, clearly comman-deered as the operator for the day. This time Hanna said nothing, and Max bit his lip as he watched his daughters race headlong into his rival's honeytrap.

Nina was standing on the terrace, watching and waiting, one arm strapped across her stomach, the other holding a cigarette. Plumes of smoke drifted into the sky as she blew out through the side of her mouth, eyes narrowed as they slowly approached, awed into silence.

'Nina,' Hanna said evenly, stopping directly in front of her on the steps. 'How are you? It's been ages.'

'Hasn't it?' Nina drawled, allowing a kiss on each cheek before she turned her attention to Max. 'Now you I *really* haven't seen in a while.'

'It's good to see you, Nina.'

'Is it, though?' she laughed drily, though her eyes danced. She looked at Bell. 'Hello again.'

'Hello.'

'You're dressed this time!'

Bell's mouth opened in astonishment, and she saw Hanna's head whip round. 'I . . . It wasn't how that sounds,' she said quickly. 'I can explain.'

This time Nina did laugh properly. 'Oh, please don't! Life's far more interesting if you never complain, never explain. *Let* them wonder.'

Bell looked at Hanna and Max with wide eyes, feeling curiously silenced. To deliver a comprehensive explanation somehow felt more damning.

'Mmm,' Nina smiled with relish, seeing how they had collectively paused, all of them on the back foot, as though held in abeyance. 'This is going to be *fun*.'

'Where is he, Nina?' Hanna wasn't smiling now.

'Linus? He's gone to his b—'

'Emil.'

'I'm here.'

They all looked over. He was leaning just inside the frame of the French doors. He looked pale but still punch-in-the-stomach handsome, his eyes burning as he took in the group gathered on his terrace. Beside her, Bell felt Max tense, the air around him somehow changing, becoming paler, thinner, less substantial.

Slowly, Emil walked over to them. Bell thought he looked like he was in pain; there was a hesitancy to his movements, a tightness across his face. She lowered her gaze, wishing she could disappear, become spectral. But he wasn't looking at her, or Hanna.

The two men stared at one another – similar in height, but where Max had the pale skin and soft muscles of the office worker, Emil was spry and tanned, looking older than his thirty-one years. It seemed somehow innately understood that Emil would be the one to break the silence and lead the conversation. This was his birthday, his home, his island, his family, after all. It seemed an age before he held out a hand. 'Hello, Max.'

Max shook it. 'Emil.'

'You look older.'

'You look well.'

A tiny smile half-cocked Emil's mouth. 'I caught up on my beauty sleep.'

The same half-smile tipped Max's mouth, but the humour hadn't risen to their eyes, not yet, and the atmosphere remained tense in spite of the civility.

'It's good of you to have gone to this effort for the girls,'

Max said, waving a hand in the general direction of the lawn amusements.

'Shame the weather isn't quite playing ball,' Emil nodded. 'But I wanted to make them feel at home.'

His words were light, courteous even, but the threat glinted just below the surface like a vein of steel. Home. Here. Bell realized she was holding her breath as the men kept their gazes steady.

'Come, let's have a drink while the girls play,' he said suddenly, breaking into the gracious smile of 'mein hoste' and leading them towards the large round table on the terrace. It had been set with a dark-grey linen tablecloth and a low bowl arranged with pale-pink dahlias, a bottle of champagne chilling in an ice bucket to the side. 'It's my birthday, after all. We should be celebrating. I slept through the last seven.'

Måns, who had been standing unseen by them all, stepped forward as though into physical being and elegantly unpopped the cork as they walked over.

'Hanna, why don't you sit here, next to me,' Emil said, motioning to the chair beside him. All eyes swivelled in his direction. 'That way, the girls will see their mother chatting and laughing beside me and know I'm not a big scary monster.'

'Right,' Hanna said, looking wan, her eyes sliding between both men, but Max was looking away, pretending to admire the gardens. Bell knew he was only pretending because she could see the ball of his jaw, clenched in tension.

'I'd better go and check on Linus,' she said, stepping back away from their group. She wasn't a guest here, after all, but an employee.

Emil's eyes flashed towards her – the first time he'd looked at her since arriving, the first time since that night, across the bedroom – *I'm awake* – and she felt frozen to the spot by their burning intensity. He released her again in the next moment, and she turned away with a gasp.

'So, thirty-one today,' Hanna said behind her with forced levity, her voice strained with the desperate urge to see today pass without hitch. 'My, my.'

'Well, I still haven't decided yet whether I should consider this my thirty-first or my twenty-fifth . . .' she heard Emil saying as she stepped into the house.

Out of sight, Bell sagged against the wall and closed her eyes, trying to recover. The way Emil had looked at her so angrily, as though he hated her too . . . Did he despise her for her act of defiance in refusing to return? He was bristling with a hostility that was made worse by concealing it beneath a veil of manners. Outright contempt, anger and swinging fists would have been preferable to that.

She found Linus in his bedroom, sitting against the far wall beside the open window. He had his head on his knees and was rolling the Corvette back and forth on the ground, listening to the murmur of adult conversation below, the occasional shrieks drifting up of his little sisters having fun without him. Dozens of books lay face down on the floor, some of the pages ripped out and scattered around him.

'Hey.' He looked up, his face tear-streaked, and she felt her heart break. 'Oh darling,' she whispered, rushing over to him and enveloping him in a hug.

'I'm fine,' he said defiantly, allowing himself to be held nonetheless as she kissed his hair and rubbed his shoulders, the way he liked her to when he was sick.

They sat in silence for several minutes. She wouldn't push him if he didn't want to talk about it.

'How was yesterday?' she whispered. It had been his first full day alone here when Hanna had come back to Summer Isle, and Bell had refused to return. Already she hated herself for it.

'. . . It was okay,' he said eventually, his voice thick. 'We helped get the garden ready and then we went on the helicopter.'

'Wow, you're so lucky. I've never been on one. Was it amazing?'

'Yeah.'

She gave a little smile. 'That didn't sound very convincing.'

'I'm just tired,' he sighed, closing his eyes as a few tears silently slipped past his lashes.

'I know you are,' she murmured, feeling the knife twist in her heart and ruffling his hair with her fingers. 'It's been a busy time lately. The girls have missed you so much.'

'Mmm.'

'They went straight onto the carousel. Have you had a ride yet?'

'No. I'm ten.'

'Ah, yes. The fire-breathers are cool, though.'

He sighed, impatient with her attempts at conversation.

'We could go for a walk if you like. Get away from here for a bit. We could go swimming on the far side.'

His shoulders convulsed under her hands, and she realized he was sobbing.

'What's going to happen?' he asked, his voice thick.

'. . . I just don't know, sweetie. I don't think anyone does.'

'Mamma loves him.'

She swallowed. 'Of course. She and your dad were married. They had *you*. They'll always love each other.'

'But she loves him *now*.' He looked back at her, and she knew he somehow knew his parents were a couple again. What had he seen? Please God, not what she had. 'So what about Pappa?'

Her mouth opened, but no words would come. What was she supposed to say? 'Well, that's why it's complicated, because Mummy loves him too. They fell in love when they were both sad about your dad, and then they had the girls. So although that isn't your dad's fault, it's not your pappa's either. No one's a bad guy here.'

He lay his head back down on his knees, looking younger than his ten years, tears continually pooling and overflowing in his clear green eyes.

'. . . Will I have to choose?'

'Choose? Oh no, darling! Oh no, no, no, no, of course not. Emil and Max both love you very much. There's room in your life for both of them.'

'But there's not room in their lives for each other, is there?' he cried. 'They're enemies. They hate each other. And which-ever one I choose, the other one will hate me too.'

'Linus, no,' she whispered desperately. 'They could never hate you.'

But he squeezed his eyes shut, shutting her out. 'I just want to go home.' His voice was small, the wish even smaller.

Bell flinched, unable to reply. What if he already was?

They lapsed into silence, the band playing 'The Bear Necessities' down the lawn, snippets of conversation drifting to the window like fragments of burnt paper in a bonfire, the flames pushing them ever upwards.

'Now let me guess. You must be . . . Tilde,' she could hear Emil saying. 'And you're Elise.'

'No!' The girls squealed excitedly, and Bell could hear their feet jumping up and down on the spot on the terrace.

'Gah,' he grimaced, seemingly smacking his thigh with his hand, panto-style.

'It's your birthday today,' Elise informed him, lest he should have forgotten.

'Well yes, it is.'

'How old are you?'

'Actually, I've got a choice, perhaps you can help me decide. Should I be twenty-five or thirty-one?'

'Five!' Elise shouted.

'All right then! That's what I'll be. And how old are you?' he asked.

'We're three! I'm older by nine minutes!' Elise shouted. They were shouting a lot today, their nerves on edge.

'Ah!' he said interestedly. 'And when will you be four?'

'October the eleventeenth.'

He laughed, light-hearted and relaxed. 'Lucky you. That's the best date in October.'

'Off you go now, girls, have a go on the helter-skelter,' Hanna said. A moment later, as the girls could be heard tearing over the lawn, she added, 'Emil, do you want to lie down? You look pained.'

'You are as white as a sheet,' Max said, chipping in.

'I'm fine,' he replied in a flinty tone. 'What I *want* to do is talk.'

There was a deafening silence, and Bell realized, from her spot scrunched up on the floor, that she was holding her breath too. This was it. He was doing it. He was going to tell Max everything and blow apart their little family unit, even as the girls played just metres away.

She wished she could get on her knees and peer over the windowsill to see Hanna's face right now. Was she reaching for his hand under the table, beseeching him not to do it, to give her more time? Because she wasn't ready yet, Bell knew that. She was confused, certainly, balancing on a tightrope in storm-force winds, but to choose between them . . . Emil might have the certainty of his convictions, but Hanna didn't. Not yet.

There was the sound of a gasp again, a chair being scraped back.

'Right, that's it.' Nina's voice intruded. 'You're coming with me. The talking can wait. We've got all day for that. You need to lie down, even if only for ten minutes.'

'I'm *fine*.'

'No. You're not.'

There were more sounds of scraping, a low groan followed by irritable tuts. Footsteps, retreating.

A silence.

Then Max's voice, calm, measured, tight. 'So, are you going to let *him* tell me what the hell's going on, Hanna? Or do you want to get in there first?'

Ingarso, Stockholm archipelago, 24 June 2012

The pen rested in the cradle of his finger and thumb, the teal ink showing through on the front side of the receipt. It was tiny. Innocuous. Unremarkable. But he already knew that scrap of paper and those four words were going to change all their lives.

The hidden beach, midnight.

Chapter Twenty-Seven

Bell stopped on the landing as the two dark-haired heads appeared above the top stair.

'Come on. You were getting worked up, I could see it,' Nina panted, Emil's arm around her shoulder as they climbed slowly together. 'You had that crazed glint in your eyes you always got when you were about to swear at me as kids.'

'I was not about to swear at you,' he muttered.

'No, but you were about to do something else just as mad. Now take a ten-minute time-out and cool yourself down.'

'I'm not a child!'

They stepped onto the landing and Nina glanced up, as though sensing her presence. Bell suspected she had the finely tuned instincts of an attack dog. 'Oh. You're there, Bell.'

'Yes, I was just in with Linus,' Bell said, seeing how Emil looked wracked with pain. She frowned. 'Is he okay?'

'Not really. The headaches are making him crazy.'

'I'm not crazy.'

'You were about to be,' Nina sniffed. She looked back at Bell. 'Could you help me get him into his room? He's being obstinately heavy.'

'I'm *not*. I just can't see that well right now. Everything's fuzzy round the edges.' He was mumbling.

'Just take his other arm, would you?' Nina instructed.

Bell did as she was told, draping his arm over her shoulder, the scent of him wrapping around her like a fur boa. She closed her eyes, trying to pretend he wasn't him.

'For chrissakes, I'm not an invalid. I don't need you both to help me walk,' he resisted, trying to remove his arm from her.

'No, you're quite right,' Nina said glancing across at the two of them. 'You can manage with just one of us. Fine, trot along then,' she said, ducking out of the way herself. 'I'll get back to our *treasured* guests.'

They both watched her go, feeling they'd been somehow played, but not quite sure how. Or why.

'Well . . .' Bell said after a heavy pause. 'Let's get you resting, then.'

'I don't need—'

'Oh just stop,' she snapped, losing patience with his continual protestations. 'You're clearly not well. Just accept the help, okay?' And when she saw his astounded expression. 'What? *You're* not my boss.'

They continued down the landing and into his bedroom. Bell kept her eyes down as they crossed the floor, helping him onto the side of the bed. 'You should lie down,' she said.

He sat instead.

She refused to even look at the room – she had resolved never to return here, to the scene of her humiliation – but walked straight over to the table by the window and poured him a glass of water from the carafe. 'Here, drink that. It's important to keep hydrated with headaches.'

He obeyed, watching her as he drank. 'You're angry with me.'

'Why should I be angry at you?' He arched an eyebrow but didn't reply, which only served to make her . . . angry.

354

'Do you need some painkillers? I think it's very clear you do,' she said briskly, giving him no time to answer.

'I'll get them—' But she was already heading across the room again, towards the bathroom. 'Fine, invade my privacy then,' he called after her.

She walked through to the en-suite. It was easily the size of her bedroom in the apartment, white strip-wood floors, a walk-in shower, a marble-topped vanity unit. She pressed the push-doors of the wall cabinet and scanned the contents – deodorant, toothpaste, comb, moisturiser, various vitamins.

'They're in a bag. New prescription,' he called through.

She crouched low and opened the cupboard, her eyes falling to a white paper bag on the top shelf. She grabbed it and peered in, finding what she was looking for, but as she was withdrawing, she caught sight of the sheer number of pill boxes and bottles in there. It was like a pharmacy stockroom, evidence of the vast chemical formulations that had been needed to put his body back together and now keep him functioning, pain-free. No wonder he hadn't wanted her to see this; it was evidence of his frailty.

Like Jack's. Just the sight of it threw her straight back into her own past, the medical detritus building up – more pills, more drugs – as the doctors had battled to keep him alive. Battled in vain. Jack had lost, and she had been lost with him.

'Any time before I die of a brain haemorrhage would be good!' he called, bringing her back to the moment.

She walked through a moment later and handed him the pills. 'As someone who I understand had to undergo a craniotomy yourself, that's not a particularly funny joke to make.'

'Yes, well, I wouldn't remember that.'

'Hanna told me.'

'It must be true, then,' he muttered, slamming them in his mouth and swallowing them with a gulp of water, his eyes fixed upon her as she looked everywhere but at him. '. . . You're particularly edgy today. How's it going with Mats?'

'That's none of your business,' she said, taking the glass from his hand – a little water left in the bottom – and walking it back to the table.

'You looked like you were having a good time on Saturday night.'

'Yes. We were.'

'Are you going to see him again?'

'That's none of your business,' she repeated.

He watched as she moved back across the room.

'I'm going to check on Linus,' she muttered, refusing to be drawn into whatever game he was playing with her. He thought he could be the cat to her mouse again? No chance.

'Things are going well between Linus and me, thanks for asking,' he said to her back.

She turned around and gave a laugh that would have made Nina proud. 'Don't kid yourself. You've got his attention only because you're dazzling him with flashy boats and helicopter rides and private screenings.'

His mouth tightened. He didn't like hearing the truth, but nor did he try to deny it. 'Perhaps. But that's all I can give him that Max can't. I missed out on all his formative moments, I wasn't there, he grew up without me – so now I'm having to create special memories with him myself.'

'But that isn't what he needs from you. He needs to feel safe. He needs to know you "see" him. You can't just *buy* him.'

'I'm not trying to.'

'Yes, you are!' she cried. 'Of course you are. You think you can have whatever you want. Nothing is denied to you!'

'You are!' He sprang up from the bed with a suddenness that made her jump. 'I don't have you, do I?' The words had seemingly left him without permission – no filter – as he looked back at her with an anger and resentment she couldn't understand. He slumped, slightly, as though something had been pulled from him, leaving him exhausted. Empty. 'I don't have you, Bell.'

'As I recall, *you* made the decision on that.' Bitterness reflected off her words like bright lights.

'Yes. I did.' He walked slowly towards her. 'Because it was the only decision I could make. It was the right one. I want my family back. I don't want to want you.' She could see the tension in his mouth as he spoke, emotions running across his face as he stopped just feet away. 'It's not supposed to be you! *She* was the last thing I saw before the accident. *She* was all I could think about when I woke up. She's the reason I got back to this point. She's the mother of my child. She's the only woman I've ever loved. I can't . . . I just can't . . .' His eyes roamed her face, kissing her without touch.

'. . . Fall for the nanny?' she finished for him, feeling flattened. Because she got it, she did. A one-night hook-up couldn't be allowed to derail a marriage, a family, a life. 'I know.'

'But you don't.' His voice was hoarse. 'Because when I close my eyes now, I see you. When I was with her, I saw you. When you didn't come back, I missed you.' He clutched his head, the fingertips blanched white as he squeezed hard against his skull, as though the thoughts, the feelings, the pain, could be forced out. 'I missed you and everything's wrong. It was so clear before, what I had to do. Ever since I woke up, it's always felt like . . . something's missing, a part of me. And it has to be them. It must be. They're my family.' His hands dropped down as he looked back at her, looking defeated. Worn down. 'It can't be you.'

'. . . I know,' she said again, not daring to move. Her heart was pounding like a jackhammer, the shock of his words still rebounding through her body like pinballs. 'I'm sorry.'

They stared at one another, unable to move closer, unable to pull away in an unbearable fixed tension that couldn't be broken. 'Today's the day I'm getting them back,' he said slowly, decisively, though she couldn't tell if he was convincing her, or himself. 'I'm not waiting another hour. When I go back down there, I'm telling Max everything.'

She nodded, feeling his eyes travelling over her skin like fingertips, touching her, feather-light. 'Okay.'

Their eyes locked and the magnetic attraction sprang to attention again. He waited. And waited. '. . . This is where you tell me that she's happy with him.'

Bell swallowed. 'She was. But now she's happy with you.'

He waited, his stare becoming more fixed, resolute. 'This is where you tell me that I'll never be half the father Max is.'

She forced herself to look back at him. 'You love your son. That's all he needs.'

A small sound escaped him, something between a groan and a plea. 'And this is where you tell me that when you were with Mats . . .' His voice cracked. 'That you didn't think of me.'

Reflexively, she looked away, the lie lodged in her throat, immovable, untellable. Because the truth was, eyes closed, he was all she'd seen and all she'd felt.

'Bell –' There was heat in the word, shape to a need, as he stepped towards her . . .

But she stepped away. 'No. You're doing the right thing,' she whispered, her eyes shining with tears as he stared back at her, so close and yet a world away. 'It's not me.'

He lay on the bed and stared at the ceiling, waiting for the pain relief to kick in and trying to still his mind; but the headache and his emotions had fused into some kind of vortex

358

whirling through him, a roar of images and sounds and feel-ings that he could neither control nor contain.

Seeing Max had been harder than he'd anticipated, dredging up feelings and memories he didn't want. Friendship-boyhood-adventure-fishing-drinking-weddings – Hanna.

Hanna. Always her.

He closed his eyes and she filled his head again. Flash of blonde. Pale skin. Blue eyes. Blackness. The last thing he saw and the first thing he saw. Blue eyes crying. Pale skin. Blonde . . .

His mind stopped, automatically rewound. Flash of blonde. Pale skin. Blue eyes crying. The last thing he saw. Blue eyes crying . . .

He stared at the ceiling, feeling his heart pound like it was going to burst from his chest, his body held captive to his mind, pain spearing through him as he lay rigid on the mattress while the memories played on and on in a loop – successive, continual. Stuck. Blue eyes crying. Blackness. The last thing he saw.

Blue eyes crying. Blackness.

Blue eyes crying. Black.

Blue eyes crying. Black.

Blue eyes crying.

. . .

Black car.

Ingarso, Stockholm archipelago, 25 June 2012 – midnight

She lay in his arms, both of them watching the full moon drift slowly above, framed by the almost perfect circle. The crater walls were ragged and frilled like a jellyfish, the dark water glimmering darkly just a few metres from their feet, hissing into the sand in rhythmic breaths.

She had already been in the water when he'd arrived, her skin so pale she could have been a mermaid. They had swum, they had chased and they had succumbed, over and over. Those years of abstinence, of doing the right thing, had done nothing to dull their appetite for one another; on the contrary, they had heightened it and he understood what a half-life he had walked through till now, thinking it could be enough to inhabit the periphery of her world.

They watched the sky brighten with every breath and he felt a spasm of panic. The sun was winning the fight, painting up the day and drawing her back. Away from him.

'I want to freeze time,' she whispered, holding him more tightly again, reading his mind. 'I want to make this the day and not the night.'

He kissed her lips, knowing wishes didn't come true. He was a realist. He knew that she could never be his, not truly. It was an unwinnable fight. 'So do I.'

She looked up at him with self-reproach. '. . . I left it too late, didn't I?'

He bit his lip. They had both been too late, permanently behind the clock from the start. 'You tried to do the right thing. We both did.'

She looked up at him, knowing what he was saying. For all her fighting talk about leaving, she was trapped. They both knew she had too much to lose now. 'I will tell him one day. When it feels . . . safe. It won't always be like this, I promise.'

'No, I want you to promise it will be,' he said, stirring and shifting on top of her again. 'I want you to promise it will always be like this.'

Chapter Twenty-Eight

She sat on the bottom stair, staring out at the idyllic scenes playing out in the garden. Linus had finally left his room to join his sisters, too intrigued by their giddy shrieks to stay upstairs, and the three of them were coming down the helter-skelter together – Tilde in front, Elise in the middle and Linus at the back, his longer legs stretching past theirs and keeping them safe as they whirled down the slide. Hanna was waiting at the bottom to catch them with outstretched arms, Max sitting at the table still and photographing them on his phone.

It was a perfect moment. They looked like the perfect family. And yet it was a mirage, no more real than Jack walking through her dreams. Upstairs was a man – a husband and father – who was preparing to take back what he had lost as he lay unconscious for all those years, and who would bet against him getting it? He was the man who had defied all odds just to be back in that room. It was the promise of reclaiming his family, and that alone, which had propelled him back to life and nothing – not Max, not her – would get in the way of that. Nothing should.

Her heart juddered at the still-hot memory of what had just passed between them and she gave another silent gasp, at what could have been, at what might have been, her shoulders hoisting up to her ears as she hid her face in her hands. Twice now, in that room, temptation had made them both buckle – but not fall. He had resisted her and now she had resisted him, though it had taken everything in her to do it.

She watched Hanna blankly through the long windows, serene in a white blouse and oatmeal linen shorts, looking for a sign that she too was about to switch worlds – these were the dying moments of her and Max's life together – but there was nothing. Here she was the Madonna and not the whore, an adoring mother playing with her children, no hint of the unfaithful wife who had slept naked upstairs in those twisted sheets.

Bell sniffed and wiped the tears away with the back of her hands. She knew she had to go back out there; she knew what she had to do. Somewhere through this heady summer, the Mogerts' lives had become fully hers and she had lost sight of herself. Become lost in a family that wasn't hers, no matter how much she might wish it –

'Don't let him get to you. He can be a difficult bugger. Always was. That's just about the one thing we can't pin on the accident.'

She looked up to find Nina leaning against the newel post, her drink held languidly in the palm of one hand.

Hurriedly, Bell dried her face as best she could. 'Oh no, I'm fine really.'

'Ha!' Nina barked. 'You're beginning to sound like him.'

Bell didn't reply and Nina took her silence as an invitation to join her on the bottom step. She shuffled over politely, making room.

'I'll be honest, I was rather hoping you'd be in there longer than you were.'

'Excuse me?'

'Oh, look, deny it if you want, but I know my brother and he's been nothing but agitated since you turned up on the scene. You're quite the cat among the pigeons, Bell.' Her eyes narrowed as she watched the Mogerts play. '. . . I don't mind telling you I was really rather banking on you steering him off this course he's so hell-bent on taking. I thought you were my wild card.'

Bell didn't reply. She couldn't. How on earth could Nina know about them? Had Emil told her?

'Does Hanna know?' Nina asked instead.

Slowly, uncertainly, she shook her head.

'No.' Nina sighed; compassion seemed to drain her. 'I'd be the first to tell her if I thought it would make a damned difference, but Emil just won't be deterred. As far as he's concerned, I'm just a dog barking at the moon.'

'I don't know what –' Bell faltered, worried that just to speak would incriminate her.

'Sure you do. He's got a second chance at life and he's fixing his entire future to a false memory of his past. It's such a shame. He's worked so hard to get here; he thinks that getting his life back means having his *old* life back. He can't see what a misstep he's taking.'

Bell bit her lip. 'But he loves Hanna.'

'No. He thinks he does. He just doesn't remember how it really was.'

'What do you mean?' she frowned.

Nina gave a sigh, sounding weary. It was a foreign sound for her to make, like a giggle or squeak. 'Because Hanna was the last thing he saw, the first thing he saw, whatever, he thinks that means they had this great love. And Hanna is exploiting him into continuing to think that.'

'Exploiting him?' It was a strong word to use. 'Are you saying they didn't have a great love?'

'To begin with, sure. They were as besotted as twenty-year-olds tend to be; first love, and all that. But by the time of his accident . . .' She trailed off.

'Things were tricky between them?'

'More than that,' Nina scoffed.

Bell frowned harder. 'Was it over? Were they going to divorce?'

Nina looked over at her with laser-sharp eyes that didn't say no. 'What he's chasing is just an idea, a warped memory.' She took a deep gulp of her drink. 'But perhaps I shouldn't say too much; not if she is going to be my sister-in-law again . . . God, discretion's *such* a fucking pain,' she muttered.

Bell watched her, trying to figure her out – she was direct and yet oblique too. 'So because the marriage was on the rocks – that's why you don't like Hanna?'

'Oh, I never did, I won't lie. I always thought he was more in love with her than she was with him. She was going out with a friend of his when she met him. She was that sort of girl, always climbing up, up, up . . . I thought she was with him for the –' She twirled her hands in the air, indicating the house and everything it represented: their family, fortune, lifestyle.

'But Hanna's got a good job,' Bell protested. 'She earns her own money. She doesn't need Emil's.'

Nina laughed her laugh. 'Oh, Bell, do you really think they could afford that house on her and Max's salaries?'

Bell didn't know how to reply. She was Generation Rent; she'd never thought too much about the cost of townhouses in the best district in town. It was a problem she was never likely to have for one thing, not to mention she had no actual idea of what kind of money Max and Hanna made. It had always seemed to her that as long as you had enough for what you needed, surplus was . . . surplus.

'The family trust set up a provision for her and Linus after Emil's accident, to give them financial security.' She arched an eyebrow. 'Why do you think she never changed Linus's name?'

'She did. He's registered as Mogert at school. It's on his school books, his name tapes . . .'

Nina shook her head slowly. 'Those are not the legally binding records, they are discretionary only, for his day-to-day purposes. You can be sure somewhere in the school files is a form that lists him as Von Greyers. Have you ever seen his passport?'

'. . . No.'

'Well, if you did, you'd see it's still in our surname. Max never officially adopted him – it was tricky, obviously, on account of Emil still being technically alive all those years. But let's not be fooled – it is also because he's an heir to an impressive fortune, and that name is as much a key to the money as a PIN.'

Bell was quiet for a moment, digesting the news. 'Hanna's never mentioned anything about that to me,' she said uneasily, trying hard to remain loyal to her boss. Whatever difficulties they had endured recently, whatever conflicts of interest they unwittingly shared on a private level, she had been a good employer for the past three years; they were friends, of a sort. 'She never mentions money.'

'No need to when it's being pumped in,' Nina shrugged.

'Well, if you think she's all about the money, then why hasn't she left Max already? It's been six months since Emil woke up.'

Nina looked thoughtful, her gaze still pinned to the twins. 'That's what I can't quite figure out.'

'You just don't like her.'

'No, there's something else too, I know there is. I just can't put my finger on it. She's been keeping him close –'

'Yes, because they share a son.'

'But not so close that she had to make any difficult decisions. She's kept her options open all this time – until he got hurt again. But she's been all over him like a rash ever since his concussion.'

'Maybe it helped clarify things for her, being confronted with the possibility of losing him again.'

Nina glanced at her. 'Doesn't she strike you as . . . jumpy?'

'I think *you* make her nervous.'

'Yes,' Nina laughed, flashing a sudden smile. 'But then I always did . . . No, this still feels like something more.' His eyes narrowed. 'Hanna's up to something.'

Bell remembered them in bed together, skin on skin, limbs intertwined, and she inhaled sharply. 'It's the guilt. She still loves Max and she feels torn, she's been trying to do the right thing by them both, but I think she's made her choice.'

'Emil certainly has,' Nina muttered.

'Whatever happened in their past, things are different between them now and I think the accident has, in some perverse way, saved their marriage – *if*, as you say, it was previously failing,' Bell said. 'Hanna told me herself Emil's a different man to the one she married; in the process of dealing with his recovery, it seems they've fallen for each other all over again.'

Nina dismissed her theory with a horsey toss of her head. 'He's fallen for you, Bell, he's just too pig-headed to face it because you don't fit into his "masterplan".' She made quote marks with her fingers. 'And you've fallen for him too. There's not many other reasons to be sitting crying on the stairs.'

Bell looked away, not wanting to hear it, other words still echoing in her head. *It can't be you.* Nina tutted disappointedly. 'You should be fighting for him.'

I want my family back. I don't want to want you. 'He wants

Hanna,' she said flatly. It was a simple and undeniable truth. 'Hanna and Linus, and nothing – and no one – will stop him from getting them back.'

Nina fell quiet, distracted. 'Hmm. Actually . . . that may not be strictly true,' she murmured. 'There's likely someone who knows more than he'll tell.' She was watching something further down the long hall, and Bell followed her gaze. Måns was watering a pale peach potted rose.

'You think Måns . . . ?' Bell looked back at Nina, wondering why she was so determined to believe there had to be another reason for Hanna being with Emil. Why couldn't she accept that if they'd fallen in love once before, it could have happened again?

'He knows something, possibly.'

'Then speak to him.'

Nina gave a frustrated exhale. 'He'd never tell me something about my brother's private life.' She gave a mirthless bark. 'Ha, he'd only tell Emil himself if Emil actually asked the right question.' She shook her head. 'Like I said, discretion's *such* a fucking pain.'

They watched Måns carefully tend to the plant, both of them seeing different things – to Nina, he was a keeper of secrets; to Bell, he was just an elderly man dead-heading with gentle fingers.

'I should go,' Nina sighed after a moment. 'I don't want Hanna relaxing too much in my absence.' She rose, giving a sharp-eyed smile. 'I may not be able to stop this fiasco but I have to be allowed my sport at least.'

Bell watched her go, feeling a stab of pity for her boss. But it seemed to Bell that beneath the sleekly threatening exterior, Nina was more Labrador than Doberman. And she loved her little brother, that much was undeniable.

She dropped her head in her hands, dreading going back out there too and rejoining the macabre party, all of them waiting for the moment Emil came back down and finished what he'd started. Finished, once and for all, the love triangle between him, Hanna and Max.

She watched Max, grey-faced and sitting stiffly at that table as his daughters enjoyed the private fairground set up on the lawn; keeping a dignified silence as he was forced to accept the hospitality of the man he knew wanted to rob him of *his* family.

Rob him back, Emil would argue.

She sighed, exhausted by the circular argument. There were no villains to rail against, no fair way out of this. Max wasn't the bad guy here, but neither was Emil and when all was said and done, he had lost more and been hurt more than anyone. Forget what his family and connections and wealth could get for him; surely the universe *owed* him some sort of recompense? Who could possibly deserve a happy ending more than him?

Max knew he deserved it, it was why he was here, and she knew it too. It was why, in that bedroom, against all her instincts, she had walked away. It was why she was going to walk out there and do it again, hand in her resignation with immediate effect. Because what was best for Emil was worst for her. She couldn't stay. Working with or for him simply wasn't an option, they both knew that; it didn't even need to be said. He needed a clear run at his future with Hanna if they were going to make it work this time round.

And she needed a clean break. She knew what it was to be alone, to have her heart broken. She had lost love before but she had survived it, and now she would do it again. The roots that had grounded her after Jack's death now felt tight and constrictive. She had to break free. Be free.

Drawing a slow, determined breath, she stood, her gaze

steady upon the small group outside, fidgeting and pretending to be at home. Then she walked back out to the garden to do what had to be done – unaware she was being watched.

Ingarso, Stockholm archipelago, 25 June 2012 – dawn

He walked through the trees, twigs snapping underfoot, the sea an inky ribbon glimpsed in snippets. It was not yet five but the moon was dipping, and across the calm waters of the lagoon, an elk was swimming between the isles. He could see the rowboat bobbing on a slack line, the jetty a shadow on the silvered surface.

He stepped onto the beach and over the weathered boards, their rattles percussive in the silence. Nothing had changed, and everything had. Four years of walking the wrong path had been corrected, and he felt a solidity within his body he'd never known before. He inhabited himself now; his soul had settled like a weight, anchoring him to the ground, the earth, this life. Her.

He approached the boat, squinting as he drew nearer and caught sight of something white on the bench seat. An envelope.

He looked around him in alarm but no sound came from the dark woods, no eyes flashing from the shadows. He stepped down and picked it up. Inside was the receipt, crumpled yet with a precise fold line across the middle. She must have dropped it – and someone else had found it.

Someone who knew his writing.

Because written on the front was a short-three letter word. His name.

Chapter Twenty-Nine

'You'll be pleased to hear my headache has cleared.'

The conversation stopped and they all turned as one to find Emil standing at the doorway to the terrace. Bell looked up from her spot on the steps with Linus and the twins. They were eating off their laps as a treat, too excitable to sit at the table today, even for ten minutes.

The sky had clouded over in his absence, thick clouds stealing shadows off the ground, an ominous wind ruffling their hair and shirts.

'Good!' Hanna said, sounding pleased. Relieved. There was an edge of mania to her brightness. 'Come and quickly have some birthday lunch, then. I'm afraid we had to start without you. The children were getting restless and it's trying to rain, so we might need to move indoors shortly.'

He walked over, Nina catching his eye. 'You *do* look better,' she said, regarding him almost suspiciously. 'I told you you needed to lie down.'

'You are always right. I should listen to you more.'

His sister frowned, puzzled by his rare obedience as he sat down in the chair beside her. 'Have I missed much?' His eyes flickered over the group – Hanna, Max, her . . . Quickly back to Nina again.

Bell felt herself flinch. She was cast out already. Here but not.

'We were just discussing the European elections,' Nina said in a sangfroid tone that came with an invisible eye-roll.

'Ah.'

The conversation resumed, Hanna seeming particularly engaged on the topic – Nina significantly less so – as Måns came over with a plate of poached salmon and cucumber salad and set it down before him. Bell watched Emil eye it without appetite, knowing that even if he could taste it, none of them were here for the food. He picked up his fork but held it limply in one hand and she could see the words building up inside him, like steam in a kettle. His eyes kept darting between Hanna and Max as they all tried to eat, and Bell noticed how the Mogerts didn't make eye contact or address each other in his presence; there were none of the intimacies or endearments, touching hands or shared laughs that characterized their home life. Was it out of courtesy to Emil? Or because it was all over? Bell couldn't tell. Everyone was on guard, playing games . . . They might as well have been strangers, and she realized that the last time the three of them would have eaten a meal together, Hanna would have been Emil's wife and Max their guest. But now, the cards had been shuffled, the deck rearranged . . .

Emil ate a mouthful of the salmon, his stony expression reflecting the deadening of his senses, as around him, the conversation steadily died. Even Nina was unable to sustain a lively repartee in the face of his implacable quiet. Pretence was impossible. They all knew the moment was upon them. All he wanted was to talk.

Emil dropped his fork with a clatter, onto the plate as, beside him, Hanna flinched. *Jumpy.* 'Max, I owe you an apology.'

Max stopped eating, his fork poised in mid-air. It wasn't the statement any of them had been expecting.

'Yes, I'm truly sorry if my recent . . . woes have proved

troublesome for you. I expect you must have been somewhat disquieted with Hanna staying here over the weekend. Playing nurse to me.'

It was the first shot, whistling through the silence like a cannonball on the dawn battlefield. Nina sighed and reached for her drink.

Max looked back at him, steadily. 'Not at all. Hanna's a great nurse. I'm glad she was able to help.' He placed the forkful in his mouth, but Bell was certain he wasn't tasting his food any more either. His skin was looking almost grey with the stress.

A small smile played on Emil's lips. 'Oh yes. She was a great . . . a really great . . . help.' He glanced over at Hanna as the stress landed on the innuendo; she wasn't even attempting to eat, staring at him with a horrified plea in her eyes, a dawning realization that she had no control over this situation after all. She was out of time . . .

'Emil –' she whispered, but Emil's attention was already back on Max.

Max continued to chew, but more slowly now. He looked over at Bell. 'If the children have finished eating, they can go off to play . . .' he said in a low voice.

It was like asking the ladies to leave the room before the men pulled out their revolvers and Bell could only shrug feebly in reply, for the three of them were already halfway down the lawn anyway, heading for the bouncy castle again, their cleared plates on her lap. She knew she should take them to the kitchen and steer well clear of this toxic scene, but her feet wouldn't move. She had to know how this was going to play out. Like some kind of sadist, she needed to watch the man *she* wanted get back the woman *he* wanted.

A cold wind barrelled up the garden, parting the flowers and carrying salt from the sea.

'You know,' Emil said, sitting back in his chair, elbows splayed and lacing his fingers together. 'People think that being in a coma for seven years is the most terrible thing, but actually, there are upsides.'

Bell glanced across at Hanna, her long hair streaming across her face. *No filter for one*, she thought.

Nina spluttered on her drink. This was her kind of humour. 'There's time to think?'

'There's less thinking going on than you may suppose,' he grinned. 'But it is very peaceful. There's a lot to be said for that. Cutting out all the noise, the chatter, the distractions . . . It's been one of the more disconcerting things to have to readapt to; life is so loud.' He sighed, letting his shoulders rise and fall, looking amiable and relaxed. 'No, more than anything, I think, if you are lucky enough to pull through it all, you emerge with Perspective. With a capital P. What's life all about? Why are we here? What *really* matters?' He threw his hands out questioningly, looking round the table at the faces looking back apprehensively. Bell realized it was actually a question. 'It's not that –' He waved a hand indicating the house. 'Forget all this –' He jerked his head towards the private fairground on the lawn, the parked helicopter, the large, lush, mature garden on a tiny Baltic island. 'All it boils down to is love.'

No one spoke. They didn't disagree. They just didn't want to go where this conversation was heading. Not Nina, not Max and not – from the look of barely controlled panic on her face – Hanna. She really wasn't ready for this, Bell realized. The way Emil had spoken to her in the bedroom, so certain of his plans, she had assumed Hanna was complicit, that they had discussed this. But there was no disguising the fear on her face now. Her eyes were shining with tears as she looked between the two men. It was clear Emil was going rogue, off-book.

'And I have always loved this woman.' He covered Hanna's hand with his own, drawing it into him and holding it against his heart. Bell stared at it there, remembering how she had lain with her head in that exact spot, for just one night. 'You know that, Max. You were one of the first people I told that I'd met the girl I was going to marry! Remember it? I introduced you to her that day in Vardshus, in the garden? You were on your lunch break and we'd piled off the ferry with some friends; it was the start of the summer – party, party, party. Life was good, eh? You remember?' He nodded, never letting go of Max's gaze. And Max, likewise, both men held in a lock. 'Of course you do. You were my best man. The best man I knew.'

Bell looked at Max in surprise. He'd said they'd been friends, that he'd gone to their wedding – but to have been best man? That wasn't just a detail, it was a statement.

Emil tapped the side of his head. 'Which brings me to another coma upside – clarity. Capital C. Some things now, from years ago, I can recall like they happened this morning. Not everything – there have been things that were just . . . just out of reach.' He tapped his head again. 'Hence the headaches, you see.'

Hanna was pressing her lips together, her body held in the contracted state before a sneeze, or a sob.

'And when I look back now, I think I knew you were in love with her too. I think I did know it,' he said thoughtfully. 'I just . . . refused to see it. I didn't want to see it. I mean, my wife and my best friend.' He made a crazy face. 'Who the hell wants to see that, right?'

Max didn't reply but he had stopped eating now, his cutlery returned to the plate, his arms splayed on the carver chairs as he sat back, listening. Waiting.

Bell couldn't take her eyes off him. Max had been in love

374

with Hanna for all those years, before Emil's accident? He'd been their best man?

'So maybe I can't blame you for *swooping* in while I lay there, not dead but certainly not alive for seven years. Maybe I'd even have done the same. All's fair in love, right, especially when the other guy's . . . you know . . . a vegetable.'

Hanna gasped. Bell winced at the savage language.

'But again – upsides!' He smacked the table with his palm, an almost jocular gesture were it not for the fact that the look in his eyes in no way matched the words coming from his mouth. 'You took care of my family and that's a good thing. I mean, I know they were more than adequately provided for financially, thanks to Nina's efforts setting up the trust.' He gave a silent clap to Nina and she nodded her acknowledgement warily. His anger threaded every word and she looked as worried as the rest of them now. 'I know you set up home together in a house that my family paid for, but you were a father to my son. You kept my wife warm at night. I should be thankful for that. You . . . minimized their suffering.'

'Emil –' Hanna faltered, but he silenced her with a look. Of course, there was no real gratitude in his eyes, but there was something else missing too. No . . .

No . . . ?

Bell gave a shiver of trepidation at his steeled manner. Everything felt 'off', somehow. There was a chilling calculation to all of this that was far removed from the passion, the desperation he had shown upstairs. He wanted his family back, she understood that, but did that mean destroying Max first? Humiliating him? And why wasn't Max fighting back and defending himself? If everything Emil said was true, there were also mitigating circumstances. Max wasn't a monster.

The wind gave a low moan, like a dog turning over, just

as Emil gave a sigh. 'But of course, the thorn in everyone's sides is that I somehow, against the odds – against the gods! – inconveniently recovered. And so now I'm back, and everything's got to change again.' The silence yawned as the statement hung in the air like smoke after the bullet's left the gun, both men staring at one another. 'Because you know, Max, of course you know, that Hanna's mine again. You knew it when she heard I'd been hurt again and she ran out in that storm.'

Emil didn't rush his words. He was almost lingering on every statement, like it was a blade over flesh and he was waiting for the beads of blood to appear.

Bell felt sick. *This* was sick. Max looked wretched, every muscle in his body tensed and braced as his eyes slid between Emil and Hanna, settling on her.

'Max, it's not what you think!' Hanna cried as Max stared at her with a broken look, his breathing coming heavily as he struggled to stay calm.

'Of course it was,' Emil cut in with cruel insouciance. 'She was very concerned about me, Max; I was amazed, actually, at just *how* concerned she was. She kept checking on me, making sure I was okay.' He picked up her hand and squeezed it again. 'All through the night, and all over the weekend – she scarcely left my side.' He smiled cruelly at Max. 'Naturally, I assumed it was because she loved me.'

Bell felt her ears prick at the implied contradiction. Huh?

Hanna heard it too, growing even paler than she already was. If that was possible. 'Emil, please, now's not the time—'

But Emil was too quick for them both, always one step ahead. He regarded Hanna again with that look, the one Bell couldn't place. 'There is no other time, Hanna. We are all gathered here, together, for the first time in almost eight years.

A lot has changed.' He cast a sardonic wave around the table. 'Clearly we need to talk.'

'But the children –'

'Are not here.' He jerked his chin towards the girls still bouncing on the inflatable castle.

She fell back, staring sightlessly at the flower bowl, but he reached for her hand again. 'This was what you wanted, surely? For me to say for you what you can't. I know you feel torn, but we can't avoid this. Someone has to get hurt. Someone already has been hurt. For seven years, that someone was me, lying in a hospital bed.' He paused, waiting for her to meet his eyes. Eventually she did, nodding slowly. 'I was critically hurt, Hanna. More dead than alive.'

A tear slid down Hanna's cheek. 'Please, stop . . .' She looked away.

'*You* hurt me, Hanna –'

Her face whipped back to him, her eyes black with panic.

'– You and him. Before the car ever hit me.'

Bell swallowed, still not keeping up. *What?*

'I didn't remember it,' he said quietly, as though he was talking to a child. 'And the people who love me – I mean, *really* love me – they thought it was a kindness not to remind me, because they believe in second chances and loyalty. Because they're discreet –'

Bell looked up at the word to find Nina already looking across at her.

'– And perhaps I never would have thought to ask the question, but those who know me well have always been able to . . . guide me, even when I haven't wanted it.'

Nina looked back at Emil and Bell saw how their eyes met in silent acknowledgement, how – for the first time since he had come out here – a flicker of warmth glowed in his eyes.

377

He'd overheard their conversation at the bottom of the stairs. He'd overheard Nina telling her Måns knew something about his past. The question was – had Nina known he was listening?

She saw Nina wink at him and had her answer. She knew exactly how to get her brother to listen to her after all.

A few spots of rain landed, bleeding into the tablecloth, and Bell looked up at the darkening tumult in the sky.

'– And of course, the headaches I've been getting – so much worse with the concussion . . . it turns out they weren't random. My brain wasn't breaking down, as I feared. It was reaching out. Searching for the memories that would explain the black hole that's been in the very centre of me since I opened my eyes. It was why I can't sleep, why I can't . . . forgive. Something deep inside me knew it was what put me here in the first place.' He stared at Hanna intently. 'Do *you* remember?'

'I don't know what you're talking about,' she whispered, looking cowed.

'Sure you do. There was a strong breeze that night – like today – and you didn't quite push the door fully on the latch. It was banging a little; not much, but Måns has never been a heavy sleeper. And when he went to check, he found on the floor, just inside the door, a small piece of paper with a note on it.'

Bell felt her breath catch. What note? When? What was going on?

'Well, you know how fastidious Måns is. He wouldn't simply ignore something like that. For security reasons, we can't have . . . unexpected guests on the island.' Bell watched as he bit his lip, the emotion getting to him. 'Imagine his disappointment when he saw what he saw.'

'No –' Hanna protested, shaking her head vociferously, her eyes filled with tears.

'Oh no,' he said quickly, patting her hand. 'It wasn't *you* who disappointed him, Hanna.' Bell watched her expression change from fearful to suspended fear. But in Emil's face . . . she saw now what it was that was missing. No . . .

'No, no, no. He said he wasn't somehow surprised about you.'

. . . No love.

Emil lifted his eyes off her. 'But you, Max . . . when he saw your boat roped up.'

Clarity dawned like a thunderclap, and Bell gasped so loudly, Emil's concentration was broken as he looked over at her. Had he forgotten she was there? Hanna broke into wretched sobs, hiding her face in her hands, as Max's jaw clenched with dangerous intensity.

'It could have started a lot earlier than it did!' he exclaimed, his hands flat on the table, arms bent out and elbows pointed like a dragon's wings. 'She was miserable with you for *years* and you didn't even notice because you were too busy playing empires, trying to impress your father!' He furiously jabbed a finger towards him. 'So don't play the victim with me, Emil! I was a loyal friend to you. For far longer than you deserved!'

Emil stared back with an inscrutable expression, but Bell could see some of the bombast had been taken out of him by the honest ferocity of Max's words. No denials. No excuses. Had Emil expected guilt-ridden capitulation?

'She wanted a divorce and you did too. You did too, until you found out about us! And that tore you up! You couldn't bear that she loved me and not you. That she always had.'

'Always had?' Emil mocked with a shrug, but the gesture lacked the flippancy of even a few minutes ago. 'Then why did she marry me?'

'Take a fucking guess! You had decided you were going to

marry her and that was that. Nothing was going to stop you and nothing could! Look familiar?'

Bell flinched at his ferocious anger – she'd never heard Max swear before – scarcely able to keep up with the chicanes of their past. She'd had no idea about their interlocked pasts, none . . . She heard something rustle behind her and turned to see a camellia bush, its leaves splaying in the wind, a bird, hopping about.

'– But let me tell you something! She's been happier with me these past seven years than she ever was with you! We're a family now. You can't destroy us. You won't. *I* won't let you! Hanna has tried to deal with you kindly. Compassionately. But this stops here, right now.'

Emil sat quietly across the table, allowing Max his bite-back, giving him his voice. But as his calmness extended ever further, Bell sensed something unsettling in the unexpected generosity of that. Max's words should have been body-blows to him, everything he never wanted to hear. He should have been retaliating with more insults, more anger, blows even. Max, his best friend, had been having an affair with his wife. He was entitled to be angry about that. But to give Max his moment so calmly . . .

'Did you never wonder why she was *so* anxious that I shouldn't remember your affair?' he asked after a moment, in a collected voice.

'Because she knew you'd be a fucking psychopath about it!'

Emil shook his head slowly. 'No. It wasn't that. It was worse than that.'

'Don't give me that! You're obsessed with her. You've pinned your whole life's worth on getting her back because you can't bear that she fell in love with me and she's *still* in love with me!'

He held his hands up in docile surrender. 'You're right,

Max. I was obsessed with her. She was all I could ever see. I didn't know why, she just filled my head – awake, asleep, *all* the time. She was the last thing I saw before the car hit.'

'Yeah-yeah-yeah, here you go again!' Max snarled, out of patience and at the end of his tether now. 'The last thing you saw. The first thing you saw.'

'She was the last thing I saw before the car hit.'

Max stared at him, picking up on the pointed echo. He gave a frustrated shrug, as if to say, 'So?'

'That was why she didn't want me to remember your affair. It was why she came over here in a storm when she heard I'd had another blow to the head; it was why she didn't leave my side. She was terrified I might start to remember things. She was terrified I might remember *why* she was the last thing I saw before the car hit.' Emil's eyes narrowed as he slowed his words right down. 'Ask me why she was the last thing I saw before the car hit.'

'Emil –' Hanna cried, jumping up from the seat. Her voice was thin and high, as though reeded.

Oh God! Bell gasped, her hands flying to her mouth as Max stayed rebelliously silent.

Emil's voice was quiet, when it came. 'It was because *she* was driving the car, Max.'

'No!' The word was a scream, Hanna crumpling against the table, a denial and an admission all at once.

Bell heard a sound behind her again, but she couldn't move, couldn't react. This couldn't be true. But she knew it was as she saw the contempt in Emil's face as he looked at the woman he loved . . . *She* had hit him? Because she wanted to be with Max?

Max stared at Hanna in disbelief, his face visibly draining of blood. '. . . Hanna?'

No one could speak. Not even Nina, her mouth hanging

open slackly. None of them could process it all. It was too much – Hanna and Max's affair; Hanna, desperate to leave her marriage . . . responsible for putting Emil in the coma?

'Hanna, you've got to talk!' Max said urgently, running around the table and pulling her up by her arm, but she was limp, her head shaking, legs buckling as she wept and sobbed. 'Is this true? You were in the car?'

'Yes!'

The wind gusted again, whipping her hair upwards like a flickering flame.

'You hit him?' Max whispered, looking ashen.

'No!' She looked back up at him with wild eyes.

He frowned, looking bewildered. Overwhelmed. 'But you just said –'

'I know! And I was in the car! I was driving! Because I was chasing after him!'

Bell frowned. It was all nuance. Semantics. She was in the car. The car was the last thing he saw –

Hanna gathered strength suddenly, or rage, her body stiffening and straightening her up as the truth aired for the first time, stretching out, taking up space. She glowered at Emil with a look of pure hatred Bell had never seen before. '. . . If you've remembered what happened that day, then you'll also recall what you said to me before you got on your bike and left the house. Won't you?' she demanded, as Emil stared back at her.

He didn't stir.

'You had threatened to take away my child! You said you were going to drag me through the courts and destroy me! That you'd make sure he grew up hating me!'

Bell swivelled her eyes from Hanna to Emil. He was looking shaken by her words. It was clear he hadn't remembered; that yet again, he only had half the memories, half the facts . . .

'What kind of a man does that? What kind of father?'

Yes, what kind did? Bell wondered, feeling herself recoil. Wasn't this an echo of her own accusations that he was failing? He was a bad father now – but he'd also been a bad father then? She swallowed, seeing him with fresh eyes. So much had been clouded by his accident – his vulnerability, the unfairness of it all, the attraction that existed between them like iron filings to magnetic north. But he was a bad father and now, it seemed, a bad husband too.

Hanna grew stronger. 'I was sobbing on the floor, begging you not to do it. I told you I didn't want your money. I didn't want anything from you. It wasn't like you even wanted me any more. You just didn't want me to be with Max! You couldn't bear that he and I loved each other, and you knew that in taking Linus, you were hurting me in the worst possible way. And there wasn't any doubt you would do it. You left that house with the absolute certainty that your family, with all their money and all their connections, would be able to rob me of my child! Just like you've tried to do again! You've always used money to try to control me, just like I've always used sex to control you.'

It was Emil's turn to pale now as her mouth twisted suddenly into a sneer, fear transformed into white-hot rage. 'But it meant nothing. Don't delude yourself it was anything more than manipulation, because you're absolutely right – I *was* frightened you were going to remember the fight that day and my affair with Max, but only because it would fire you up again into taking Linus away. So I kept you close and I gave you what you wanted only because I was buying time, figuring out how to make you see we could never go back – because I won't lose my child. I won't. Not for either one of you.' She looked back at Max evenly, laying down her terms to him too. He had to accept what she'd done for her son . . . This was not an apology.

Max was quiet, emotions running over his face like colours – anger and resentment marbled with a grudging look of possible understanding. 'What happened in the car?' he asked eventually. 'I need to know everything.'

Hanna looked back at Emil, tucking her hair behind her ears as the wind toyed with her like sprites. Her voice was calm again, all the fury that had bleached it white now spent, colour coming back as the tear tracks dried on her cheeks. 'I never touched you. I got in the car and chased after you because I was going to make you talk and listen, that was all.' She flinched, remembering fully, falling back into that moment. 'I drew up alongside you at the lights and you looked over at me and saw me through the window, calling to you to pull over, begging you. I was desperate just to talk. But instead, you jumped the light and turned the corner. You hit a pothole, just as the tram was coming . . .' A single sob escaped her, the horror still too vivid to suppress. 'It looked like a puddle, and threw you straight into the path . . . You couldn't have known, no one could.'

Max put his arms around her and she slumped against his chest, crying quietly into his neck.

Bell looked on, scarcely able to believe what she'd learned as the two men stared back at each other, both stunned, both spent, and there was the sense of an ending in the silence. She'd thought there were no villains in this story, but the truth was, they all were. They'd each behaved badly, treacherously, in their own ways.

Emil sat watching as Max comforted his – *their* – wife. He looked utterly alone, Nina sitting on the opposite side of the table with shining eyes, her hand pinched over her mouth, knowing she couldn't interfere or save her little brother this time. This was his mess. He'd made it, he had to tidy it up.

No one spoke for a very long time. Then slowly, Emil scraped back the chair and walked over to them both. He put his hands on each of their shoulders. Max's. Hanna's. Hanna's head lifted as she looked back at him.

'I'm sorry,' he said quietly. 'For everything.' The words chimed with heavy sincerity.

'Really?' she asked. Disbelief crackled her voice, like a child being told Christmas could be repeated.

'We'll work this out,' he nodded, meeting Max's gaze. 'We will. Everything's as it's meant to be. I can see that now.'

Bell saw the tension break in Max, many more than seven years' worth of guilt washing through him in waves, and she knew he'd suffered long before Emil ever had. But it was over. At long last, the truth was out, and –

She saw Emil's head turn in her direction, his remarkable stare coming to rest upon her and looking for – what? An option? A back-up? A future?

But she didn't register it. Something else was pushing to the forefront of her mind, her attention snagging on a detail that had meant nothing in all the noise. Slowly she twisted back, glancing behind, because her eye had caught sight of something before – a tiny wink of red in the long grass, by the camellia bush.

She peered closer, and saw it was a toy Corvette.

'Bell?' She heard the concern in Emil's voice as she lifted her gaze and stiffly scanned the garden, looking over the helter-skelter, the carousel, the bouncy castle . . . She felt her blood run cold as she looked back at them all watching her, frozen like statues.

'Where are the children?'

Chapter Thirty

They split up, one in each direction, Hanna sprinting towards the jetty, certain they'd be taking the boat back to Summer Isle. Bell could hear their shouts shake through the trees, the children's names being called out with bald-faced terror.

Bell knew Linus had heard everything. He'd been hiding in the bush, listening to every word – hearing how his mother had fallen in love with another man, how his father had threatened his mother with losing him, how his mother had chased his father in the car, both of them angry, reckless, dangerous . . . He had been frightened of having to choose but now he had chosen – and he hadn't chosen any of them. He had taken his sisters and he was taking them to safety, away from all the so-called grown-ups who professed to love them.

She knew all this because she knew him. She loved him, actually, that was the truth of it. She loved him like he was her own, though he wasn't. She was the nanny. Just the nanny. And yet she'd always been more than that. They'd demanded more from her and she'd given it because she'd needed a family, a home, when she had been alone and stranded in the world.

She tore through the trees, her palms slapping against bark as she pushed off against them, running blindly, past the birches and pines, the blueberry bushes and the hawthorns that scratched her legs.

She came to the water's edge, the sea suddenly there like a bear saying 'boo', the levels much higher than usual, dredged up by the low pressure of the coming storm. She stared out, screaming their names, but it was hard to see and hear – the water was being whipped up by the wind, the standing waves in the strait making it hard to spot a small rowing boat or a kayak. Please God, not a kayak, not out there, not in these conditions . . . She scanned up and down the shore, stumbling on the rocks as she surveyed the water, straining to hear for cries over the wind, but there was nothing . . .

She decided to keep to the perimeter and walk round. It was the water that was the danger. As long as they didn't go in the w—

Suddenly she stopped.

She knew exactly where they were.

The others had realized it too, Hanna still sprinting as Bell met her on the rocks, their feet slipping in their panic. The wind was blowing their hair around, blinding them for moments, Hanna's slight frame sinewy and rigid with tension.

They got to the crater and stared down the sheer drop, Hanna giving a cry as they saw the basin was full of rough, slapping water, no sand visible. No beach.

'Linus!' Hanna screamed, her eyes white like a horse's in battle. 'Tilde! Elise!'

Max was ahead of them, on the far side, already scrambling down the rill. Emil was maybe a hundred metres behind him – not as fast, not as strong.

'I can see them!' Max yelled, his voice faint as the wind conspired against them and threw his words back over him. 'They're okay! They're on a ledge! They're okay!'

Hanna gasped, her body giving out at the news, adrenaline

387

overwhelming her, and she sank to the ground. Bell rushed over, holding her. 'It's okay, Hanna. Max has got them. They're safe now.'

'I can't lose them, Bell.'

'I know, and you won't. Max is getting them. It's all going to be okay.'

'Oh God, my babies,' she moaned.

Bell looked down and saw Hanna's hand curled over her stomach. A mother's instinct. 'They're safe. But this one needs protecting too. You've got to look after yourself.' And she placed her hand over Hanna's.

Hanna stared back at her, the question pale on her lips. 'How . . . ?'

'I saw the pregnancy test in your drawer, that day when you'd lost the ring.'

Their eyes met. They both knew now it had never been lost at all. Hanna had already been trying to control Emil the only way she felt she could, keeping her love for Max a secret still, buying time.

'. . . I only took the test yesterday. I knew confirming the pregnancy would only complicate it all further and I wasn't sure how far I would have to go to keep Emil on-side . . .' She swallowed, looking ashamed. 'You must think I'm terrible, to have done what I did.'

'I think you were desperate, Hanna. Anyone would have been. You were protecting your family.'

'As soon as it came up positive, I knew I couldn't keep trying to persuade him or fool him anymore. I had resolved to tell him once we'd got through today. I was prepared to go to court over it.' A tear slid down Hanna's cheek as she bit her lip, trying to master her emotions. 'But it wasn't all an act. I do still love him, you know, in my own way. In spite of it all. How *could* I hate him? He gave me my son.'

Bell bit her lip. 'Just try to relax now. The kids are safe, Max is getting them and you heard Emil – it's all going to be okay. They're going to work it out.'

Hanna gave a weak smile and nodded, closing her eyes as they both waited for the men – the two fathers – to bring the children back up.

Bell felt herself trembling too, her own body unwittingly depleted by the frantic chase across the island and as she sat on the ground, she closed her eyes, trying to control her shock. She did what she'd done after Jack had died and closed the world down to darkness and just sounds – she listened to Hanna's still-frightened breathing, the birds singing, the wind moaning, the sea's rhythmic slapping . . .

And then one more – unexpected, unwelcome, unnatural.

A scream.

In the final moments of his life, it was her face that filled his mind. Images spun round and round, of the light catching their pale spun hair, heads thrown back in laughter, his three girls, his three graces. Everything about them was radiance and beatific grace, as though they were not solid at all but heavenly conceits, constellations of stardust fallen from the skies into deft, perfect forms . . .

In seeing all this, there was much that he missed – the frond of strife dropped by a passing gull, the slickness left by a high wave, the ragged gasps that pulled brokenly at the air and tore down the archipelago's sky. He knew none of it.

For him there was only light.

And then darkness.

Epilogue

Auckland, NZ, four months later

'Emergency! We're out of milk!' Bell yelled in panic.

'But I only got some yesterday!' Mats replied, his voice – and then bewildered face – appearing through the galley door.

'Yeah, but did you have more of your shakes last night and this morning?'

Realization dawned as he gave an apologetic grimace. '. . . Oh.'

Bell rolled her eyes, not even knowing why she was surprised. 'They're going to be here in a few hours; I'll go to the shops. Do we need anything else?'

'Babe?' Mats called, swinging himself down the short staircase by the ladder and landing softly like a cat. 'Need anything?'

Justine walked through, wrapping her hair up in a towel. 'We're pretty low on peanut butter.'

'Okay, peanut butter,' Bell repeated, checking her purse was in her bag. She wasn't strictly sure peanut butter was a vital ingredient for tonight's coq au vin, but she supposed come breakfast . . . 'The one with the seeds?'

Mats pulled another face as Justine sidled up to him. 'Why

can't we just have peanut butter with peanut butter in it? I don't want seeds in my butter. I'm not a frickin' canary.'

'It's added goodness, babe,' Justine grinned, hooking an arm around his neck and kissing him on the mouth. She was three inches taller than him, and often took advantage of the fact. The kiss became more involved –

'Right, well, I'm off then,' Bell groaned. It had been twenty-two days exactly since they'd met and she was looking forward to the month mark, when Mats said he usually began to calm down. 'Be done by the time I'm back, please!'

'Oh, he will be,' Justine joked.

'Oi!' Mats protested, picking her up.

Bell skipped up the stairs and jumped off the boat, onto the concrete gangway. It was very wide and stable, something of a relief after three months at sea, although she preferred the rickety swaying of the wooden sort. Of the Swedish archipelago . . .

She immediately pushed the memories aside, refusing to let them settle. She had been disciplined and done a great job of outpacing her past, and she didn't intend to let it catch up with her now.

She glanced up at the sky as she walked quickly through the marina, past the hundreds of glossy white boats, sails bound, masts swaying in the wind; it wasn't called the City of Sails for nothing. Black clouds were billowing overhead like witches' skirts, the forecast storm arriving pretty much on time.

The sight of it made her smile. She did her best to smile every day, refusing to sink back into the clutches of despair. She might have been here before, but Tove had sent her off with the actually wise wisdom that 'life isn't what happens to you, but how you choose to react to it'. So in the aftermath of those awful final weeks in the summer, she had first chosen freedom – and now she was choosing happiness. They weren't inextricably linked yet, but she hoped one day they might be.

'Hi! Hi!' she called out to the increasingly familiar faces as she passed by their boats, hand raised in a friendly wave.

'Hey, Bell!'

'How's it going, Bell?'

Their answering calls had different accents to the one she'd known during the summer, but the same carefree smiles and wind-whipped hair.

She turned onto the main strip, glancing in through the open door of the harbourmaster's office as she passed, walking with a long stride. 'Hi, Dan,' she called.

'. . . Hell?'

She stopped walking like it was a command. 'Kris?' she shrieked as a scraped-up man-bun on top of a very handsome head appeared around the door frame, swiftly followed by Tove's electrified perm. 'Tove?'

'We were literally just getting your berth details!' he laughed, running over and picking her up in a bear hug, swinging her around so that her legs swung out. 'Jesus, there's a lot of boats here! It's Sandhamn on steroids!'

She laughed with delight, feeling like a little girl as he swung her round, the Swedish language like music to her ears after her Kiwi hiatus. 'But I wasn't expecting you for hours yet! I'm out of milk!' she cried, effortlessly speaking Swedish back and feeling very over-excited as he put her down and Tove swooped in for her hug.

'Travelling winds,' Tove said into her hair.

'Huh, I could have done with some of those myself,' she said, pulling back and taking in the happy sight of them both. They hadn't changed a bit. Admittedly, it had only been four months, but in that time, her entire world had changed.

'Yeah? You're okay? You made it across safely?' Kris asked, forever concerned.

'Well, I'm here, aren't I?' she laughed.

'It couldn't come a moment too soon as far as I was concerned. He was fussing constantly,' Tove said, rolling her eyes. 'Kept checking the charts, looking at wind speeds . . .'

'Aww, my mother hen,' Bell grinned, leaning into his arm and squeezing it. 'I told you I'd be fine. I was in good hands.'

'I hope you don't mean that literally,' he said.

She threw her head back and laughed. 'Oh, trust me, no! That ship has very definitely sailed. Mats is currently loved up with a bikini model from Brisbane.'

'Well, you could be one of those. Just look at you!'

'*If* I grew a pair of legs,' Bell quipped, holding a hand several inches above her head. 'Short-arse here.'

'But you're so thin!' Tove frowned. 'Were you even allowed to sleep?'

Bell laughed again, feeling the emotional release of being with old friends. She had missed it more than she'd realized. 'Turns out sailing nine and a bit thousand nautical miles is all you've got to do to get a bikini body. There's no coffee and cake shops in the middle of the Pacific!'

Kris chuckled. 'Well, you look amazing, but then you always did. Curves are good, I don't know why women don't get that.'

'Shame that *you* don't,' Tove muttered.

'And Marc couldn't make it?' she asked sympathetically.

He gave a sad pout. 'Exams coming up. But he sends his love.'

'Ah, poor thing.' She looked at him enquiringly, still worried about him in turn. 'And it's all good with you guys?'

Kris winked. 'Better than good. We're keeping the apartment warm and stocked up on humous and pot plants until you return.'

'But that's not the main news. Tell her the main news,' Tove prompted impatiently.

Kris grinned. 'Marc asked me to marry him and I said yes.'

Bell gasped. 'Oh Kris!'

'The wedding's set for next June. *Midsommar*'s, in fact.'

'Oh –' Bell's mouth parted, the word an immediate link to her heartache, images flashing through her mind on a silent reel – his eyes; the fireworks; *Impressed yet?*; the first press of his lips . . .

She saw them both watching her, seeing her freeze, like she had a pause button they could press. That easily, sending her back . . .

'Ask who his best man is,' Tove said, pressing play again.

She gave a quizzical shrug, shaking the moment off. 'Who's your best man?'

'You're looking at her,' Tove said, giving a dramatic bow.

'Oh dear God!' Bell exclaimed in shock – also feeling crashingly disappointed. She knew it wasn't a competition, but Kris had always felt like *her* special friend. 'This is going to be the speech of all speeches, you know that, right? No mercy.'

Kris gave a hopeless shrug. 'What could I do? She wants to wear a tux.'

'I've always wanted a tux,' Tove agreed.

'You're mad, both of you,' Bell said, hoping her dismay didn't show.

'Have you ever worn a tux?' Kris asked, one eyebrow arched.

'Me?' Her eyes widened as she saw the smile in his eyes. She gasped. '*I* get one too? *I'm* your best man too?' Her hands flew up to her mouth in surprise.

'How is that even a question?' he demanded, outraged. 'Of course you are!'

'Well, I didn't want to assume. I mean . . . I'm down here now, for one thing.'

'Yeah, but not *forever*,' Tove said, looking panicked.

'No, but –' She shrugged. 'Nothing's fixed. It could be five months. Could be five years.'

'I do *not* think so,' Kris said sternly. 'I'm not losing my sister by another mister on account of Mr Right getting it wrong.'

Bell frowned, shifting weight, her easy mood deadening. 'He wasn't Mr Right.'

'No?'

'He was . . . Mr Right For One Night. That was it.'

Kris arched an eyebrow. 'That wasn't what you said when you got back to the city. You were in pieces.'

'Yes, well, it was an emotional time. After everything that happened with Max, and Hanna and the kids . . . I was all over the place.'

They were both watching her closely, scrutinizing her for lies. '. . . Have you spoken to him?' Tove asked.

She shook her head. 'Clean break, you know. Best thing. Definitely.'

'Along with switching hemispheres. Just to be on the safe side.'

'Exactly,' she said, realizing a moment too late it was intended as a joke. She gave a delayed smile.

'Hmm,' Kris intoned, looking thoughtful.

'Hmm?' she queried.

He looked at Tove. 'Could be awkward,' he said in a low voice, not moving his lips.

'I told you. I did say,' Tove hissed back. 'She's stubborn as fuck. She's not gonna be down with this.'

'Down with what? What's going on?' Bell demanded,

feeling a flutter of anxiety. She didn't like it when they ganged up against her.

Tove put a hand on her shoulder. 'Just promise you won't get mad, okay?'

'Will I have a reason to get mad?'

'No. None at all. We've done this from love.'

'*For* love,' Kris interrupted. 'And because they wouldn't stop doorstepping us.'

'*Doorstepping?*' The press? Had they found out she was the Von Greyers' nanny? One quick Google search had been enough to confirm that Hanna and Emil's divorce was now all over the Swedish papers.

Their gazes collectively rose to a point beyond her shoulder, and she slowly turned. There, standing twenty metres away, was a man in a baseball cap – and beside him, a boy with a skateboard.

'Oh my God!' she cried, stepping back, her hands flying to her mouth at the sight of them here. All the way down here.

'He *literally* wouldn't stop calling,' Tove murmured, watching her like she might fall. 'I had to pick up for the sake of my sanity.'

In a flash, Bell understood where her friends had got the money for the tickets. She should have known they didn't have the spare cash to fly across the world to see an old friend and a boat race.

'You're not mad, are you?' Kris asked, seeing how she had paled. 'We tried to brush him off at first by saying you were with Mats. He didn't care. He said he had to see you and talk to you in person. So we truck a deal, but with conditions: he's promised to stay out of the way if you don't want to see him. He said we can bring the kid to see you every day and he'll go sightseeing or something . . . Say you're not mad.'

'. . . No, I'm not mad,' she whispered, seeing how tightly

Emil was gripping Linus's shoulder, holding him in place; how Linus was straining forward; both of them waiting for a cue . . . Her arms raised up reflexively, held out wide, and in the next instant, the boy had broken free, dropping even his beloved board, and was sprinting towards her.

'Bell!' He rushed into her arms, his own around her waist and his head against her heart. 'I missed you.'

'I missed *you*,' she gasped, not able to believe this was happening, her hands squeezing him, running over his hair, checking he was real. 'Oh my God, I missed you so much! You're really here? I'm not . . . I'm not hallucinating?'

He looked back at her, nodding happily. 'No! We flew for a day and a half to get here. We wanted to surprise you!'

'Well, you did that, all right!' she cried, half laughing, a sob of shock escaping her as she looked up to see Emil, closer now but still hanging back, holding his son's skateboard. He had his baseball cap on, but no shades; she could see his eyes, those eyes . . .

'So, are we good? Is this all good?' Kris murmured, scanning the seemingly happy reunion. 'Cos we can go to the hotel or we can stay here with you. For support. Back-up. Whatever you want.'

'. . . It's fine, this is good,' she murmured, smiling down at Linus as he beamed back at her. A sunbeam that had landed in her arms.

'Okay. Well, laters then, we'll give you some time,' he whispered, kissing her temple.

'Later, alligator,' Tove said, touching her arm lightly.

Bell looked back at Linus again, barely aware of her friends leaving. 'You've grown! My God, I can't believe how much you've grown! Just straighten up.' She measured the top of his head against her jaw. 'Oh my God, half a neck! You were down here when I saw you last!'

'I know!' he laughed excitedly. 'Dad thinks I'm going to be taller than him.'

'Well, I think he might be right.'

She glanced at Emil again, her heart beating fast. He was another few steps closer. He'd travelled halfway around the world, only to stop short the last six feet? Still, she couldn't talk to him yet. Not yet. She needed time to recover, to process what was going on.

'How was the voyage?' Linus asked, helpfully bringing her attention back to him again.

'Oh, long! Tiring! We've been resting since we got here. We did it in nine weeks in the end. As feared, we hit the doldrums in the ITCZ.'

'The what?'

'The Inter-Tropical Convergence Zone. Remember I told you about that once? It's near the equator.'

'Oh.' Linus nodded thoughtfully, clearly drawing a blank. 'Guess what!'

'What?'

'We flew economy. Dad's never flown coach before. But Mamma made him. She said it was a condition for this holiday. And we watched films all the way over. Back-to-back, we didn't stop, did we?'

'Nope, we didn't,' Emil sighed.

Bell couldn't stop a bemused smile at the thought. She could see, now he was closer, he looked exhausted.

A few fat drops of rain fell onto the ground – weighty, forceful – and she eyed the sky again. She figured they had less than a minute –

'Where's Mats? I want to see him.'

'He's, uh . . . busy,' she said quickly. 'But don't worry, you will. He won't be long.'

Linus eyed her warily. 'Is he still your boyfriend?'

'He never was, Linus. He was my special friend, remember?'

'Bell, I'm not a baby. I know that's just a different way of saying he's your boyfriend.'

'Oh!' She tried to look put out. 'Well, for *me*, it means he's sort of like a boy best friend. More than a normal friend, not quite my brother.'

'Huh.' He gave a careless shrug. 'I'm going to have a brother!'

'And how amazing is that?' she gasped, holding her hand up for a high five.

'Mamma says I can help choose his name.'

'Very cool. Although I'm thinking *not* Blofeld. Or Oddjob.'

He laughed. 'Pappa chose those for the cats, not me. Besides, I'm nearly eleven now.'

'Yes, you are,' she sighed, ruffling his hair again. 'Can't you slow down a little? You're making me feel old.'

He looked at her again, then dropped his head against her once more. 'I missed you.'

A throb of tears pressed from nowhere. 'I missed you,' she said in a thick voice. 'So much.'

A sudden clap of thunder made them all jump as the sky's bucket was tipped and the rain began falling at double time, raindrops pelting the ground, the boats, them . . . Linus yelped with delight, scarpering to the relative cover of the awnings of the marina cafe, beside the harbourmaster's office. But Emil didn't move and neither did she as they stood staring at each other through the rain for several moments. The sky had become dark, the clouds almost black, and yet the light had taken on an almost glowing quality so that everything felt saturated, more deeply itself.

He walked over at last, breaching the last small gap, hesitation in his eyes. '. . . Hi.'

399

'Hi.'

'I hope you don't mind us . . . stopping by like this.'

Stopping by? He had his sister's way with words. 'No, of course not.' She stared into those eyes that had caused her so much trouble. Heartache. 'It's a lovely surprise,' she swallowed, looking away. 'How's Max?'

'Fine now. Pretty much fully recovered.'

'Oh, I'm so glad!' she said, relieved, looking straight back at him. The offer to sail south with Mats had been perfectly timed for a clean getaway for *her*, she couldn't stay, not for an extra minute, not for another tragedy, but no sooner had Stockholm disappeared from sight than she had berated herself for leaving when he had still been so sick. 'I felt so bad . . .' She didn't finish the sentence, not that she needed to. He knew he was the reason why she'd gone, and he didn't say anything for a moment as he read the unsaid words in her eyes. '. . . It turned out it was his heart, not his head.'

She looked at him in surprise. 'But the fall . . . ? He hit his head on the rocks.'

'Yes, but he fell *because* of the heart attack. All the stress . . . he had an undiagnosed condition apparently.'

She winced, remembering that awful day and what Emil had put him through. He had the decency to look ashamed about it now. 'It was just as well the helicopter was there,' she said neutrally.

'Yes.'

'And you, of course. You kept the compressions going. You saved his life.'

'He would have done the same for me.'

She looked at him, seeing the calmness in his face as he spoke about the man marrying his ex-wife. 'And Hanna? How is she?'

'Blooming. She's taken a sabbatical to look after Max and have time with the girls before the baby comes.' He said the words with a fluent ease, as though he could have been talking about an aunt or a mutual acquaintance. 'She sends her love. She misses you, though. We all do.'

Oh. Was that why he was here? Was this a charm offensive designed to drag her back to her old job? 'Well, I think I'm done with nannying for a bit,' she said shortly, looking away. She felt a sudden, strong urge to get away from him, for Kris to come back. She didn't want this after all – she had been doing just fine. Fine-ish.

'Bell –'

She looked back at him, her heart aching with the pain that came from just looking at him. 'You know, you could have just emailed. You didn't need to get on a plane and fly for a day and a half. In *economy*.'

He hesitated, seeing her agitation. 'Well, apparently it's good for me. Although my back would disagree.'

They were getting soaked, but neither of them appeared to notice. He took a step closer to her but she instinctively stepped back.

'Bell, I'm not here because we want you back as our nanny,' he said, reading her with an expert eye. 'Nor am I here because I've caved in to Linus's daily pleas that we come to see you. I am a strict father these days. I have *boundaries*.' He arched an eyebrow slightly, sounding rather like his sister. 'I also have a very strict pocket-money policy, much to Linus's dismay.'

She watched him, sensing his attempt at levity. Brightness. Does he still believe he owns a boat?'

'I'm afraid not.'

'Well, that sounds positive.'

'He didn't think so.'

401

A small smile escaped her, but she flattened it down again. 'Look, Emil—'

'I know you probably won't believe this,' he said quickly, cutting her off, hearing her tone. 'But there are a lot of things that are positive now. Things that might have seemed impossible in the summer.'

'. . . Good. I'm glad.'

'Max nearly dying clarified everything. Suddenly none of it mattered. It was just ego and fear and half-memories, I know that now. Hanna and I – we went to couples counselling.'

She frowned. '*Couples* counselling? But—'

'We did it to "devolve our relationship and try to build a new platform for our relationship going forward".' He gave speech-mark fingers, an almost-smile in his eyes.

'Oh.' It all sounded very Gwyneth Paltrow. 'Did it work?'

He blinked. 'Yes. We do brunch.' That wry tone he shared with Nina hovered in the corners of his words.

'Okay.'

'And we talk about you. A lot. What we did, dragging you into something so toxic. We wanted to make it up to you, but didn't know where you'd gone.'

'I couldn't stay.'

'I know. I also thought I knew what loss was – until you disappeared.'

The words stripped back her defences, peeling back the layers she had worked so hard to close. 'Emil –'

'I had to basically beg your friends to tell me where you were. When they wouldn't, I resorted to bribery.' He shrugged. 'It's not the sort of thing the New Me would condone, but I was desperate. Tove calls me her stalker although I actually think she's quite pleased to have one . . .'

It was a quip, but she couldn't smile. Her emotions were

rushing through her like floodwaters, and the smile in his eyes faded too. 'When they said you were with Mats.'

'Not like that.'

'I know that now.' His eyes burned. 'But I wouldn't have blamed you if it had been like that. The way I treated you . . . rejecting you, pushing you away, trying to pretend you meant nothing when in reality, you were everything. I was chasing an idea, something that, deep down, I knew I didn't want – but it was all I knew . . .' He took a step in again, but this time she didn't retreat. 'I felt so alone after I woke up properly. I didn't remember the meeting with Linus at all and I couldn't understand why he wouldn't come. I knew something was wrong but I didn't know what. Hanna kept making excuses, saying I needed to get better first, so I channelled everything into that. Getting back to my family, becoming well enough that they would see me again . . . It became my entire life. My only focus. It was absolutely impossible for me to imagine that there might be another path. And even when you were right there, showing me . . . I couldn't trust in it.' He swallowed. 'Not until it was too late, and I'd ruined it all.'

Rivulets of rain ran down the planes of his cheeks and she knew what he was leading up to.

'Emil, I get it, really,' she said sadly. 'I understood it then, too. But even if you and Max and Hanna are all good now, it's still too complicated for me to go back to. Hanna was my boss. Linus was the child in my care. I can't . . . step out of being the nanny to them.'

'You can.'

'No.'

'Yes, they already know—' he blurted. 'I told Hanna. About us. About how I felt about you.'

403

Bell's mouth parted. 'You did *what*?' she gasped. '*Why* would you do that?' She glanced across at Linus, seeing him watch them closely from the safety of the awnings.

'Well, for one thing, I had to account for why Linus and I wanted to cross the world to find you. For another, I thought she should have fair warning before I did everything in my considerable power to bring you back.'

It was seemingly another joke, something to buy time as she absorbed the news that Hanna knew. Hanna knew. She ran her hands over her – wet – face. 'Shit – oh my God, what was her reaction?' she winced, wanting and not wanting to know all at once.

He inhaled slowly. 'Shocked at first, naturally. But then . . .' He shrugged. 'After a while, she said she could see it.'

'*See* it?' she repeated, dumbfounded, peering at him through her fingers.

'Us. Together. She thinks we'd be good for each other. She knows you won't stand for my bad behaviour, for one thing. And she knows that Nina likes you, which is little short of a miracle because she really does abhor most humans. And she knows that you love Linus, of course.'

'Well, of course. But –'

'And that Linus and I both love you.'

It was such a simple statement, and yet it contained a world within its words. She stared at him in stunned silence, oblivious to the rain pouring down her neck as he stepped in to her, closing the gap between them finally. They loved her? *He* loved her?

He hooked his finger and trailed it lightly over her cheek. 'Bell, I know I'm no catch. I'm never going to be perfect. I was a flawed man before the accident and I'm always going to be, no matter how much therapy I have. I don't deserve you but I will do everything in my power to *try* to deserve you.' He shrugged. 'Can't you take a chance on me?'

Could she? she wondered, staring into his remarkable eyes. He wasn't the easy option by any stretch. He was difficult and stubborn and had no filter. But she'd felt something on that *Midsommar* night, when his hand had cupped her head and his lips had first kissed hers – she had understood in that moment of perfect stillness, that since Jack's death her heart had been like a frightened bird beating its wings frantically against a cage, and he, he had been a warm pair of hands around her. He had woken her up again and they were both awake now.

'Hey,' she said quietly, realizing something else.

'What?'

'You're speaking in English.'

A smile curled his beautiful mouth, enlivening his eyes. Those eyes. 'Impressed yet?'

She took off his cap, pressed her hands to his cheeks and kissed him; she kissed him though the rain was dripping off their noses and eyelashes, and running in sheets over their cheeks. She kissed him though she knew this was a point of no return for her heart. There would be no turning back. 'I love you both too,' she whispered, seeing how his eyes burned and his fingers clutched against her waist, the flame between them flickering and beginning to dance again.

Linus darted out from the safety of the awning, cheering with pumping fists, and they both jumped, having forgotten him momentarily. 'Dad wants you to be his girlfriend but he told me not to say anything!'

She laughed. 'You did very well to keep it a secret. I never would have guessed.'

Emil reached for him, hugging Linus into them both in a happy huddle. A little family. He looked up at the cascading sky, closing his eyes and feeling the rain on his face. 'You know what?'

'What?' she smiled.

'. . . I think we should go for a walk.'

'In the rain?' Linus gasped, eyes shining at the contrariness of it.

'Of course – this is the very best time,' he said, cupping her head and kissing her again. He pulled away, his eyes burning brightly. Fiercely. 'It reminds you you're alive.'

Acknowledgements

My loyal readers will know I visit every location I write about, and I usually do enough research beforehand that I know what I want to see before I get there. This time, it was different. I have several good friends of Swedish descent and they'd shared enough stories over the years that I knew I wanted to set a book in Stockholm; it's one of the coolest cities in the world, so young, so colourful, so techy . . . What I hadn't expected was to fall in love with the wet, wobbly bit beside it, speckled with scattered crumbs of land. The archipelago was a revelation to me – it's desolate, I'm sure, through the winter, but through the summer months, utterly stunning isolation! Grand old houses on rocky outcrops, regattas, pine forests, picnics and, of course, teeny tiny cabins. If you've read even one other of my books, then you'll know I'm a sucker for a ramshackle hut, be it on a mountain, a fjord or a beach. I fell in love with the Swedish way of summering, feeling a genuine regret that this was not part of my own life story, and I really hope I've been able to impart some of its rustic purity and simplicity to you. If you can't get there yourself, hopefully the story within these pages is a good second best.

Emil's story was inspired by a real news story that seemed almost too good to be true. I looked into traumatic brain injuries further, and certainly such a recovery is sadly a freak rarity, bordering on the miraculous, but it is possible, and by then, my interest had been peaked with this thought: imagine waking up and finding yourself a stranger in your own life; everyone you loved has moved on . . . It's chilling and tragic, and I honestly didn't know how I was going to answer that question. However, my editor Caroline Hogg and agent Amanda Preston were both quick to see the appeal, keeping me calm when the collywobbles invariably set in and feeding back with observations and suggestions that really tightened up and refined the story. I honestly could not put a book out into the world without their eyes on it first. Thank you, both.

A huge debt is also owed to the Pan team at large – the copy- and sub-editors who tirelessly fine tune the details so that the story rings true and feels authentic; the marketing and advertising and comms teams who make sure that you get to know the book is out there; the sales teams who ensure it's actually on bookshelves so that you can buy it; the art department who make sure you want to pick it up from the bookshelf when there's a thousand other alternatives . . . you get the point. It really does take a village and I'm just so grateful that all these talented people are working on my side and not the competition's!

This is also the time to thank my friends. I really do go to ground when I'm writing these books. I say 'no' to most things, don't call, forget to reply to texts. I'm well and truly off the grid, the world's worst friend, and it is always such a relief that they allow me to just pick up where we left off, without recrimination, when I re-enter the real world.

Finally, above all and always, my family. They are my beating heart and although I spend my days creating new worlds, nothing would exist for me without them. They are my beginning, my middle and my end. The end.